Deception

Exposed Series

Book 1: Exposed
Book 2: Deception
Book 3: Betrayal

Books by Naomi Chase

Deception

Betrayal

Published by Dafina Books

Deception

NAOMI CHASE

Kensington Publishing Corp.

http://www.kensingtonbooks.com

ISBN-13: 978-0-7582-5323-1
ISBN-10: 0-7582-5323-0
First Kensington Trade Edition: March 2012
First Kensington Mass Market Edition: April 2015

eISBN-13: 978-1-61773-875-3
eISBN-10: 1-61773-875-1
Kesington Electronic Edition: April 2015

10 9 8 7 6 5 4 3 2 1

Printed in the United States of America

*To everyone who has ever wanted
a second chance to make things right*

ACKNOWLEDGMENTS

I owe a huge debt of gratitude to the readers, reviewers, book club members, and bookstore employees who enthusiastically recommended *Exposed* to others. Thank you for all the love and support you have given me. I truly hope that *Deception* will live up to your expectations!

To my loving husband and children, who endure months of neglect while I'm buried deep in my cave, trying to meet deadlines. Thank you for understanding, and for always being there for me. Words can't express how much I love and appreciate all of you.

To fellow authors Angie Daniels and Adrianne Byrd, thank you so much for your unwavering friendship and support. Thank you for brainstorming with me, motivating and encouraging me, and patiently enduring my frequent bouts of insanity. I don't know where I'd be without sister-friends like you!

A very special thanks to Ann Christopher, who generously shared her legal expertise with me. Any mistakes made or liberties taken in the name of fiction are my own.

Chapter 1

Tamia

Houston, Texas
November 4, 2011

Tamia Luke's heart pounded violently as she watched the twelve jurors file into the jury box and reclaim their seats. She was so nervous, she wanted to throw up. These men and women held her fate in their hands. Their verdict would determine whether she spent the rest of her life in prison or walked out of this courtroom a free woman.

She searched their faces, hoping for something—*any-thing*—that would give her insight into the decision they had reached. But their expressions were unreadable, and none of them would make eye contact with her. Not even Juror Number Eight, an attractive, middle-aged black man who'd hardly been able to keep his eyes off her throughout the trial.

But today he seemed to go out of his way not to look at her.

Like the other jurors.

With mounting anxiety, Tamia leaned over and whispered to her attorney, "They won't look at me. Why won't they look at me?"

"Relax," Brandon murmured soothingly. "It doesn't mean anything."

Tamia hoped to God he was right. She'd spent the past five months behind bars, serving time for a crime she hadn't committed. She didn't know *what* she would do if the jury found her guilty of Isabel Archer's murder. It was unthinkable.

When the judge emerged from his chambers, Tamia and Brandon rose from the defense table. Her insides were shivering, and her legs were so wobbly, she thought she'd collapse to the floor. Without thinking she grabbed Brandon's hand and held tight, comforted when he squeezed her back.

"Ladies and gentlemen of the jury," said the judge, "have you reached a verdict?"

The jury forewoman stood. "We have, Your Honor."

As the judge read the folded note that contained the jury's verdict, the silence that had permeated the packed courtroom was now deafening. You could literally hear a pin drop.

The judge looked at the forewoman. "What is your verdict?"

Tamia closed her eyes, her heart slamming against her rib cage as she braced herself for the woman's next words.

"We, the jury, find the defendant—"

Tamia held her breath.

"—not guilty."

Pandemonium erupted in the courtroom, loud cheers from Tamia's supporters dueling with shouts of protest from Isabel Archer's outraged relatives. The judge banged his gavel, calling for order. But it was the sight of Brandon's beaming face that gave Tamia permission to believe the verdict she'd just heard.

"WE WON!" she screamed, throwing her arms around Brandon's neck as he laughingly lifted her off the floor. As he spun her around, she caught a glimpse of Dominic Archer, seated behind the plaintiff's table across the aisle. He looked so stunned that Tamia might have felt sorry for him—if she didn't despise his motherfucking ass.

"Thank you, Brandon," she said earnestly as he set her back down on her feet. "Thank you for believing in me. Thank you for saving my life!"

"You're welcome," he told her. "I never doubted your innocence."

"I know. And that meant *everything* to me."

His expression softened. "You know I—"

"Congratulations," a new voice interrupted.

Tamia and Brandon turned to encounter a pretty, brown-skinned woman dressed in a navy Dolce & Gabbana skirt suit that hugged her slender figure. Her dark, lustrous hair flowed past her shoulders in a way that made Tamia more desperate than ever to get into her stylist's chair. Sporting months of nappy new growth and wearing a pantsuit that did nothing for her shape, she felt raggedy next to Cynthia Yarbrough—the scheming hussy who'd stolen Brandon from her.

She forced a smile. "Hey, Cynthia. You're looking well."

"Thank you, Tamia." Cynthia didn't insult her intelligence by returning the compliment. "Congratulations on your acquittal."

"Thanks." Tamia smiled gratefully at Brandon. "I couldn't have done it without this man's amazing legal prowess. I don't know if I can ever repay him, but I'm determined to try."

Brandon chuckled. "You might feel differently after you receive my final bill."

Tamia laughed, then leaned up and kissed his smooth, clean-shaven cheek. She didn't miss the way Cynthia's eyes narrowed with displeasure.

Don't get it twisted, heffa, Tamia mused. *He was my man first!*

Soon she was surrounded by a group of supporters who'd been there for her throughout the trial. Lou Saldaña scooped her up and swung her around, while her best friend, Shanell Jasper, took one look at her attire and promised to take her shopping ASAP. Distant cousins Tamia hadn't seen in ages had shown up, along with a few of her neighbors.

Everyone who mattered was there.

Except Fiona.

And she *doesn't matter anymore*, Tamia thought darkly.

"YOU BITCH!"

The enraged outburst came from the other side of the courtroom, where a sobbing woman was being restrained by several members of Isabel Archer's family. As Tamia watched, the woman pointed at her and screamed, "You're gonna burn in hell for what you did to Isabel!"

Before Tamia could open her mouth to defend herself, Brandon silenced her with a warning look. "Don't say anything. The jury has spoken for you, and that's all that matters."

Nodding grimly, she watched as the hysterical woman was led out of the courtroom. Although Tamia knew she was innocent, it bothered her that there were people who would always believe the worst of her, that she'd killed her lover's wife in a jealous rage. The worst part was that she *knew* who the real killer was—and there wasn't a damn thing she could do about it. She'd sworn not to tell anyone, and no matter how horribly she'd been used and betrayed, a promise was a promise.

After accepting more congratulatory hugs and kisses, Tamia followed her small entourage out of the courthouse and into the bright November afternoon. She and Brandon were met by a buzzing swarm of reporters who shouted questions at them.

"Miss Luke, do you feel vindicated by today's verdict?"

"Mr. Chambers, do you stand by your strategy to por-tray Dominic Archer as the real killer?"

"Do either of you believe he really murdered his wife?"

"Miss Luke, do you regret having an affair with a mar-ried man?"

Taken aback by the barrage of questions, Tamia looked askance at Brandon. He gave her a reassuring smile, then stepped to the cluster of microphones. Calmly he surveyed the crowd, waiting for the noise to die down before he spoke.

"Miss Luke and I are pleased that justice was served today. I commend the men and women of the jury for weigh-ing all the evidence and coming back with the only verdict they could have: not guilty."

The reporters fired more questions at him.

"With all due respect, Brandon," one voice rang out above the rest, "how difficult was it for you to defend the woman who cheated on you? Throughout the trial, you were forced to hear the lurid details of Miss Luke's affair with Do-minic Archer. How in the world did you remain objective?"

Tamia's face heated with shame, while Brandon didn't so much as flinch. "My prior relationship with Miss Luke wasn't on trial," he answered evenly. "If I didn't think I could handle hearing the 'lurid details' of her affair, as you put it, I wouldn't have taken her case. But I did, because I believed in her innocence. Clearly the jury did, too."

Tamia beamed at him.

"Is there any chance that you and Miss Luke might rec-oncile?"

Brandon paused, giving Tamia a sidelong glance.

She met his gaze, holding her breath as she waited for his response.

After several moments he turned back to the reporters, chuckling and shaking his head. "You guys are always look-ing for a romantic Hollywood ending. All I want to do is celebrate this victory, which reaffirms my belief that the justice system can and *does* work."

"Given your winning track record," someone retorted, "I'd say the system works just fine for you."

Brandon grinned as laughter swept over the crowd.

Tamia was also grinning, but not for the same reason as everyone else. For the first time in several months, she had reason to hope that all was not lost between her and Brandon. Because whether he realized it or not, by dodging the reporter's question, he'd left the door open for the possibility of him and Tamia getting back together.

Today's verdict had given her back her life. Now that she was a free woman again, nothing would stop her from trying to reclaim the only man she'd ever loved.

Nothing.

And no one.

Turning her head, she saw Cynthia standing off to the side by herself.

Their gazes met.

Tamia smiled.

Cynthia's eyes narrowed with suspicion.

That's right, bitch, Tamia thought. *I'm taking back what you stole from me. And this time, I'm never letting him go!*

Chapter 2

Tamia

The downtown nightclub was thumping by the time Tamia made her grand entrance that evening. The dance floor was packed with bodies grinding to the hypnotic rhythm of Nicki Minaj's "Moment 4 Life," and the flashing strobe lights suspended from the ceiling made the dancers appear electrified.

Tamia bobbed her head to the music as her senses came vibrantly alive. After spending the past five months trapped inside a prison, stepping into the noisy, crowded club made her feel as rejuvenated as if she'd just stumbled upon paradise. It didn't hurt that she looked positively fierce in a red Gucci halter dress that molded to her luscious curves and showed off her long, toned legs. On her feet were five-inch stilettos with ice-pick heels. Her hairstylist had tamed her nappy roots with a fresh relaxer that had her sleek, shoulder-length bob lying like silk against her scalp.

She didn't miss the appreciative stares she was receiving from several men, their lustful gazes undressing her from head to toe. Though she played it cool, she couldn't help but soak up all the attention. After the ordeal she'd been through, she needed to feel beautiful again. Desired.

"You looking good, mamacita. *Real* good."

Tamia turned her head and smiled at Lou, who'd generously footed the bill for her makeover as well as tonight's homecoming party. "Thank you, papi. For everything."

He smiled. "You know I got your back."

"I know. You're so good to me."

"That's what friends are for." He winked at her. "You ready to get this party started?"

Tamia grinned, tucking her arm through his. "Lead the way."

They navigated through the gyrating throng of bodies, making their way up to the second-floor VIP lounge Lou had reserved for the night. When they reached the entrance to the large suite, a chorus of voices yelled out, "Welcome home, Tamia!"

She beamed with pleasure as she surveyed the sea of smiling faces. She recognized only a handful of the guests, including Shanell and her husband, Mark. The rest were strangers, ranging from scantily clad females to tattooed ballers dipped in designer gear and platinum jewelry.

As Tamia moved through the crowd accepting congratulations on her acquittal, she couldn't help searching for Brandon. She'd invited him and Cynthia to the party, secretly hoping that he would show up alone. But so far there was no sign of either of them.

Swallowing her disappointment, Tamia followed Lou through the lavish lounge, which featured low lighting, plush sofas, a private bar, and a small dance floor near the back. There was a table laden with gourmet cheeses, caviar, shrimp cocktail, crab cakes, buffalo wings, and exotic-looking meatballs. A plasma television mounted against one wall was showing BET music videos, but most of the guests had wandered over to the balcony, preferring to watch the dancers below.

As Tamia and Shanell sat down on a low sofa tucked into a private corner, Lou asked, "What's your poison, ladies?"

Tamia grinned. "I'll have a Blue Motherfucker."

"Oooh, that sounds good." Shanell winked at Lou. "Make that two."

"I got you."

"And I'll fix you both a plate," Mark offered.

"Thank you, fellas," cooed Tamia and Shanell.

After Lou and Mark departed, Shanell grinned broadly. "Men who believe in catering to their women. Now *that's* what I'm talking about."

Tamia grinned, crossing her legs. "It *is* nice, isn't it?"

"Hell, yeah." Shanell gave her an approving once-over. "Girl, you are wearing the *hell* outta that dress."

"Thanks, girl. You're working your outfit, too," Tamia said, admiring the silk shorts jumper that showcased Shanell's ample cleavage and thick thighs. "Thanks again for taking me to the Galleria this afternoon."

Shanell waved off her gratitude. "You know how much I love shopping, especially with someone who has a platinum card. Speaking of which, I thought you told me that Lou's film studio went bankrupt."

"It did."

"Sure as hell coulda fooled me." Shanell gestured around the luxurious suite. "Only a serious baller could afford all this."

Tamia shrugged, tapping her foot to the music of Keri Hilson. "He told me he's doing well with a new business venture."

"What kind of business venture?" Shanell asked suspiciously.

"I don't know. He didn't elaborate."

Shanell frowned. "I hope it's nothing illegal. The last thing we need is for your homecoming party to be interrupted by a police raid."

"Believe me," Tamia said grimly, "I have *no* desire to go back to prison."

Although Lou had been evasive about his new line of work, he'd assured Tamia that everything was legit. Earlier that year, he'd learned that the FBI was secretly investigating him in order to get to some of his Mexican mafia associates. His house and phone had been bugged, and two agents had been assigned to follow him everywhere he went. They'd even brought him in for questioning, hoping to intimidate him into cooperating with their investigation. But Lou was smarter than that. He knew the feds had nothing concrete on him, so he'd retained Brandon to get the motherfuckers off his back—which Brandon had done, earning Lou's gratitude and the nickname "the rainmaker."

"I can't believe she's not here."

Pulled out of her reverie, Tamia gave Shanell a blank look. "Who?"

"Your sister. I can't believe she's not here to celebrate with you. As if it weren't bad enough that she missed your big day in court this morning."

Tamia's mood darkened at once. "Fiona's not here," she said tightly, "because she wasn't invited. And I told her not to show up at the courthouse today."

Shanell frowned. "Why would you do something like that?"

Tamia said nothing.

"I know you told me that you and Fiona had a big falling out," Shanell continued, "but I didn't think either of you would carry it this far. I mean—damn, Tamia. You're sisters. What if the jury had found you guilty? Don't you think Fiona should have been there for that?"

Tamia was spared from answering when Mark returned with two plates filled with food. After Tamia and Shanell thanked him, he told his wife, "I'm going downstairs to say hello to a friend. I haven't seen him since we graduated from basic, so I'll be back in a little while."

"Okay, baby," Shanell said distractedly, using her fork to cut into a crab cake. "Have fun catching up."

As Mark walked away, Tamia eyed her friend incredulously. "Wow."

Shanell glanced up from her plate. "What?"

"You and Mark have such a trusting relationship. You didn't even ask him the name of the friend he was going to see."

"So?"

Tamia hesitated. "Mark's an attractive guy. Some women might think twice about letting their husbands out of their sight in a club filled with half-naked hoochies."

Shanell chuckled dryly. "Girl, please. Mark just returned from Iraq. If he wanted to cheat on me, he had a whole year to do so. And I don't think he did."

After another hesitation, Tamia couldn't resist asking, "How do you know for sure?"

"Because I trust my man." A wicked gleam entered Shanell's cognac-colored eyes. "And because ever since he got back, he's been fucking me like he ain't sniffed pussy since the dawn of the millennium."

Tamia shrieked with laughter. *"T-M-I!"*

Shanell grinned unabashedly, forking up another bite of crab cake and chewing for a few moments. "Look, I'm not naive. I know that military men have a reputation for being dogs. But I can honestly tell you that my boo's not like that. We've been married for five years, and he's never given me any reason to even suspect that he's cheating. And while he was deployed, we made damn good use of our computer webcams and cell phones. You'd better believe I gave that brotha *plenty* to look forward to when he came home."

Tamia chuckled. "I bet you did, hussy. It's always the

ones sitting up in church every Sunday who're the biggest freaks."

Shanell grinned. "Don't hate."

"Whatever." But Tamia *was* feeling somewhat jealous. It had been more than five months since she'd gotten laid. She missed the feel of a man thrusting between her legs. But since she was on a mission to win back Brandon, she'd made a pact with herself not to sleep with anyone but him—no matter how long it took her to convince him to give her a second chance. After the way she'd betrayed him with Dominic, depriving herself of sex was the least she could do.

But looking around at some of the buff, tattooed biceps on display, she wondered how long she'd be able to hold out.

"Sorry to keep you waiting, ladies." Lou had returned with two drinks, which he passed to Tamia and Shanell before lowering himself onto the sofa beside Tamia. "I got held up talking to one of my clients."

Shanell pounced on the word. "Clients?"

"Yeah." Lou snagged a buffalo wing from Tamia's plate and took a bite, chewing appreciatively. "Mmm, that's good."

Shooting a quick glance at Tamia, Shanell asked casually, "What kind of work do you do, Lou?"

"The kind that pays the bills." He winked at Tamia, who grinned and shook her head at Shanell.

"I think that's his polite way of telling you to mind your own business."

Shanell scowled. "I was just trying to make conversation. Damn."

Tamia and Lou laughed.

"Excuse me," interrupted a sultry female voice.

Everyone glanced up to encounter a voluptuous, honey-toned beauty with a weaved mane that hung down to her ass and D-cup breasts pouring out of her black leather minidress.

She was staring at Tamia with an awestruck expression. "I'm so sorry to bother you, but aren't you Mystique?"

Tamia instantly stiffened. Setting her plate down on the small table beside the sofa, she said coolly, "I used to be."

"Oh, my God!" the young woman squealed excitedly. "It's such an honor to meet you! I'm a *huge* fan of your work."

Tamia inwardly groaned. The last time she'd heard similar words, she'd gotten caught up in a web of deceit and betrayal that ended with her being framed for murder.

"I've watched all of your *Slave Chronicles* videos," the girl gushed. "You were amazing! Honestly, you're the reason I got into the business."

"Is that right?" Tamia glanced at Lou, who looked decidedly uncomfortable as he tugged on his thick black ponytail. "Did you also work for Voyeur Productions?"

"Sure did." The girl stuck out a manicured hand. "My name's Halima, but I go by Honey."

"Hello," Tamia said, accepting her handshake. "It's nice to meet you, Honey."

"Have you seen any of my movies? Lou says I remind him a little of you."

"Does he, now?"

Honey nodded, smiling slyly. "The way you used to—"

Lou cleared his throat loudly, cutting the girl off.

Tamia gave him an amused sidelong glance before returning her attention back to Honey. "Now that the studio is no longer in business, what are you doing with yourself these days, Honey?"

Please say you're in college trying to make something of yourself, Tamia silently prayed. *Please don't tell me you're still doing porn.*

"Oh, I'm still working for Lou."

"Really?" Shanell interjected, eyeing Honey with undisguised interest. "Doing what?"

"I'm one of—"

Lou jumped up as if the sofa had suddenly caught on

fire. "That reminds me, baby girl. There's someone I want you to meet."

"Okay," Honey agreed. "But can I have Mystique's autograph first?"

Lou looked askance at Tamia. "If she's okay with that."

Tamia hesitated, biting her lower lip. She'd spent the past eight years trying to distance herself from her days as the underground porn star famously known as Mystique. But Dominic Archer's intrusion into her life had blown the lid off her scandalous secret. Anyone who'd followed Tamia's criminal trial—as most Houstonians had—already knew the salacious details of her past. So what harm was there in signing one measly autograph?

She mustered a smile. "Got a pen?"

She'd barely gotten out the words before Honey whipped out a Sharpie and passed it to her.

"Paper?" Tamia asked.

Honey shook her head, bending down until her voluptuous cleavage was mere inches from Tamia's face. "I want you to autograph my titties."

Shanell sucked her teeth. "Who the hell do you think she is? Nicki Minaj?"

Tamia laughed, scribbling her alter ego's name across the soft mound of Honey's breasts.

The girl beamed with pleasure. "Thank you *so* much, Mystique. I can't tell you how much this means to me."

"No problem," Tamia said, handing back the Sharpie.

Honey remained in her face. "If you're ever interested," she purred, "I'd *love* to have a threesome with you sometime."

Tamia chuckled. "Thanks for the offer, baby girl, but I'm strictly dickly."

"So am I." Honey winked at her. "But I'd make an exception for you."

Leaning back against the sofa, Tamia drawled, "I'll keep that in mind."

"I hope you do." The girl licked her glossy lips and smiled, then slipped her arm through Lou's as he led her away, his hand resting lightly on the thick swell of her ass.

Shanell stared after them, shaking her head in disgust. "I bet he's fucking her."

Tamia laughed. "Knowing Lou, that's probably true."

"She looks barely twenty-one."

Tamia sipped her drink. "That's how he likes 'em. Young, but not young enough to be considered jailbait."

Shanell's eyes narrowed shrewdly on Tamia's face. "Did you ever—"

"No," Tamia said, already anticipating the question. "I never slept with Lou."

"Good," Shanell said with such vehemence that Tamia laughed.

"Damn, girl. He's not *that* bad."

"Um, yeah, he is. I mean, don't get me wrong. I definitely think he's sexy. He reminds me of a younger Benicio Del Toro, right down to those hazel eyes and juicy lips. Girl, the first time he showed up to testify at your trial, I thought he *was* Benicio."

Tamia chuckled. "He gets that all the time."

"I'm not surprised." Shanell frowned. "But as fine as he is, there's something about him that rubs me the wrong way. I don't trust him, Tamia, and I don't think you should, either."

Tamia sucked her teeth. "What're you talking about? Lou and I are old friends. He's always been there for me."

Shanell gave her a look. "Just because he made you a porn star—"

Tamia took umbrage. "It was more than that. He really looked out for me."

"Of course he did. You were making him money."

"What about *after* I left his studio?" Tamia challenged. "He protected my identity even when he didn't have to anymore."

"Are you sure about that?" Shanell countered. "You said yourself that you still don't know who gave Dominic your real name. For all you know, that scheming motherfucker might have paid Lou off. Or am I the only one who doesn't think it's just a coincidence that Lou shut down his film studio shortly after you went to prison—and now he's living large?"

Tamia shook her head in vehement denial. "You're wrong, Shanell. Voyeur Productions meant *everything* to Lou. He hated losing the studio, but he couldn't afford to stay in business anymore."

"Or maybe he was ready to conquer new territory and the payoff he received from Dominic opened new doors for him."

Tamia took a long sip of her drink, wishing that she could dismiss her friend's ugly suspicions. But Fiona's devastating betrayal had taught her that she couldn't put anything past anyone, including those who were closest to her. She didn't want to go through the rest of her life questioning people's motives, but if she couldn't trust her own flesh and blood, who the hell *could* she trust?

"And that's another thing," Shanell continued doggedly. "How much you wanna bet that Lou's 'new business venture' involves pimping out young girls like Honey?"

Tamia set her glass down with a thud and glared at Shanell. "This is supposed to be my homecoming party, but all you've done is talk about shit that's bringing me down. Can you please give it a rest?"

Shanell looked taken aback. "I just—"

"I'm serious, Shanell. Don't make me ask one of Lou's bodyguards to escort your black ass outta here."

Shanell's eyes narrowed. "You wouldn't."

"Think I wouldn't?"

They stared each other down, then simultaneously burst out laughing.

Sobering after several moments, Shanell sighed and shook her head. "You're right," she said contritely. "I don't mean to ruin your celebration. It's just that I can't help worrying about you. You've been through hell, Tamia, and I don't want to see you get hurt again. You need to be careful."

"I know," Tamia said soberly. "And I truly appreciate your concern, Shanell. You've been more like a sister to me than Fiona, so I know you've got my back. But I've been looking forward to this night for months. So I just want to relax and enjoy myself. All right?"

Shanell nodded. "All right."

"Thank you." Tamia grinned, reclaiming her drink. "By the way, I think you may have missed your calling. For a minute there, I thought I was being cross-examined by a damn lawyer."

Shanell smiled, but she was no longer looking at Tamia. "And speaking of lawyers . . ."

Tamia followed the direction of her friend's gaze.

When she saw who stood at the entrance to the VIP lounge, her heart thudded.

Brandon had arrived.

And he was very much alone.

Chapter 3

Tamia

"Hey, the rainmaker's here!" Lou announced boisterously.

Brandon grinned and shook his head as a loud chorus of cheers and applause swept through the crowd. He sauntered into the lounge, oozing so much swagger that Tamia's nipples hardened and her pussy creamed. She watched as he stopped to shake hands and chat with Lou and several members of Lou's entourage.

After what seemed an eternity—but was probably less than three minutes—Lou pointed out where Tamia was seated. When Brandon looked over and met her gaze, Tamia's pulse quickened. He flashed a lazy smile, and damn if her panties didn't get wetter.

As he started toward her, she couldn't help admiring his appearance. He'd changed into a fitted Versace suit over a stark white shirt with the top three buttons undone. He looked so delicious that Tamia couldn't even blame the females whose lustful gazes tracked him across the suite.

"Dayuum!" Shanell exclaimed appreciatively. "That brotha is *hella* fine."

"You ain't never lied," Tamia murmured.

When Brandon reached them, he bent and kissed Tamia's upturned cheek. The feel of his soft, full lips had her clit throbbing at the memory of his mouth buried between her legs. She would have given *anything* to feel his long, thick shaft stroking her walls until she shattered and screamed in ecstasy. Making love to Brandon was all she'd thought about while she was locked up. That—and getting free.

"Wassup?" He greeted Tamia, sitting down beside her.

"Hey," she said softly. "You made it."

"Of course. Hey, girl," he said warmly to Shanell.

She beamed at him. "Hey, Brandon."

"Where's your husband?" he asked her.

"Around here somewhere."

"Why don't you go see what he's up to?" Tamia suggested.

Shanell eyed her blankly. "Why?"

Tamia gave her a pointed look.

After another moment, Shanell got the hint. "Um, yeah, let me go see what my man's up to. That's a *great* idea." She set her plate down on the table and rose from the sofa, then winked at Tamia and Brandon before striding quickly away.

Brandon chuckled softly, watching her departure. "Subtle."

Tamia didn't respond. She was too busy soaking up all his fineness—six two with skin the color of dark chocolate, smooth black hair cut low to his scalp, deep midnight eyes, sexy dimples, and a manicured goatee that framed the most succulent lips Tamia had ever kissed.

Suddenly she realized that Brandon was staring right back at her.

"What?" she said self-consciously.

"That's what *I* should be asking you," he drawled. "You're looking at me like I've got something on my face."

Nothing but deliciousness, Tamia mused with a smile. "Nah, you're good. By the way, I've been meaning to tell you that I really like your new goatee. But I thought facial hair was strongly discouraged at the firm."

"It is," Brandon said, stroking his chin. "But now that I've made partner—"

"—you can do whatever the hell you want, right?"

He grinned, flashing dimples. "Pretty much."

Tamia laughed, shaking her head at him. "So it's like that, huh?"

"Damn straight." He nodded at the glass in her hand. "What're you drinking?"

"A Blue Motherfucker."

"*What'd* you call me?"

Tamia's smile faded. "That's the name of the—"

Brandon laughed. "Relax. I'm just messing with you."

Tamia grinned, punching him playfully on the arm. It felt good to be on such friendly terms with Brandon again. After the way she'd hurt and betrayed him, she knew how lucky she was that he was even speaking to her.

Just then they were approached by an attractive young woman balancing a drink on a small tray. "This is for you, Mr. Chambers," she purred, handing the glass to Brandon. "A neat scotch from Mr. Saldaña."

Brandon looked across the suite. Meeting Lou's eyes, he nodded and raised his glass in a small toast.

Lou nodded back and smiled.

Tamia watched as Brandon sipped his scotch, looking smoother than James Bond. One of the things she admired most about him was his versatility. Although he'd grown up in one of the wealthiest zip codes in Texas, he didn't have a pretentious bone in his gorgeous body. He could discuss foreign affairs and commodity futures with the good ole boys at his law firm, then turn around and chill with the hoodest of hood rats. He was comfortable in his own skin, and he made no apologies for who he was—a proud, powerful black man who was on course to take the world by storm.

Cheating on Brandon was by far the stupidest thing Tamia had ever done in her life. But she had every intention of rectifying that mistake. Starting tonight.

"I'd like to propose a toast." When Brandon met her gaze, she elaborated, "For the past several months, we've been so focused on the trial that I haven't really had a chance to congratulate you on making partner. I know how hard you worked to achieve that goal, and no one deserved it more than you. So I just wanted to tell you how amazing I think you are, and how proud I am of you."

Brandon's expression softened with gratitude. "Thank you, Tamia," he said quietly. "I appreciate that."

"I meant every word." She raised her glass. "Here's to you."

"And you. This is *your* night."

"Which was made possible by you."

Brandon smiled. "Okay, then. Here's to both of us."

Tamia liked the sound of that. "To both of us."

They clinked glasses and sipped their drinks, staring at each other.

"I'm glad you came," Tamia said.

"I told you I would."

"I know, but . . ." She trailed off uncertainly.

"But what?"

"I thought you might change your mind."

"Nah. I wouldn't have missed your celebration."

"Thank you." Tamia hesitated. "Cynthia couldn't make it?"

"No."

"Oh," Tamia murmured. "That's too bad."

Brandon gave her a knowing look.

Smothering a smile, Tamia set down her glass and picked up her plate. She speared a meatball and brought it to Brandon's mouth. "Taste this," she said, watching as his lips closed around the fork. "How is it?"

He chewed slowly. "Delicious."

"Yeah? They *look* delicious."

"You haven't had one yet?" When she shook her head, Brandon grinned. "Oh, so now you're using me as your taste tester?"

"Yup." She laughed and fed him another meatball, then deliberately licked the fork as he watched her. Satisfied that she had his undivided attention, she leaned back against the sofa and crossed her legs, observing the way his dark gaze lowered to her thick thighs. When he unconsciously bit his bottom lip, it was all she could do not to hop onto his lap, yank down his pants, and impale herself on his rock-hard dick.

Ignoring the hungry throbbing of her pussy, she ate one of the meatballs and asked conversationally, "How's your father's election bid going?"

Slowly Brandon lifted his gaze from her thighs. "Hmm?"

Tamia hid a knowing smile. "I asked about your father's campaign. How are things going?"

"So far so good," Brandon answered, settling more comfortably on the sofa with one arm draped across the back. "Since the election's a year away, he hasn't gotten into the heavy campaign season yet."

"Not that he'll need to do much campaigning," Tamia drawled, setting aside her plate. "Everyone knows he's the front-runner."

Brandon smiled, sipping his scotch.

His father was lieutenant governor Bernard Chambers, one of the most powerful men in Texas. Earlier that year, he'd formally announced his plans to run for governor. Many Houstonians expected him to win the election in a landslide.

"And how's your mother doing?" Tamia asked politely.

"She's doing well," Brandon replied.

"That's good."

Tamia knew that Bernard and Gwen Chambers had adamantly opposed Brandon's decision to represent Tamia during the murder trial. They'd already believed that she wasn't good enough to date their son. Once Tamia was arrested and sent to prison, they'd fully expected Brandon to wash his hands of her. But he'd defied their wishes, proving that he was his own man.

Which was another reason Tamia would always love him.

Glancing across the lounge, she noticed a group of scantily clad females huddled near the bar. Every last one of them was shamelessly eyeballing Brandon.

Tamia frowned, hoping she wouldn't be forced to act a damn fool at her own homecoming party.

As subtly as possible, she moved closer to Brandon on the sofa, letting the pack of vultures know that he wasn't available. While a couple of them smirked at her, the rest had the sense to look away, no doubt realizing that if Tamia really *had* killed her lover's wife, she was the last one they wanted to be fucking with.

Seemingly oblivious to what was going on, Brandon smiled softly at Tamia. "So what are your plans now?"

"You mean now that I'm a free woman?"

"Yeah."

"Well, for starters, I'm moving out of my house."

"Really?" Brandon looked surprised. "Why?"

She hesitated. "I need a change of scenery." She couldn't tell him the truth, that after what Fiona had done to her, there was no way they could continue living under the same roof. Tamia wanted absolutely nothing to do with her sister. The sooner she severed ties with Fiona's treacherous ass, the better.

"Where are you moving to?" Brandon asked.

"Lou found an apartment for me. I haven't seen it yet, and he won't tell me where it is, but he assures me that it's perfect for my needs."

Lou knew she couldn't afford much. Her legal fees had

all but depleted her bank account. After her final payment went through, she'd have just enough money to cover her rent for two months. She needed to find a job ASAP, but she knew this wouldn't be easy now that she had a criminal record. And she could pretty much forget about landing another advertising job. No reputable ad agency would hire someone who'd just been acquitted of murder.

Observing her downcast expression, Brandon reached over and cupped her chin in his hand. "Look at me."

Tamia met his gaze.

"Five months ago, you didn't think you'd be sitting here tonight—a free woman. But you are. So don't worry about what may or may not happen tomorrow. Enjoy this moment, and believe me when I tell you that everything's gonna be just fine. All right?"

Tamia nodded, fighting back tears. "Thank you, Brandon. I couldn't have gotten through any of this without you." She hesitated, swallowing hard. "I'm so sorry for—"

Brandon pressed his finger to her lips, silencing her. "You don't have to keep apologizing, Tamia. What happened between us is in the past. I've moved on, and so should you."

Tamia stared at him, her mind flashing on an image of Cynthia bent over his desk as he fucked her from behind. The memory of what she'd seen that night still haunted Tamia, overtaking her thoughts when she least expected it. After the way she'd cheated on Brandon, she knew she had no right to feel betrayed because he'd slept with another woman. But that was exactly how she felt, and nothing would ever change that.

"Tamia."

Jarred out of her painful musings, Tamia blinked at Brandon.

"You okay?" he asked gently.

She nodded quickly, then picked up her glass and drained

the contents just as Keyshia Cole's "Take Me Away" began playing.

"Oooh, that's my song. Dance with me, Brandon."

Before he could respond, she set down her empty glass, grabbed him by the hand, and led him over to the small dance floor, which was already packed with other couples. Tamia moved close to Brandon, sliding her arms around his neck as his big hands encircled her waist.

As they began swaying to the music, she looked into his eyes. "Do you know what this reminds me of?"

He smiled down at her. "Our first date."

She nodded. "You took me to dinner at Da Marco, then we went dancing at your frat brother's new club." She smiled, reliving the memory of what had come afterward. They'd checked into a luxury hotel downtown, then spent the rest of the night fucking like the world was coming to an end.

Tamia sighed. "What a night."

Brandon merely smiled again.

As they danced together, his hard, muscled chest rubbed against her breasts, making her nipples tighten. She cuddled closer to him and buried her face against his neck. The scent of his Clive Christian cologne teased her nostrils, smelling so damn good she wanted to drag her nose along his throat and inhale his skin off.

She sang along with Keyshia, bringing her lips close to Brandon's ear as she crooned the lyrics that told him how much she loved him.

When the mellow jam melted into a faster number, Tamia and Brandon picked up the pace. He was a good dancer, confident and smooth. As they grooved together, effortlessly matching each other's rhythm, Tamia twirled around and curved her arm around the back of his neck. His hands slid around her waist, holding her closer as his warm breath caressed her nape.

Tamia shivered with pleasure. She provocatively gyrated her hips, delighted and aroused by the feel of Brandon's hard dick pressed against her ass. As they ground against each other, the sweaty bodies around them seemed to fade away until she and Brandon were alone on the dance floor, transported back to the night of their first date. A night filled with passion and excitement, when their future together had been filled with endless possibilities.

When Brandon turned Tamia in his arms, she looked into his dark eyes and realized that he wanted to make love to her as much as she wanted him to.

She opened her mouth. "Baby—"

"Listen up, party people!" Lou announced over a microphone, his voice cutting through the loud music. "It's time for us to make a special champagne toast to our guest of honor. I've got servers handing out glasses of Cristal, so be sure to grab one so you can toast to Tamia. Mamacita, can you bring your sexy self over here for a minute? And bring the rainmaker with you."

Tamia and Brandon looked at each other, then walked slowly off the dance floor.

As they made their way through the steamy crowd, Tamia found herself smiling so hard her cheeks hurt. Because for the second time that day, Brandon had given her reason to hope that they would be together again.

The past five months had been a living nightmare, but tonight no one could tell Tamia that she wasn't the luckiest woman in the world.

Chapter 4

Brandon

It was after two a.m. by the time Brandon stepped through his front door.

After leaving the club, he'd driven around for a while trying to clear his head and get his raging erection under control. Dancing with Tamia had done a serious number on him. During the months leading up to her trial, he'd managed to stay focused on the case by constantly reminding himself that he and Tamia were over. She'd betrayed him in the worst possible way, so giving her a second chance was out of the question.

But the moment he arrived at the party tonight and saw her voluptuous body poured into that fuck-me dress, he'd nearly lost his damn mind. It didn't matter that she'd broken his heart and destroyed their relationship. When he took her into his arms for that slow dance, she'd felt so right he'd almost forgotten that she didn't belong there anymore.

Brandon leaned against the closed door and blew out a deep breath, disturbed by his conflicting emotions. He had no business indulging feelings for Tamia. He was with Cynthia now, a good woman who loved him and would never deceive him. No matter how sexy Tamia had looked tonight, and no matter how badly Brandon wanted to fuck her, he couldn't betray Cynthia like that.

And just because he'd forgiven Tamia didn't mean he'd ever forget the way she'd played him.

Grimacing, he pushed away from the door and moved silently through the darkened condo to his bedroom, where he found Cynthia waiting for him. Well, not exactly *waiting*. She'd fallen asleep amid a pile of legal tomes she'd been studying in preparation for an upcoming trial.

Pausing in the bedroom doorway, Brandon propped his shoulder against the doorjamb and watched her sleep. He remembered how stunned she'd been when he'd asked her to move in with him. Truth be told, he'd been pretty shocked himself. They'd been dating for only two months, and after everything he'd just gone through with Tamia, living with another woman should have been the *last* thing on his mind. But it had seemed like the most natural thing in the world to shack up with Cynthia. They already spent long hours together at the office. At the end of an interminable, stressful day, it was nice to have someone to unwind with. Someone who could relate to the demands of his job. Someone who was fun enough to play video games with—and freaky enough to go down on him as they sat in the back of a half-empty movie theater.

At the memory of those steamy encounters, Brandon grinned at Cynthia. She lay curled on her side with her long, slender legs tucked toward her body. She wore one of his Longhorn T-shirts and a pair of red boy shorts that had ridden up her ass. As Brandon stared at her round butt cheeks, his dick hardened again.

He walked over to the enormous bed and leaned down

to kiss Cynthia. Her lips were soft, plump, and warm, like the ones nestled between her legs.

As she slowly opened her eyes, Brandon pulled away and smiled down at her. "Hey, sleepyhead."

"Hey," she murmured. "You're back."

"I'm back." He sat on the edge of the bed and reached over, running his hand up her smooth thigh to cup her ass. She gave him a look but didn't move away.

"How was the party?" she asked.

"Good." He hesitated. "You should have come."

She snorted. "I don't think so. We both know Tamia didn't want me there."

Brandon didn't deny it. He hadn't missed the way Tamia's face lit up when he'd arrived at the club alone. Although she'd told him to bring Cynthia, Brandon knew she would have resented Cynthia's presence at her celebration. He'd done the right thing by leaving Cynthia at home, but that didn't make him feel any less guilty about it.

Trying to change the subject, he nodded at the books scattered across the bed. "Get a lot of reading done?"

"Not really." Cynthia sat up, pushing her disheveled hair off her face. A slight frown marred her brows. "I had a hard time concentrating."

Uh-oh, Brandon thought. But he had to ask. "Why's that?"

She hesitated, biting her lower lip the way she did whenever she was uneasy about something. "I couldn't stop thinking about you . . . and Tamia."

He said nothing, waiting for her to elaborate.

Which she did. "She wants you back, Brandon."

Of course he knew that. He'd known for months. But he couldn't admit that to Cynthia, or she'd start questioning his motives for taking Tamia's case. And he didn't need—or want—that kind of scrutiny from her. Not when his own feelings for Tamia were still unresolved.

He rose from the bed and started across the room toward the walk-in closet. "Tamia and I aren't getting back together."

"Are you sure about that?" Cynthia challenged.

Brandon paused, glancing over his shoulder at her. "What's that supposed to mean?"

She frowned. "I was there today, Brandon. I saw the way Tamia was looking at you, like you were her whole world. And you went out of your way not to answer the reporter's question about reconciling with her."

"That's because I didn't want to embarrass Tamia," Brandon said calmly. "She's been through hell these past months. Today was her big day. Nothing else mattered."

Cynthia regarded him for a long, tense moment. "I don't think you understand how difficult these past five months have been on *me*, too."

"Of course I do," Brandon said quietly.

When everyone from his parents to his best friend had tried to talk him out of representing Tamia, Cynthia was the only one who'd supported his decision. He knew it hadn't been easy for her. As Tamia's attorney, he'd been required to spend a lot of time at the prison with her, preparing her for trial and trying to keep her morale up. They'd talked for hours on end, growing closer than they'd ever been before. She'd called him at all hours of the day, frequently interrupting his evenings with Cynthia.

One night, he and Cynthia had been making love when Tamia called. In hindsight, Brandon knew he should have ignored his ringing cell phone. He was in no condition to give any legal counsel or pep talks.

Resenting the interruption—and wanting to punish Brandon for taking Tamia's call—Cynthia had rolled him onto his back and straddled him. After lowering herself onto his dick, she'd started riding him with long, sensual strokes. And then she'd done something new with her pussy, something that made him lose control. By the time he regained his composure and picked up the fallen cell phone, Tamia had already hung up. The next time he saw her, she'd been clearly upset. He'd felt guilty, but that was the last time she'd ever called him after eight p.m.

"Brandon?"

Pulled out of his reverie, he blinked at Cynthia. "I'm sorry, baby. What did you say?"

She frowned, shaking her head at him. "Just because my father's a minister doesn't mean I'm a saint. I get jealous and paranoid like any other woman. Having to share you with your ex-girlfriend was no damn picnic, but I dealt with it because I love you, Brandon, and I know your conscience would have eaten you alive if you hadn't helped Tamia. But now that you've done your part and gotten her acquitted, I don't want to share you anymore. And I shouldn't have to."

"You won't," Brandon assured her, retracing his steps to the bed. "Believe me, sweetheart, I know how trying this whole situation has been for you. I wouldn't have blamed you for walking out on me months ago."

"Don't think I didn't consider it," Cynthia muttered, picking up one of her textbooks.

Brandon smiled. "But you didn't leave," he said, his hip touching hers as he perched on the edge of the bed. "You hung in there with me, and that means more to me than you can imagine. As for me and Tamia getting back together, have you ever heard that old song by Chicago, 'If She Would Have Been Faithful'?"

Cynthia looked faintly amused. "Chicago?"

Brandon grinned. "Don't laugh. You know how Kessler's always playing eighties music on his computer?"

She nodded.

"Well, one night we were working late in his office

when this Chicago song came on the radio. I'd never heard it before, but the words captured my feelings about the way things worked out between us. If Tamia hadn't cheated on me, you and I wouldn't have hooked up. If she would have been faithful, I would have missed out on being with you."

Cynthia's expression softened. "Do you really mean that?"

"Of course." But even as the assurance left Brandon's mouth, he wondered whether he really *had* meant what he'd just told her. Did he honestly believe that losing Tamia was for the best, or was that just wishful thinking on his part?

Frowning inwardly, he reached over and cupped Cynthia's cheek, as though touching her would silence his doubts.

She smiled, tears misting her eyes as she rubbed her face against his palm. "You're just trying to sweet-talk your way into my panties," she teased.

Brandon grinned weakly. "Is it working?"

"Maybe."

"Maybe?" He leaned over and kissed her, feeling her nipple harden as he caressed one of her breasts. "What about now? Is *this* working?"

"Mmm . . ." Suddenly she pulled away. "No."

"Why not?"

"Because you need to take a shower. I can smell Tamia's perfume all over you." Cynthia eyed him suspiciously.

Guilt assailed Brandon at the memory of dancing with Tamia, grinding his dick against her juicy ass until he almost nutted in his pants.

Watching him carefully, Cynthia frowned. "Is there something you're not telling me?"

Brandon met her gaze. "Like what?"

Her frown deepened. "What, exactly, happened at that party?"

"Nothing."

"Nothing?" Cynthia repeated skeptically.

"Yeah, baby. Nothing."

They stared at each other, two lawyers trying to see who would back down first.

After several moments, Cynthia smirked at him. "Let me give you a word of advice, *baby*. The next time you want to seduce me, don't come home smelling like your ex-girlfriend. Trust me, it's an automatic mood killer."

Brandon frowned. "Come on, Cynthia—"

"I'm serious, Brandon. No shower, no action." She returned to her book, leaving no room for debate.

Sighing heavily, Brandon rose from the bed and made his way to the walk-in closet. He sniffed at his suit jacket, then inwardly groaned. Cynthia was right. He smelled like he'd spent the entire night in Tamia's arms. Which wasn't far from what he'd been tempted to do.

Grimacing, he removed his jacket, shirt, and pants, then set them aside to be dry-cleaned.

Unless Cynthia decided to burn them first.

When he emerged from the closet moments later, she didn't even glance up from her book, though she'd never been able to resist the sight of his naked body. Despite his demanding schedule, he always made time to work out. The result of his efforts was a hard, muscular physique that turned female heads wherever he went.

Not now, though. He might as well have looked like Fat Albert, for all the attention Cynthia was paying him.

Damn, Brandon mused. *My black ass is* really *in the doghouse!*

He headed toward the master bathroom, then changed his mind and abruptly reversed direction. Cynthia's eyes widened as he bore down on the bed, his jaw set determinedly.

"What are you doing?" she demanded. "You're supposed to be taking a—"

"I will. We can shower together, after we're both good and sweaty."

She swallowed visibly. "Brandon—"

He bent and kissed her hard, silencing her protests. As she melted against him, he reached down and swept the book off her lap. It landed on the floor with a heavy thud.

He lowered himself to the bed, covering her body with his as he tugged off the T-shirt she wore, baring her breasts. They were small but plump, crowned with pretty chocolate nipples. He leaned down and flicked his tongue over one, then the other.

Cynthia groaned and arched her back, breasts thrusting upward in sensual invitation. He palmed them, pushed them together, and took both nipples into his mouth.

"Ummm," Cynthia moaned with pleasure, eyes rolling closed.

When he'd finished sucking her tits, Brandon grasped the waistband of her skimpy boy shorts and eased them down her legs, revealing a narrow patch of black pubic hair. His dick throbbed at the sight of her fleshy lips glistening with arousal.

He draped her legs over his shoulders and lowered his head, then drew her clitoris into his mouth.

She let out a strangled cry as her hips arched off the bed.

Brandon nibbled and sucked her clit, then began eating her pussy as she writhed against him and grabbed fistfuls of the bedcovers. Within seconds she was climaxing, damn near suffocating him as her thighs squeezed his head.

After several moments, when her body had stopped bucking and trembling, she collapsed against the bed and exhaled a deep, shaky breath. "That was *so* unfair."

Brandon chuckled, the sound muffled against her damp abdomen. "Don't hate the playa, baby. Hate the game."

She sputtered indignantly, swatting at his head.

He laughed, catching her wrists and pinning her arms above her head. She squirmed beneath him as he rose over her, settling his body between her thighs. Their stares locked, smiles dissolving as their mouths met in a deep, carnal kiss flavored with Cynthia's juices.

With his free hand, Brandon reached down and wrapped his fingers around his hard dick. As he began stroking himself, Cynthia ground her hips against him, urging him to take what was his. When he'd teased her enough, he guided his shaft to her slick opening.

"I'm going commando," he told her, because he didn't want to stop the flow to retrieve a condom. "That all right?"

Cynthia nodded quickly. "You're good, soldier."

The words had barely passed her lips before Brandon thrust into her, burying himself deep. They both groaned with pleasure.

He looked downward, watching himself slide out of her, then slowly back inside. Cynthia moaned and tugged at her captured wrists. As soon as Brandon released her, she grabbed his ass, fingernails digging into his skin. He began pumping into her with long, deep strokes that she met with hungry thrusts of her own.

"Damn, woman," he whispered, sweat collecting on his forehead. "You feel good."

"So do you, baby," she breathed, licking at his lips. "You're banging the *hell* outta my spot."

"Yeah?"

"Oh, yeah."

"Should I stop?" he teased.

"You'd better not!"

His laughter dissolved into a groan as she tightened her

thighs around him, locking him into place. As he closed his eyes and pounded her pussy, the force of his thrusts made the bed frame shudder and sent Cynthia's books bouncing across the mattress.

Reopening his eyes, he gazed down at Cynthia. One moment he was looking at her small breasts bouncing up and down. A moment later the image changed to big, luscious tits with dark caramel nipples pointed straight toward him.

Shit! Brandon thought, squeezing his eyes shut again as he tried to block out the familiar vision of Tamia's breasts. But the more he tried not to think about them, the more he wanted to lick and suck them. When he leaned down and wrapped his mouth around Cynthia's nipple, she moaned with pleasure. But it was Tamia's throaty purr he heard, Tamia's hot pussy he was drilling like a piston.

Seconds later Cynthia screamed in ecstasy as he exploded inside her, his dick spurting violently, another woman's name nearly spilling from his lips. He clenched his jaw, head thrown back, arms trembling as they supported his weight. He felt Cynthia's chest heaving beneath his as they both gasped for air.

After several moments he collapsed beside her on the bed. She sighed contentedly and rolled onto her side, facing him with a satiated smile. Ignoring a sharp pang of guilt, he gathered her into his arms, enjoying the dampness of her skin pressed against him.

Hooking one leg across his hip, she murmured, "I love the way you feel inside me."

Brandon smiled. "Good, 'cause I love *being* inside you. Speaking of which, are you ready to take round two to the shower?"

She laughed. "In a minute. I need to catch my breath first."

He grinned, stroking her thigh. "Can't hang, huh?"

"Oh, don't even try it. You *know* I can hang."

"No doubt," Brandon agreed.

Who would have guessed that beneath her prim and proper demeanor, Cynthia was a straight-up freak who could get down and dirty with the best of them? *He'd* certainly never suspected. But he should have. After all, she *was* a pastor's kid.

At the thought of Joseph Yarbrough, Brandon casually asked, "Does your old man still have a problem with us living together?"

Startled, Cynthia stared at him. "Where'd *that* come from?"

Brandon shrugged. "I'm just wondering."

"Are you serious? You just fucked my brains out, and all of a sudden you're wondering what my father thinks of us shacking up?"

"Well . . . yeah."

Cynthia chuckled, shaking her head at him. "Way to kill the mood, bringing up my father after sex."

Brandon grinned sheepishly. "Sorry."

"You should be. Now you're gonna have to work extra hard just to get me back in the mood."

"That's cool," Brandon drawled, letting his fingers wander between her legs. "I like working hard."

"And you're so good at it, too. But to answer your question"—Cynthia shivered as he strummed her clit—"no, my dad isn't too crazy about our living arrangement. He thinks we should—" She broke off with a gasp as Brandon slipped his middle finger inside her.

"He thinks we should what?"

Cynthia groaned, closing her eyes as he stroked her pussy. "N-Nothing, baby. It's not important."

But Brandon knew what she'd been about to say. Their parents had made no secret of the fact that they wanted the two of them to get married. Brandon had resisted the idea for years, telling himself that he and Cynthia were better off as friends. But everything had changed, and he now realized how special she was. But was she special enough to—

"Brandon?" Cynthia purred, interrupting his thoughts.

He met her eyes. "Yeah, baby?"

She smiled wickedly. "I'm ready for round two."

Chapter 5

Fiona

Later that morning, Fiona Powell was awakened by the sound of voices outside her bedroom. Opening her eyes, she peered groggily at the alarm clock on her nightstand. It was 8:26 a.m.

Frowning, she rolled over in bed, encountering the muscled warmth of a man's naked body. She eyed him blankly for a moment, trying to remember who he was and how he'd gotten there.

As a kaleidoscope of images flashed through her mind, the memories came rushing back. Last night she'd driven to a popular downtown club hoping to crash Tamia's homecoming party. But she'd been turned away at the front entrance by a big, beefy bouncer who'd checked the clipboard in his hand and informed her that she'd been placed on a "Do Not Enter" list, as if she were some fucking terrorist.

Enraged and humiliated, Fiona had cussed the dude out before taking her ass to another club, where she'd hooked up with a sexy, caramel-toned brother who'd bought her drinks and shared his weed. They'd worked it out on the dance floor, then returned to her house for a serious fuckathon that had lasted into the wee hours of the morning.

Since Fiona didn't have any appointments scheduled until noon, she'd hoped to sleep in late.

So much for *that* idea.

Hearing the shuffle of heavy footsteps in the hallway, she frowned and jumped out of bed, naked breasts bouncing. She snatched her panties off the floor and tugged them on, then strode to her closet and grabbed her robe.

"What's going on?" came a drowsy mumble from the bed.

"Nothing." *What the hell is his name again?* "Go back to sleep."

He did just that, pulling the covers over his head as Fiona quickly left the room and started down the short hallway.

When she reached the living room, she was stunned to encounter bare walls, windows without curtains, and missing furniture. As she stood there gaping around, two young Hispanic guys strolled into the house, walked over to the remaining sofa, and lifted it onto their shoulders.

"Hey!" Fiona yelled, rushing over to them. "What the fuck do y'all think you're doing?"

They stared at her with confused expressions.

"What? Y'all motherfuckers don't speak English? That's my shit you're stealing!"

"Actually," a voice said coolly, "it's mine."

Fiona whirled toward the front door.

Tamia sauntered into the house looking like she'd just stepped off the set of a BET music video. Her long bob was swinging, and she wore a pair of designer sunglasses, skintight jeans, and strappy stiletto sandals.

Fiona glared at her. "What the hell's going on, Tamia?"

"What the hell does it look like? I'm moving out, and I'm taking my shit with me."

"What?" Fiona exclaimed in shock. "You didn't tell me you were moving!"

"I just did." Tamia signaled to the two men, who carried the sofa out the front door.

"Wait a minute!" Fiona protested vehemently. "They can't take that!"

"Says who?" Tamia countered. "*I'm* the one who bought that sofa, not you. Matter of fact, I bought practically everything in this damn house. Which is why I'm taking everything with me."

Fiona stared at her. "What do you mean?"

"I don't think I stuttered," Tamia said coldly, pushing her sunglasses off her face as she started across the room. "But since your stank ass is obviously high or hung over, let me make myself clearer. When I leave this house today, everything that belongs *to* me is going *with* me."

Fiona panicked. "You can't do that!"

"Oh, yeah?" Tamia challenged, advancing on Fiona until their faces were separated by mere inches. "Who's gonna stop me?"

Fiona swallowed hard as something like fear crept over her. "Don't move out, Tam-Tam," she said plaintively. "Stay here with me. It'll be like old times again."

Tamia eyed her incredulously. "*Are you out of your fucking mind*? How can you even open your mouth to say some outrageous shit like that to me? You let me take the fall for a crime *you* committed! After everything I've done for you, you were willing to let me spend the rest of my life rotting in prison. As if that weren't fucked up enough, you threatened to have me killed if I told anyone the truth about what really happened! Do you have *any* idea what the past five months were like for me? Constantly looking over my shoulder, sleeping with one eye open, inspecting my food, wondering which of those crazy bitches would walk up to me one day and shank my ass because my own sister told them to. And now you have the audacity to stand there and talk to me about old times? It will *never* be like old times again, Fiona! Do you hear me? *NEVER!*"

Guilt assailed Fiona, bringing tears to her eyes. "I never meant to—"

"Save your fucking apology," Tamia snarled furiously. "Nothing you can say will ever make up for the way you betrayed me. So, yeah, bitch. I'm taking all the furniture, linens, pots and pans, silverware—every damn thing that I bought with *my* hard-earned money. And I wish you would try to stop me."

Fiona gulped hard, blinking back tears. "Fine," she mumbled. "Be that way."

"I will, fuck you very much."

Fiona hesitated, then couldn't resist adding snidely, "It's not like I can't replace everything. I make good money now."

Tamia smirked. "Only because Brandon asked his brother to hire you as a favor to *me*. But how long do you think you'd keep that job if they found out that you killed Isabel Archer?"

Stricken, Fiona stared at Tamia. "You wouldn't."

"Maybe I would."

"But you promised not to!"

"Maybe I've had a change of heart." Tamia jabbed an accusing finger at Fiona. "You killed a woman for no reason. We both know your psycho ass should be locked up, not working at one of the top sports agencies in the country. My conscience has been bothering me for months. So maybe I'll wake up tomorrow morning and decide it's my civic duty to turn you over to the police, like I should have in the first place."

The blood drained from Fiona's head. She couldn't go back to jail. She'd rather die than see the inside of another prison cell. "You promised," she whispered.

A malicious gleam filled Tamia's eyes. "Some promises are meant to be broken."

Fiona's heart thudded. "If you tell—"

"You'll do what? Put out a hit on me? Do what you gotta do." Tamia leaned closer, eyes narrowed menacingly. "But you'd better make damn sure the motherfucker gets the job done. 'Cause if I'm still standing when the dust settles, I'm coming for you. And when I get through with your black ass, you'll wish you'd never met me."

Shaking from the inside out, Fiona watched as Tamia slid her sunglasses over her eyes and smiled coldly, then turned and headed toward the door.

Fiona knew she should just let her leave. But she couldn't—not when there was a chance that Tamia would walk out that door and go straight to the police.

"What about Brandon?" Fiona blurted desperately.

Tamia stopped walking but didn't turn around. "What *about* him?"

"He broke up with you because of all the lies you told him. How do you think he's going to feel when he finds out that you sat by and let him defend you in court when you knew all along who the real killer was? Even if you try to explain that you were just trying to protect me, he'll see it as one more lie you told him. And he'll never trust you again, let alone take you back."

Tamia turned slowly around.

Sensing that she'd gained the upper hand, Fiona smiled tauntingly. "Isn't that what you want? To get your man back? Haven't you spent all these months plotting how to take him away from Cynthia? Haven't you tortured yourself thinking about him going home to her every night, eating her pussy, fucking her doggy style the way he used to fuck *you*?"

When Tamia said nothing, Fiona laughed. "I know you have. And I also know you have every reason to worry about Brandon and Cynthia. They're getting serious about each other. So serious that their parents have started planning their wedding." Fiona paused, watching with satisfaction as the corners of Tamia's mouth tightened. She'd gotten under her skin. Good.

"If you want one last shot at getting Brandon back," Fiona warned coolly, "you'd better keep your damn mouth shut about what really happened that night."

Tamia regarded her in silence for several moments, then slowly retraced her steps across the room. When she and Fiona stood face-to-face, Tamia asked very calmly, "Are you finished?"

Fiona's chin lifted in defiance. "Actually—"

Quick as a striking snake, Tamia backhanded her across the face.

Pain exploded inside Fiona's head as she fell backward, landing hard on the floor. As another burst of pain shot up her spine, tears spurted from her eyes. She brought a hand to her burning cheek and stared up at her sister with a look of wounded disbelief.

Tamia pushed her sunglasses off her face, then crouched down beside Fiona. She'd never seen her sister's eyes filled with such hatred and fury.

"Listen, bitch," Tamia snarled, viciously grabbing a fistful of Fiona's long hair and wrenching her head back. "After today, I don't *ever* want to see your face again. Don't call me, don't try to visit me, don't even speak my fucking name. Because as far as I'm concerned, you're dead to me."

Fiona eyed her piteously, tears rolling down her face. "But we're sisters—"

"*Sisters* don't use and betray each other," Tamia spat venomously. "*Sisters* don't let each other take the blame for their crimes. And *sisters* sure as hell don't put out hits on each other."

Fiona whimpered as Tamia's ruthless grip tightened on her hair. "I know you showed up at the club last night and acted a damn fool when you got turned away. So let me repeat myself since your ass is stuck on stupid. You and I aren't sisters anymore. Got that? I want absolutely nothing to do with you. If I catch you anywhere near me again, I'ma fuck you up, then call the police on your stalker ass. If you think I'm playing, just try me."

Fiona cried out as Tamia gave her hair one last vicious yank, then slid her sunglasses back into place and rose to her feet.

"What the hell's going on out here?" asked a slurred voice.

Fiona and Tamia glanced across the living room. Dude from the club stood there butt naked, eyes bloodshot, nappy dreadlocks hanging to his shoulders.

He looked Tamia up and down, lewdly admiring her big breasts and ass. "Dayuum!" he exclaimed, licking his lips as he stroked his short, fat dick. "You fine as *hell*, baby. Did she bring you here for me?"

Tamia peered at him over the top of her shades, then rolled her eyes in disgust and muttered, "Nigga, please."

As she sauntered out the front door, he stared after her departing ass. "Dayuum," he repeated, glancing down at Fiona for the first time. "Was that your *sister*?"

She glared at him, trembling with pain and outrage. "Get out."

He frowned at her. "What'd you say?"

"I said GET OUT!" Fiona screamed, lunging to her feet and charging toward him with tightly balled fists.

He backed away, holding up his hands as he eyed her incredulously. "Wait a minute. Why you trippin' just 'cause I said your sister's fine?"

"You dumb motherfucker!" Fiona raged, following him into her bedroom. "I don't give a damn about that! I just want you to get your shit and get the fuck outta my house! *NOW*!"

Calling her all kinds of a crazy bitch, he hurriedly threw on his clothes and grabbed his stash of weed, then bounced.

After he left, Fiona ran to the kitchen and flung open the cabinets and drawers. They were bare as a bone, not even a fork to be found.

With mounting hysteria, she turned and raced down the hallway to Tamia's bedroom.

It was empty!

Fiona turned slowly in a circle, her stunned gaze sweeping around the room. Her sister hadn't been bluffing. She really *had* moved out, leaving Fiona completely alone.

Alone. The word ricocheted through her mind.

For the first time in her life, she was truly on her own.

As reality sank in, she opened her mouth and screamed at the top of her lungs before crumpling to the floor, her body wracked with sobs of anguish and fury.

If Tamia thinks she's heard the last of me, she silently raged, *she'd better think again!*

Chapter 6

Tamia

Tamia stared out the window at the white shotgun house that squatted on a small patch of lawn. The house—with its sagging porch, rickety swing, and peeling paint—was the only home she'd ever known. She'd always dreamed of the day she would move out and never look back. But now that that day had finally come, she found it harder to leave than she'd expected.

As she gazed at the old house, childhood memories replayed in her mind's eye. She saw herself chasing Fiona around the small yard, their faces glistening with sweat, barrettes bouncing at the end of their braided pigtails as their grandmother looked on from the porch. When Tamia caught Fiona and playfully wrestled her to the grass, their mother would step from the house and call out warningly, "Be careful now! Don't hurt your baby sister."

And Mama Esther would cluck her tongue at her daughter. "Oh, hush. Tamia won't hurt that chile. She loves Fiona more than anyone else in the world."

"Tamia?"

Snapped out of her bittersweet reverie, Tamia turned from the window to meet Lou's concerned gaze.

"Are you okay?" he asked gently.

She nodded, relieved that her sunglasses concealed the moisture in her eyes. "I'm fine."

She and Lou sat in the luxurious backseat of his Escalade while they waited for the movers to finish loading up the truck. While Fiona was at work yesterday, Tamia and Shanell had come to the house to pack up the kitchen and Tamia's bedroom. They'd transported everything they could to Shanell's place, where Tamia had spent the night. Early that morning, Lou and his movers had picked her up and driven her back home to retrieve the furniture and the rest of her belongings.

Just when she'd begun to think that Fiona might sleep through all the commotion, her sister had showed her face. From there it was on and popping. Tamia's hand still stung from how hard she'd slapped Fiona, trying to snap her damn head off her neck.

"Did you get everything you came for?" Lou asked her.

"Yeah," Tamia answered, her gaze returning to the window. She watched as the two Puerto Rican guys closed the back door of the moving truck, then climbed inside.

Lou's driver glanced in the rearview mirror. "Are we ready?"

Lou eyed Tamia expectantly, waiting.

She took one last, lingering look at her childhood home, then swallowed tightly and turned away.

Staring straight ahead, she said with quiet finality, "Let's go."

Twenty minutes later, Lou ushered Tamia through the front door of her new apartment. Since he'd insisted on blindfolding her before they reached their destination, she had no idea where they were or what the place looked like.

"Come on, papi," she said, laughing. "The suspense is killing me."

Lou tsk-tsked. "So impatient."

"*Impatient*? You've had me blindfolded for—"

He removed the strip of cloth and announced, "Welcome to your new home."

Opening her eyes, Tamia looked around and gasped.

The apartment boasted rich hardwood floors, beautifully painted walls, and a collection of modern furniture and tasteful artwork. The ceilings were high, and a row of picture windows overlooked the downtown skyline.

It was absolutely stunning.

"Whose apartment is this?" Tamia whispered, staring incredulously at Lou.

He grinned. "Yours."

"Don't play with me."

"I'm not. This is your new crib, mamacita."

"What?" Tamia glanced around in shocked disbelief. "I can't afford this!"

"You don't have to. Not for a while, anyway."

She looked at Lou as if he'd lost his damn mind. "Come again?"

He chuckled softly. "The apartment is leased by one of my clients, who had to leave unexpectedly for Singapore. When I told him I was looking for a place for you, he offered to let you stay here while he's gone. The lease is already paid up through a year, so all you have to cover are your utilities."

Suppressing a thrill of excitement, Tamia gave Lou a suspicious look. "It sounds too good to be true. What's the catch?"

He laughed. "Why does there have to be a catch?"

"*Are you serious*? I just got out of prison. I have no money and no job, yet you're telling me that I can post up in this fully furnished luxury apartment—rent free—for a whole year? Come on, Lou. Do you honestly expect me to believe there's no catch?" She eyed him skeptically, lips twisted to one side.

"Why are you being so suspicious?" he protested, shaking his head at her. "Haven't I always looked out for you? When you told me you needed to find a new place to live, did you think I'd let you move to the projects or some low-rent apartment complex? You deserve better than that." He gestured grandly around. "You deserve One Park Place."

At the mention of the ritzy address, Tamia's eyes widened. "Is *that* where we are? One Park Place?"

Lou grinned. "That's right."

As if needing confirmation, Tamia hurried over to the windows and gazed out at the glistening skyscrapers that defined the downtown skyline. When she worked at Richards Carruth, she'd often fantasized about living in one of the luxury high-rises that she passed on her way to the office every day. She couldn't believe her fantasy was about to become a reality. There *had* to be a catch.

As Lou joined her at the windows, she remarked, "Your client must be pretty wealthy to afford a place like this."

"He is," Lou confirmed. "But the company he works for is paying for the apartment, not him."

"Ohhhkay," Tamia said, drawing out the word slowly. "So since they sent him to Singapore for the next year, won't they want a refund on the lease?"

"Nah. You know how these corporations work. They get huge tax write-offs for leasing corporate apartments. Besides, my client told them he wants to keep the place for his mistress." Lou grinned. "Having a love nest is one of the perks of being a top executive."

"I guess so," Tamia said sardonically. "But he'd better not show up here one day expecting to get some pussy."

Lou laughed, kissing the top of her head. "He won't, mamacita. He knows better."

"Good." Tamia hesitated, searching Lou's hazel eyes. "When are you going to tell me about your new business venture?"

He held her gaze for a long moment, then said, "Come on. Let's have a seat."

He took her hand and led her over to the white sofa, which was so elegant and pristine that Tamia was almost afraid to sit down. As she did, she ran her hand over the plush fabric and realized that she could get very used to living here.

Don't get ahead of yourself, an inner voice warned. *Hear what Lou has to say before you make any decisions about taking the apartment.*

Still holding on to her other hand, Lou looked her in the eye and said, "I run an escort agency."

Tamia blinked at him. "You run a *what*?"

"An escort agency."

"Are you serious? *That's* your new line of work?"

"Yup." Releasing her hand, Lou leaned back against the sofa and stretched out his long legs.

"How did *that* happen?" Tamia asked.

"When the studio went bankrupt, I found myself stuck with all these beautiful actresses who still wanted to work for me. So that's when I came up with the idea to start an escort agency. And let me tell you, it was one of the best ideas I've ever had. You wouldn't believe what some dudes are willing to pay for just an hour with one of my girls."

Tamia eyed him knowingly. "Like Honey?"

"Yeah." Lou grinned. "As a matter of fact, she's my most popular escort."

"That doesn't surprise me." Tamia frowned, her mind flashing on an image of the young, voluptuous beauty who'd boldly propositioned her at the party. "How old is that girl, Lou?"

"Old enough." He winked at her.

Tamia wasn't amused. "I'm really surprised at you.

With all the heat you've been catching from the feds, I would have expected you to lay low for a while. You know they're looking for any reason to lock you up. If they find out that you've traded porn for prostitution—"

"Hold up," Lou interjected, taking umbrage. "Last I checked, escort agencies aren't illegal in this country. I'm running a perfectly legitimate business and providing a valuable service to the community—"

Tamia snorted. "Be serious, Lou."

"What?"

She gave him a look. "If your girls are having sex with their clients, you know damn well that qualifies as prostitution. And if the feds find out, they're gonna be all over your ass. Why even take that risk?"

"First of all," Lou countered calmly, "the feds aren't gonna find out shit because my agency doesn't offer sexual services—not officially, anyway. The no-sex policy is spelled out clearly on the website, and my escorts know that they have to be discreet. Not only that, but my clients sure as hell aren't gonna talk. Some of these guys are powerful CEOs and politicians with wives and reputations to protect. And if the feds try to conduct some bullshit sting operation, my lawyer has contacts who will tip him off to the investigation."

Tamia arched a brow. "Your lawyer?"

"Yeah. Brandon. Don't forget that he's the one who got the fucking Feebs off my back in the first place. And all he had to do was make a phone call to someone at the Justice Department—some higher-up who's hoping that Brandon's father will appoint him to his cabinet after he's elected governor." Lou grinned broadly. "I don't think even *you* realize just how connected your boy is."

Tamia said nothing, remembering how Brandon had used his father's powerful connections to sabotage Dominic's business deals. If there'd been any doubt in her mind before, she'd realized then that Brandon was the absolute *last* person she'd ever want as an enemy.

"His father plays golf with President Obama," Lou continued. "And according to some of my clients who move in those political circles, the old man wants to appoint Brandon to attorney general when he becomes governor."

"Really?"

"Yeah, really." Lou laughed, shaking his head with an awed expression. "The Chamberses are like the fucking Kennedys or something. So as long as Brandon's got my back, you think I'm worried about the feds coming after me? Hell, no."

Tamia chuckled. "I see your point," she conceded, leaning back against the cushy sofa and crossing her legs. "It's great to have friends in high places. But I still think you need to be careful."

"I am." Lou paused a moment. "And you can help me."

"What do you mean?"

Holding her gaze, he reached over and took her hand again. "I want you to come work for me, Tamia."

Caught off guard, she stared at him. "Are you asking me to be one of your *escorts*?"

"No. I want you to run the agency for me."

Tamia frowned. "I don't understand."

"I have a receptionist who schedules the appointments with clients, but I need someone to manage the escorts for me. Someone who's smart, sexy, and knows how to carry herself with class. Someone the girls already respect and would listen to." Lou brushed his lips across the back of Tamia's hand, smiling into her eyes. "That someone is you, mamacita."

"Ah." Tamia nodded wisely. "So *that's* what this is all about. The new wardrobe, help from the movers, the swanky apartment. You're trying to bribe me."

"No, I'm not," Lou insisted. "I bought you new clothes

and got you this place because we're friends, and friends look out for each other."

Tamia eyed him knowingly. "So you *weren't* trying to bribe me?"

"Of course not." Lou hesitated, then grinned sheepishly. "Maybe just a little."

"Umm-hmm. That's what I thought."

"Did it work?"

"No."

"Why not?"

Tamia sighed heavily. "Don't get me wrong, papi. I'm flattered by your job offer. But I don't know anything about running an escort agency."

"Neither did I, but that didn't stop me from starting one anyway. I'm telling you, Tamia, you're perfect for this job. You've already proved that you have a head for business, so you'd know how to interact with my clients. Not only that, but all of my girls already know who you are. They've watched your movies and they look up to you."

"They look up to Mystique," Tamia corrected. "And I'm not her."

Lou groaned. "Come on, mamacita. If you worked for me, you'd make a killing. You could afford to buy a new car and lease this apartment on your own next year."

"Damn," Tamia marveled, staring at him. "So it's like that? You're really making *that* kind of paper?"

"Hell, yeah. I wasn't lying when I said that starting an escort agency was one of the best ideas I've ever had. That shit is recession-proof." Lou grinned broadly, looking pleased with himself.

Again Tamia sighed. "I won't lie. Your offer is very tempting, because after I pay off my legal bills, I'm gonna be flat broke. So I need a job ASAP."

"Then come work for me."

"I can't." She grimaced. "No offense, Lou, but I'm not interested in going back into the sex industry."

"This is different—"

"Maybe in some ways, but sex is still the main focus of your business."

Lou smirked. "So what? You got something against sex now?"

"Not at all," Tamia said wryly. "In fact, getting laid is all I've been thinking about since I left the courthouse yesterday."

"Why didn't you say so?" Lou wiggled his brows suggestively. "You know I can help you out with that."

Tamia grinned. "Um, no, that's okay."

Yet she found herself staring at his full lips and remembering what her fellow porn stars used to whisper about his bedroom skills. If she hadn't made a vow to hold out for Brandon, she would have been seriously tempted to give Lou some pussy. She needed her back blown out like nobody's business.

Pushing the thought aside, Tamia said humorously, "I appreciate the offer, papi, but I value our friendship too much to take advantage of you like that."

"Take advantage of me," he urged. "Really. I don't mind."

They both laughed.

Sobering after several moments, Tamia smiled softly at Lou. "For real though, papi. I'm glad that business is going so well for you, and I'm flattered that you'd entrust me with managing your agency. But I love working in advertising, so I'm really hoping that I can find another job in that field. Starting Monday morning, I'll be scouring every job search engine that's out there and sending out my resume. With any luck," she added ruefully, "I'll find an employer who doesn't know, or doesn't care, that I was just acquitted of murder."

"You will," Lou said with such certainty that Tamia gave him an amused look.

"How can you be so sure?" she asked.

"That you'll find a job?"

"Yeah. I mean, given my recent legal troubles—combined with a bad economy and an even worse job market—you have to admit that the odds are seriously stacked against me."

"They are," Lou gently agreed, his hazel eyes boring into hers. "But you're a survivor, Tamia. No matter how many curveballs life throws at you, you're always gonna come out on top. Remember that, and believe it."

Chapter 7

Tamia

As Tamia returned to her apartment that evening, her cell phone went off.

After Brandon broke up with her, she'd changed her special ringtone for him to Melanie Fiona's "Gone and Never Coming Back," a song that made her cry every time she'd listened to it, which had been often. But hearing it now brought a huge, delighted grin to her face.

Because it meant that Brandon was calling.

After retrieving the phone from her new leather purse, she answered warmly, "Hey, you."

"Hey, yourself." The sound of Brandon's deep, sexy voice made her pussy clench as she walked to the kitchen. "What're you up to?"

"Nothing much," she replied, her heels clicking smartly on the hardwood floor as she crossed to the refrigerator, opened the door, and placed a Styrofoam container on the top shelf. "I just got back from dinner with Shanell and Mark, and his army buddy Gavin."

"Yeah? Where'd you guys go?"

"Pappadeaux. I've been craving seafood for months."

"Sounds good," Brandon said. "What'd you order? Your usual?"

Tamia smiled as she reached for a bottle of chardonnay that had been a housewarming gift from Shanell. "What's my usual?"

Brandon chuckled softly. "You think I don't remember just because it's been a while?"

"Yup."

"Well, you're wrong."

Tamia grinned, retrieving a wineglass from the cabinet before hunting down a corkscrew. "Prove it."

"What? You're testing me or something?"

"Maybe," Tamia teased, thoroughly enjoying their light-hearted banter. "You're pushing thirty-four, boo boo, so your memory's probably starting to fail you."

Brandon laughed. "Oh, you got jokes?"

"Yup."

"That's a'ight. I'ma remember that when you hit the big 3-0 next year."

"Oooh! Hater!"

This time they both laughed.

Cradling the phone between her shoulder and ear, Tamia uncorked her bottle of wine and poured herself half a glass. "Well?" she prompted.

"Well what?"

"I'm still waiting for you to tell me what I ordered for dinner."

Brandon heaved an exaggerated sigh. "Since you insist on testing my memory, little girl, I'll play along. You had a house salad with chili lime vinaigrette, the crawfish platter, and a slice of key lime pie for dessert."

Tamia smiled with pleasure. "You remembered."

"Of course." His voice softened. "I remember every-thing."

Tamia's smile faded. Given the disastrous way their relationship had ended, she couldn't be blamed for wishing he didn't have such a photographic memory.

"Anyway," Brandon continued after a few moments, "I was calling to find out how the move went today."

"Everything went well," Tamia said, carrying her wineglass over to the long breakfast counter and perching on one of the high-backed barstools. "The movers were really efficient and professional. And they didn't even get mad when the plans changed and they had to make an extra trip to Goodwill to drop off my furniture."

"You donated your furniture to Goodwill?"

"Yup. Turns out I didn't need any of it where I was going."

"What do you mean?"

"Remember how I told you that Lou found an apartment for me?"

"Yeah."

"Well, I had no idea that he'd hooked me up with an apartment at One Park Place."

Brandon whistled softly. "One Park Place, huh? *Nice.*"

"Tell me about it," Tamia agreed, unable to keep the excitement out of her voice. "This apartment is off the chain, Brandon. It has two bedrooms and a study. It's beautifully furnished, and it has the most amazing views of downtown. And don't even get me started on the gourmet kitchen," she gushed, admiring the room's custom cherry cabinets, granite countertops, and stainless steel appliances. "I can't *wait* to start cooking in here. As a matter of fact, I'd love to make you dinner sometime, Brandon. It's the least I can do after the way you came through for me. Just say the word, and I'll start planning the menu. I'm thinking—"

"Whoa," Brandon interrupted with a soft chuckle. "Slow down and take a deep breath, baby girl. I can't keep up with you."

Tamia's face heated with embarrassment. "I'm sorry," she said sheepishly. "I didn't mean to ramble on like that. It's just that . . . well, this is the nicest place I've ever lived. And you know what happens when you take folks like me outta the hood. We don't know what to do with ourselves."

Brandon was silent for a long moment. "Tamia."

"Yes?" she mumbled.

"You have no reason to be ashamed of your humble beginnings," he said so tenderly that tears welled in her eyes. "Who you are isn't determined by what you had, or didn't have, growing up. What you do with your life—the choices you make—is what defines you as a person."

Tamia swallowed tightly. "I know. I didn't at first, but . . . I do now."

"I believe that," Brandon said quietly.

"You do?"

"Yeah." He hesitated, as if he were trying to decide how much he should say. "I've watched you change over these past several months, Tamia. You let your guard down, and you opened up to me in ways you never had before. I wish . . ." He trailed off.

Tamia held her breath, waiting.

But he didn't pursue that train of thought. "What you went through never should have happened, but I've always believed that what doesn't kill you can only make you stronger. I think you're much stronger today than you were five months ago."

"I think so, too," Tamia whispered.

"Good," Brandon said gently. "And as for your humble beginnings, not having the so-called finer things in life will only make you appreciate them more when you get them. Like that apartment."

She smiled softly. "You're right. I'm definitely appreciating the new digs." She chuckled, adding, "I've been hearing *The Jeffersons* theme song in my head all day. *Fish don't fry in the kitchen—*"

Brandon crooned, *"Beans don't burn on the grill—"*

"Took a whole lotta tryin'—"

"Just to get up that hill—"

"Now we're up in the big leagues—"

"Getting our turn at bat—"

Together they sang, *"As long we live, it's you and me, baby. There ain't nothin' wrong with that. Well, we're movin' on up!"*

They both burst out laughing.

A few minutes later, wiping tears from the corners of her eyes, Tamia took a sip of her wine and sighed. Until that moment, she hadn't realized just how much she'd missed Brandon's friendship, missed laughing with him and having fun together. If he gave her a second chance, she'd make damn sure she never again took him for granted.

Holding her glass, she slid off the stool and started from the kitchen. "By the way," she said curiously, "where are you, Brandon?"

"At the office, catching up on some paperwork."

"That's no way to spend a Saturday evening," Tamia gently scolded. "Besides, I thought one of the perks of making partner was working shorter hours."

"Not quite." Brandon chuckled dryly. "There's an old saying in the legal community that practicing law is like a pie-eating contest. When you make partner, the prize is more pie."

"Damn," Tamia said with a rueful grin. "No rest for the weary, huh?"

"Nah. But it's all good. I'm meeting the fellas for dinner in half an hour."

"Oh, that's nice." Tamia paused, then couldn't resist asking casually, "Where's Cynthia?"

"She went to her cousin's bridal shower."

No wonder, Tamia mused. If that clingy bitch had been around, there was no way she would have allowed Brandon to call Tamia, let alone stay on the phone for so long.

Reaching the living room, Tamia opened the sliding glass door and stepped out onto the balcony. Excitement coursed through her veins as she beheld the panoramic view of the night skyline, which was dominated by a glittering array of skyscrapers. Thirty stories below, the shimmering oasis of a pool flanked by palm trees made her feel as though she were vacationing at a tropical resort.

Standing at the banister, she closed her eyes and raised her face to the sky as a gentle, balmy breeze caressed her skin. She couldn't help wishing that Brandon were there beside her, sharing her enjoyment of the breathtaking view.

On the other end of the line, he murmured, "Are you still there?"

She smiled, slowly opening her eyes. "I'm still here. I just stepped outside to check out the view from my balcony."

"How is it?"

"Spectacular." She sipped her wine. "Are you at your desk?"

"Yeah."

"I want you to do something for me."

"What?"

"Get up from your chair and stretch your muscles, then walk over to the windows."

He chuckled softly. "Why?"

"You'll see." She paused, giving him time to follow her instructions. After several moments, she asked, "Are you there?"

"Yeah." Humor threaded his deep voice. "What now?"

She smiled. "Tell me what you see."

He hesitated. "Buildings. Tall office buildings."

"What else?"

"Cars moving down the street."

"Look up." Tamia paused. "*Now* tell me what you see."

"The sky."

Lips twitching at his cryptic descriptions—typical lawyer—she prodded, "What *about* the sky?"

"There's a half moon. And a lot of stars." His voice softened. "It's beautiful."

"It is." Tamia smiled quietly, staring toward the heavens. "Do you know why we never see a full moon surrounded by stars?"

"No. Why?"

"Because bright moonlight scattered by the atmosphere tends to outshine nearby stars. So if you ever happen to see a circle of stars around a full moon, you've witnessed something truly phenomenal."

"Really?" Brandon sounded both amused and fascinated. "I didn't know that. Have you taken up astronomy now?"

Tamia grinned sheepishly. "While I was incarcerated, I did a lot of reading on lunar eclipses and the winter solstice. Don't laugh," she added when Brandon chuckled. "It was actually pretty amazing stuff."

"No doubt. What you just shared with me was very interesting."

Tamia smiled, warmed by the sincerity in his voice. "After learning all those things about the solar system, I vowed never to take another sunrise or full moon for granted. So that's why I asked you to get up and look out your window. I wanted you to enjoy the same view I'm enjoying."

"Thank you, Tamia," Brandon said quietly. "Thank you for reminding me to appreciate the simple things."

"You're welcome." She closed her eyes, her heart overflowing with such love for him that she could barely contain it. Swallowing hard, she said reluctantly, "Well, I won't keep you any longer. Have fun with the fellas, and don't be a stranger."

"Same to you."

In the ensuing silence, Tamia sensed that he wanted to say more.

She waited, breath trapped in her lungs.

But after several seconds, all he said was, "Good night, Tamia."

Disappointment washed over her. She didn't know what she'd expected him to say. Maybe she'd wanted him to prolong their conversation, or ask her out on a date, or tell her how much he loved her and missed being with her. But she knew that was asking too much. Reclaiming his love would take time. She hadn't lost him overnight. So she couldn't expect to win him back overnight.

But that's okay, because I'm in this for the long haul.

Smiling to herself, Tamia said softly, "Good night, Brandon. I definitely won't be a stranger."

Chapter 8

Brandon

After ending the call with Tamia, Brandon exhaled a deep, shaky breath and closed his eyes, tapping the phone against his forehead. His chest was tight with emotions he didn't want to identify. Didn't want to feel.

Despite his resolve to keep Tamia at arm's length, he'd found himself picking up the phone and calling her tonight. He'd told himself that he was just checking up on her as a formality. But deep down inside, he knew the real reason was that he'd wanted to hear her voice. Once upon a time, their phone conversations had been the highlight of his day.

Apparently the more things changed, the more they stayed the same.

"It's not *that* bad, is it?"

Brandon opened his eyes and glanced over his shoulder. An attractive brunette leaned in the doorway of his office with her arms folded across her ample breasts. She wore jeans tight enough to cut off her circulation, and on her feet were pink flip-flops that showed off a French pedicure.

She was watching Brandon with an expression of amused curiosity.

He smiled briefly. "Hey, Addison. How's it going?"

"Good. Which is probably more than I can say for you. You look like you've got the weight of the world on those broad shoulders." She smiled teasingly. "Don't tell me you already regret making partner."

Brandon chuckled. "Not at all," he said, returning to his chair behind the enormous mahogany desk he'd recently inherited—along with a plush corner office, a $500,000 salary, and the prestige of being named an equity partner at one of the top law firms in the country.

Addison eyed him speculatively. "So it's *not* the job that had you looking so miserable a minute ago?"

"Nah."

"You must be having woman trouble, then."

Brandon gave her a wry look. "If I were, do you honestly think I'd tell *you*?"

Addison grinned unabashedly. "I guess not, considering that your girlfriend and I aren't exactly BFFs."

That was an understatement if Brandon had ever heard one. Cynthia and Addison had been bitter adversaries for as long as they'd worked at the firm. Although both women were talented, hardworking, and ambitious, they had zero respect for each other. Being drastically outnumbered by their male colleagues hadn't united them either. If anything, their minority status made them even more hostile and vicious toward each other, like two feral lionesses fighting over the last scrap of unconquered territory.

It didn't help that Addison had made no secret of her attraction to Brandon. Every time she looked at him, he half wondered whether he had a sign stamped across his forehead that read MANDINGO. He'd often caught her checking out his crotch and licking her lips, as if she were visualizing his big, black dick ramming into her pussy. When he made partner, she'd invited him out for drinks to celebrate. But Brandon was no fool. He knew that she had more than whiskey shots on her mind, so he'd turned her ass down. Even if he'd been tempted to cheat on Cynthia, he wouldn't have fucked around with Addison. Though she was smart and attractive, he wasn't interested in white women. Never had been, never would be.

"Speaking of Cynthia," Addison said casually, glancing around as she wandered into the large room, "where *is* she tonight?"

None of your damn business hovered on the tip of Brandon's tongue. But he decided not to be rude. "She's at a bridal shower."

"Ah." Addison nodded, lowering herself onto the sleek leather sofa near his desk. "I see."

Something in her tone had Brandon's shoulders tensing. "What does that mean?"

Wide green eyes blinked innocently. "What? I didn't say anything."

"You said plenty."

Addison shrugged, twirling a strand of hair around her finger. "I probably shouldn't mention this, but a lot of people around here think Cynthia's starting to lose her edge."

Brandon frowned. "By 'a lot of people,' I assume you're talking about associates."

"Yeah." Addison smirked. "You know, the lowly grunts who've been toiling away at this firm for years, hoping to join the exalted ranks of partner like you did."

Brandon didn't rise to the bait. He knew that many of his colleagues resented him for achieving the coveted brass ring of partnership. Some even believed that his wealthy, powerful parents had pulled strings for him. But Brandon knew better. Over the past eight years, he'd worked his ass off to reach his goal of making partner. He'd endured the long hours at the expense of a social life, had won the tough court cases, and had generated more business for the firm than any of his peers, bar none. He'd more than earned his promotion, and anyone who thought differently could go fuck themselves.

Which brought him back to the matter at hand.

"Why do people think Cynthia has lost her edge?" he asked, keeping his tone carefully neutral.

Addison sighed, as if it pained her to be the bearer of bad news pertaining to her rival. "Well, for starters, she hasn't been logging as many billable hours as she used to. And over the past month, we've all noticed her leaving the office earlier than usual."

"Not that it's anyone's business," Brandon calmly interjected, "but she's been helping with the preparations for her cousin's wedding."

"That may be so," Addison countered, "but the perception is that ever since she started dating you, she's gotten comfortable. She seems more interested in having lunch with you than scheduling meetings with her clients. It's almost as if she assumes that she's got it made because you're her boyfriend, and now that you're an equity partner, your vote will sway the others into making her partner next summer."

Brandon laughed, shaking his head at Addison. "So that's the meme that's going around."

She frowned at him. "What are you talking about? What meme?"

"The talking points everyone will recite to discredit Cynthia when she makes partner. You guys will say she was chosen because she's dating me. Just like *I* supposedly benefited from who my parents are."

Addison stared at him, a slow flush crawling up her neck to spread over her face. "Are you pulling the race card, Brandon?"

He met her gaze directly. "Are *you*?"

She looked affronted. "First of all, no one in their right mind would say you didn't deserve to be made partner. If you hadn't been chosen, *I* would have started a riot. Not only are you a kick-ass trial attorney, but you bring more revenue and prestige to this firm than most of the senior partners! You know how to network and schmooze with clients like nobody's business. And, like it or not, it doesn't hurt that your father will probably be the next governor, and Bey-oncé—*BEYONCÉ!*—personally calls you up to have lunch whenever she's in town. Are you kidding me, Brandon? The partners would have been crazy not to promote you, and whether they admit it or not, everyone knows that!"

By the time Addison had finished speaking, her face was beet red.

Brandon gave her a long, assessing look.

After a prolonged silence, a small, crooked smile lifted one corner of his mouth. "I guess you told me."

Addison gaped at him for a moment, then burst out laughing.

Brandon chuckled. Addison might be Cynthia's worst enemy, but one thing he'd always appreciated about her was that she wasn't afraid to speak her mind. He always knew where he stood with her, which was more than he could say about most of the other sharks he worked with.

As her laughter subsided, Addison sighed and shook her head at Brandon. "Seriously though, Chambers. I know you may think your girlfriend is being unfairly persecuted, but I've heard grumblings even from people who happen to be huge fans of hers. If my colleagues believed *I* was slacking, I'd want to know. So at the very least, I think you should give Cynthia a heads-up."

Brandon inclined his head. "Maybe I will. Thanks."

"Any time." Addison grinned. "You know, Kessler was wrong about you."

"What do you mean?"

"Well, he said once you made partner, you'd start acting like you were better than the rest of us."

Brandon scowled. "Fuck Kessler."

Addison snorted. "Not even if you paid me."

They both laughed.

Brandon's cell phone rang. Seeing his best friend's number on the caller ID, he plucked the phone off his desk and answered, "Wassup."

"Yo," Dre greeted him. "I'm about five minutes away."

"Cool. I'll meet you downstairs at Stogie's. Justin and Cornel are running late—as usual."

Dre said slyly, "So I'll have you all to myself for a while?"

"Man, chill with that down-low shit before I tell Leah."

As Brandon hung up on Dre's raucous laughter, Addison snapped her fingers. "Damn. I was hoping you didn't have any plans tonight so I could talk you into having drinks with me."

Brandon sent her a wry smile. "Come on now," he drawled.

"What?" she asked, rising from the sofa.

"You know you and I are never gonna have drinks together."

"Why not?"

"Because around here, 'having drinks together' is code for fucking. And no offense, Addison, but I'm not interested."

Her green eyes glinted wickedly. "Are you sure?"

"Positive."

She sighed. "Can't blame a girl for trying," she quipped before sashaying from the office.

Five minutes later, Brandon had just boarded the elevator to head downstairs when Addison called out breathlessly, "Wait up!"

He instinctively stuck his hand between the sliding

brass doors to prevent them from closing as Addison raced inside, a leather briefcase in one hand and a small gym bag slung over her shoulder.

"Thanks," she panted with a throaty laugh. "I ran as fast as I could to catch you before you got away. With the elevator, I mean."

"No problem." Brandon pressed the buttons for the lobby and the underground parking level.

As soon as the doors slid closed, Addison began peeling off her skintight jeans.

Brandon stared at her. "What the hell—"

She laughed as she nearly lost her balance and had to lean against him for support to finish removing her pants. She quickly stuffed them inside her bag, then reached for the hem of her T-shirt.

"What the fuck are you doing?" Brandon demanded.

"Relax, handsome." Her amused voice was muffled as she tugged off her shirt to reveal pale, melon-sized breasts barely contained by a skimpy lace bra. "I'm meeting some friends at the club, and I forgot to change before I left the office."

"Likely story," Brandon muttered, averting his eyes to stare up at the electronic monitor above the doors. But he was aware of Addison shimmying into a strapless black tube dress and stiletto heels, her sensual gaze willing him to watch her in the polished brass of the doors.

After what seemed an eternity, the elevator reached the lobby.

As Brandon stepped off, Addison said, "Oh, wait, I forgot to ask you something."

He glanced back at her.

Pressing the button to keep the doors open, she grinned at him. "Aren't you impressed by my perfect timing?"

"Sure," Brandon said drolly. "You must have a lot of practice undressing in elevators."

She laughed, combing her fingers through her tousled dark hair. "Not exactly. I just know how to multitask." And she gave him a look meant to make him wonder how many *other* things she could do at once.

"What did you want to ask me?" he prompted, impatience edging his voice.

But she was suddenly staring across the lobby.

Following the direction of her gaze, Brandon saw Dre striding through the double glass doors and heading toward the entrance to Stogie's.

"Isn't that your friend Deondre?" Addison asked.

"Yeah."

"Wow, he looks great. Not all black guys can pull off a baldie like he can. And he looks really buff, too. Has he been working out a lot?"

Before Brandon could shoot off some smart-ass remark, Dre glanced over and saw Brandon and Addison standing at the elevator. When Addison smiled and waved at him, Dre looked her up and down before raising his brows at Brandon.

Addison snapped her fingers. "Damn. Just that quick, I forgot what I wanted to ask you."

"Then it probably wasn't that important," Brandon said wryly.

"Maybe. Maybe not." Addison grinned coyly at him. "If it comes to me tomorrow, I'll give you a call."

At the look Brandon shot her, she laughed. "Just kidding. Have a good time with your friends tonight."

"Thanks. You too." He sauntered off without a backward glance.

When he reached the other side of the lobby, Dre grinned slyly at him. "What was *that* about?"

"What?"

"You and your girl Addison, coming downstairs together on a Saturday night." A suggestive gleam filled Dre's dark eyes. "Were you up there tappin' her off?"

Brandon scowled. "Hell, nah. You know I ain't down with no swirl action."

Dre chuckled. "Just checking, bruh. Even from a distance, I could see the way she was looking at you, like she wanted you to fuck the shit outta her. And I can't really say I'd blame you," he added, casting another glance toward the elevators as if Addison were still there. "Shorty was looking sexy as *hell* tonight."

Brandon made no comment as they entered the dim interior of Stogie's.

Boasting mahogany-paneled walls, plush leather upholstery, and a bar stocked with top-shelf liquor, the swanky establishment had the look and feel of a gentlemen's cigar club—which, technically, it still was. Though membership had been opened to women more than thirty years ago, females rarely ventured into the bastion of masculinity that was Stogie's. The exception was on Saturday nights, when guys wanting to impress their dates brought them to the upscale restaurant.

After greeting Brandon and asking about his father's gubernatorial campaign, the maître d' escorted him and Dre to the circular leather booth Brandon had reserved for the evening. A solicitous waiter appeared with their humidors and took their drink orders—a neat scotch for Brandon and cognac for Dre.

As the waiter moved off, the two friends cut the caps off their vintage cigars and lit up.

"So," Dre began conversationally, grinning at Brandon across the glossy mahogany table, "how many times has wifey called you tonight?"

Brandon puffed on his cigar, savoring the taste and aroma of the smoke before slowly exhaling through his nose. "What're you talking about?"

Dre laughed. "Nice try. You know damn well what I'm talking about. How many times has Cynthia called you while she's been at the shower? And don't say she hasn't called, 'cause I know better."

Brandon shrugged, lounging against the plush leather cushions. "I've only heard from her once."

Dre eyed him knowingly. "Does that count text messages?"

"Man, shut up."

Again Dre laughed, shaking his smooth bald head. "I knew she couldn't go an entire night without checking up on you."

Brandon frowned. "She just wanted to say hello and see how my evening was going. What's wrong with that?"

"Nothing." Dre puffed on his cigar, eyes glinting with amusement behind a veil of smoke. "Remember how we used to tease her about being one of those independent, career-obsessed, don't-need-a-man sisters?"

Brandon nodded.

"Well, that was *before* you started tapping that ass. Now you got her so wide open, she'd probably forfeit her law degree if you asked her to."

Brandon was silent as Addison's words echoed through his mind. *She seems more interested in having lunch with you than scheduling meetings with her clients.*

He couldn't pretend that the remark hadn't bothered him. When he and Cynthia first began dating, he'd worried that their relationship would interfere with their jobs. But Cynthia had assured him that she could successfully balance the demands of both, and he'd had no reason to doubt her. But now, in light of his conversation with Addison, he had to wonder whether he'd become a distraction to Cynthia. The last thing he wanted to do was jeopardize her chances of making partner after she'd worked so hard to achieve that goal.

The waiter returned with Brandon and Dre's drinks and

asked them if they wanted to wait for the other members of their party before placing their dinner orders.

"Yeah, thanks," Brandon said, overriding Dre's protestations of being hungry.

After the waiter departed, Dre downed some cognac before grumbling, "I wish those niggas would learn to show up on time for once."

Brandon chuckled. "Come on, now. We've known Justin and Cornel since high school. Have they *ever* been on time for anything?"

Dre grunted. "Good point."

Brandon sipped his scotch, then took a lazy drag on his cigar. "So how are things going with Leah?"

"Man." Dre pushed out a deep, weary breath. "It's been rough."

"Why? What's going on?"

Dre glanced around the restaurant before confiding in a low voice, "Leah's work schedule is taking a serious toll on our bedroom action."

Brandon's lips twitched. "How serious?"

"Let's just say if I don't run up in some pussy soon, my dick's gonna shrivel up and fall the fuck off."

"Damn, bruh," Brandon commiserated. "That *is* serious."

Dre glared at him. "So why the hell are you grinning?"

"My bad." Brandon covered his mouth, but the laughter escaped anyway.

"You think this shit is funny?"

"Nah," Brandon rasped, laughing so hard that his words came out in fragments. "Believe me . . . I understand what . . . you're going through."

"Nigga, please," Dre scoffed. "Don't patronize me. I know Cynthia be giving up the pussy on the regular. Not only do you two live together, but then you see each other all day at work. I still remember that time she was sitting on your phone while you were tappin' her off on your desk, and the phone accidentally dialed my number. Man, I coulda *killed* your ass for rubbing your sexcapades in my face like that."

"Sorry," Brandon said, using his free hand to wipe tears of mirth from the corners of his eyes. "For the last time, bruh, we didn't know she was sitting on the phone."

"That's even worse, 'cause that means the shit was so good, your girl didn't even notice a hard object poking her in the ass."

Brandon grinned wickedly. "The only 'hard object' she cared about—"

Dre groaned loudly, holding up his hand. "Don't say it. *Please* don't say it. Damn. I walked right into that one."

Brandon laughed. "You sure did."

Dre shook his head, scrubbing both hands over his face. "I'm telling you, man. I'm so damn horny I've even caught myself checking out Fiona, and you know how I feel about *her* motherfucking ass."

"Dayuum," Brandon exclaimed, torn between amusement and incredulity. "You *are* in bad shape."

"Tell me about it. I've lost my damn mind, lusting after an ex-con who also happens to be one of our employees." Dre scowled at Brandon. "I blame you and your damn brother for hiring her in the first place."

Brandon grinned, blowing out a thick curl of smoke.

Last year, after resigning from his job at a corporate law firm, Beau Chambers had approached Brandon and Dre about partnering with him to form a sports management agency. He'd envisioned a one-stop-shop facility that would house the contract management offices, a barber shop, and a wellness center that could be overseen by Dre, who had a Ph.D. in sports medicine and worked as an athletic trainer for the Houston Texans.

Brandon and Dre had been so impressed with the scope of Beau's vision that they'd agreed to pool their financial resources to become his business partners. One year later, Pinnacle Sports Group represented several professional and collegiate athletes, and the wellness center had become so popular that Dre planned to leave the NFL after this season to devote more time to the center's clients.

Unlike Brandon, who functioned as a silent partner, Dre was very involved in the agency's daily operations, which included making personnel decisions. When Tamia's sister, Fiona, lost her booth at the hair salon where she'd worked for years, she'd come to Brandon for help. Remembering the great haircut she'd once given him when his regular barber was out of town, Brandon had called a meeting with Beau and Dre to recommend that they hire Fiona.

Dre had been adamantly opposed to the idea, although his objections had more to do with who her sister was than Fiona's criminal record. He hadn't forgiven Tamia for the way she'd betrayed Brandon, so he considered Fiona guilty by association. But Brandon and Beau felt differently, and because they outnumbered Dre, Fiona had been hired.

Dre bitched about their decision every chance he got, but his complaints fell on deaf ears. Fiona was one of the shop's best barbers, and the clients enjoyed having a beautiful woman around. So she wasn't going anywhere.

Pointing his cigar at Dre, Brandon warned, "Don't even think about pushing up on that girl."

Dre shot him a look of disgust. "Nigga, please. I'm not *that* desperate. Shorty may be fine, but she's young and hood as hell. And I'm not even sure she's playing with a full deck," he added, tapping a finger against his temple.

Brandon grimaced. "She strikes me as more naive than anything else. I mean, yeah, she's rough around the edges. But she has this childlike innocence about her, you know? It's like she's a little girl trapped inside a woman's body."

Dre snorted derisively. "Yeah, and you should see the way she flaunts that body in front of the customers."

Brandon grinned. "I don't hear anyone else complaining, bruh. So methinks you doth protest too much."

Dre sucked his teeth. "Whatever."

Brandon chuckled, sipping his scotch. "Anyway, cut Fiona some slack. She's been through a lot and she's trying to turn her life around, so I don't mind helping her."

Dre eyed him knowingly. "Like you helped her sister?"

"Sure."

"So that means you're gonna hook Fiona up with a luxury apartment, too?"

Brandon went still, staring at his best friend. "What're you talking about?"

Dre barked out a laugh. "You know damn well what I'm talking about. You've got Tamia staying over at One Park Place."

Shit, Brandon thought grimly. "How do you know about that?"

"I overheard you and Lou making the arrangements a few weeks ago. And before you accuse me of ear hustling, it wasn't even like that. Remember the night I met you at your office so we could ride to the Rockets game together?"

Brandon nodded tightly.

"Well, you had me waiting in the reception area for so long that I decided to head back to your office to see what was the holdup. You were on the phone with your back to the door, and that's when I overheard your conversation with Lou. I didn't say anything to you 'cause I figured if you wanted me to know about your plans, you would have told me." Dre frowned, shaking his head at Brandon. "What the hell were you thinking, putting Tamia up in an apartment?"

Brandon shrugged, tapping his cigar ashes into an ashtray. "She needed a new place to stay."

"And how is that *your* responsibility? Last I checked, bruh, she's not your wifey anymore."

"I know that. I just wanted to do her a favor."

Dre snorted. "You already *did* her a favor. You got her ass out of prison, which is probably more than she deserved. But that's another topic for another day."

Brandon scowled. "Yeah, please don't start, 'cause I'm not trying to hear that shit tonight."

"Of course you don't wanna hear it," Dre retorted. "You've got blinders on when it comes to Tamia. And I see you like living dangerously, too. Do you have any idea how Cynthia will react if she finds out that you dropped over a hundred grand on rent and furniture for your ex-girlfriend's love nest?"

Brandon's temper flared. "Damn, nigga, why the hell are you all up in my wallet? Are you my accountant or something? I'm a grown-ass man, so I can spend my money however the fuck I want."

The two friends glowered at each other across the table.

"If it's really like that," Dre challenged, "then why all the secrecy? Why not tell Tamia that *you're* the one paying for the apartment?"

"Because it's not important," Brandon growled. "If I told her, she'd feel like she owes me. And she doesn't. I don't want anything from her."

Dre regarded him skeptically. "You don't want anything from her."

"That's what I said."

"So you didn't get her the apartment because you still love her and you wanna take care of her? And you're not planning to go over there and fuck her the first chance you get?"

Brandon took a long pull on his cigar, then blew out a stream of smoke on the word, "Nope."

Dre scoffed. "Come on, B. This is *me* you're talking to, remember? I've known you since we were eleven years old. So you can sit there all you want and tell yourself whatever makes you feel better. But don't expect me to believe a word you're saying, 'cause I know it's pure bullshit."

Clenching his jaw, Brandon glanced toward the entrance to the restaurant. He'd never been more relieved to see that Justin and Cornel had arrived. Maybe now Dre would shut the fuck up.

As if he'd read his mind, Dre frowned. "Let me just leave you with some food for thought."

Brandon leveled a glare at him.

Dre glared right back. "Before you and Tamia pick up where you left off months ago, just remember how devastated you were when you found out that she'd been cheating on you. Remember how hurt and angry you felt—and then ask yourself whether you can justify doing the same thing to Cynthia."

Chapter 9

Tamia

Brandon stood by the windows, his tall, muscular frame bathed in soft moonlight.

Dressed in spiky heels and nothing else, Tamia sauntered toward him as Kelly Rowland's "Motivation" played seductively in the background.

Brandon turned and watched her, his hungry gaze getting her so aroused that the whisper of air against her naked flesh nearly made her come.

When she reached him, she cradled his face between her hands and kissed his succulent lips. He moaned softly and slid his hot, silky tongue into her mouth. She sucked him, savoring his taste and texture like a wine connoisseur.

From his mouth she kissed her way down to his hard chest, her tongue tracing the outline of his muscular pecs and abs as she sank to a crouch before him, her thighs spread wantonly open. Brandon stared as she reached down and stroked her swollen clit, coating her fingers with the sticky nectar dripping from her body.

"Let me taste you," Brandon whispered.

She lifted her hand to his mouth, shivering as his lips closed around her fingers.

"Mmm," he moaned appreciatively, sucking off her juices. "Damn, you taste good."

"You missed this pussy?"

"You *know* I did."

Tamia smiled with naughty satisfaction.

As his mouth reluctantly released her wet fingers, she grasped the waistband of his dark boxers. As she pulled the shorts down his powerful legs, her gaze was riveted by the hard, chocolate dick that sprang free. It was long and thick, blessed with a curved tip that discovered secret G-spots like a highly specialized homing device.

Raising her eyes to Brandon's face, she wrapped her fingers around the base of his shaft and eased all that delicious goodness into her mouth.

Brandon groaned, his eyes rolling closed as his head went back. "Shit, baby. That feels *so* good."

She licked around and over the head of his cock, lubricating him with her saliva. He sank his hand into her hair, gripping the back of her head as she expertly deep-throated his ten inches.

"Ahhh," he moaned with pleasure.

"You like that, baby?"

"Fuck, yeah."

Suddenly Tamia felt a whisper of movement behind her. Pulling Brandon's dick out of her mouth, she glanced over her shoulder.

Another lover had joined them.

He knelt behind Tamia, head bent as his hands roamed down her back and caressed the swell of her ass cheeks.

Her heart thudded with recognition.

"Dominic?" she breathed.

He lifted his head and grinned—that slow, wicked grin she remembered all too well.

"Welcome home, Mystique," he whispered, then rammed into her.

Tamia bolted upright, the sound of her own scream echoing around the dark bedroom.

Her heart was slamming against her ribs, and sweat dampened her skin.

Swallowing hard, she glanced toward the moonlit windows, half expecting—*hoping*—to see Brandon standing there. But she was alone.

Frowning, she eased back against the pillows and stared up at the ceiling.

She'd been having another one of her erotic dreams about Brandon. But tonight, for the first time, the dream had been invaded by Dominic.

Tamia exhaled a deep, shaky breath and closed her eyes.

Seconds later—unable to resist—she reached beneath the covers, parted her legs, and touched herself.

As usual, her pussy was drenched.

Biting her lower lip, she slid a finger into her wetness, first imagining it was Brandon's dick . . . then Dominic's.

And then they were both inside her, one thrusting into her asshole while the other tore up her pussy.

Suddenly her cell phone went off.

Her eyes flew open, and she snatched her finger out of her body as if she'd just been caught masturbating by her grandmother.

Her cell rang again, a burst of sound in the silent room.

Frowning, she reached across the nightstand and picked up the phone, checking the caller ID.

Unknown number.

Who the hell is calling me at 2:45 in the morning? she wondered.

Pressing the talk button, she answered hesitantly, "Hello?"

There was no response.

"Hello?" she repeated.

Silence.

She pressed the phone to her ear, straining to listen. After several moments, she heard soft breathing on the other end.

She swallowed nervously, the fine hairs rising on the back of her neck. "Who is this?"

Still no answer.

Heart pounding erratically, she whispered, "Dominic?"

The line went dead.

Chapter 10

Tamia

It had been ten years since Tamia stepped through the hallowed doors of a church.

A decade ago, at the age of nineteen, she'd attended the funeral of her grandmother, who'd been robbed and brutally murdered by a home intruder who'd never been caught. As she'd stood weeping beside her beloved grandmother's casket, Tamia had wondered how God could allow such an unspeakable tragedy to befall a woman who'd faithfully served Him all her life. Inconsolable with grief, she'd rejected the gentle platitudes of other mourners who'd told her, "Mama Esther's in a better place now" and "The Lord works in mysterious ways."

A week after the funeral, she'd landed her first starring role in a porn video, becoming the masked dominatrix known as Mystique. After that, she saw no reason to continue attending church and worshipping a God who'd robbed her of the most important person in her life.

But while she was incarcerated, she'd begun dreaming about her grandmother. Sometimes Mama Esther would be rocking gently on the porch swing and knitting a blanket, or braiding Tamia's hair. Other times she'd be stirring a pot of grits on the stove, or painting her fingernails as she hummed along to her favorite hymn. No matter how varied the dreams, they always ended with Mama Esther imploring Tamia to renew her faith and seek the Lord for deliverance. And Tamia always awakened with her grandmother's name on her lips, her hand outstretched to empty air.

She began reading the Bible again, and during one of Shanell's weekly visits, Tamia promised to attend church with her if God allowed her to get out of prison.

So there she was, seated beside Shanell and Mark as they listened to Joseph Yarbrough warn his congregation about the dangers of lust and sexual immorality.

Tamia had apparently chosen the wrong Sunday to make her return to church.

"The Bible tells us that those who sow to the flesh will *not* inherit the kingdom of God," the bishop thundered from behind the pulpit, his theatrical baritone soaring to the roof. "Apostle Peter exhorts all believers to abstain from the passions of the flesh, which wage war against our very souls!"

Grimacing at the reminder of last night's erotic dream, Tamia leaned over and whispered to Shanell, "Are you sure you didn't tell him you were bringing me today?"

Shanell cracked up, earning a censorious look from an elderly woman seated in front of them.

As the bishop's fiery sermon raged on, Tamia found herself gazing around the sanctuary, torn between awe and disgust. The enormous hall was equipped with plush upholstery, balcony seating, high-tech lighting, and three giant flat-screen televisions that flanked the large stage and projected Bishop Yarbrough's image to every corner of the packed arena.

The powerhouse megachurch boasted 40,000 members that included high-profile athletes, entertainers, and politicians. That Sunday morning, the most prominent congregant in attendance was lieutenant governor Bernard Chambers, accompanied by his wife and eldest son. The impeccably attired couple enjoyed a special place of honor onstage behind the pulpit, while Brandon sat in the front row beside Cynthia, his arm draped casually over the back of her chair.

The sight of them together sent a dagger through Tamia's heart. They looked like the quintessential buppies—educated, upwardly mobile, prosperous yet socially conscious. The kind of young black couple that donated to worthy causes, had tickets to the theater, and owned a tastefully furnished house in an upscale suburb.

Tamia would have preferred being waterboarded to watching her boo play house with another woman. It didn't help that Cynthia seemed to be paying more attention to Brandon than her own father's sermon. Every five minutes, she leaned close to Brandon and whispered something in his ear. Something that brought a slow, lazy smile to his mouth and left Tamia feeling less and less optimistic about her chances of getting him back.

And then came an unexpected ray of hope.

When Bishop Yarbrough cracked a joke that sent a wave of laughter through the congregation, Brandon casually glanced over his shoulder.

When he saw Tamia seated several rows back, his eyes widened with surprise.

As their gazes locked, Cynthia's father exhorted loudly from the pulpit, "So I say unto you, my sons and brothers. Heed the words of Proverbs six, verses twenty-five through twenty-six: 'Keep away from the immoral woman, from the smooth tongue of the wayward harlot. Do not lust in your heart after her beauty, or let her captivate you with her eyes. For the prostitute reduces you to a loaf of bread, and the adulteress preys upon your very life.' "

Brandon and Tamia stared at each other.

He winked.

She winked back.

As he returned his attention to the stage, Tamia kept watching him. When he discreetly removed his arm from the back of Cynthia's chair, she wanted to jump up and dance in the aisles.

His subtle withdrawal didn't go unnoticed by Cynthia, who regarded him quizzically before glancing over her shoulder.

When her gaze met Tamia's, she frowned, eyes narrowing with displeasure.

Tamia shrugged as if to say, *What can you do?*

Cynthia glared at her, then angrily turned away.

Catching the entire exchange, Shanell shook her head and muttered under her breath, "Girl, you are a mess."

"I know." Tamia grinned broadly. "And God loves me anyway."

After the service, while Mark excused himself to check the scores of today's NFL games, Shanell insisted on waiting in the long receiving line to greet Bishop Yarbrough and the first lady.

As she and Tamia inched down the aisle, Tamia's gaze followed Brandon around the bustling sanctuary. He and his father expertly worked the crowd—shaking hands, slapping backs, kissing babies, and conversing with Bernard's constituents in an effort to shore up votes for next November's election.

At one point, Brandon looked right over at Tamia and mouthed, *Don't go anywhere.*

Delighted that he'd apparently been aware of her presence the entire time he'd been schmoozing, Tamia smiled and mouthed back, *I won't.*

He grinned, flashing those sexy dimples.

Shanell looked from one to the other, then glanced heavenward and sighed. "This is gonna get *so* messy. Lord help us all."

Tamia grinned at her. "Why do *you* need help?"

"Because I'm gonna get caught in the middle between you and Cynthia, and I'll probably end up having to find another church home."

"That might not be such a bad idea," Tamia muttered.

Shanell arched a brow at her. "What's that supposed to mean?"

"I don't know." Tamia gestured around the opulent sanctuary, her nose wrinkling with distaste. "This place just seems so over-the-top and fake."

"You're not feeling the megachurch experience, huh?"

"Not really."

Shanell chuckled. "It takes some getting used to, I'll admit. But Bishop Yarbrough knows how to preach the word. I always come away feeling like he was speaking directly to me."

Tamia snorted. "Oh, I *definitely* felt like he was speaking to me. Every time he mentioned Jezebel, I swear he looked right at me."

Shanell laughed, reaching inside her purse for a pack of peppermint gum. She offered a piece to Tamia before unwrapping one for herself.

Tamia folded the stick of gum into her mouth, then smiled softly at her friend. "Thank you."

"For what? The gum? *I'm* the one whose breath was kinda tart."

Tamia laughed. "Your breath was fine. And I wasn't thanking you for the gum. I was thanking you for being supportive, and for not telling me to give up on Brandon. I know you and Cynthia are friends, so this whole situation has probably been pretty awkward for you."

"It has," Shanell admitted, smiling and waving at someone across the sanctuary. "I like Cynthia and I have a lot of respect for her. But you're my girl, Tamia, so you know I got your back. Besides, Brandon was your man first. You deserve a second chance to make things right." She gave Tamia a meaningful look. "As long as you don't do anything crazy to get that brotha back."

"I won't," Tamia vowed. "Believe me, I've learned my lesson."

"Good."

As they moved up in line, Tamia observed Joseph and Coretta Yarbrough as they greeted their adoring congregants. The charismatic minister was tall, lean, and attractive, with a walnut complexion and a neatly groomed natural and mustache. In contrast, his wife was short and heavyset—homely in a way that no amount of professional makeup, expensive jewelry, and designer clothes could disguise.

Tamia had already met the couple earlier that year at Bernard Chambers's campaign launch party. They'd been coolly polite toward her because she was Brandon's girlfriend, which interfered with their plans to marry their daughter off to him. Tamia knew they'd rejoiced in the streets when she and Brandon broke up, clearing the path for Cynthia.

When Tamia and Shanell finally reached the front of the line, Shanell hugged the Yarbroughs and told the bishop how much she'd enjoyed his sermon.

"I'm so glad to hear that, Sister Jasper." Joseph's dark gaze shifted to Tamia. "And what about you, Sister Luke? I hope you received God's word today."

Tamia forced a smile. "I did, thank you."

"That's good." His answering smile was as sanctimonious as his next words. "I thank the Lord for using me as a vessel to shed light in the darkness of sinners' souls."

Being the sinner in question, Tamia had nothing to say.

He continued piously, "You should know that our congregation kept you lifted up in prayer throughout your incarceration. As the Bible says, 'The prayers of the righteous availeth much.' "

"Thank you for your prayers," Tamia said smoothly. "Of course, it didn't hurt that I was represented by the best defense attorney in town."

"Ah, yes," Joseph agreed, exchanging proud glances with his beaming wife. "Our Brandon is a very gifted young man. Coretta and I look forward to welcoming him into our family, although he's practically one of us already."

Tamia's heart sank at his words, which had obviously been his intent.

Before she could respond, Shanell gushed excitedly, "Oh, my goodness! Are congratulations in order, Bishop Yarbrough? Has Brandon proposed to Cynthia?"

The man's smug smile wavered. "Well, not yet—"

"But we all know it's only a matter of time," his wife interjected haughtily.

Shanell grinned. "Well, please be sure to let the congregation know *as soon* as it's official. I want to get them a really nice wedding gift, but I don't want to spend my money until a wedding date's been set."

Joseph and Coretta smiled tightly. "Of course."

As Shanell and Tamia said their good-byes and walked away, Tamia mumbled, "Thanks, girl."

Shanell draped a comforting arm around her waist. "Any time."

Tamia sighed heavily. "I hate to worship and run, but can we get out of here? People have been staring at me all morning, like they can't decide whether to approach me for an autograph or keep their distance in case I'm packing a piece. Not only that, but I don't want to run into Brandon's parents, and I know I'm the absolute *last* person they want to see."

"That's probably a safe assumption," Shanell agreed ruefully.

They left the main sanctuary and made their way through the crowded lobby. The sprawling facility housed a bookstore, a day care center, office suites, a banquet hall, and a restaurant, where Mark and several other men had flocked immediately after service to watch football on the plasma television.

Tamia and Shanell had nearly reached the restaurant when a deep voice cut through the crowd, "Didn't I tell you not to go anywhere?"

Both women turned to watch as Brandon sauntered toward them.

Tamia's heart gave an excited bump. He hadn't forgotten about her!

"Hey, Brandon," she and Shanell chorused.

"Wassup, ladies." He hugged them each in turn, making Tamia laugh as he lifted her slightly off the ground before setting her back down. The delicious contact with his body had her shivering with arousal.

Pulling away, he smiled into her eyes. "I didn't know you'd be here today."

She grinned impishly. "I made a pact with God that I'd start going to church if He got me out of trouble."

Brandon chuckled. "Smart woman."

"Yup." She tapped her clutch purse against the shapely curve of her thigh, noting the way Brandon's gaze lingered there. "Shanell told me you've been coming to church regularly. So it looks like I'm not the only one who's had a spiritual awakening, huh?"

He grinned wryly. "I wouldn't exactly say that."

"No?" Tamia teased. "So does that mean you got convicted by today's sermon? Have you been lusting in your heart, Brother Chambers?"

Brandon rubbed his goatee, eyes glinting with amusement. "I plead the Fifth."

Tamia and Shanell laughed.

"*There* you are."

Tamia's good mood evaporated as they were joined by Cynthia, who wore a stylish pink dress with a scooped neckline and a hem that flared at the knees.

"Hey, girl." She greeted Shanell with a hug and a chaste kiss on the cheek. "How are you?"

"I'm good." Shanell ran an admiring eye over Cynthia. "I like that dress you're wearing. Wait—don't tell me. Marc Jacobs?"

Cynthia laughed, nodding her head at Shanell. "You are *such* a fashionista."

Shanell grinned. "I've been called worse, so I'll take it."

Cynthia chuckled before transferring her attention to Tamia with obvious reluctance. "Hello, Tamia. Thanks for visiting today."

"No thanks necessary. I enjoyed the service. In fact," Tamia added almost as an afterthought, "I might even decide to join the church."

A quick flash of anger narrowed Cynthia's eyes before she recovered and plastered on a bright smile. "Really? That's wonderful. We're always happy to welcome new members."

Tamia smiled just as sweetly. "I'm glad to hear that."

"Of course," Cynthia continued, linking her arm possessively through Brandon's, "if you change your mind and decide to attend church somewhere else—or not at all—no hard feelings." She glanced at Brandon. "Right, baby?"

Lips quirking as he held Tamia's gaze, Brandon murmured, "She won't change her mind."

Cynthia forced out a laugh. "How do you know?"

"She made a pact with God."

Brandon and Tamia smiled at each other.

Cynthia frowned at being excluded from their private joke.

"Hey," Shanell spoke up, trying to distract Cynthia. "We're meeting one of Mark's friends for lunch this afternoon. Why don't you and Brandon join us?"

Cynthia made a face. "Thanks for the offer, but we're having lunch at Opal's Landing to celebrate my brother's birthday."

"Oooh, that fancy restaurant on the water? Girl, I've been dying to check out that place for months. Can we come, too?"

It was obvious that Shanell had only been joking, but Cynthia answered sharply, "No."

Taken aback, Shanell exchanged glances with Tamia and Brandon. "Ohhhkay."

Realizing that she'd spoken too harshly, Cynthia hastened to make amends. "Girl, you know I didn't mean it like that. I'd love for you guys to come, but the reservations were made weeks ago, and the celebration's really only for family. You understand, don't you?"

"Of course," Shanell said breezily. "It's all good. And it's probably best that you and Brandon have other plans anyway. Mark's friend is really feeling Tamia, so I'm sure he wouldn't appreciate having her ex-boyfriend around." She playfully nudged Brandon's arm. "You know how it is."

"Of course." Brandon smiled lazily at Tamia. "Is that the same dude you had dinner with last night?"

Flustered, Tamia stammered, "Um, well—"

"Yup, that's him," Shanell intervened. "Gavin just got back from Afghanistan. Mark says he's been asking about Tamia ever since they were introduced to each other at the club on Friday. After you left the party, Brandon, that brotha wouldn't let Tamia out of his sight. He's the one who suggested dinner on Saturday, then lunch this afternoon." She grinned slyly. "After today, I'm sure he'll want Tamia all to himself."

Cynthia beamed with delight. "Sounds like a love connection," she said gleefully.

Tamia glared at Shanell. "I wouldn't go that far."

Shanell shrugged. "You never know what could happen. Anyway, we'd better go find Mark so we can get going. Definitely don't want to keep Gavin waiting." She smiled cheerfully at Cynthia and Brandon. "Have a good time at lunch."

"You too." Cynthia gave Tamia a knowing glance. "Especially *you*."

"Thanks." Tamia glanced at Brandon, who merely inclined his head.

As she and Shanell walked away, Tamia hissed, "What the hell are you doing?"

"Girl, watch your language. We're in the Lord's house, remember?"

Tamia ignored the rebuke. "Why the hell did you volunteer all that information about Gavin? I already told you I'm not feeling him like that. And I don't want Brandon to think I'm interested in seeing another man. Another man is what broke us up!"

Shanell chuckled. "Don't worry. I got this."

"Got what? What are you—"

"Brandon told you to move on, right?"

Tamia frowned. "Yes."

"So that's what you're doing. See, you have to let him believe that you respect his relationship with Cynthia and you're willing to move on, which means dating other guys. You don't want him to think you're sitting around waiting for him to give you a second chance, even though we both know you are. Men don't like desperate, clingy women—which Cynthia's about to learn the hard way." Pausing midstride, Shanell removed a compact mirror from her purse and held it up, checking her hair and makeup.

Or at least that's what Tamia *thought* she was doing until a slow, satisfied smile curved Shanell's lips. "Umm-hmm. Just as I thought."

"What?"

"Brandon keeps looking back at you. When I count to three, casually glance over your shoulder. One, two—"

On *three*, Tamia did as Shanell had instructed.

Brandon and Cynthia were heading back toward the sanctuary. As Tamia watched, Brandon looked over his shoulder and met her eyes.

They stared at each other.

Tamia offered a hesitant smile.

Brandon nodded shortly before disappearing through the sanctuary doors.

Tamia swallowed hard, returning her gaze to Shanell. "He didn't look too happy."

Shanell grinned smugly. "That's because he's jealous."

"You think so?"

"Absolutely."

Tamia sighed, and hoped to God that her friend was right.

Chapter 11

Fiona

"Why you ain't got a boyfriend, sexy?"

Fiona arched a brow at her client as she guided her buzzing clipper along the sides of his hair. "How do you know I don't?"

Dark eyes searched hers in the full-length mirror that ran along one wall. "Do you?"

A coy, mysterious smile curved Fiona's lips. "That's for me to know and you to keep guessing."

Monte Shaw groaned laughingly in protest. A power forward for the Houston Rockets, he was one of the first clients who'd signed with Pinnacle Sports Group after the agency opened last year. At six ten, with a wide, flat nose and skin as black as tar, he'd never be voted the best-looking player in the NBA. But what he may have lacked in conventional good looks, he more than made up for with a seven-figure salary and a cool swagger that attracted groupies wherever he went.

That Monday afternoon, he was sprawled in Fiona's chair with his long legs stretched out as she tightened his fade. Over the past three months, he'd become one of her regulars, defecting from his longtime barber after watching Fiona work her clipper magic on another customer's head. She'd made a believer out of him and every other patron who'd wrongly assumed that women couldn't cut men's hair. She now had as many clients as the shop's other four barbers, and only *she* was known for having a "velvet touch."

As she edged the back of Monte's head, she bopped to the bass-thumping rhythm of Lil Wayne's latest single. Monte watched her in the mirror, admiring her flawless mocha complexion, doe eyes, model-perfect cheekbones, juicy lips, and the glossy black hair that hung halfway down her back—all natural, thank you very much.

"For real though, shorty," Monte drawled. "When you gon' lemme take you out to dinner?"

Fiona laughed. "Now, you know I never mix business with pleasure."

"Why not?"

"You're my client, boo," she explained. "If we started messing around and things didn't work out between us, you'd take your business elsewhere. And if that happened enough times, I'd find myself out of a job."

Of course, that was only *part* of the reason Fiona didn't date her clients. The main reason was that she had her sights set higher than becoming the mistress of a professional athlete. She had her sights set on snagging her boss, the big dog himself.

Beau Chambers was the ultimate catch. Not only was he fine as hell, but he was worth millions and belonged to one of the most powerful political dynasties in Texas. His family name, combined with his talent and ambition, would undoubtedly take him very far—maybe all the way to the White House.

Why would Fiona settle for being the trophy wife of a basketball player who was one injury away from retirement when she could someday be First Lady? And what better way for her to get back at Tamia than by marrying into the family that had shunned her? Tamia had fucked up her one chance to become Mrs. Brandon Chambers, but Fiona wouldn't be stupid enough to make the same mistake. She knew that sleeping around with the agency's clients was *not* the way to capture Beau's heart. She had to prove to him that despite her troubled past, she could become the woman he needed—a woman he'd be proud to call his own.

So she'd set out to reinvent herself by enrolling in college and severing ties with all the losers who'd once polluted her life. She'd started reading nonfiction books to expand her vocabulary, and she stayed up on current events so she'd be able to hold an intelligent conversation with Brandon and Beau, who had to be the smartest brothas she'd ever known.

When it came to snaring a Chambers man—and, really, either one would do—Fiona was determined to succeed where her sister had failed. So no matter how tempted she was to ride a baller's dick and let him be her sugar daddy, she had to keep her eye on the prize.

But that didn't mean she couldn't enjoy teasing and flirting with her customers. Nothing drove a nigga crazier than being tempted with pussy he couldn't have.

Amused at the thought, Fiona moved in front of Monte to shape the edges of his hairline. As expected, his eyes latched onto the luscious swell of her cleavage exposed by her low-cut cashmere sweater. He licked his lips and flexed his big hands, as if he were trying to restrain himself from grabbing her titties.

Fiona inwardly laughed.

Without taking his eyes off her breasts, Monte asked, "You gon' watch my game tomorrow night, right?"

She smiled. "As soon as I get out of class, boo, I'ma run home and turn it on."

Monte gave a satisfied nod. "That's what's up."

Although the barber shop was closed on Mondays, Fiona had accommodated his request for an appointment because he'd be on the road for the rest of the week. As she cut his hair, the easy silences between them were filled with the sounds of Lil Wayne combined with voices droning from the large plasma television mounted in one corner.

As Monte watched a roundtable of ESPN sportscasters analyze the results of yesterday's NFL games, Fiona's gaze wandered across the lobby to the glass-fronted wellness center. She could see a few customers browsing around the general nutrition store, mulling over the wide range of vitamins, supplements, and energy and bodybuilding products.

When Dre suddenly emerged from the back offices, Fiona scowled.

That baldheaded motherfucker had been a thorn in her flesh from the day she'd started working at the barber shop. She knew he'd tried to talk Beau and Brandon out of hiring her, and he was still pissed because he hadn't gotten his way. Every time Fiona turned around, he was mean-mugging her ass or making some snarky comment. She'd told herself to let his hateful attitude roll off her back, but it bothered her to be judged and condemned by someone who didn't know the first thing about her, didn't know the hell she'd suffered her whole life.

As if sensing Fiona's glare, Dre glanced over at her.

Their gazes clashed in a tense standoff that crackled in the space between them.

Sucking her teeth, Fiona cut her eyes at him and returned her attention to Monte before she fucked up his hair.

Moments later, she was caught off guard when Dre came strolling into the barber shop.

Even as she found herself annoyed by his sudden appearance, she couldn't help admiring the way he looked. His skin was the delicious color of a dark chocolate Hershey bar, and his heavy-lidded eyes always gave him the look of a man who'd just finished fucking. He wore dark slacks and a black polo shirt that hugged his muscular chest and showed off thick, sculpted biceps. He wasn't quite as tall or handsome as Brandon and Beau, but he had the body of an ex-con whose religion had mandated pushing weights.

As he approached Fiona's chair, Monte grinned broadly and called out, "Wassup, Dr. Dre?"

"Yo, wassup," Dre responded.

Fiona watched as the two men exchanged brotherly handshakes. She didn't bother to greet Dre, nor did he acknowledge her presence.

"So the Heat is on tomorrow night," he remarked to Monte, referencing the Rockets' upcoming opponent. "You ready for LeBron and D-Wade?"

"Hell, yeah," Monte retorted with a cocky grin.

As they began discussing game strategy and stats, Fiona found herself stealing peeks at Dre. He stood with his feet braced apart and his arms folded, a thick vein running through each bulging bicep. The nigga was so cock diesel, he *had* to be working with a little dick.

Fiona snickered to herself, catching Dre's attention.

His eyes narrowed on her face. "Something funny?"

"Yup."

"Care to share?"

"You don't want me to. Trust." She finished Monte's hair and gave his neck the Clubman Talc send-off, then removed the black cape draped over his body.

He stood and admired his reflection in the mirror. "Damn, that's tight. Where you been all my life, baby girl?"

"That's what *I* should be asking you," Fiona purred.

He laughed, peeling off two crisp Benjamins that he tucked into the back pocket of her jeans before swatting her playfully on the ass.

She beamed up at him. "Thank you, Big Daddy. Have a good game tomorrow night. I'll be watching."

"Then I'ma dunk on LeBron *just* for you," he promised.

"You do that."

Monte winked at her, then slid on a pair of Gucci shades and sauntered out of the shop with Dre.

Fiona had just finished sweeping the floor when Dre returned minutes later, his eyes flashing with anger as he stalked toward her.

"Is it asking too much for you to behave like a professional who doesn't swing around a pole for a living?" he demanded.

Taken aback, Fiona stared at him. "*Excuse* me?"

"You heard me," he snarled. "If you wanna pop your pussy and give lap dances, go work at a fucking strip club. We're trying to run a respectable business around here."

"What the hell are you talking about?" Fiona spat, nostrils flaring with indignation. "When have you ever seen me popping my pussy and giving lap dances?"

"You might as well have! I've watched the way you carry on with the customers—pushing your breasts all up in their faces, pretending to drop things so you can bend over and let them look at your ass. And what the fuck are you wearing?" he snapped, pointing an accusing finger at her exposed cleavage. "Did you leave the rest of that sweater at home or something?"

Dropping the broom, Fiona thrust her hands onto her hips. "Who the fuck do you think you are? You can't tell me how to dress!"

"No?" Dre challenged, raising his brows. "Last I checked, *you* work for *me*. So if I decide to enforce a dress code, you'd better follow that shit!"

"Or what?"

"Or you can go work somewhere else!"

"Oh, yeah?" Fiona jeered. "Why don't we see what Beau has to say about that when he gets back from his trip to New York. Or better yet, let's call Brandon right now and ask him if *he's* willing to fire me over some bullshit dress code you just made up."

She watched with vicious satisfaction as Dre clenched his jaw so hard she thought his teeth would break. Taunting him further, she pulled out her cell phone and held it up. "I've got Brandon on speed dial. Shall we call him?"

Dre just glared at her.

She smirked. "I didn't think so."

"You need to check yourself," he warned.

"No, *you* need to check yourself," she spat.

"What the hell are you talking about?"

"For someone who's supposed to be running the wellness center across the lobby, you sure spend a lot of time looking over here and watching *my* every move. And now you wanna lecture me about the way I dress? Nigga, please! You're just jealous 'cause I ain't pushing my breasts all up in *your* face."

Dre laughed scornfully. "Don't flatter yourself. If I'm watching your every move, it's because I wanna make sure you don't steal anything. You *did* serve time for armed robbery."

Fiona's face burned with humiliation and fury. "Listen, you motherfucker—"

"Is there a problem here?"

The two combatants spun around to find Dre's girlfriend standing there, her eyes narrowed with suspicion as she watched them.

"Hey, baby." Quickly stepping away from Fiona, Dre walked over and kissed Leah on the cheek. "What're you doing here?"

"I just got off from work and decided to swing by to see if you'd had lunch yet." Leah frowned, tucking her hands into the pockets of her lab coat as she divided a speculative glance between Dre and Fiona. "I'm obviously interrupting something."

"Nah, it's all good," Dre assured her. "Fiona and I were just having a minor disagreement about a new personnel policy."

"Didn't sound 'minor' to me. Unless I heard wrong, she called you a motherfucker." Leah looked Fiona up and down, lips twisted disdainfully. "If that's the way you speak to all of your employers, no wonder you lost your booth at the other salon."

Fiona sucked her teeth. "Bitch, whatever."

Leah's eyes widened with outrage. "Who're you calling a bitch?"

"The bitch I'm looking at," Fiona retorted.

As Leah lunged forward, Dre grabbed her arm and held her back. "Come on, baby," he said urgently. "Let's go to lunch. I'm starving."

Ignoring him, Leah and Fiona stared each other down.

The first time Fiona met Leah, she'd been surprised by how average looking she was. Other than her light skin and pretty amber eyes, there was nothing special about her. She had a freckled nose, thin lips, and a pointy chin, and her blue hospital scrubs hung loosely on her tall, narrow frame. Fiona would have pegged Dre as the type of brotha to have a dime-piece on his arm, not some skinny heffa who could pass for Olive Oyl's high-yellow half sister. No wonder the man was so obsessed with Fiona's luscious titties and phat ass. His girlfriend had neither.

Cutting her eyes away from Fiona, Leah scowled at Dre. "You and your business partners really need to be more selective in your hiring decisions."

"I know. I'm working on it." Shooting one last glare at Fiona, Dre hustled Leah out the doors.

Seething with fury and resentment, Fiona finished straightening her area, then closed up the shop and bounced.

Dre's parting comment had her feeling some type of

way. *I'm working on it*, he'd said, implying that he was still trying to get Fiona fired.

"Motherfucker!" she screeched, banging her fist on the steering wheel of her candy-apple red Nissan Murano.

Although Brandon and Beau stood behind their decision to give her a job, Fiona knew their feelings could change at any time. If Dre kept complaining about her and hounding them to get rid of her, the two brothers might eventually decide that Fiona wasn't worth the aggravation.

Then all of her carefully laid plans would be ruined.

She couldn't allow that to happen.

She wouldn't.

One way or another, Dre was going to back the hell off.

She'd make damn sure of it.

Chapter 12

Tamia

When Tamia sat down at her laptop to check her bank balance late Friday morning, she was surprised to discover that her final payment to Chernoff, Dewitt & Strathmore still hadn't been deducted from her account.

Puzzled, she picked up her cell phone and called Brandon, secretly welcoming an excuse to contact him. Because she hadn't spoken to him since Sunday, she'd spent the entire week worrying that Shanell's ploy to make him jealous had backfired. If Brandon wound up proposing to Cynthia because he mistakenly believed that Tamia had moved on, she'd never forgive Shanell.

After letting the phone ring five times, Tamia was about to hang up and try again later when Brandon answered. "Hello?"

"Hey," Tamia greeted him warmly.

"Tamia?"

"Yeah. Don't tell me you've already forgotten what I sound like."

Brandon chuckled softly. "Of course not. I didn't recognize the number."

"Oh, that's right. I meant to tell you that I got my number changed this week."

"Everything okay?"

"Not really. I got a few calls from reporters who wanted to interview me about the trial, and they wouldn't take no for an answer. I also got a crank call on Saturday night, and it creeped me out a little."

"What'd the caller say?"

"Nothing. All I heard was breathing, then the person hung up."

Brandon was silent, contemplating her words.

"It was probably just a wrong number," Tamia added, though she wasn't entirely convinced.

"Probably," Brandon agreed. "But if you get another call like that, let me know. All right?"

"All right." Tamia smiled, enjoying his overprotectiveness. "Anyway, the reason I was calling—"

"Hold on, Tamia." His voice grew muffled as he spoke to someone in the background.

Tamia waited, glancing around the spacious study that was as tastefully furnished as the rest of the apartment. She still couldn't believe that this was her new home. She kept waiting for someone to knock on the front door and tell her this had all been a huge mistake. When she passed the front desk attendant on her way back from running errands every day, she half-expected to be stopped and escorted off the premises.

After a few minutes, Brandon came back on the line. "Sorry about that."

"It's okay. I know how busy you are, so I won't hold you up. I just wanted to call and find out why my final payment hasn't gone through yet." She grinned. "If y'all wait too long, I'ma mess around and spend that money."

Brandon laughed. "Actually, I wanted to talk to you about that."

"About what? My retainer?"

"Yeah. Have you had lunch?"

"Me?"

"No. Your doorman." He chuckled. "Of course I meant you. There's something I wanted to discuss with you, so I thought we could meet for lunch. That is, if you're free."

"I'm free," she said quickly, not caring how eager she sounded. She wasn't about to pass up an opportunity to spend time with Brandon.

"Good. Where would you like to go?"

"I don't know." Struck by a sudden inspiration, Tamia casually suggested, "Actually, would you mind coming over here for lunch? I went grocery shopping, so I can whip up something for us to eat." When Brandon hesitated, she hastened to add, "I've been eating out at restaurants all week, so I kinda need a break."

"I know the feeling," Brandon said ruefully. "I take clients to lunch so often that I practically live in restaurants. But I don't want you to go to the trouble of making lunch, so I'll pick up something on my way there. Got any requests?"

Tamia grinned. "Now that I've satisfied my seafood craving, can you guess what else I've been feenin' for?"

Brandon chuckled. "I think I've got a pretty good idea. See you soon."

"I'll be waiting."

Tamia disconnected the call, then let out a squeal of excitement. Unable to contain herself, she sent off a quick text message to Shanell: *My boo's coming over for lunch!*

By the time she got up and rushed to her bedroom to get dressed, Shanell had called.

"See?" her friend gloated. "And you were worried that

you'd pushed Brandon away by going out with another guy. I *told* you that brotha was jealous!"

Tamia grinned, shimmying out of the spandex halter and shorts she'd donned that morning to head downstairs to the fitness center—a trip she'd never made. "He said he wants to discuss something with me."

"Really? What?"

"I'm not sure. Something about my retainer."

"Your retainer?" Shanell sounded puzzled.

"That's what he said. I guess I'll find out when he gets here. Anyway," Tamia said, hurrying over to her walk-in closet, "I was so excited that I just had to let you know."

"Are you gonna fix him lunch?"

"No, he offered to pick up something."

"Then I guess you can provide dessert." Shanell chuckled lasciviously. "Nothing like some love in the afternoon."

Tamia laughed. "Only if I'm lucky. Holla at ya later, girl."

"You'd better. I'm gonna want details."

Grinning, Tamia snapped her phone shut and set it down on a silk footstool. After surveying the rows of clothes that lined the large closet, she grabbed a fitted pink T-shirt and a dark pair of True Religion skinny jeans that molded her voluptuous curves. She'd been dressed similarly the first time she and Brandon met, and he hadn't been able to resist her. With any luck, she'd get the same results today.

By the time she'd put on some makeup, flat-ironed her hair, and lightly spritzed herself with Jo Malone's pomegranate noir, the doorbell rang.

Anticipation quickened her pulse.

It was all she could do to walk, not run, to the front door.

The sight of Brandon's sexy chocolateness had her pussy throbbing instantly. She watched as he slowly looked her up and down, his dark eyes glittering with blatant appreciation.

"Hey," he murmured.

Tamia smiled. "Hey, yourself." She leaned up and hugged him, enticing him with the scent of her sweet perfume and the lushness of her breasts. She pulled away in time to see him inhale a shaky breath and close his eyes for a moment, as if he were fighting for self-control.

She felt a thrill of satisfaction. She wanted nothing more than to take him by the hand and lead him to her bedroom, where she'd spend the rest of the day and night showing him just how much she'd missed him.

Patience, girlfriend. Don't rush this, or you'll scare him off.

When Tamia glanced down and saw that Brandon was holding a carryout bag from their favorite barbecue joint, she exclaimed delightedly, "You remembered!"

He smiled lazily. "Why are you surprised? Haven't we already established that I remember everything?"

Tamia laughed, taking the bag from his hand and closing the door as he entered the apartment. She led him down the long entryway to the living room, saying over her shoulder, "Welcome to my not-so-humble abode."

Brandon glanced around, nodding approvingly. "Very nice."

"That has to be the understatement of the year," Tamia teased.

He chuckled, following her into the kitchen. "I'm glad you're still enjoying the place."

"What's not to enjoy? The gourmet grocery store? The swimming pool with a waterfall? The concierge and valet services?"

Brandon grinned, removing his suit jacket and rolling up his sleeves. "Point taken."

Tamia retrieved two plates from the cabinet and began opening the carryout containers. "Mmm," she breathed, savoring the mouthwatering aroma of barbecue ribs, brisket, pinto beans, and creamed corn. "You knew *exactly* what I wanted."

"Of course." Brandon met her gaze across the breakfast counter. "That hasn't changed."

Tamia smiled at him. "I hope it never does."

They stared at each other until Brandon's cell phone suddenly rang. Tamia watched as he pulled it from his pants pocket and glanced down at the caller ID. Although his expression didn't change, Tamia instinctively knew the call was from Cynthia.

"Do you want some privacy?"

"Nah," he murmured, turning off the phone before tucking it away. "I'm good."

Shanell's words ran through Tamia's mind. *Men don't like desperate, clingy women—which Cynthia's about to learn the hard way.*

She hoped Shanell was right.

As Tamia piled food onto two plates, Brandon poured them each a glass of the restaurant's sweet tea.

"It's a beautiful day," Tamia said. "Mind if we eat outside?"

"Not at all," Brandon agreed.

They carried their meals to the small table on the balcony, where they could enjoy the gorgeous view while they ate.

"So," Brandon began almost as soon as they were seated, "are you dating that dude now? What was his name again?"

"Gavin?"

"Yeah. Him."

Tamia smiled, biting into a juicy rib and chewing slowly. Brandon watched her, waiting. "Well?"

"I wouldn't exactly say we're dating," Tamia answered vaguely.

"You've gone out with him twice."

"With Shanell and Mark."

"He hasn't asked you out alone yet?"

Tamia polished off her rib. "He has."

When she offered no more, Brandon raised a brow at her. "And?" he prompted.

Tamia hesitated, then decided to opt for the truth. "And I told him that I'd rather just be friends for now. He's a really nice guy, but I'm not ready for another relationship." She paused. "Honestly, I'm not over you yet, Brandon. And I don't know when, or *if*, I ever will be. So while it may have been easy for you to move on, *I* need more time."

Brandon was silent for several moments, pondering her heartfelt words.

As she stared at her plate of food, he said quietly, "It *wasn't* easy."

Tamia glanced up, meeting his solemn gaze. "What?"

"It wasn't easy getting over you. Moving on."

"But you did," she countered, unable to keep the hurt and accusation from her voice. "I know I made a terrible mistake, and I betrayed your trust. But I never expected you to fall in love with another woman so quickly. I guess you must have loved her all along."

Brandon said nothing, neither confirming nor denying what she'd said.

Tamia gave him a small, mirthless smile. "I applaud Cynthia for patiently biding her time, waiting for the right opportunity to make her move. I can't really say I blame her, because if *I'd* been secretly in love with you for two years, I might have been just as sneaky and manipulative. As they say, all's fair in love and war."

Brandon frowned. "Tamia—"

She held up a hand. "It's okay. I'm not trying to start an argument with you by rehashing the past. In fact, that's the *last* thing I want to do."

"I don't want to argue with you, either," Brandon murmured.

"So let's not. Let's enjoy this delicious barbecue, the beautiful view, and the pleasure of each other's company. Agreed?"

He smiled faintly. "Agreed."

"Good."

A few minutes after they'd resumed eating, Brandon asked conversationally, "How's the job search going?"

Tamia grimaced. "Not well," she admitted. "I've been looking all week, and it's slim pickings. I've only found a few openings for advertising jobs."

"Did you submit your résumé?"

"Yeah, but I'm not very optimistic. Image is everything in the world of advertising, and my image isn't exactly unblemished. Even the headhunter I consulted had some serious concerns about my employability."

Brandon looked sympathetic. "Don't get too discouraged. It's only been a week."

"I know. That's what I keep telling myself." Tamia sighed heavily. "If all else fails, I suppose I could always go work for Lou."

Brandon frowned, eyes narrowing. "At the escort agency?"

"Yeah. He offered me a job."

"Doing what?"

Tamia laughed at Brandon's suspicious tone. "It's not what you think. He wants me to run the agency and manage his escorts. He said I'd be well compensated."

"And what'd you tell him?"

"I told him thanks, but no thanks. I'm not interested in working as a madam."

Brandon nodded. "Glad to hear it."

Tamia grinned ironically. "Of course, if I get desperate enough, I might change my mind."

"No, you won't," Brandon said with such conviction that Tamia arched a brow at him.

"How do *you* know I won't change my mind?"

"Because you'll be working for me."

She blinked at him, thinking she'd heard wrong. "Excuse me? Did you just say I'd be working for *you*?"

"Yeah." Brandon met her stunned gaze. "That's what I wanted to discuss with you. How would you feel about becoming my legal assistant for the next three months?"

Tamia stared at him, excitement pulsing through her veins. "Are you serious?"

"Yeah."

"But you already have a secretary *and* an assistant."

"I share a secretary with several other partners," Brandon clarified. "And my personal assistant, Noemi, is going on maternity leave in two weeks. Rather than hire a temp, I'd like to give you the job."

"Wow," Tamia whispered, shaking her head in disbelief. "This is so unexpected, Brandon. How can you hire me? I don't even have any legal experience."

"Didn't you intern at a law firm for two summers while you were in college?"

Tamia nodded, surprised that he'd remembered such a minor detail about her.

"Then, technically, you have legal experience." Brandon chuckled. "Seriously, Tamia. You're more qualified than you may think. You worked at one of the top advertising agencies for over seven years. You're smart as hell, organized, detail oriented, great at research, and you're definitely not afraid of hard work. Noemi will give you a crash course in legal writing before she leaves. And since you'll be reporting to my secretary, she'll be able to answer any questions you'll have."

Tamia eyed him wonderingly. "I don't even know what

to say, Brandon. You've already done so much for me, and I haven't even finished paying off my bill."

Brandon sipped his drink. "Don't worry about the rest of your retainer."

She frowned. "What do you mean?"

"I'm not collecting your final payment."

Tamia stared incredulously at him. "You're going to forgive the rest of my debt?"

"Yeah."

"Oh, my God! Are you serious? Can you even *do* that?"

"Of course."

Tamia hesitated for a moment, then shook her head. "Thank you, Brandon, but I can't let you do that for me. You'd catch hell from the other partners."

He chuckled dryly. "Let me worry about that."

"Brandon—"

"Look, you need help getting back on your feet, and you also need to keep that money in the bank in case it takes you a while to find another job once Noemi comes back. Stop me when I start lying."

Tamia smiled wanly. "Everything you've said is true. But I don't feel right about not paying you what you rightfully earned. You worked your ass off to get me acquitted, and I know for a fact that the hourly fees you *did* charge me were pro-rated."

Brandon gave her a blank look. "I don't know what you're talking about."

She laughed. "Yeah, right! We dated for nine months, Brandon. I know the kind of fees you command, and I know that I got off cheap."

"Whatever you say."

"Brandon—"

"Listen, baby girl," he gently interrupted. "The way I see it, we're doing each other a favor. You need a job, I need a reliable assistant, and that's all that matters right now. So are you gonna sit there arguing with me about retainers? Or are you gonna say yes to my job offer?"

A slow, delighted grin spread across Tamia's face. "Yes."

"Yes, what?"

Yes, I'll marry you! "Yes, I accept your job offer."

Brandon smiled approvingly. "Good. I'll take care of everything when I get back to the office."

"Okay." Tamia couldn't believe her good fortune. She couldn't have prayed for a better opportunity to ease her way back into his life. "Thank you, Brandon. Thank you *so* much."

"Don't thank me just yet," he drawled humorously. "In the interest of full disclosure, I have to warn you up front that I can be a real hard-ass as a boss. I'm demanding as hell, and you may feel that some of the tasks you're given are beneath you."

Tamia sent him a wry look. "I just got out of prison, and I'm on the verge of applying for unemployment benefits. Trust me, I won't think *anything's* beneath me."

Brandon grinned crookedly. "We'll see if you're still singing the same tune three months from now."

Tamia just laughed.

They spent the remainder of lunch discussing everything from the Houston Texans' playoff chances to sharing their favorite memories of local parades and festivals they'd attended as children. The conversation was so lively and enjoyable that they lost track of time, one hour slipping into two.

It was Tamia who happened to glance down at Brandon's platinum Rolex and exclaim, "Goodness! It's after two o'clock!"

Brandon unhurriedly followed the direction of her gaze. "Mmm. So it is."

Tamia gaped at him, shocked by his blasé response. "Don't you have to get back to the office?"

"Sure." But he made no move to get up, lazily contemplating the downtown skyline.

Tamia studied him for a few moments, her head tipped thoughtfully to one side. "Wow."

Brandon looked at her. "What?"

She smiled softly. "You're so much more relaxed nowadays."

"Think so?"

"Definitely. Once upon a time, you were too busy to take personal lunch breaks, let alone *extended* breaks. Six months ago, this scenario"—she gestured around the balcony—"never would have happened."

"You're right," Brandon agreed with a rueful expression. "Lunch breaks were a luxury I couldn't afford."

"And now look at you. Sitting here chillin' like you don't have a care in the world." Tamia grinned at him. "I think making partner may have been the best thing that ever happened to you, Brandon."

He smiled faintly. "Time will tell, I guess."

As they rose and began clearing the table, Tamia wished she'd kept her mouth shut about the time. She didn't want Brandon to leave. She wanted him to stay and chill with her for the rest of the day, just the two of them, keeping the rest of the world at bay.

When they returned to the kitchen, Brandon helped her put away the leftover food. When they'd finished, he rolled down his sleeves and refastened the buttons on his shirt cuffs before walking over to the barstool where he'd draped his suit jacket. As he shrugged into it, Tamia moved behind him and impulsively wrapped her arms around his broad back, embracing him.

Brandon tensed with surprise, but only for a second.

Tamia closed her eyes as he took her hands and placed

them over his heart, which was beating as fast as her own. She swallowed hard, her chest tightening with emotion.

After several moments, he brought her hands to his lips and gently kissed her knuckles, making her shiver with longing.

"Brandon . . ."

Turning slowly in her arms, he leaned his forehead against hers and stared down into her eyes. Their uneven breaths mingled, fanning each other's faces. Tamia's nipples were so hard they ached, and her wet pussy had begun throbbing.

"I have to go," Brandon whispered.

"I know," Tamia whispered back. "But I don't want you to."

"Neither do I. And that's why I have to."

She nodded slowly, even as her hips rubbed against his thick, hard dick and made him shudder. "I'm so wet for you, baby."

"*Shit*," he swore gutturally. "Don't tell me that."

"But it's true."

Nostrils flaring, eyes glittering fiercely, Brandon grabbed her face between his hands and crushed his mouth to hers.

Tamia moaned with pleasure, sucking his soft, succulent lips as he sucked hers.

His big hands roamed the curves of her body before cupping her ass, grinding his heavy erection against her. Her pussy rained as they kissed with deepening hunger, mouths exploring, tongues slurping and feasting.

Abruptly Brandon pulled away and staggered backward, his chest heaving as he fought to catch his breath. Scrubbing a shaky hand over his face, he whispered hoarsely, "Fuck."

"Yes," Tamia panted, staring at his bulging crotch, "let's do that. *Please*."

Brandon stared at her for a moment, then made a sound

that was part laugh, part groan. As she watched, his hooded eyes traveled from her kiss-swollen lips to her hard nipples protruding through her T-shirt.

Shaking his head, he discreetly turned away to adjust his pants.

Tamia licked her lips, still tasting his deliciousness. "I want you to know something, baby."

Brandon glanced over his shoulder and met her intent gaze.

She said boldly, "I want you back. In my life, in my arms, in my bed. I'm not gonna sleep with any other man until you come back to me, no matter how long it takes. So whenever you're ready, boo, I'll be waiting. But just know that the longer you make me wait, the more I'ma wear your ass out with this starving pussy. Believe that."

Brandon's eyes widened with a combination of lust, surprise, and anticipation. He held her gaze for several scorching seconds.

Tamia waited, pulse pounding like a drum.

Finally he growled, "I'll call you tomorrow."

She nodded, then watched as he turned and strode purposefully from the kitchen.

As soon as she heard the front door close, she unzipped her tight jeans and shoved her hand down her panties. They were so wet that the silky material clung to her skin like Saran Wrap.

Closing her eyes, she thrust two fingers inside her pussy and groaned softly. Bracing one hand on the countertop, she stroked her fleshy insides until she found sweet release, coming so hard and fast her knees buckled.

Gasping, she slid weakly to the floor.

A minute later she let out a soft, shaky laugh.

As horny as she was, she must be out of her damn mind to even *think* she could abstain from sex much longer. But she had to. She'd made a promise to herself, and now to Brandon. So no matter what happened, or however long it took him to put her out of her misery, she'd keep her promise.

Because she knew beyond a shadow of a doubt that he was worth the wait.

Chapter 13

Brandon

Later that afternoon, Brandon's concentration was shot to hell as he sat in the weekly litigation partners meeting. Boasting a roster of seven hundred attorneys—which included two hundred partners—Chernoff, Dewitt & Strathmore was so large that most leadership meetings had to be divided by practice areas.

Seated at the glossy mahogany conference table, Brandon half listened as his colleagues griped about unnamed partners who hoarded clients to drive up their own billable hours. The accusations didn't apply to Brandon, who'd already established himself as a team player who fairly delegated work and mentored associates. So since he wasn't on the offensive, it was easy for him to let his mind wander.

And wander it did . . . right back to Tamia.

He couldn't stop thinking about her. Since leaving her apartment, he'd been in serious need of an arctic-cold shower. He should have known better than to go to her place for lunch. The moment she'd opened her front door and he got an eyeful of her bodacious body squeezed into those jeans, he'd been in trouble. He'd wanted to toss her over his shoulder, carry her to her bedroom, and lose himself deep inside her sugar walls till the cops came knocking. And that little speech of hers had fucked him up big-time. Every time he replayed her words, his dick hardened painfully.

I want you back. In my life, in my arms, in my bed. . . .
But just know that the longer you make me wait, the more
I'ma wear your ass out with this starving pussy.

Dayuuummm!

"Are we boring you, Mr. Chambers?"

Snapped out of his reverie, Brandon glanced around the large conference table. Twenty-four pairs of eyes stared back at him, including those belonging to Mitch Perkins, managing partner of the firm's litigation department and his former supervisor.

Brandon grinned sheepishly. "Sorry. It's Friday," he offered by way of explanation.

Everyone laughed.

Everyone but Russ Sutcliffe, one of the firm's senior partners who'd made it clear from day one that he was no fan of Brandon's. With his meticulously groomed hair and icy blue eyes, Russ was your typical good ole boy—a staunch Republican who undoubtedly believed that minorities had no business working at blue-chip law firms, let alone sharing a slice of the partnership pie. He'd vigorously campaigned against the election of the current governor and his running mate, Bernard Chambers.

So there was no love lost between him and Brandon.

"I'm sorry," Russ drawled, his voice dripping with sarcasm. "Are we interfering with your exciting weekend plans, Mr. Chambers? Should we reschedule our meetings to another day of the week that better suits your attention span?"

"Actually, that wouldn't be such a bad idea," Brandon quipped.

Laughter swept around the room.

"He's got a point," another partner spoke up. "I've always said that Friday afternoons are a lousy time for meetings."

As more voices chimed in, Mitch laughingly held up his hands. "Before this turns into a mutiny, let the record show that I'm open to suggestions for alternate meeting days."

"You have *got* to be kidding me." Russ sent an exasperated glance around the table. "Just because *Chambers* has a problem, suddenly we're all willing to rearrange our schedules to accommodate him? Since when does a newly minted partner call the shots around here?"

Brandon deadpanned, "Oh, you didn't get the memo?"

Another round of laughter filled the room.

Russ wasn't amused. "Ah, yes," he drawled sarcastically, "Behold young Mr. Chambers, flush with victory after winning not one but *two* big court cases this year. Let us all bow in submission to his greatness."

Brandon tsk-tsked, wagging his finger at the other man. "Jealousy doesn't become you, Russ."

"*Jealous*? Of *you*?" Russ snorted derisively. "Don't flatter yourself, kid. I was a rainmaking partner at this firm while you were still captain of your high school debate team. I've got too many years of litigation experience under my belt to feel threatened by some upstart who's feeling his oats after winning a couple of cases that I could have easily handled."

"Really?" Brandon challenged. "Is that why *you* were entrusted with the Quasar Diagnostics lawsuit? Hmm? Oh, wait, that's right. You weren't. The case was assigned to *me*, a lowly associate with less than half the years of litigation experience that you have. So I have to wonder, Russ. Does that say less about me—or *you*?"

Russ's face flushed beet red as a tense silence settled over the room.

Eyes glinting with humor, Mitch interjected, "At the

risk of interrupting this pissing contest, which has been highly entertaining—"

Russ held up a hand, interrupting Mitch as he gave Brandon a narrow, condescending smile. "You seem to be forgetting that you're only a *junior* partner."

"A junior partner," Brandon countered evenly, "who brought $2.6 million of new revenue to the firm last year as an *associate*." He paused, pinning his adversary with a direct gaze. "What was your haul, *partner*?"

He stared Russ down, watching with satisfaction as the man's face turned an even brighter shade of red.

Throats cleared and papers shuffled around the table. Everyone knew that Russ was an underperforming partner whose neck was on the chopping block. He was dead weight in one of the firm's top revenue-producing departments, so his days were rumored to be numbered.

Mitch glanced around the room. "Before we adjourn the meeting, are there any other items we need to discuss?"

Brandon spoke up. "I just wanted to let everyone know that Tamia Luke will be filling in for Noemi during her maternity leave."

A shocked silence followed his announcement.

Not surprisingly, Russ was the first to recover and sneer. "Tamia Luke? As in, the former porn star who was just acquitted of murder? As in, your client?"

Brandon met Russ's reproachful stare. "My *former* client."

Mitch frowned at him. "How did this, ah, development come about?"

Brandon shrugged. "Miss Luke needs a job, and I need a temporary assistant."

He'd made the decision on Sunday afternoon during lunch with Cynthia's family. Throughout the festive celebration, he'd found himself struggling not to dwell on thoughts of Tamia dating other guys. As Cynthia fed him a spoonful of crème brûlée, he'd come up with the idea to hire Tamia, which would not only help her out financially but also give him the means to keep tabs on her.

"While we're on the topic of Miss Luke," Russ jeered, breaking into Brandon's thoughts, "has she even settled her retainer yet?"

"She doesn't have to. I'm writing off the rest of what she owes."

Russ's brows shot up to his receding hairline. "You're *forgiving* her debt?"

"That's what I said."

Russ scoffed, glancing incredulously at the other attorneys seated around the table. "Are we running a charity or a law firm?"

Brandon heaved an impatient sigh. "Come on, Russ. My successful representation of Quasar Diagnostics just netted this firm $128 million in revenue. Are you seriously gonna rake me over the coals for retiring a $15,000 debt?"

Russ clenched his jaw, impotent with fury because he knew he couldn't refute Brandon's point.

Mitch diplomatically intervened, "Brandon, no one's disputing that you're one of our top rainmakers—"

"*That's* an understatement," someone muttered in agreement.

Mitch chuckled dryly before continuing, "Russ is just expressing concern that hiring a former client could present a conflict of interest."

"It's downright unethical," Russ snapped.

Brandon raised a brow at him. "Are you gonna report me to the bar? Or are you planning to sell an exposé to the *Houston Chronicle*?"

Someone snickered. "Don't give him any ideas."

This set off another wave of laughter that was interrupted by a new voice. "Hiring Miss Luke *does* seem rather unsavory."

Brandon looked across the table, meeting the censorious gaze of Gibson Sorrell, the litigation department's only other black partner. The man rarely spoke during meetings, and notoriously refused to render an opinion on any controversial issue—a reputation that had earned him the nickname "Clarence Thomas Junior."

It figured that he'd break his long-running silence to oppose a fellow black colleague.

Brandon smirked at him. "What was that, Gibson? I didn't catch what you said."

The brotha pressed his lips together, quickly backing down.

I didn't think so, Brandon mused. *Fucking coward*.

After shooting Gibson a look of disgust, Russ returned his attention to Brandon. "Surely even *you* can acknowledge that hiring a client—a former murder defendant, at that—is a huge violation of ethics."

As Brandon's patience finally snapped, he growled, "Miss Luke's trial is over, she's no longer a client, and quite frankly, I can hire whoever the hell I want."

Russ laughed scornfully, shaking his head as he leaned back against his chair. "I gotta tell you, Chambers. For all the trouble you've gone through for this woman, the putang must have been *really* something."

Brandon clenched his jaw, eyes narrowed on Russ's smirking face. He wanted to lunge across the table, grab the smug motherfucker by the throat, and throw his ass out the window.

Checking the violent urge, Brandon said coolly, "Unlike you, Sutcliffe, my mother raised a gentleman. So out of respect to Edna and Nancy"—he glanced at the two female attorneys in the room—"I won't dignify your crassness with a response."

Russ scowled.

"And you seem to have misunderstood me," Brandon

continued in the same mild tone. "When I made my announcement, I wasn't asking for permission."

"Wonderful," Russ mocked, looking around the room. "So let's all go around forgiving clients' debts, and when our profits take a nosedive, we'll see how the golden child feels about *that*."

The snide suggestion elicited some chuckles.

Unfazed, Brandon shrugged. "To be perfectly honest, Russ, I'm making enough money from the sports agency that I could take pro bono cases for the next two years and not lose any sleep at night. Hell, maybe I should just leave and help my brother negotiate multimillion-dollar NBA contracts. You wouldn't *believe* the perks."

As his colleagues exchanged nervous glances, he snapped his fingers. "Or better yet. Maybe I'll just start my own firm and take all my clients with me."

Dead silence.

He glanced around the table, looking each of the partners in the eye.

Russ glared back at him, while Mitch merely grimaced and shook his head.

Satisfied that he'd made his point, Brandon flicked his wrist and checked his watch. "I don't know about the rest of you," he drawled, "but I've got some billable hours to run up."

No one spoke as he unhurriedly got to his feet, fastening the last two buttons of his suit jacket. He looked around the room and said, "Gentlemen," then inclined his head toward Edna and Nancy. "Ladies."

The two women nodded at him, their eyes glimmering with amusement and respect.

And with that, Brandon turned and sauntered out of the conference room.

Chapter 14

Fiona

"*Oooh, Daddy*," Fiona moaned lustily, breasts bouncing up and down, hips working frantically as she rode the stiff shaft of her current lover. "This dick is *sooo* good!"

"So is this pussy," Shane panted beneath her, gripping Fiona's butt so hard she just knew he'd leave permanent handprints. "I don't think I can . . . last much longer."

Of course you can't, Fiona thought with wicked satisfaction.

"This pussy too much for you, Daddy?" she taunted, seductively rocking her hips as she fingered her hard clit. "You can't handle all this good punanny?"

He shook his head quickly, squeezing his eyes shut. "Oh, shit," he groaned hoarsely as she flexed her inner walls. "Shit, baby, I'm . . . *coming*!"

"So am I!" Fiona yelled exultantly, busting her nut at the same time that she felt his dick pumping rapidly inside her, spilling semen into the condom he wore.

Laughing breathlessly, she collapsed on the bed beside him and rained kisses down his neck and heaving bare chest.

"Ummm." He smiled contentedly, caressing her damp back. "That was amazing."

Not quite, Fiona mused as she snuggled against him. *But it's good enough for now.*

"I *love* it when you do that thing with your pussy muscles." He shuddered. "Gets me every single time."

Fiona smiled coyly. "So that should *definitely* earn me an A on the final exam, right?"

Shane laughed, his warm breath fanning her face. "You don't need to seduce me to get good grades in my class, Fiona."

"What?" she exclaimed, feigning shock. "You mean I've been fucking you all this time for nothing?"

They both laughed.

Shane was her economics professor at Rice University. She'd been attracted to him from the very first day of class, although he wasn't her usual type. He was light skinned, for starters, and he didn't have a thuggish bone in his body. But he was handsome in a scholarly, neo-soul kind of way. With his short, neat twists and the rimless frames he sported, he reminded her of the singer Maxwell.

At the beginning of the semester, she'd found herself paying more attention to the way his jeans hugged his ass than to what he was teaching. By the second week of classes, she'd been totally lost. So she'd gone to him for help.

She'd already known that he was attracted to her. She'd caught him checking her out several times, his eyes sliding over her thick ass and thighs when he thought she wasn't looking. He'd been only too happy to oblige her request for after-hours tutoring. Halfway through their first session in his office, she'd had him down on his knees, his face buried between her legs as he enthusiastically ate out her pussy.

They'd been hooking up secretly ever since.

"You're a beautiful woman, Fiona," Shane murmured,

stroking her tousled hair. "But you should never feel that you have to use your body to get what you want out of life."

Fiona went still, Shane's words presciently echoing what her grandmother had told her many years ago. *God blessed you with beauty, chile, but He never intended for you to use it as a weapon.*

A familiar ache of sorrow and regret swept through her at the memory of Mama Esther, who'd meant everything to Fiona and Tamia. After her tragic death, their lives had never been the same again.

"You're a lot smarter than you think you are," Shane continued when Fiona remained silent. "Didn't you just ace a history test that most of your classmates tanked?"

Fiona beamed, the painful memories from the past evaporating. "Yup. I sure did."

"See? And I know you're *definitely* not sleeping with Professor Wozniak."

"Hell, nah!" Fiona exclaimed, her nose wrinkling in disgust at the thought of even *touching* the old, liver-spotted relic who sprayed spittle when he lectured. "No amount of money in the world could convince me to fuck *that* dude."

Shane laughed. "That's good to know."

Fiona grinned, running her fingers through the thick swirls of hair covering his chest. "Why aren't you married, professor?"

He sighed dramatically. "No woman will have me."

Fiona snorted out a laugh. "Stop playin'! You know damn well that's not true. Have you seen the way your female students look at you? Every last one of them wants to fuck the shit outta you. If they knew about us, they'd be so damn jealous."

Shane eyed her alertly. "But they don't, right? I mean, you haven't told anyone about us, have you?"

"Of course not! I'm not stupid. I know you don't wanna lose your job." She scowled. "Even though they'd be dead wrong for firing you. It's not like I'm some damn teenager. I'm twenty-five years old. A grown-ass woman."

"You most certainly are," Shane agreed, squeezing her butt cheek.

Fiona grinned, cuddling closer to him. "Anyway, why did you say no woman will have you? Have you been in a lot of bad relationships?"

"Not really." He paused. "I just always seem to attract women whose hearts belong to someone else. Like the last woman I dated. She was smart, beautiful, accomplished, and we really had a lot in common."

When he fell silent, Fiona prompted, "But?"

Shane grimaced. "But she was in love with another man."

"Damn," Fiona commiserated. "That's fucked up. I can tell you were really feeling her."

"I was," he admitted.

"What was her name?"

He hesitated. "Cynthia."

"Cynthia, huh? Well, she was a damn fool for letting you go."

Shane chuckled, kissing the top of Fiona's head. "In all fairness to her, the guy she was pining for just happened to be Houston's most eligible bachelor. So it's not like I lost out to some ugly, broke-ass chump off the street. *That* would have made me feel worse."

Fiona had been tracing lazy patterns through the soft mat of Shane's chest hairs. At the mention of "Houston's most eligible bachelor," her hand stilled. Lifting her head, she stared at Shane. "Are you talking about Brandon Chambers?"

He made a pained face. "Unfortunately, yes."

"Wait a minute. You dated Cynthia Yarbrough?"

"Yeah." Shane eyed Fiona curiously. "Do you know her?"

"Not personally. But I know who she is. Her father's megachurch is even bigger than T.D. Jakes's. And everyone in town knows she's dating Brandon Chambers." Fiona was reeling with shock. She couldn't believe that the man she'd been sneaking around with had once dated her sister's nemesis. Talk about six degrees of separation!

"Have you ever been to Bishop Yarbrough's church?" Shane asked her.

She hesitated. "No, but my boss has started going."

"You mean the owner of the barber shop where you work?"

Fiona nodded.

She hadn't told Shane very much about her background. So he didn't know that she'd spent two years behind bars, that she worked for the lieutenant governor's sons, that she was related to the former porn star whose scandalous murder trial had made national headlines. And he sure as hell didn't know about the harrowing night that Fiona had taken another woman's life, a transgression that would haunt her for the rest of her life.

As far as she was concerned, the less Shane knew about her, the better.

Glancing at the clock on the nightstand, Shane grimaced. "Damn, it's already after five. I'd better head home and change so I won't be late to the faculty reception."

"Okay." Fiona sighed. "I wish I could go with you."

"No, you don't," Shane retorted, climbing out of bed to get dressed. "You'd be bored to death, standing around eating finger food and making small talk with the most pretentious assholes you've ever met. Trust me, if I weren't seeking tenure, I'd skip the damn reception tonight and stay right here with you."

Fiona grinned. "Well, you're more than welcome to come back when it's over. And just in case you need a little mental stimulation to get you through the boring evening . . ."

Slowly she spread her legs to show him the plump, glistening folds of her pussy.

Shane stared down at her, his Adam's apple bobbing as he swallowed hard.

Smiling seductively, Fiona dipped a finger inside her wetness and purred, "*This* is what will be waiting for you."

Shane glanced at the clock, then back at her, torn between lust and duty.

Fiona provocatively licked her finger. "Mmm."

Shane's nostrils flared. "Fuck it," he muttered.

As he tossed aside his shirt and dove on top of her, Fiona could only laugh in wicked triumph.

After Shane left an hour later, Fiona lit up a blunt, reached inside her Coach bookbag, and pulled out her history test. She beamed at the score scrawled across the top of the page. Ninety-seven. She'd only gotten one answer wrong, and only because she'd second-guessed herself. The questions had been difficult, but she'd studied hard and had come prepared.

She was damn proud of herself.

Wanting to share her accomplishment with the one person who'd always believed in her, Fiona grabbed her cell phone without thinking and called Tamia.

She frowned as an automated voice informed her that the number she'd reached was no longer in service.

Hanging up, she took a long drag on her blunt and exhaled a shaky breath. When her eyes watered, she blamed it on the smoke. But she knew better. Her feelings were hurt. Tamia had obviously changed her number in a cruel attempt to sever all ties with Fiona.

I don't think so, she mused darkly, speed-dialing another number.

When Brandon answered the phone, she momentarily

forgot why she was calling him. His deep voice was hella sexy, sending delicious shivers down her spine.

"Hey, baby girl," he said, sounding distracted. "Is everything all right?"

"Um, yeah."

"Cool. I'm on the phone with a client, so can I call you back?"

"Sure, but you don't have to. I just wanted to know if you have Tamia's new number."

"Yeah." He paused. "She didn't give it to you, huh?"

"No. And I really need to talk to her. I'm thinking about putting our house up for sale," she lied, "and Tamia has the deed and all the other paperwork."

Brandon was silent.

Fiona imagined him frowning into the phone, eyes narrowed as he tried to determine whether she was telling the truth.

She waited, toking nervously on her blunt.

"One of these days," Brandon muttered grimly, "I'ma get to the bottom of what *really* went down between you two."

Fiona's mouth went dry. She knew that if anyone could ferret out the terrible secret she and her sister shared, Brandon could.

"I have to go," he said, "so here's Tamia's number."

Fiona jotted down the digits on the back of her history test. "Thank you, Brandon," she said sweetly.

"No problem. Later, girl."

After he hung up, Fiona inhaled a deep, steadying breath and let it out slowly. When she felt calmer, she dialed her sister's new number.

Tamia answered on the fourth ring.

"I thought I told you not to call me," she said, her voice so chilling that Fiona would have sworn the temperature had suddenly plummeted below zero.

She gulped hard. "Hey, Tamia," she croaked.

"How the fuck did you get this number?"

"B-Brandon gave it to me. I told him I needed to talk to you—"

"I don't talk to ghosts, and you're dead to me. Remember?"

Tears welled in Fiona's eyes. "Come on, Tam-Tam. I *miss* you. The house isn't the same without—"

There was a sharp click.

Seconds later, all Fiona heard was the rude drone of the dial tone.

With tears streaming down her face, she flung aside the phone and blindly crushed out her blunt in an ashtray on the nightstand.

As a seething rage built inside her, she snatched her history test off the bed and viciously ripped the pages apart, then hurled the shredded pieces into the air like confetti.

After retrieving her jeans and sweater from the floor, she dressed quickly and grabbed her car keys.

As she slammed out of the house moments later, she had only one destination in mind.

Chapter 15

Tamia

Tamia was livid.

She couldn't *believe* Fiona had called her! What part of "I want absolutely nothing to do with you" did that bitch not understand? What made her think for one damn second that Tamia was ready to forgive her—especially when it had only been a week since she'd been acquitted for a murder that *Fiona* had committed?

"Un-fucking-believable!" Tamia hissed furiously.

After hanging up on her sister, she'd tried to return her attention to the *Legal Writing for Dummies* guide that she'd been reading before she was interrupted. But she couldn't concentrate on a damn word. After perusing the same passage for the third time, she'd tossed down the book in angry frustration.

She was debating whether to drive over to the house to lay hands on Fiona when a loud knock sounded at her front door.

Heart thumping into her throat, Tamia snatched off her earrings and lunged from the sofa. "This bitch thinks I'm playing," she ranted, marching from the living room. "Don't let me find her standing on my doorstep, or I'ma whup her fucking ass like I shoulda done in the first place!"

She reached the front door and yanked it open, her fists balled in preparation.

But it wasn't Fiona who stood there with disheveled hair and a busted lip, her eyes concealed behind dark sunglasses and the strap of her Louis Vuitton purse dangling off one shoulder.

Tamia froze, staring in shock. *"Honey?"*

The young woman nodded quickly, darting a glance over her shoulder before returning her gaze to Tamia. "Can I come in?"

Tamia hesitated, eyeing her warily. After all the shit she'd recently gone through, the *last* thing she wanted was to get involved in someone else's mess, and Honey was clearly in some mess.

"Please?" the girl implored.

Tamia wavered another moment, then took Honey's hand and pulled her inside, glancing up and down the empty corridor before closing and locking the door.

"I'm sorry to show up at your place like this," Honey mumbled, nervously twisting her hands as she faced Tamia, "but I didn't know where else to go. Lou always says how cool you are, and he told me I could come to you about anything."

"Um, that's fine," Tamia said, folding her arms across her chest. "But how did you get past the front desk attendant? They're supposed to call me whenever I have visitors."

Honey looked sheepish. "Don't get mad. I begged him not to call you because I wasn't sure you'd let me up."

Tamia frowned at her. "What's going on?"

Honey exhaled a shaky breath, then reached up and slowly removed her sunglasses.

When Tamia saw the swollen flesh around the girl's left eye, she gasped. "Who the hell did that to you?"

Honey grimaced. "I got into a fight with my boyfriend, Keyshawn."

"And he *hit* you?"

Honey nodded, her eyes glistening with tears. "He was really upset."

Tamia scowled. "That doesn't give him the right to put his fucking hands on you." Moving closer, she examined Honey's bruised eye for a moment, then sucked her teeth and took the girl's hand, leading her to the kitchen.

"Have a seat," she instructed, motioning toward one of the barstools at the breakfast counter.

Honey did as she'd been told, watching as Tamia quickly assembled an ice pack. "You have a really nice place."

"Thanks." Tamia walked over and gingerly pressed the ice pack against Honey's swollen eye, her mind flashing back to the times she'd tended to her mother's injuries after one of Lorraine's brawls with Fiona's father. Tamia had despised Sonny Powell, whose volatile temper had made their lives a living hell until the day he left and never came back.

Shoving aside the traumatic memories, Tamia frowned at Honey. "What the hell was your boyfriend so upset about?"

Honey grimaced. "He was going through my things, and he found an engraved diamond bracelet that one of my clients gave me. He went off, demanding the dude's name and asking me how long I'd been fucking him. When I refused to tell him, he started punching me." She blinked rapidly, fighting back tears. "He's hit me before, but tonight was the first time he's ever threatened to kill me. When he went into the bedroom to get his gun, I was so scared I just grabbed my purse and got the hell outta there."

Tamia nodded grimly. "You did the right thing."

"I know." Honey swallowed hard. "I've never seen

Keyshawn so mad before. I really think he was gonna shoot my ass. I know he's out there looking for me right now, tracing my tags and shit. That's why I parked on the other side of town and caught a cab here. Thank God Lou told me where you live."

Tamia had gone still. "Hold on. Back up." She stared alertly at Honey. "What do you mean your boyfriend is tracing your tags? Is he a cop or something?"

Honey nodded reluctantly.

"Aw, hell, nah!" Tamia exclaimed, stepping back so quickly she nearly dropped the ice pack. "I'm sorry, baby girl, but you gotta leave. I just got out of prison, so I don't want no trouble with the po po."

"There won't be any trouble," Honey assured her.

"How do you know? If that nigga is as crazy as he sounds, there's no telling *what* he might do. I don't want him showing up here—"

"He won't!" Honey insisted. "He doesn't even know where I am. That's why I didn't go to any of my friends' apartments. I knew those were the first places he'd look for me. And I didn't go to Lou's because I didn't want him to see me like this. He already told me that the next time Keyshawn lays a hand on me, he's gonna come up missing."

Tamia frowned. Given Lou's ties to the Mexican mafia, there was no doubt in her mind that he'd make good on his threat. But if he went after a cop and things went awry, all hell would break loose.

Tamia wanted no parts of that. But as she looked at Honey's swollen eye and split lip, she couldn't help feeling sorry for her. Wearing no makeup and pink Hello Kitty sweatpants, Honey looked even younger than Tamia remembered.

"I've got a spare bedroom, so you can crash here for the weekend," she said gruffly. "But I can't promise anything beyond that."

"I understand," Honey said meekly. "Thank you, Tamia."

"Don't mention it." Tamia crossed to the fridge and grabbed two Black and Tans. She'd bought Brandon's favorite brand of beer so he'd feel right at home every time he came over.

As she returned to Honey and handed her a frosty bottle, she asked, "Are you hungry? I was gonna order some Chinese for dinner."

Honey grinned, then winced and gingerly touched her busted lip. "Chinese sounds good."

After they reviewed the menu and Tamia placed their order, they headed into the living room with their beers.

"Look at that amazing view," Honey marveled, walking over to the windows to stare at the glittering night skyline. "I feel like I can see the whole city from up here."

Tamia smiled, sitting down on the sofa. "Are you from Houston, Honey?"

She shook her head. "New Orleans. My family got bussed here after Katrina."

Tamia nodded. Her hometown had taken in the largest number of evacuees after the hurricane. "Are they still here? Your family?"

"Nah. They missed home too much, so they went back three years ago."

Tamia quietly observed her. "You must miss them a lot."

Honey nodded, a shadow of pain crossing her face.

"Why didn't you go back with them?" Tamia asked gently.

"I couldn't. I mean, I didn't *want* to." Honey sighed, gazing out the windows. "I needed to start over someplace new, take my life in a different direction. As much as I miss New Awlins, there's nothing there for me. Know what I mean?"

"I do," Tamia murmured, shaken by how much of herself she saw in Honey—a tough, street-savvy young woman whose need for survival would prove to be her greatest salvation, or her ultimate downfall.

Honey continued, "I'm trying to save as much money as possible so I can convince my family to come back to Houston. If they're living in a big house with a swimming pool and driving nice cars, maybe they won't miss home so much." A rueful smile curved her lips. "That's what I'm *hoping*, anyway."

Tamia returned her smile. "Sounds like a plan to me."

Sipping her beer, Honey wandered over to the sofa and sat down. Her gaze was instantly drawn to the coffee table, where Brandon and Beau Chambers graced the cover of the latest issue of *GQ* magazine. Impeccably tailored in three-piece Armani suits, the two brothers stood back to back as they puffed on expensive cigars. Their dark eyes were narrowed almost menacingly, making the headline STEP INTO THEIR CHAMBERS seem like a dare. They oozed so much swagger, arrogance, and sex appeal that Tamia's nipples hardened every time she glanced at their photo, which had been often.

"Wow," Honey breathed, picking up the magazine and staring at the cover with openmouthed appreciation. "Excuse my language, but these brothas right here are some *foine-ass mothafuckas*! *Got-damn!*"

Tamia grinned. "You ain't never lied."

"Okay, um, please tell me you have another copy of this?"

"Nah, girl. I got the last copy on the stand. The bookstore manager told me they sold out their entire stock in less than two hours. And, of course, most of the buyers were women."

"No doubt." Honey ogled the cover another moment, then held the magazine to her chest and sighed dreamily. "I think I just slipped and fell in love."

Tamia laughed. "With which one? And you'd better not say Brandon, 'cause I've already got dibs on him."

"I know." Honey grinned at her. "Don't forget I was at your homecoming party. I saw the way you two were coochie-grindin' on the dance floor. I just knew y'all was about to start a fire up in that club!"

Tamia chuckled, sipping her beer.

Sobering after another moment, Honey said quietly, "I hope you get him back, Tamia. I can't speak for the general public, but me and all my girlfriends who followed the trial are rooting for you and Brandon to work things out."

Tamia met Honey's earnest gaze and smiled softly. "Thank you. I really appreciate that."

Honey held up her beer. "To second chances."

"I'll *definitely* drink to that."

They clinked bottles and sipped, grinning at each other like two coconspirators.

Holding up the *GQ* magazine, Honey said slyly, "So, um, can you hook a sista up with an introduction to Beau Chambers?"

Tamia laughed, shaking her head. "Girl, you need to handle your business with Keyshawn first. Speaking of which, how does he feel about you working as an escort? I can't imagine *any* boyfriend being cool with that, let alone one who's a cop."

"You're right," Honey agreed with a pained grimace. "Key *hates* that I'm an escort. He bitches about it every damn day. But at the same time, he enjoys spending my money, and he sure as hell didn't refuse the new truck I bought him for his birthday."

Tamia smirked. "Surprise, surprise."

"I know. He's such a hypocrite, right?" Honey sucked her teeth, rolling her eyes in disgust. "I don't even know why I'm still with him. All we do lately is argue about my job."

"It doesn't help that you've got clients giving you expensive gifts," Tamia pointed out wryly.

"I know." Honey sighed heavily, setting her bottle down on the table. "I've tried telling this particular client to stop buying me things, but he won't listen. And it's not just the gifts. He calls all the time to tell me that he's thinking of me and he can't wait to see me again. And before we get off the phone, he always begs me to talk dirty to him so he can jerk off." She snickered. "It never takes very long."

Tamia chuckled. "Damn, baby girl. You got that man pussy-whipped."

"I know. It's crazy." Honey's expression turned grim. "Sometimes I feel guilty because he has a wife and children who think the world of him, and I know they'd be devastated if they ever found out about us. I've even asked him to consider going to marriage counseling, but he just laughed and said that wasn't an option for a man of his stature." She spread her hands wide, palms upturned in a helpless gesture. "What could I say? I need the money, so I'm not about to turn away one of my best-paying customers."

"I hear you," Tamia agreed sympathetically. "But it sounds like your relationship with this client may be more trouble than it's worth. Have you told Lou?"

Honey vigorously shook her head. "Lou doesn't even know that this man uses the escort agency. Dude sets up our dates through a third party, he pays under a fake name, and he hires his own driver to pick me up and take me to our secret meeting spots."

"Damn, girl," Tamia exclaimed. "That's some serious cloak-and-dagger shit right there! Who the hell is this client? The Pope?"

Honey got an odd look on her face. "Not quite."

Tamia stared at her, eyes narrowed speculatively.

Honey nervously moistened her lips. "You know I'm not supposed to reveal the identity of my clients—"

"I know. And you probably shouldn't start now."

"I know. But for real, though? I've been *dying* to get this secret off my chest. I trust you, Tamia. If I tell you the client's name, I know you won't breathe a word to another soul, no matter how tempted you might be." Her eyes tunneled into Tamia's. "Right?"

Tamia hesitated. "Right."

"I'm dead serious, Tamia. This information absolutely *can't* go public. I didn't tell my grandma that I'm an escort because she has a weak heart. She survived Hurricane Katrina, but this shit right here would kill her."

Damn, Tamia thought. *Now, why did she have to go there when I have a soft spot for grandmothers?*

"So do you promise to keep my secret?"

Again Tamia hesitated, wondering if this was how Linda Tripp had felt before hearing Monica Lewinsky's scandalous confession.

"Tamia?" Honey prompted.

She nodded. "I promise."

"Okay." Honey paused to take a deep breath, as if to shore up her courage.

Seconds passed.

Unable to take the suspense any longer, Tamia suddenly blurted, "Girl, please don't tell me you're fucking Bernard Chambers!"

Honey shook her head slowly. "Wrong father."

Tamia eyed her incredulously as comprehension dawned. "Oh, my God."

"Yup." Honey smiled ironically. "My client is Bishop Yarbrough."

Chapter 16

Brandon

"HAVE YOU LOST YOUR DAMN MIND?"

Brandon swiveled around in his chair to watch as Cynthia came charging into his office, her face suffused with fury, hands planted on her hips.

When she saw that he was on the phone, she abruptly pulled up short. But it was too late.

After murmuring an apology to the prospective client he'd been counseling, Brandon hung up the phone and calmly regarded Cynthia.

She had the grace to look sheepish. "I'm sorry. I didn't know you were—"

"Close the door."

"Brandon—"

"Close. The. Fucking. Door."

She flinched, nostrils flaring as she moved to comply.

Facing him once again, she began defensively, "Look, I—"

He cut her off. "First of all, don't you *ever* barge into my office like that again. Matter of fact, don't even cross the threshold without knocking first."

Her eyes widened with disbelief. "Brandon—"

"I'm talking."

She snapped her mouth shut, face reddening with humiliation.

"Second of all," Brandon continued, his voice never rising above a low growl, "don't you *ever* come at me like you just did, shrieking at the top of your lungs like you just lost your fucking mind. I won't stand for that shit here at the office, or at home, or any-fucking-where else. You feel me?"

Cynthia stared at him for a stunned moment, then suddenly burst into tears. "I can't believe you're sitting there scolding me over a harmless mistake!" she sobbed. "After what I just found out, *you* should be apologizing to *me*!"

Brandon scowled. "What the hell are you talking about?"

"You know *damn* well what I'm talking about!" Cynthia raged, charging over to his desk and slapping her palms down on the surface. "How *dare* you offer Tamia a job without consulting me first?"

Brandon arched a brow at her. "I wasn't aware that I needed your permission to make hiring decisions," he said coolly.

"*Are you serious*? Are you really going to sit there and tell me that you see absolutely *nothing* wrong with hiring your ex-girlfriend to be your assistant? Do you *really* expect me to be okay with seeing Tamia around this office every day, doing everything in her power to break us up? And don't you *dare* open your mouth to tell me she won't do that, because we both know better!"

Brandon silently regarded Cynthia. Her face was ravaged by tears, her nose was running, and her lower lip was flecked with spittle.

He grimaced, torn between revulsion and guilt for reducing her to the emotional wreck that now stood before him. Whatever happened to the strong, sexy, confident woman he'd turned to after Tamia betrayed him? Where had *that* Cynthia gone?

She sneered at him. "So you have nothing to say for yourself?"

Brandon reached across his desk, picked up a box of Kleenex, and wordlessly offered it to Cynthia.

She snatched two tissues out of the box, then whirled away from the desk to swipe at her face and blow her nose.

He silently observed her slender back, firm butt, and toned calves accentuated by a pair of designer pumps. She was too attractive, and had too much going for her, to cling so desperately to him or any other man.

"Look," Brandon said, keeping his voice level, "I don't want to argue with you."

Cynthia rounded furiously on him. "Then why the hell did you do it? Why did you hire that bitch when you knew damn well how I'd feel about it? To add insult to injury, you didn't even have the decency to tell me! I had to find out from *Addison*, of all people! And only because she and another associate were just laughing and gossiping in the restroom about how you totally owned Russ Sutcliffe during the partners' meeting today. My God, Brandon, do you have *any* idea how humiliated I'm going to feel when your ghetto-ass ex-girlfriend starts sashaying around here like she's the queen of the castle? *Do you?* Or do you even care?"

Brandon scowled. "First of all, chill with all that 'ghetto' bullshit. You may not like Tamia, but you know damn well she's got more class than any of the pompous assholes who work at this law firm. I've checked your ass about that shit before. I'm not gonna tell you again."

Cynthia eyed him incredulously. "I don't believe this. After *everything* I just said to you, your only response is to chastise me for calling Tamia *ghetto*? Are you fucking serious? Why are you so offended by me speaking the truth? I mean, what else do you call a social-climbing fraud who lies about living in the hood and having jailbird relatives, who engages in public brawls—"

Brandon tightened his jaw. "Cynthia—"

"—and cavorts with low-life porn directors. What else do you call a cheap whore who'd go to any lengths to hide the fact that she used to fuck complete strangers for a liv—"

Brandon lunged from his chair so suddenly that Cynthia jumped back with a startled squeak, her eyes wide with alarm.

He glared at her. "Shut. The. Fuck. Up."

She swallowed audibly, staring at him as if he'd suddenly sprouted horns and begun speaking in ancient tongues. "What the hell's going on, Brandon? Why are you defending her? And why are you behaving like *I've* done something wrong here? *You're* the one who has totally disrespected me and showed no regard for my feelings. Like I said before, *you* owe *me* an apology."

Brandon just looked at her, jaw tightly clenched, blood pressure escalating.

Cynthia folded her arms expectantly across her chest. "I'm waiting."

A stab of guilt pricked Brandon's conscience, telling him that she was right. He *should* apologize to her, and not just for hiring Tamia. For kissing her, holding her, and wishing like *hell* that he didn't have to stop there.

Unlocking his jaw, he said levelly, "I'm sorry that you're so upset, and I'm sorry that you had to learn about my decision from someone else."

"And?" Cynthia prompted.

He frowned. "And what?"

"And you're sorry for offering Tamia a job, which you will rescind *immediately*."

"No." Brandon shook his head firmly. "That I won't do."

"What do you mean?" Cynthia protested shrilly. "She can't work here, Brandon!"

"She can, and she will."

Cynthia glared at him, her face contorted with outrage. "You know what? Contrary to what you may believe, *Mr. GQ*, you're not the only game in town! And you're not the only one in this relationship who has options. I can have *any* guy I want! Do you know how many celebrities and wealthy CEOs I've met through my father's church? Do you know how many men have gone to my father and practically begged for my hand in marriage? And let's not forget about Shane. Remember him? He still calls me on a regular basis. If I wanted to, I could have him back"—she snapped her fingers "*just* like that. So don't get it twisted, sweetheart. I have *plenty* of options."

Unfazed by the threat, Brandon spread his hands wide and drawled, "By all means, please feel free to exercise them."

Cynthia flinched, her face flushing with anger and indignation.

Quickly recovering her composure, she raised her chin and looked him squarely in the eye. "Maybe I will."

"Do what you gotta do."

"I will." Fuming, she spun on her heel and stalked to the door, snatched it open, and stormed out of the office.

Exhaling a deep breath, Brandon sat back down and calmly reached for the phone receiver to call back the man whose consultation had been interrupted by Cynthia's outburst.

Before he'd finished dialing the number, Cynthia came marching back into the room, her face set with determination as she shoved the door closed behind her.

Brandon couldn't suppress a mocking smile as he set down the receiver. "What happened to exercising your options?"

"Nice try," she said darkly, rounding his large desk, "but

I'm not giving up on us that easily. That's *exactly* what Tamia wants, but I won't play into her hands."

Brandon sighed. "Look, maybe it'd be best if we—"

"*No*. Don't even go there." Cynthia hitched up her pencil skirt and quickly climbed onto the chair, straddling his lap. Her red-rimmed eyes bored into his. "Hear me out before you say another word, okay?"

He hesitated, then nodded slowly.

"I *love* you, Brandon Chambers. I love you so damn much it's ridiculous. Prior to April, I'd been waiting two whole years for you to see me as more than just a colleague and a friend. Two long, excruciating years of pretending I wasn't interested in you like that. When you met Tamia and started dating her, I was devastated. I felt cheated, like she'd come out of nowhere and taken something that rightfully belonged to me."

Brandon frowned. "Cyn—"

She pressed a finger to his lips, silencing him as she continued, "Obviously I *know* you didn't belong to me. I'm just explaining my state of mind at the time. I was also frustrated with myself for lacking the courage to tell you how I felt about you. I tortured myself with a thousand *what if*s. What if I'd dressed more sexy around the office? What if I'd possessed more of that street vibe you find so damn irresistible in Tamia? What if I'd simply acted on my feelings *before* you met her? I drove myself fucking crazy with the *what if*s, Brandon. But I respected your relationship. I didn't try to come between you and Tamia, even as I realized that you were getting serious about her. No matter how hard it was, I didn't make a move on you." She paused, shaking her head at him. "It's not *my* fault that Tamia didn't appreciate the good thing she had."

Brandon held her gaze for a long moment, then glanced away, his eyes landing on the yellow legal pad where he'd scribbled notes during his phone consultation. A ghost of a smile touched his mouth at a memory of Tamia teasing him about being old school and cajoling him to buy a OneNote tablet so that he could join the twenty-first century. Maybe one of these days he would.

"Brandon?"

When he didn't respond, Cynthia framed his face between her hands, gently drawing his attention back to her. Her expression was earnest. "You know what, baby? Some of my friends think I should have just left you alone, because rebound relationships are doomed to failure. But I don't care what they say, because I know damn well that not *one* of them would have given you up if they were in my shoes." She paused. "I'm not stupid, Brandon. I know you still have feelings for Tamia. But I also know that she's not right for you, and if given the opportunity, she'll hurt you again. I don't intend to give her that opportunity, and neither should you."

When she'd finished speaking, Brandon raised a brow at her. "Are you done?"

She frowned, her hands dropping limply from his face. "Is that all you have to say after I just poured out my heart to you?"

Brandon sighed heavily. "Look, baby, if you're so confident that Tamia's not right for me, then you have nothing to worry about. Right?"

She hesitated, biting her lower lip.

"Right?" he repeated.

"I suppose," she reluctantly conceded.

"Good. I'm glad we had this talk." He briskly patted her ass. "Now get up so I can return this phone call before it gets too late."

"Not so fast," Cynthia protested softly, looping her arms around his neck and kissing him. "We just had a big argument, so now we're supposed to have really hot makeup sex."

Brandon couldn't help smiling against her mouth. "Later," he promised.

"Why put off until later what we can do right now?" she purred, provocatively gyrating against his crotch until his dick began to rise.

As he tried to pull away, Cynthia followed, pinning him against the chair as she nuzzled his throat.

He closed his eyes. "This isn't a good time, sweetheart."

"Since when? Have you forgotten that the very first time we made love was in your office on a Friday night?" She laughed coyly. "Seems to me that this is the *perfect* time. And do you realize that you've been partner for three months, and we have *yet* to christen your new office?"

"Really?" Brandon murmured. "I didn't realize that."

"I did." She nibbled his earlobe. "I've been dying for you to fuck me on this huge desk and all over that cushy leather sofa."

Brandon grimaced. "Not tonight."

"Why not?"

"I'm all out of condoms," he lied.

"That's okay. I've been on the pill now for two weeks, so we should be good. Besides, you weren't worried about not using protection when you went commando last week."

"That was last week," Brandon said, exasperation sharpening his voice.

Cynthia tensed against him, then slowly lifted her head and searched his face. "What's going on, Brandon?"

"What's going on," he said with forced patience as he lifted her off his lap and set her on her feet, "is that I was in the middle of an important conversation with a prospective client when you came barging in here. I'd like to resume that conversation before Mr. Humphrey decides to take his business elsewhere. So as much as I'd love to let you have your way with me, I'm gonna have to request a rain check. You feel me?"

Cynthia pouted, smoothing her skirt. "Yeah, I feel you. Not where I *want* to feel you, but—"

Brandon laughed. "Later, I promise."

"It'll have to be *much* later. I'm spending the night at my aunt and uncle's house, remember?"

Brandon eyed her blankly. "You are?"

Cynthia shot him an exasperated look. "Hello? Tomorrow is Lynn's wedding. I'm her maid of honor, remember? She wanted all of her bridesmaids to spend the night so we can all get our hair and nails done at the same time, then get dressed together for the ceremony." She shook her head at Brandon. "I hope you won't forget what time the wedding starts tomorrow afternoon."

"How could I?" he countered wryly. "You've been reminding me for the past three weeks, you added the date and time to my BlackBerry, and you taped the invitation to the bathroom mirror this morning."

Cynthia grinned unabashedly. "Just covering all my bases."

"Umm-hmm." Brandon reached for the phone, signaling that the conversation was over. "Have a good time at Lynn's."

"Oh, I will." Cynthia smirked. "We'll probably hit the strip club since the fellas will be face deep in tits and asses at the bachelor party tonight."

The bachelor party she'd begged Brandon not to attend, he mused.

"That's cool," he said easily. "Make sure you take plenty of singles to tip the dancers."

She gaped at him incredulously. "You mean you don't mind that the girls and I will be hanging out at a strip club? You don't care that a bunch of buff, oily guys will be gyrating all over me and shaking their dicks in my face?"

"Nope. 'Cause we both know the only dick you wanna ride is right here."

Cynthia shook her head at him. "You really think you're the shit, don't you?"

"Nah, baby. That's *your* job."

Sputtering with angry indignation, she spun on her heel and marched away from his desk. When she reached the door, she paused and glanced back at him, her eyes glinting with challenge. "Just remember what I said, Brandon. I have options."

"No doubt." He paused. "And that goes both ways."

Their stares locked across the room.

After several tense moments, Cynthia turned and stormed out, leaving in much the same manner that she'd arrived.

Chapter 17

Fiona

Fiona's pulse was pounding as she crept stealthily through the old cemetery.

As she walked, she shone the beam of her flashlight on the gray marble tombstones around her, illuminating the names of the departed souls whose ghostly voices whispered to her as she passed.

When she reached the tombstone she'd been looking for, she set down the flashlight and reached inside her jacket, removing the bottle of Patrón she'd picked up on her way to the cemetery.

Her hands trembled as she uncorked the bottle and took a long swig of tequila, needing liquid courage for what she was about to do.

She'd come to the graveyard to make atonement, though she knew that confessing her sins to a cold headstone couldn't begin to absolve her of what she'd done.

But it was a start. Because ever since that unspeakable night when her life had changed forever, she hadn't dared utter the truth to anyone.

She was guilty.

Guilty of deception.

Guilty of murder.

Guilty.

And she'd gotten away with it because no one had suspected her. She'd kept her silence, and she'd allowed others to believe that someone else was responsible.

After all this time, the least she could do was unburden herself to the victim of her treachery.

Drawing a deep, shaky breath, Fiona stared down at the tombstone she'd been seeing in her nightmares since that harrowing night.

"Hello." Her voice was as thready as her pulse. "I know I'm probably the last person you wanna see at your final resting place, but I had to come. It . . . it was time."

She paused to collect her fragmented thoughts.

"I've never stopped thinking about you. But it's been even more intense ever since Tamia got out of prison. I guess because seeing her reminds me of you."

She swallowed tightly as tears crept into her eyes. "You have to know that I never meant for you to get hurt. But you were going to—"

The sudden snap of a twig made her whirl around, heart lodged in her throat.

Her eyes scanned the darkness, the gray tombstones taking on ghostly shapes in the moonlight.

"Who's there?" she whispered sharply.

Though she saw nothing, she swore she could feel a pair of sinister eyes watching her.

A chill ran through her. "Is someone there?"

Silence.

As a clammy sweat broke out on her skin, she took an unsteady swig of tequila and cautiously turned back to the headstone, which had now taken on the same eerie glow as the others.

She swallowed hard, knowing that she shouldn't stay there much longer.

"Everyone who knew and loved you misses you so much. If I could bring you back, I would. But I can't, and for that I am *truly* sorry."

Fiona took one last sip of the Patrón, then poured the contents of the bottle across the foot of the tombstone with the solemnity of a tribesman observing a sacred ritual.

When she'd finished, she dropped the empty bottle on the ground and sank to her knees. Slowly she reached up and lovingly traced her fingers over the inscription etched into the cold, gray marble.

ESTHER VIOLA COPELAND
Beloved wife, mother, grandmother, and
faithful servant of God

"I'm sorry, Mama Esther," Fiona whispered, tears rolling down her face and seeping into the corners of her mouth. "I'm sorry I got you killed."

Chapter 18

Brandon

"Mort Chernoff tells me that you've been making enemies at the firm."

Brandon stood with his arms folded and his feet braced apart, watching through mirrored sunglasses as his father moved into position behind a white golf ball teed up in front of him.

"I have no idea what Mort's talking about," Brandon drawled.

Bernard chuckled, then swung the iron club with an expert flip of his wrist. He and Brandon watched as the ball sailed through the air before bouncing three hundred yards down onto the meticulously landscaped grounds.

It was Saturday morning. After meeting for breakfast at the River Oaks Country Club, father and son had headed to the private golf range so that Bernard could hit some practice balls for an upcoming charity golf tournament that he was headlining. Of course, everyone knew that the lieutenant governor needed no practice. He, like his father and grandfather before him, was an excellent golfer whose single-digit handicap made him the envy of his peers.

Though it was expected of him, Brandon had yet to acquire a taste for golf. His preference for basketball was an ongoing source of frustration for his father, who subscribed to the old cliché of "swinging one's way to power." As he often lectured Brandon and Beau, "Deals are made on golf courses, not basketball courts."

After hitting another ball, Bernard sent Brandon an amused glance. "So you *didn't* make a complete ass of Russ Sutcliffe during the partners' meeting yesterday?"

"No, sir," Brandon said lazily. "Russ did that all on his own."

Bernard laughed uproariously. "Going toe-to-toe with the firm's biggest racist," he declared with affectionate pride. "That's my boy."

Brandon smiled wryly. "Now that I've made partner, I suppose it's too much to expect that Mort Chernoff will stop reporting my every move to you."

Bernard guffawed. "Come on, now. Mort and I go way back. We were playing golf together when you were still in diapers. Of course he takes a personal interest in you. You're like a son to him. Besides"—Bernard sent another ball soaring through the air—"it's not *my* fault that an old friend of mine happens to be one of the founding partners of the firm you chose to lend your talents to."

Brandon snorted. "Considering how many people you know, Dad, I'm sure that would have been the case at *any* firm I went to work for."

Bernard grinned unabashedly.

He was a tall, handsome man with smooth, dark skin and graying temples that he wore as debonairly as an Armani tux. Already one of the most powerful men in Texas, he was fast becoming a rising star on the national political scene, thanks in no small part to his friendship with President Obama. The president was expected to campaign on Bernard's behalf. In exchange, Bernard had promised to do everything in his power to deliver his conservative state to Obama during the next presidential election. It didn't matter that no Democrat had won the Lone Star State since 1976. When Bernard Chambers made a promise, absolutely no one doubted his word.

"As much as I enjoyed hearing about how you handed Sutcliffe's ass to him," Bernard drawled, "I must confess that I was surprised at the particular reason."

Here we go, Brandon thought resignedly. He'd been waiting all morning for his father to broach the subject of Tamia.

"Would you care to tell me why you hired that girl to be your assistant?" It wasn't a request, and Brandon knew it.

He shrugged, and gave the same explanation he'd been parroting since yesterday. "Tamia needs a job, and I need an assistant."

His father let out a sharp bark of laughter, wagging his head at Brandon. "Look at me, son. Do I look like I was born yesterday? We both know damn well why you hired Tamia, and it's got nothing to do with her needing a job."

Brandon couldn't deny it.

"You're trying to have your cake and eat it, too," Bernard said knowingly. "But I'm here to tell you that it doesn't work that way. And, quite frankly, after everything Tamia put you through, I can't understand why you'd even *want* it to work."

Brandon heaved a weary sigh. "Can we talk about something else? I'm bored with this topic."

"Not bored enough, apparently." Bernard hit another ball, his golf club slicing through the air with a soft *whish!*

"You know," he continued, "it's a testament to your litigation prowess that you were not only able to persuade that jury of Tamia's innocence but you turned her into something of a feminist hero—a woman whose only crime was succumbing to a blackmailer in order to protect her youthful indiscretions and hold on to the man she loved." He made a snort of disgust. "You had those silly female jurors eating out of the palm of your hand and fawning over what a loving, forgiving boyfriend you are. Is it any wonder Tamia was acquitted?"

"She was acquitted because she's innocent." Brandon smiled narrowly. "But my defense strategy certainly didn't hurt her chances."

"My point exactly, son. You're far too talented to be throwing your life away on one woman."

Brandon scoffed. "Come on, Dad. How am I throwing my life away by giving Tamia a *job*?"

"It's more than just a job, boy, and you know it."

Before Brandon could respond, a country club employee materialized with a new bucket of golf balls and proceeded to tee them up for Bernard. Several yards away, members of the lieutenant governor's security detail looked on with stoic expressions.

When father and son were alone again, Bernard continued, "You need to start looking at the big picture, Brandon. I've got great plans for you. Appointing you to attorney general is just the beginning—"

"With all due respect," Brandon interrupted, "when did I ever say I wanted to become attorney general?"

His father gave him a look of grave disappointment. "You're a Chambers. Achieving greatness isn't an option—"

"—it's a birthright," Brandon finished, reciting the familiar credo that had been passed down through four generations of Chamberses. "Yeah, Dad, I know all that."

"Do you?" Bernard challenged, eyeing him shrewdly.

"Because ever since you told us about Tamia, I've often wondered if you've forgotten your priorities."

"My priorities are right where they need to be," Brandon countered evenly. "But thanks for your concern."

Bernard glared at him before turning away to whack at another ball. "I haven't told your mother about this latest stunt of yours. She's still recovering from your decision to represent Tamia during the trial, and she was livid that Tamia showed her face at Bishop Yarbrough's church last Sunday."

"The *audacity* of the woman, showing up at church to hear God's word," Brandon exclaimed with mock indignation.

His father shot him one of those quelling looks that used to have Brandon and his siblings ducking for cover.

Now Brandon merely chuckled.

Bernard wasn't amused. "Your mother isn't the only one who was upset. She had to console Cynthia for quite a while after the service."

"That's unfortunate," Brandon said blandly.

Bernard scowled. "You know what else is unfortunate? Your complete lack of judgment and shortsightedness when it comes to Tamia Luke." His lips twisted scornfully. "You think Barack would have made it to the White House with some hood rat on his arm? Hell, no! He chose an educated, articulate, sophisticated woman that mainstream America could accept and admire. If you have any serious political aspirations—and that's not even up for debate—Cynthia Yarbrough is the woman you want by your side. You got that? *Cynthia* is the one who will help take you all the way, not Tamia."

When Brandon made no comment, his father shook his head in angry exasperation. "But since you seem hell-bent on having that damn woman, at least be discreet about it, for God's sake! Flaunting her in Cynthia's face is the quickest way to get your fucking balls chopped off in the middle of the night."

This startled a laugh out of Brandon.

"You think I'm joking?" Bernard nodded at his golf club. "Ask Tiger Woods if he was laughing after his wife swung one of these at his head."

Brandon sobered. "I see your point."

"Hell hath no fury like a woman scorned, son. Always remember that."

"Thanks. I will." Brandon gave his father a sardonic look. "So does this mean you'd condone me having an affair with Tamia?"

"Hell, no. But you're a grown man, and I know you're gonna do what you want. Or should I say, *who* you want."

Brandon frowned. "I haven't done anything."

"*Yet*. But you will," Bernard said knowingly. "Tamia's a sexy, beautiful woman. The moment I met her, I could see how you'd gotten turned out."

Brandon scowled. "I'm not turned out."

Bernard snorted, swinging at another ball. "Don't kid a kidder, son. That girl had your number from day one. She's your kryptonite. But take heart. All great men throughout history have had mistresses. David had Bathsheba, JFK had Marilyn, Bill had Monica—"

"Please don't tell me Barack has someone."

His father smirked at him.

"Never mind," Brandon muttered, holding up a hand. "I don't wanna know."

"What? I didn't say anything. Anyway, the bottom line is that next to your mother and Bishop Yarbrough, you're my most important campaign surrogate. So I can't afford to have you caught up in some sex scandal or any other nonsense that could compromise my campaign. The Republicans are gunning for me in the worst way, so even the slightest misstep could torpedo my candidacy."

"I'm aware of that," Brandon said levelly.

"Good. So go ahead and enjoy Tamia as your mistress. But be discreet about it." Bernard jabbed a warning finger at Brandon. "And for God's sake, don't get any crazy ideas about making her your wife."

Chapter 19

Tamia

Twenty-four hours after hearing Honey's shocking revelation, Tamia was still reeling. She couldn't believe that Joseph Yarbrough—pastor of the largest black megachurch in Texas and a devoted family man—had been secretly paying an escort for sex.

It wasn't his shady behavior that shocked her. After all, it seemed that every time she turned on the television, there was news of some prominent politician or minister who'd been caught in a sex scandal. So she wasn't necessarily stunned to learn that Joseph Yarbrough, like many powerful men, had a problem keeping his dick in his pants.

What angered and appalled her was that he'd stood behind the pulpit and railed against the dangers of lust and sexual immorality while *he* was secretly banging a woman young enough to be his daughter. Tamia's temper flared every time she remembered the way he'd condescendingly looked down his nose at her and spouted that sanctimonious bullshit about being used as a "vessel to shed light in the darkness of sinners' souls."

Fucking hypocrite!

"How do I look?"

Pulled out of her dark musings, Tamia glanced up from her laptop. Honey stood in the doorway of her study wearing a slinky black cocktail dress that showed off her ample cleavage and voluptuous curves.

Tamia smiled. "You look good, baby girl."

"Good enough to eat?" Honey asked with a wink.

Tamia laughed. "I'm sure your client will think so. And don't give me that look. I've already told you I'm strictly dickly. If you try any shit with me, I'ma whup your ass and call Keyshawn to come get you."

Honey laughed. "Damn, Tamia, that's messed up! It's not my fault I have a crush on you."

"Bitch, whatever."

Honey grinned, her stiletto heels clicking on the hardwood floor as she walked over to Tamia's desk and perched her hip on the corner, her manicured fingers wrapped around her cell phone. "Thanks again for taking me shopping today, and for hooking up my makeup. You can hardly even see the black eye."

Tamia nodded. "I still think you should have taken the night off."

"I can't. I already switched with another girl last night. If I call in sick again, Lou will get suspicious. Besides, I need the money."

Tamia heaved a resigned sigh. "All right."

Honey smiled softly. "I really appreciate your concern, Tamia. I always wanted an older sister who'd look out for me."

Tamia couldn't help thinking of Fiona. After everything she'd done for that heffa over the years, Fiona had repaid her with an unspeakable act of betrayal. For that reason alone, Tamia had no interest in becoming someone else's big sister.

She eyed Honey suspiciously. "How old are you anyway?"

The girl bit her lip, looking sheepish. "Lou told me not to tell you."

"*What*? Why the hell—"

"Are you thinking about going to law school?" Honey asked abruptly.

Caught off guard by the question—which was an obvious diversion tactic—Tamia frowned. "No. Why?"

Honey nodded at the stack of legal tomes that Tamia had purchased from the bookstore yesterday.

"Oh. Those." Tamia smiled. "I'm cramming for a new job."

"At a law firm?"

"Yes, but not just *any* law firm. I'm going to be working with Brandon."

Honey's eyes widened. "For real?"

"Yup." Tamia beamed. "He asked me to be his assistant yesterday."

"*Are you serious*? That's wonderful, Tamia!"

"I know. I couldn't believe it."

"When do you start?" Honey asked her.

"Monday. I'll be part-time until his assistant goes on maternity leave." Ever since Brandon called Tamia that morning to confirm the details, she'd been floating on cloud nine.

An amused gleam filled Honey's eyes. "You know Cynthia probably had a damn *fit* when she found out."

"I know." Tamia grinned with wicked satisfaction. "I'd have *loved* to be a fly on the wall when Brandon told her. She's about to find out how *I* felt when she was always hanging around him, wandering into his office for no reason, acting all innocent when I knew damn well she wanted to fuck my boo."

"Can you really blame her? Your boo is fine as hell."

"That's not the point."

"I know." Honey grinned wryly. "I've never met Cynthia, but the way her father goes on and on about her, you would think she was as pure as Snow White."

Tamia snorted derisively. "Ain't nothing 'pure' about that bitch. She's a fraud just like her father."

Honey grimaced. "I probably shouldn't have told you about me and Bishop Yarbrough. Now that you'll be working at the firm with Cynthia, you're gonna be tempted to rub her face in what you know."

"You're right," Tamia admitted darkly. "I *will* be tempted. It'd give me great satisfaction to knock that heffa off her high horse. But I promised to keep your secret, and I intend to keep that promise. All right?"

"All right." Honey sighed. "I *do* feel a little better now that I've told someone. Does that make sense?"

Before Tamia could respond, Honey's cell rang. "That's my driver," she said, glancing at the caller ID. She answered the phone and let him know she was on her way downstairs, then hung up and smiled ruefully at Tamia. "Showtime."

After seeing Honey off, Tamia padded into the kitchen and poured herself a glass of wine. She'd just taken a sip when the doorbell rang. Assuming that Honey had forgotten something, she went to open the door.

The moment she saw who stood there, the blood drained from her head.

It was the last person she'd expected to see.

The last person she'd *wanted* to see.

"Hello, Mystique." A slow, mocking smile crawled across Dominic's face. "Miss me?"

Tamia stared at him for a stunned moment.

As she moved to slam the door, his arm shot through the narrow opening.

Tamia pushed against him, but he was too strong for her. As he forcefully shoved the door open and barged inside, she stumbled backward, heart knocking against her rib cage.

"What the fuck are you doing here?" she hissed furiously. "And how did you find me?"

"Come now, love," Dominic drawled, closing and locking the door behind him. "You know I can *always* find you, as I proved the very first time we met."

Tamia glared at him. After the way he'd ruined her life, she hated that she still found him sexy as hell, with his copper-brown complexion, sleepy dark eyes, and full, sensuous lips. His tall, muscular frame was covered in a black turtleneck and black jeans that made him look like a cat burglar, which seemed fitting under the circumstances.

After the trial, Brandon had filed a restraining order against Dominic to protect Tamia from further harassment or retaliation. He wasn't supposed to come anywhere near her.

"You're violating the restraining order," Tamia coldly informed him. "If you don't leave right now, I'm calling the police."

Dominic tsk-tsked. "Is that any way to treat your old lover? And after I went to the trouble of tracking you down?"

"Listen, you motherfucker," Tamia snarled. "I have *nothing* to say to you!"

"Oh, but I have *plenty* to say to you." His eyes roamed appreciatively over her body, lingering on the swell of her breasts. "Before we talk, maybe we can get . . . reacquainted."

"You're out of your damn mind," Tamia spat, even as she mentally flashed on an image from the erotic dream she'd had. "I wouldn't touch you if you were the last man on earth."

He laughed softly. "We both know you don't really mean that. You've been locked up for the past five months, so I know good and damn well you've been feenin' for some dick." He smiled suggestively, coming toward her. "Remember how great we were together? Remember how much you *loved* having this Crucian cock ramming into that hot, wet pussy of yours?"

As her nipples hardened traitorously, Tamia folded her arms across her chest and glared at him. "I'ma tell you one more time, motherfucker. Get out, or I'm calling the police."

His smile widened. "No, you won't."

"Watch me."

As she spun on her heel, he launched at her, seizing her around the waist and wrestling her to the floor.

"Get off me!" Tamia screamed, struggling helplessly as he straddled her hips and clamped her wrists together in one powerful grip.

"Stop fighting," he barked at her.

"SOMEONE H—"

He clapped his hand over her mouth, muffling her cry for help. "Stop fighting," he warned again, "or I'll *really* give you something to scream about."

Tamia went still, staring up at him with alarm. For the first time, it occurred to her how much danger she was in, trapped alone with the conniving bastard who believed she'd murdered his wife.

As if he'd read her mind, Dominic smiled malevolently. "You got away with the perfect crime, didn't you?"

When Tamia vehemently shook her head, he let out a low, menacing chuckle that scraped her nerves raw. "Yes, you did. You killed my wife, then managed to convince the jury that *I* was the murderer."

Tamia eyed him warily, nostrils flaring as she struggled to control her breathing.

"I'm going to remove my hand so we can have a conversation," Dominic said softly. "If you even *think* about screaming for help, it'll be the last sound you ever make. Do you understand?"

Tamia swallowed hard, then gave a jerky nod.

Slowly he uncovered her mouth, his eyes daring her to defy him.

Tamia wisely remained silent.

"We both know I didn't kill Isabel," he continued. "But thanks to you and Loverboy, I'm under investigation by the police. My assets have been frozen, my company's losing money, and I can't even collect on Isabel's insurance policy as long as I'm considered a suspect in her murder. As if that weren't bad enough, my grandfather died last week, but I wasn't allowed to fly home to attend the funeral because I've been ordered not to leave the damn country."

Tamia sneered at him. "Am I supposed to feel sorry for you? You ruined my damn life. Because of you, I lost my boyfriend, my job, *and* my freedom. So spare me your fucking sob story. You deserve everything that's—"

She gasped as thick, strong fingers suddenly seized her throat.

"Stupid bitch," Dominic snarled, his eyes gleaming with malicious satisfaction as she frantically thrashed against him, gasping for air. "You always did have a problem remembering who was in charge. After all the shit I just told you, do you *really* think it's smart to antagonize me? I'm on the verge of losing everything, so what's to stop me from choking you to death right now?"

Tamia stared at him in wild-eyed terror as his fingers tightened around her neck.

"I *should* kill you," he growled. "God knows you've been more trouble to me than you're worth. You and that pussy-whipped boyfriend of yours. I should kill *both* of you. But this is your lucky day, bitch, 'cause you're more useful to me alive than dead."

As he abruptly released his stranglehold, Tamia wheezed and coughed as sweet, blessed air rushed back into her lungs.

Dominic smirked at her. "Didn't like that feeling, did

you? Thought you saw your life flash before your eyes, didn't you? Imagine how my wife felt when you pointed that gun at her and pulled the trigger."

"I didn't—" Tamia broke off, her throat raw from the prolonged lack of oxygen.

"You didn't what? Kill my wife?"

Tamia nodded vigorously.

Dominic sneered. "So you keep insisting. I have to applaud you for the brilliant performance you put on for those gullible jurors. The way you took the stand that day and talked about your poor upbringing, how you and your family had to survive on food stamps, how you always dreamed of going to college but you knew your mother couldn't afford it. You made your decision to do porn sound like the act of a fucking martyr. And don't even get me started on Juror Number Eight. Every time you just *glanced* at that nigga, I thought he was gonna nut in his pants. Speaking of which"— he deliberately rubbed his hard dick against Tamia's crotch, making her shudder with a combination of revulsion and arousal—"what do you say we take this to the bedroom, for old time's sake?"

Tamia eyed him incredulously. "If you really believe I killed your wife," she said hoarsely, "why would you still wanna fuck me?"

An amused, knowing gleam lit his eyes. "The same reason *you* still wanna fuck *me* after everything I did to you. Tell me I'm wrong."

"You're wrong."

Dominic gave her a look of mock reproach. "You should know better than to lie to me," he gently scolded, running his fingertip from her chin down to the plump cleavage exposed by her low-cut sweater. "Your nipples have been hard ever since I got here. And I know if I slipped my hand inside your panties, I'd find your pussy soaking wet for me."

Tamia couldn't resist smirking. "Actually, I was thinking about Brandon before you showed up. So the nectar is for him, *not* you."

Dominic's eyes narrowed menacingly. "What did I tell you about provoking me? You wanna get choked again?"

Tamia gulped tightly.

When she tugged at her captured wrists, he tightened his grip until she winced in pain.

"You think I'm playing around with you, bitch. But I'm very serious about clearing my name and getting my life back, and you're gonna help me."

"How?" Tamia challenged defiantly. "You have no more power over me, Dominic. Thanks to you, all my secrets have been exposed. I lost everything, and I spent five months in prison for a crime I didn't commit. So unless you plan to kill me right now, nigga, there ain't shit else you can do to me."

"Wrong," Dominic countered silkily.

"What?"

"See, Tamia, I think you've still got one or two secrets up your sleeve."

She eyed him warily. "What the hell are you talking about?"

"I watched your every move during the trial. When the prosecutors showed the crime scene photos, you looked like you were gonna be sick. At first I thought you were just pretending, or maybe you looked upset because you couldn't face the reality of what you'd done. But then I saw the way you kept looking over your shoulder, as if you were searching for someone. Someone that you felt should have been sitting at that defense table instead of you."

He paused, carefully watching Tamia's face.

Though her heart was slamming against her chest, she managed to keep her expression neutral.

A slow, cunning smile curved Dominic's mouth. "So you see, love, I've come to realize that you *were* telling the truth. You didn't kill Isabel. But I think you know who did.

And when I find out who that person is, I'm gonna make damn sure you *both* go down."

Chilled by the ominous threat, Tamia forced herself to look Dominic in the eye. "I don't know what the hell you're talking about. But even if you were right, I can't be tried twice for the same crime, remember? It's called double jeopardy."

"That may be so," Dominic countered mildly, "but if it can be proven that you deliberately concealed the identity of Isabel's killer, you can be charged as an accessory to murder. So, technically, that's a different charge than the one you stood trial for." He smirked at her. "But maybe you should ask Brandon. He'd know better than I would."

Tamia stared at him.

He stared back.

"You need to leave," she told him.

"Or what?" he taunted. "You'll call the police?"

She hesitated. "I'm expecting someone any moment," she bluffed.

"Nice try, but I saw your little roommate leave before I came up."

"That's not who I was talking about. My best friend's coming over for dinner."

As if on cue, her cell phone rang from where she'd left it on the foyer table after she and Honey returned from shopping.

Dominic glanced over at the phone, then back at her, his eyes narrowed speculatively.

"That's probably Shanell calling to say she's on her way. Do you really want her to see you here when she knows I've got a restraining order against you?"

Dominic wavered.

Tamia waited tensely.

After several moments, he slowly climbed off her and stood.

Deliberately ignoring his outstretched hand, Tamia got to her feet and marched to the door. Snatching it open, she glared at Dominic. "Get out, and don't ever come back."

He chuckled softly, taking his sweet time walking to the door. "You haven't heard the last of me, love."

"Stop calling me that," Tamia snapped. "I'm not your 'love.' I *never* was."

"I beg to differ. Despite the way things ended between us, we were good together. We turned each other out, Tamia."

She twisted her lips scornfully. "Having good sex isn't the same as having a good relationship. You blackmailed me, Dominic. Trust me when I tell you that the worst day of my life was the day I met you."

"I'm sorry you feel that way," he drawled, "because I've never met another woman who rocked my world the way you did. And that's the damn truth."

Tamia shook her head in disgust, unintentionally following him into the hallway. "You're quite the grieving widower, aren't you?"

He laughed softly. "I'm just keeping it real." He leaned down, pinning her against the wall by the door as he whispered in her ear, "You should try it sometime."

Tamia shoved at his broad chest. "You need to back—"

"What the *fuck*?"

Tamia and Dominic whipped their heads around to see Brandon coming down the hallway, clad in a black tuxedo with the shirt unbuttoned and the tie hanging loose around his neck.

The bottom dropped out of Tamia's stomach.

"Hold up." He laughed in disbelief, glancing from Dominic to Tamia. "My eyes must be deceiving me, 'cause I *know* this motherfucker has a restraining order against him."

As he neared them, Tamia panicked. "Brandon, it's not what—"

"Yes, it is," Dominic taunted, grinding his hips against Tamia's. "It's *exactly* what you think."

Before Dominic or Tamia could react, Brandon slammed his fist into Dominic's face. The force of the vicious blow sent Dominic toppling backward through the open doorway, landing on his butt.

"Brandon!" Tamia cried out as he charged Dominic again, clocking him twice on the jaw before Tamia managed to drag him back with a strength borne of sheer desperation.

Chest heaving, eyes flashing with savage fury, Brandon roared at her, *"What the fuck is he doing here?"*

Tamia suppressed a whimper. She'd never seen him so enraged before. "Baby, listen to me—"

"You crazy motherfucker!" Dominic exclaimed, cupping a hand to his bloody nose as he eyed Brandon in outraged disbelief. "Have you lost your fucking mind?"

Before Brandon could lunge at him again, Tamia jumped in front of him, holding him back. "Leave him alone, baby," she entreated. "He's not worth it. You *know* that."

Brandon's eyes narrowed dangerously on hers. "I'ma ask you one more time," he ground out through clenched teeth, deliberately enunciating each word. "What. Is. He. Doing. Here?"

Before Tamia could respond, Dominic interjected slyly, "Didn't you know? Your girl invited me over."

"What!" Tamia burst out, staring incredulously at Dominic. "That's a damn lie!"

"Is it?" Dominic got slowly to his feet, smirking at Brandon even as blood dripped from his nose. "Who're you gonna believe, bruh? Me, or the woman who's been lying to you from the day you met her?"

Brandon divided a glance between them, his eyes narrowed with suspicion and doubt.

"Don't believe him, Brandon," Tamia pleaded urgently.

"He came here to threaten me over Isabel. I tried to call the police, but he wrestled me to the floor and started choking me!"

"WHAT?"

This time she didn't stop Brandon as he grabbed Dominic and viciously jacked him up against the wall, one arm locked across Dominic's jugular like a crowbar. "Nigga, you must have a death wish," he growled.

A slow, diabolical grin swept across Dominic's battered face.

Brandon scowled. "You think this shit is funny?"

"I do now. See, before you arrived, I was just telling Tamia how I've been struggling financially thanks to *you* turning the police against me. But now, thanks to your violent temper, I'm gonna be a very rich man again after I sue your crazy ass for assault." Dominic smiled smugly. "How's *that* for poetic justice?"

Tamia sucked her teeth. "Good luck finding any eyewitnesses, asshole, 'cause *I* didn't see a damn thing."

"Ah, but *they* did." Dominic nodded down the hallway.

Following the direction of his gaze, Tamia and Brandon saw a young white couple huddled in the doorway of their apartment, watching the unfolding drama with unabashed interest.

Shit, Tamia thought.

Dominic continued smoothly, "And the best part is, I never even raised a finger in self-defense. The attack was completely unprovoked *and* uncontested." He smirked at Brandon. "So it looks like I'll be seeing you in court, Counselor."

Brandon laughed softly. "Do what you gotta do, chump. Considering that my moms and pops know every damn judge and lawyer in this town, I'd be surprised if your case ever made it to court. But even if it somehow did and you happened to win the lawsuit, it's all good because, honestly,

I have more money than I can spend in a lifetime. Matter of fact, I'd gladly write you a check right now if you promised to fight me back like a man, you punk-ass motherfucker."

Dominic's jaw hardened with anger.

"Hey, Brandon," called the guy from down the hallway. "My wife and I are huge fans. Can we get your autograph before you leave?"

Brandon gave them a lazy smile. "Most definitely." His gaze returned to Dominic's. "Now what were you saying, asshole?"

Dominic spat a mouthful of blood onto Brandon's tuxedo jacket.

Brandon glanced down at himself, then back up at Dominic. "That all you got? *Spitting*?" He shook his head in amused disgust. "Like I said. Punk. Ass. Motherfucker."

Barely able to contain her satisfaction at seeing Dominic so thoroughly humiliated, Tamia gently touched Brandon's arm. "Come on, baby. Let's go inside."

"Hold up." Calmly Brandon peeled off his jacket, removed his wallet and cell phone, then tossed the soiled garment at Dominic's face. "Keep it. It's Brioni. After you get it dry-cleaned, you can pawn it to help pay your legal fees. Lawyers can be expensive." He winked. "Take my word for it."

As he and Tamia turned and started toward the apartment, Dominic snickered. "Before I forget, Brandon, thanks for getting Tamia acquitted. I missed fucking her for you while she was locked up."

Heat stung Tamia's face.

She looked at Brandon and shook her head, silently willing him not to rise to the bait.

"She may be a cold-blooded killer," Dominic taunted, "but pussy like that don't come around every day. Now that she's a free woman, you'd best believe I intend to resume tapping that sweet ass. She already promised to reenact some of her most popular Mystique scenes for me."

Tamia whirled around. *"You lying motherfucker!"* she shrieked furiously.

Now it was Brandon's turn to hold *her* back. As he dragged her into the apartment, he shot one last warning glare at Dominic. "You're trespassing on private property and violating a restraining order," he said coldly. "I suggest you take your black ass home before I call the police."

Dominic chuckled, shaking his head at him. "You got some interesting taste in women, bruh."

Brandon's eyes narrowed. "What the fuck is that supposed to mean?"

Dominic merely smiled, nonchalantly hooking Brandon's jacket over his shoulder. "I'll be seeing you around." He blew a kiss at Tamia. *"Both* of you."

Seething with fury, she slammed the door in his face.

Chapter 20

Tamia

By the time Tamia turned around, Brandon was already punching out numbers on his cell phone.

"Who're you calling?" she asked him.

He held up a hand. "This is Brandon Chambers," he growled to someone on the other line. "I just arrived at Tamia Luke's apartment and found Dominic Archer here. Do you mind telling me how the *fuck* that happened when you're supposed to have a guy sitting on him?"

He impatiently listened to the response as he stalked from the entryway.

Tamia followed him, shaken by how quickly the situation had gone from bad to worse.

"Do that, Sergeant," Brandon barked into the phone. "Or the next call I make will be to Chief McClelland."

Snapping his phone shut, he turned to face Tamia. His expression softened with concern. "Are you all right?"

"I'm fine." She tried to smile. "I've only been living here a week, and I've already brought the hood up in here, thanks to you."

Brandon wasn't amused. Carefully examining her throat for bruising, he muttered darkly, "That crazy motherfucker could have killed you."

"I know." Tamia swallowed with difficulty. "What's gonna happen to him? Are the police picking him up?"

"Hell, yeah! He's not supposed to come anywhere near you, especially considering that he may have murdered his wife."

Guilt gnawed at Tamia's insides. "I don't want to press charges against him."

"What?" Brandon demanded, his thick brows slamming together. "Why the hell not?"

Tamia faltered, "I don't want you to get in trouble for hitting him, Brandon. If I try to press charges, he'll just counter by saying you assaulted him."

"Let *me* worry about that."

"No. I'd rather just leave things alone. At least this time."

Brandon stared at her, his eyes filled with incredulous fury. "I don't believe this shit. Are you *protecting* that motherfucker?"

"No!" Tamia cried vehemently.

"Yes, you are! After everything he's done to you—after he came over here tonight and *choked* you—you don't wanna press charges against him because you're trying to protect him!"

"I'm not—"

"The hell you aren't! But guess what, sweetheart? He violated the restraining order, so that means he's getting arrested and spending the weekend in jail whether *you* like it or not!"

"I never said I didn't—"

"WHAT IS HIS HOLD ON YOU?" Brandon suddenly roared, looking so ferocious that Tamia wanted to run and hide. "What is it, Tamia?"

"Nothing!" she insisted as tears sprang to her eyes. "He doesn't have a hold on me!"

"Why the hell did he have you up against the wall when I got here?"

"Because he was trying to intimidate me! Didn't you see me push him away?"

Brandon sneered. "Maybe you saw me coming down the hallway."

"What?"

"You heard me. Maybe you *really* did invite him over here."

"I DID NOT!" Tamia shouted, trembling with wounded outrage. "How can you even believe that?"

"Hmm. Let me think. Maybe because you used to sneak around behind my back to fuck that nigga!"

Without thinking Tamia slapped him across the face, the sound echoing sharply around the room.

"Fuck you, Brandon!" she screamed. "I've apologized a thousand times for cheating on you! If you think I'm gonna spend the rest of my damn life groveling for your forgiveness, you'd better think again, 'cause I ain't that bitch!"

Brandon glared at her, a muscle flexing in his tightly clenched jaw.

"And speaking of bitches," Tamia jeered, too far gone to stop, "shouldn't you be somewhere playing house with Cynthia? Why the hell are you here worrying about what *I'm* doing when you know that trick is waiting for you at home?" She pointed toward the front door. "Don't let that shit hit you on the—"

Without warning Brandon lunged at her, seizing her face between his hands and slamming his mouth down on hers.

Tamia gasped, her entire body shuddering with shock and instant arousal. She threw her arms around his neck as he sucked on her bottom lip, sending delicious sensations to her pussy.

"Brandon—" she whispered.

"Shut the fuck up." His hands moved down her back, roughly squeezing her butt cheeks. "You think you running shit up in here? You ain't gonna *tell* me to leave. I'll leave when I'm good and goddamn ready."

His authoritative words, combined with the pressure of his hard dick, had her pussy creaming faster than a tricked-out butter churn.

Breaking the kiss, he knelt and yanked her leggings all the way down and off her French-pedicured feet. His eyes glittered with lust when he saw that she wore no panties. She trembled as he stared at her smooth-shaven mound for several seconds, as if he were beholding a priceless work of art.

After another moment, he touched the inside of her thighs, capturing the glistening wetness that had leaked out of her body.

Lifting his feral gaze to hers, he growled, "That motherfucker got you this wet?"

"No, baby," Tamia whimpered, shaking her head. "That's *all* for you. Every last drop."

"Better be." He stroked her hard clit before easing first one, then two fingers inside her drenched pussy.

Tamia cried out hoarsely, her knees buckling just as Brandon caught her and lifted her off the floor. He carried her over to the cherry dining table and laid her down on her back, dragging her hips to the edge.

Her legs were shaking violently as he draped them over his broad shoulders and lowered his head. She watched as he inhaled deeply, his eyes closing as he savored her scent. And then he licked the plump folds of her sex, sliding his hot tongue between the creases before sucking her clit into his mouth.

Tamia's hips bucked off the table. "Ohhh shit . . . baaay-beee . . . !"

Brandon muttered unintelligibly before getting down to business, licking, nibbling, and sucking her pussy. She moaned with pleasure and writhed against him, alternately grabbing his head and fistfuls of his tuxedo shirt.

He feasted on her, using his fingers to spread her lips wider before his tongue snaked inside, devouring her nectar.

She screamed his name as she exploded in a hot rush, basting his mouth and chin with warm honey as her thighs clamped tightly around his head. And still he kept lapping at her like a hungry cat licking every last drop of cream from a bowl.

After several moments, he lowered her legs from his shoulders and hooked them around his waist as he slowly stood. His lips glistened with her juices, and his long, hard dick tented the front of his black pants. Planting his hands on either side of her head, he leaned down and kissed her, a deep, erotic kiss that had her feenin' for more.

"Brandon," she whispered pleadingly as she tightened her legs around him, "make love to me, baby. *Please*."

"Nah," he taunted her. "You told me to leave, remember?"

"I didn't mean it!"

"No?" He ran his lips down her throat. "Sounded pretty damn sincere to me."

Tamia wanted to scream with frustration. "Come on, baby. I want you, and I know you want me, too." She rubbed against his thick erection. "You gonna let all this good dick go to waste?"

"Nah. Like you just pointed out, I've got someone waiting for me at home."

Tamia felt sick at the thought of him going home to fuck Cynthia, but she didn't want to give him the satisfaction of knowing that. Summoning her pride, she propped herself up on her elbows and smirked at him. "Then I guess you'd better get going."

Brandon eyed her darkly. "What'd I tell you about that? I'll leave when I'm ready to leave."

Tamia sucked her teeth. "Well, *I'm* ready for you to leave, okay?"

"That's fine," he said mildly, stroking her face. "But you need to know something first. If I ever catch that nigga around you again, I'm gonna kill him. Straight up, Tamia. I'm taking his ass out—no questions asked. So you'd better make damn sure he doesn't get any more crazy ideas about coming over here."

Tamia scowled at him. "I told you I had nothing to do with him showing up here. I haven't had any contact with him since I went to prison!"

Brandon nodded slowly. "Okay. I'm just letting you know."

"Whatever." Hurt, angry, and annoyed, she sat up all the way and unwrapped her legs from around his waist. "Could you hand me my leggings, please?"

Brandon hesitated, his heavy-lidded eyes lowering to her pussy and lingering there.

The longer he stared at her, the more hot and bothered Tamia became. When she couldn't take anymore, she put her finger under his goateed chin and lifted his head, forcing him to meet her exasperated gaze.

"If you're not gonna fuck me," she snapped, "at least let me get dressed."

He clenched his jaw, nostrils flaring as he wrestled with temptation.

Tamia waited, pulse pounding, clit throbbing.

After several moments, Brandon turned away and walked over to where he'd dropped her leggings on the floor. When he returned to her, he knelt and slowly pulled the black spandex over her calves, up her thighs and, when she lifted off the table, over her hips and ass. It was the first time Tamia had ever been dressed—as opposed to *un*dressed—by a man, and it turned her on even more than she already was.

But she wasn't going to beg Brandon to finish what he'd started, no matter how badly she wanted him to. He'd already gotten enough pleasure from torturing her tonight.

Frowning at the thought, Tamia grumbled, "You're different."

Brandon's eyes lifted to hers. "What do you mean?"

"I mean, I've always known you had a ruthless streak, but it seems even more noticeable tonight."

Brandon looked amused. "Yesterday you told me I seemed more relaxed."

"Well, yeah, you do. But at the same time, you also seem more . . . hardened." She hesitated uncertainly. "I hope I didn't do that to you."

"Maybe." One corner of his mouth quirked upward. "Or maybe this is the real me."

Tamia frowned again. "What do you mean?"

He got slowly to his feet. "Maybe I didn't let you see the real me when we were dating. Or maybe you only saw what you wanted to see. A nice guy."

"You *are* a nice guy, Brandon."

"Am I?" A grim, reminiscent smile touched his mouth. "When I was growing up, a lot of other black kids thought I was just some corny-ass rich boy from River Oaks. So they assumed I was a punk who couldn't fight. One summer when I was thirteen, Dre and I went to this picnic around his neighborhood. Some hood rats liked my Air Jordans so much they decided they were just gonna take 'em. So when Dre and I got separated, the dudes rolled up on me, and they jumped me."

Tamia stared at him. "What happened?"

He chuckled softly. "Let's just say when the dust settled, I still had my sneakers, along with someone else's pair."

Tamia grinned. "Dayum, slugger."

Brandon made a wry face. "I didn't tell you that story to impress you."

"Too late. I'm impressed."

He gently stroked her cheek. "The moral of the story is that people aren't always what they seem. My grandfather was an amazing poker player, and he always taught me that in life, you don't show your hand until the other players show theirs. I guess that's how I've always approached relationships. I try not to let my guard down completely until the woman I'm dating shows *her* true colors."

Tamia's grin faded. Suddenly she didn't like where this conversation was going. "What are you saying, Brandon? That we dated for nine months and I never knew the real you?"

He raised a brow at her. "Did I know the real *you*?"

That shut her up.

Brandon murmured, "We've still got some walls between us, still have some relearning to do."

Tamia eyed him hopefully. "Are you saying . . . there's still a chance for us?"

"I don't know, Tamia. I'd be lying if I said I'm completely over you. I'm not, and I think you know that. But you need to understand something about me. You're the only woman I've ever let down my guard with, and I got fucked up in the process." He leaned close, his soft lips brushing her temple before moving to her ear. "So here's what I'm saying. If I find out that you're lying to me about anything—absolutely *anything*—I promise you there won't be any second chances. Believe that."

Tamia gulped hard, watching as he slowly pulled away and gave her a small, narrow smile. "*Now* I'm leaving."

And with that, he turned and walked out, leaving Tamia with a sense of dread that was all too familiar.

Chapter 21

Brandon

"Where the hell have you been?" Cynthia demanded, accosting Brandon as soon as he stepped through the front door of his condo.

As proof of how angry she was, she still had on the tacky turquoise gown that she and the other bridesmaids had been forced to wear, which Cynthia had vowed to burn as soon as the wedding was over.

She apparently had bigger fish to fry at the moment.

"I left for *twenty* minutes to help Lynn get out of her gown so she and Phillip could leave for the airport," she ranted. "By the time I came back to the reception, you were nowhere to be found! I had to catch a ride home with my parents!"

"Didn't you get my text?" Brandon asked calmly, setting his keys and cell phone on the foyer table. "I told you I had to swing by the office to fax some important documents to a client."

"That was two hours ago! Don't expect me to believe you've been at the office all this time!"

"I wasn't." He paused. "I went to Tamia's apartment."

"I KNEW IT!" Cynthia exploded, glaring furiously at him. "You went over there and fucked her, didn't you?"

"No."

"I don't believe you!"

"That's your prerogative." Craving a cold beer and a hot shower, Brandon brushed past Cynthia and headed to the kitchen to take care of the first need.

She charged after him, the loud swishing of her taffeta gown sounding like hissed accusations. "Why the hell did you go over there if you weren't planning to fuck her? And don't you *dare* tell me you didn't touch her, because I can smell her damn perfume on you!"

Brandon grabbed a Black and Tan from the fridge and twisted the cap off the bottle. Leaning back against the counter, he met Cynthia's gaze directly. "I didn't say I didn't touch her. I said I didn't fuck her."

"What!"

As Cynthia raised her hand to slap him, Brandon caught her wrist midair and shook his head once, a terse warning.

"I've had enough of that for one night."

With a strangled cry of frustration, Cynthia yanked her wrist free and shrieked, "It's bad enough that you showed up late to the wedding—"

"I told you I was with my father."

"—but then you snuck off early to be with that whore! Like you just couldn't help yourself!"

Brandon sipped his beer, silently pondering her angry words. Truth be told, she wasn't too far off the mark. When it came to Tamia, he often felt as though he had no control over himself. When he'd arrived at her apartment tonight and seen her with Dominic, he'd lost his mind. If she hadn't intervened, he probably would have killed that motherfucker with his bare hands.

"Don't you see what's happening, Brandon?" Cynthia

cried shrilly. "She's only been home a *week*, and she's already coming between us!"

Brandon said quietly, "You need to calm down and lower your voice."

"Why?" Cynthia jeered. "Afraid your neighbors will find out what a lying, cheating bastard you are?"

"I haven't lied to you, Cynthia. I told you exactly where I was."

"Like that's supposed to make me feel better! If you see absolutely nothing wrong with leaving my cousin's wedding reception to sneak over to your ex-girlfriend's apartment, then I have nothing more to say to you!"

With that, she spun on her heel and stormed out of the kitchen.

Brandon took a long sip of his beer, then heaved a deep sigh and followed her.

By the time he reached the living room, Cynthia was marching from his bedroom carrying her suitcase. He had an unpleasant flashback to the night he'd returned home to find Tamia packing her belongings after she'd caught him and Cynthia flirting with each other at the office. He couldn't help marveling at how things had come full circle.

As Cynthia strode past him, he asked, "Where are you going?"

"Where do you think?" she snapped. "I'm going home. I refuse to stay here and put up with any more of your bullshit. Unlike that bitch Tamia, *I* have standards. My parents have been happily married for forty years because they genuinely love, respect, and trust each other. So why the hell should I accept anything less from you?"

"You shouldn't."

Cynthia faltered for a moment, looking as if she hadn't expected him to agree with her.

He lowered himself onto his favorite armchair and drank

his beer, watching as she squared her shoulders and continued on her way to the front door.

"I'm sick and tired of being taken for granted. As I explained to you before, I have options. *Plenty* of them. But you obviously weren't listening to me, so I'm gonna make a believer out of you."

Reaching the door, she paused and looked over the huge, frothy bow on her shoulder. She frowned when she saw that Brandon had made no move to follow her.

"You must think I'm playing," she spat.

"What I think," he countered patiently, "is that you've been here at least an hour, so you were obviously waiting for me to come home because you want me to talk you out of leaving. But I'm not going to, sweetheart, because I actually think it's a good idea for you to go back to your house for a while. We both need some space to reassess what we want out of this relationship."

Cynthia stared at him with a stunned expression. "Are you breaking up with me?"

"That's not what I said. *Now* who isn't listening?"

She sneered. "You want space? Fine. I'll give you all the space you want. But don't be surprised if I've moved on by the time you come to your fucking senses!"

As she wrenched the door open, Brandon called out, "Cynthia."

She turned back expectantly.

"I'm going to my parents' house tomorrow after church. So you can stop by here and get the rest of your belongings. I'll instruct the doorman to let you inside."

"Don't bother," Cynthia hissed. "I can just use my damn key."

"Nah." Brandon shook his head. "You need to leave the key *now*."

She let out an affronted gasp, her face twisting with indignant fury. "Why? Are you suggesting that I'm gonna run out tonight and make a spare copy?"

He just looked at her.

Sputtering with outrage, she snatched the requested key off her key ring and hurled it across the room at him, then stormed out, slamming the door hard enough to rock the walls.

Alone, Brandon took a long swig of his beer and allowed his thoughts to drift back to Tamia.

She was the only woman he'd ever truly loved.

And if he wasn't careful, she would be his ultimate downfall.

Chapter 22

Fiona

Fiona hummed softly to herself as she sashayed through the glass doors that fronted the administrative offices of Pinnacle Sports Group. Since it was after hours on a Saturday night, the large reception desk was empty, the phone lines were silent, and the plasma television mounted against the wall was dark.

With a magazine tucked beneath one arm, Fiona left the plush reception area and made her way down a thickly carpeted corridor adorned with sports memorabilia, press clippings, and framed awards that the agency had received since opening last year.

When she reached the open door at the end of the hallway, she poked her head inside and smiled.

Beau Chambers sat behind a large, glass-topped desk talking on the phone. Spying Fiona in the doorway, he held up one finger, signaling that he'd be with her shortly.

She nodded and smiled again.

As Beau continued his phone conversation, his gaze took slow inventory of Fiona's appearance. Her long black hair was swept over one shoulder, her pouty lips were slicked with MAC's Nymphette lip gloss, and she wore a tan Juicy Couture shirt dress with matching leather stiletto boots.

She could tell by the way Beau's eyes gleamed that he liked what he saw. And the feeling was definitely mutual.

With his dark chocolate skin, ebony bedroom eyes, chiseled cheekbones, and juicy lips, Beau was so damn sexy that Fiona's coochie throbbed every time she saw him. His shoulders were as wide as Dwight Howard's, and his hands were the size of dinner plates, leaving no doubt in Fiona's mind that he had to be working with *at least* ten inches.

By the time he ended his business call and motioned her into the office, her pussy was pumping harder than her heart after a high-impact Zumba workout.

As she sauntered over to his desk, Beau leaned back in his chair and smiled at her, a diamond stud twinkling in one ear. "Wassup, girl."

"Wassup," Fiona purred, giving him her sexiest smile. "I just wanted to welcome you back and get your auto-graph."

He raised a brow. "My—? Oh," he said, chuckling as she dropped the current issue of *GQ* magazine onto his desk and pointed at the cover.

"You and Brandon look like straight-up gangstas," she teased him.

Beau grinned wryly. "Don't let my old man hear you say that. He's been bitching ever since he saw this cover, ask-ing us why we didn't choose a 'less threatening' pose. He's worried that the Republicans will find a way to portray us as thugs or some ish like that."

Fiona laughed, shaking her head. "Your pops is trippin'. I *love* that photo. You and Brandon got the coolest swagger I've ever seen. And the feature article was amazing."

"Thanks," Beau drawled, idly flipping through the mag-azine. "I'm glad you enjoyed it."

"Most definitely." Fiona grinned. "I want you and Brandon to sign my copy so I can take it to school and make all my classmates jealous."

Beau tsk-tsked. "Now, that's not very nice."

"Oh, trust. They'd all do the same thing if they knew you and your brother."

Beau chuckled, setting aside the magazine. "We're having lunch with my parents tomorrow, so I'll get Brandon's autograph for you then."

"Thank you," Fiona told him, lowering herself onto one of the visitor chairs across from his desk. She deliberately crossed her legs, noting the way his eyes followed the movement and lingered on the luscious curve of her thighs.

Hiding a satisfied smile, she asked conversationally, "So how was New York?"

"Good." His gaze slowly returned to hers. "Very productive."

Beau had flown to New York to conduct business on behalf of some of his clients. While there, he'd also met with Damarion Griggs, a star quarterback and Heisman Trophy frontrunner who was expected to declare for the NFL draft in January. Not surprisingly, every football agent in America was salivating at the prospect of signing him.

Fiona grinned at Beau. "Do you think you can lure Damarion away from the competition?"

Beau smiled lazily. "Let's just say I like my odds," he said with such confidence that Fiona's nipples hardened.

"He'd be crazy to sign with anyone but you," she asserted.

"That's pretty much what I told him."

She and Beau laughed.

As the humorous moment passed, Beau asked her, "So what's good with you? How are your classes coming along?"

"Great!" Fiona smiled shyly. "I just got an A on a history test."

"Really? That's wonderful," Beau said warmly. "Congratulations, Fiona. I'm proud of you."

She warmed with pleasure. "Thanks, Beau. I appreciate that."

He snapped his fingers. "That reminds me. I brought you back a souvenir."

"Really?"

"Yeah. It's just a little somethin' somethin' I picked up in Manhattan." He glanced around the cluttered surface of his desk, brows furrowed with exaggerated bewilderment. "Now where did I put—Oh, that's right." He reached under the desk and retrieved an elegant bag that bore the Hermès logo.

Fiona's eyes widened. "What is it?"

Beau smiled, passing the bag to her. "Open it."

Fiona peered inside, then gasped when she saw an exquisite blue crocodile Birkin handbag. "Oh, my God! Is this what I *think* it is?"

Beau's smile deepened. "Depends on what you think it is."

She eyed him incredulously. "A *little somethin' somethin'*? Beau, these handbags cost—"

"Shhh." He put his finger to his lips. "I won't tell if you don't."

Shaking her head, Fiona carefully removed the Birkin from the bag and ran her fingers over the sumptuous leather. "I heard these are only available on a limited basis," she marveled. "And they used to make you get on a waiting list. I can't believe you bought one for me. I mean, I would have been happy with an 'I Heart New York' T-shirt or keychain!"

Beau chuckled softly. "Nah, baby girl. I don't do cheap trinkets. Besides, you deserve nothing but the best for the way you keep the fellas in line down at the barber shop."

Fiona grinned, tucking the expensive designer handbag into the crook of her arm.

Beau nodded approvingly. "You wear it well."

"Think so?"

"Most definitely."

Fiona beamed. Just as she began fantasizing about being worn on *his* arm, his cell phone rang.

Murmuring a quick apology, Beau answered the phone. "Hey," he said, his deep voice dropping to a low, intimate tone as he angled slightly away from Fiona. "I'm still at the office, but I'll be leaving soon."

Fiona glanced up from admiring her handbag to watch as a slow, sexy smile curved his mouth. "Don't worry, I won't be late." Pause. "Can't wait to see you, too. Be there soon."

Disconnecting the call, he shot Fiona a sheepish glance. "Sorry about that."

"No problem." She flashed a fake smile. "Got a hot date?"

"Mmm. Something like that."

Fiona's heart sank.

Beau's womanizing reputation was another obstacle she'd have to overcome in her quest to become his wifey. Every time she turned around, there was some new trick in the picture. Unfortunately, with his dark good looks, sexy swagger, and multimillion-dollar bank account, Beau attracted even more groupies than his celebrity clients. And unlike Brandon—who'd monogamously dated Tamia for nine months—Beau showed no signs of turning in his playa card.

As he began straightening papers on his desk, Fiona suppressed a heavy sigh and reluctantly rose from the chair. "Well, I won't hold you up. Have fun on your date tonight."

"Thanks, Fiona. What about you? Got any special plans?"

"Nah. I have too much homework to do. By the way, do you mind if I use the receptionist's computer? I need to print my term paper."

"Sure. Go ahead. Dre should be around here somewhere. He said he had some paperwork to catch up on, so he'll lock up after you."

I bet he will, Fiona thought darkly.

Forcing a bright smile, she held up her new handbag. "Thanks again for the Birkin. I've always wanted one. Now I feel like I've joined an exclusive club."

Beau winked at her. "Enjoy your membership."

On her way back to the reception area, Fiona saw that the door to Dre's office was ajar. As she walked past, she heard soft kissing sounds and the low murmur of Dre's and Leah's voices.

Unable to resist, Fiona paused to eavesdrop while pretending to read a framed *Sports Illustrated* article mounted on the wall beside the doorway.

"Come on, baby," Dre was softly cajoling. "It's been over a month. I'm going outta my damn mind."

"I know you are," Leah said, "and I'm really sorry about that. But you know how exhausted I am when I get home from the hospital. This surgical rotation's kicking my butt. Most days I don't know if I'm coming or going."

"Give me one night, baby, and you'll *definitely* know you're coming."

Fiona rolled her eyes at the lame, corny-ass line.

"So come on, baby," Dre continued. "Let's go home and get down to business."

Leah sighed heavily. "I'd love to, but we can't. My period started today."

Dre groaned. "You can't be serious."

"I am, unfortunately."

"Shit. I knew that was gonna happen."

"What tipped you off?" Leah quipped humorously. "The fact that it happens every month?"

"You know what I meant." Dre let out another frustrated groan. "Let's do it anyway. I'll wear a condom."

Fiona wrinkled her nose in disgust as Leah objected, "Hell, no! You know I'm not down with that, Dre, so I don't even know why you went there."

Dre grumbled darkly, "I went there 'cause I'm horny as fuck, and my dick's about to fall off from lack of use."

Leah chuckled drolly. "That's not medically possible."

"No? Tell that to my atrophied dick."

Fiona snickered, then clapped a hand over her mouth.

But it was too late.

"Did you hear something?" Leah asked Dre.

Panicking, Fiona raced down the hallway before the couple could catch her eavesdropping.

Reaching the lobby, she sat behind the receptionist's large desk and set down her handbag, then turned on the computer.

Five minutes later Beau left for his date, looking fine as hell in a charcoal Versace suit he'd changed into inside his private bathroom. As Fiona watched him leave, she couldn't help envying the lucky bitch who'd get to ride his ten inches tonight.

Shortly afterward, Dre and Leah emerged from the back. When they saw Fiona seated at the reception station, their faces twisted with such displeasure, you'd have thought they'd just caught the hired help taking a shit on their imported silk bedsheets.

"What the hell are you doing?" Dre demanded suspiciously.

Fiona smirked at him. "What does it look like? I'm hacking into the network to steal personal data about our clients to sell to the tabloids."

After exchanging uneasy glances with Leah, Dre snapped, "Yo, that shit ain't funny."

Fiona laughed belligerently. "Was to me."

As she returned to proofreading her term paper, she saw Leah eyeballing her handbag on the desk.

"Is that a *Birkin*?"

"Yup." Fiona gave her a smug smile. "Beau bought it for me while he was in New York."

"Oh, really?" Leah shook her head, lips twisted disdainfully. "He should have saved his money. You don't have enough class to own a Birkin."

"Beau obviously thinks I do," Fiona countered sweetly. "So fuck you."

As Leah's face reddened with anger, Dre quickly intervened, "Come on, baby. Let me walk you out to your car. The sooner I finish up here, the sooner I can meet you at home."

As he began ushering Leah toward the doors, she glared back at Fiona. "I will be *so* glad when your ghetto ass gets fired."

Fiona held up her new handbag, smirking triumphantly. "Don't hold your breath, bitch."

She laughed, watching as Dre had to practically drag Leah from the reception area.

After they left, Fiona finished proofing her paper, then sent the thirty-page document to the printer. She had to provide one copy to her professor and another to his assistant.

She was standing in the small copy room waiting to retrieve her print job when Dre reappeared. She pretended not to notice him, though she'd have to be blind not to acknowledge how good he looked in a gray pullover, dark jeans, and black Timbs.

"*Now* what the hell are you doing?" he demanded impatiently.

"Minding my damn business," Fiona retorted. "I suggest you do the same."

He scowled. "If you're using the company's equipment and supplies for personal reasons, it *is* my fucking business."

"For your information," she snapped, "Beau told me I could print out my term paper."

"Ever thought of using your own damn printer at home?"

"I don't have one."

Dre raked her with a scornful glance. "Maybe if you spent less money on designer clothes, you could afford one."

"What?" Fiona spat, rounding indignantly on him. "Are you my man? No? Then it's none of your damn business how I spend my money!"

"The hell it ain't! You need to stop using this office as your personal Kinko's!"

"And *you* need to stop tracking my every move like you're fucking GPS! Why the hell are you so obsessed with me?"

Dre snorted derisively. "*Obsessed* with you?"

"That's what I said, nigga! Now tell me I'm lying!"

He glared at her.

Fiona glared right back, the air between them seething with hatred and fury.

The next thing she knew they were pouncing on each other, mouths clashing voraciously. Dre yanked up Fiona's dress and ripped her silk thong off her booted legs, then roughly lifted her onto the printer. The machine was warm, humming beneath her naked ass as the pages of her paper continued churning out.

She hurriedly unfastened Dre's jeans, her eyes bulging when she beheld his beautiful black dick. She'd been wrong about him. The nigga was packing a python!

Before she could stop to consider whether he'd even fit inside her, Dre grabbed her butt and dragged her to the edge of the printer. Their heated gazes locked as she wrapped her legs around his waist. Before she could draw her next breath, he shoved all twelve inches into her.

She screamed hoarsely, erotic pleasure mingling with pain.

Dre groaned and shuddered deeply, his cock seeming to lengthen even more as he began ramming into her. The feeling was like nothing Fiona had ever experienced before. She threw her arms around his thick neck, her calves riding the flexing muscles of his ass as he pounded her pussy. It was all she could do to keep from whimpering and coming apart like a whipped bitch.

"I hate you," she snarled against his mouth.

"I hate you, too," he snarled back.

Biting his lower lip, she panted breathlessly, "I'm sick of you . . . always being up in my business. You need to—*Oh, shit!*" she yelled as he shoved his hips against hers, ruthlessly stroking her G-spot.

His dark eyes gleamed with wicked satisfaction. "Now what the fuck were you saying?"

Fiona shuddered and closed her eyes, trying her best to outlast him even as she found herself wishing she bore his last name. What the hell was Leah thinking, neglecting all this good dick? Was that bitch *crazy*?

"I'm sick of you, too," Dre ground out, each word punctuated with a slapping thrust that echoed around the small room. "I don't trust your fucking ass."

"That goes . . . both ways!" Fiona managed to choke out.

"I think you're a sneaky—"

"—conceited—"

"—lying—"

"—meddling ass—"

"—motherfucker!" they both screamed as they came violently together.

Dre pulled out of Fiona, grabbed his dick, and sprayed the front of her dress with a hot burst of cum.

Gasping and shaking uncontrollably, Fiona fell back against the printer and released a lusty, breathless laugh.

Dre leaned over her, chest heaving, big hands braced on either side of her body as he fought to catch his breath.

After several moments, Fiona glanced down at her

ruined dress, then looked up at Dre and smirked. "That all you got?" she taunted.

A menacing grin curved his mouth. "I was about to ask you the same thing."

She sat up and quickly tugged off his pullover, her mouth watering at the smorgasbord of thick, rippling muscles that defined his massive chest.

"Dayuuummm!" she exclaimed before she could stop herself. Licking her lips, she ran her hands over his sculpted pecs and biceps, silently marveling, *This mofo is the epitome of cock diesel!*

"My turn." Dre yanked her dress over her head and tossed it aside. His eyes widened at the sight of her large, luscious breasts spilling from the cups of her skimpy silk bra. Unfastening the front clasp, he pushed her titties together and sucked her hard nipples into his mouth.

Fiona groaned with pleasure, gripping his bald head as the stroking motions of his tongue made her pussy drip.

She was on the verge of climaxing again when he suddenly grabbed her hips, flipping her over so fast it was a wonder he didn't stab himself with her stiletto heels. As he rubbed the swollen head of his dick against her asshole, Fiona instinctively tensed, bracing herself to be split in half.

"Should I come through the back door?" he murmured wickedly.

Fiona swallowed hard, jerking her head from side to side. "I-I don't think you'd fit," she admitted weakly.

Dre laughed, the sound so sexy her belly quivered. "Punk ass."

And with that, he plunged into her pussy.

Fiona screamed, her back arching as her walls stretched to accommodate his shaft.

She looked over her shoulder, watching the way Dre's taut stomach muscles contracted as he thrust into her with long, thick strokes that sent her breasts bouncing. Adrenaline and lust sped through her veins, a powerful aphrodisiac that made her feel higher than any drug could.

"Fuck me," she panted.

"Ain't that what I'm doing?" Dre challenged.

"Nah, nigga," she lied, barely able to get out the words. "You playing around with me."

"Oh, is that right?"

She cried out as he slapped her round butt cheek, making her flesh jiggle. "Fuck me, Dre," she half commanded, half begged. *"FUCK ME!"*

He began pummeling her pussy, his hips pumping furiously as his heavy balls slapped her backside. Warm beads of perspiration dripped from their bodies and splattered onto the printer.

As Dre's hand rose and fell against her ass cheeks, Fiona alternately moaned and shouted, her voice climbing in octaves as she felt another orgasm building in her loins.

Wrapping her hair around one hand, Dre yanked her head back and bent down to whisper in her ear, "Am I fucking you now?"

Fiona groaned, wishing like hell she could tell him that his dick game was whack, that she could have had a V8. But her mouth wouldn't formulate the lie, because the indisputable truth was that Dre was the best lover she'd ever had—and she'd had plenty.

His grip tightened on her hair. "Answer me, little girl."

Fiona closed her eyes. "What was the ques—"

He rammed his dick to the hilt, forcing her to scream at the top of her lungs, *"YES!"* as her body exploded, completely soaking his shaft.

He came seconds later, his guttural shout blending with her breathless cries. She shivered as he pulled out of her, splashing off on her back and ass.

Fiona collapsed on top of the printer, thoroughly spent and satiated.

After another minute, a deafening silence permeated the room.

And then Dre whispered hoarsely, *"Shit!"*

Raising her groggy head, Fiona looked over her shoulder at him. He was staring down at her with the shocked expression of a man who just realized he'd not only cheated on his girlfriend but had betrayed her with a woman he despised.

Passing a trembling hand over his head, he hissed, "Fuck."

"Okay, Daddy," Fiona purred, "but you gotta let me ride that black python this time."

Dre looked down at her luscious apple bottom glazed with pearly cum. His nostrils flared and his eyes darkened, leaving no doubt in her mind that he wanted to sex her again. And again, and again.

Feeling downright devious, Fiona reached behind her and massaged his cream into her skin, then sucked her sticky fingers one by one.

Dre swallowed visibly as his cock jerked in his hand.

Fiona rolled over on the printer, crossed her booted legs, and combed her fingers through her long black hair. As Dre stared at her, she licked her lips into a sensual smile. "Anytime you're ready, Daddy."

He stepped away from her, shaking his head as he hurriedly tucked his dick back into his jeans and zipped up. As Fiona watched in amusement, he retrieved her dress and lingerie from the floor and tossed them at her.

"Get dressed so I can clean up in here," he ordered gruffly.

Smirking, Fiona gave a mock salute. "Yes, sir."

Dre grabbed his shirt and quickly left the room, as if he didn't trust himself to be alone with her a second longer.

Smiling with satisfaction, Fiona eased down to the floor and took her sweet time getting dressed and smoothing her tousled hair. When she'd finished, she retrieved the copies of her paper from the printer tray, then calmly strolled out the door.

Dre was leaning against the wall with his head tipped back as he stared up at the ceiling, as if he were seeking absolution.

Fiona stepped right up to him.

They stared at each other.

Your secret's safe with me, she mouthed.

His expression darkened. Because he knew that her silence came with a price.

She winked at him.

He frowned.

Chuckling wickedly, Fiona turned and sauntered away, basking in the knowledge that from now on, she owned Dre Portis.

Chapter 23

Tamia

"I need your advice, Mama Esther."

Tamia sat on the porch swing next to her grandmother, watching as the old woman's nimble fingers moved her knitting needles with practiced ease.

"Speak your mind, chile," Mama Esther encouraged.

Tamia hesitated. "It's about Fiona."

A shadow crossed her grandmother's face, and for a moment her knitting needles went still as she stared off into the distance.

Tamia gently touched her arm. "Mama? Are you okay?"

Mama Esther met her concerned gaze, then nodded. "I'm fine, baby. What did you want to ask me about your sister?"

Tamia inhaled a deep breath and let it out slowly. "I don't know what to do about her."

"What do you mean?"

"She committed a horrible crime, Mama Esther. She should be locked up, but instead she's roaming free because

I never told anyone the truth about what really happened that night."

"And why didn't you?"

"You know why. She threatened to have me killed while I was in prison!"

Mama Esther eyed Tamia knowingly. *"That's not the only reason you kept your silence."*

"Yes, it is," Tamia argued.

"No, it isn't." Mama Esther offered a gentle, intuitive smile. *"You've always protected your sister. Remember when you were children and Fiona would break things around the house or sneak things out of your mother's room? You'd always take the blame for that chile because you didn't want her to be punished. It got to the point where your mama stopped whupping you because she knew you probably hadn't done anything wrong."*

Tamia smiled softly, awash with poignant memories. *"Poor Ma. She should have just whupped both of us to cover her bases."*

She and Mama Esther shared a warm laugh.

Sobering after several moments, Tamia sighed heavily. *"I can't keep protecting her, Mama."*

"I know," her grandmother agreed quietly.

"She murdered an innocent woman. Isabel deserves justice, and her family needs closure."

"I know."

"Not only that, but her husband suspects I'm hiding something. He's determined to find Isabel's killer so he can clear his name and collect her insurance policy. So I know he'll be coming after me again as soon as he's out on bail."

Mama Esther nodded, looking grim. *"That's probably true."*

Tamia groaned. *"But that's not even the worst part, Mama. The worst part is that Brandon will never forgive me if he finds out that I kept such a terrible secret from him. He forgave me for all the other lies, but finding out that I've been protecting a murderer will push him away for good."* She swallowed hard, shaking her head. *"I can't lose him again, Mama Esther. I can't."*

Her grandmother set down her needlework, then reached over and gently patted Tamia's hand. *"Don't fret so,"* she soothed. *"Brandon loves you, chile."*

"Maybe, but that could change," Tamia mumbled miserably. *"There's only but so much deception he can take."*

"Yes, but you should never underestimate the power of a man's love."

Tamia held her grandmother's gaze for a few moments, then sighed. *"I hope you're right, Mama. Because I've never loved any man the way I love Brandon. I'd be lost without him."*

"Umm-hmm."

Tamia kissed her grandmother's hand and held it against her cheek, savoring the familiar warmth and softness of the old woman's skin. *"I wish you could have met him, Mama,"* she said with a tender smile. *"I think you would have loved him. He's a good man."*

"I know he is," Esther concurred.

"How do you know?"

"You wouldn't love him if he weren't. You may have given your body to that rascal Dominic, but you knew better than to give him your heart." Mama Esther smiled sadly. *"If only your mama had guarded her heart better."*

Tamia was silent, thinking of her late father, who'd abandoned her and her mother when Tamia was a little girl. Over the years, she'd often reflected on how different her life would have turned out if Emmett Luke had been remotely interested in being a husband and father. If he'd stayed in the picture, her mother wouldn't have met Sonny Powell, the *sadistic monster who'd wreaked havoc on their lives. If Lorraine had never met Sonny, Fiona wouldn't have been born.*

And maybe that wouldn't have been such a bad thing.

Pushing aside the dark thought, Tamia watched as her grandmother's deft fingers wove blue yarn between her needles.

"What are you knitting, Mama?" she asked curiously.

Mama Esther paused, lips pursed thoughtfully as she eyed her unfinished handiwork. "I'm not sure."

Tamia laughed. "What do you mean? You don't know what you're making?"

"I think it's a baby's blanket."

"Really?" Tamia grew still. "For who?"

Her grandmother frowned, shaking her head. "I don't know."

The two women fell silent, pondering the possibilities.

After another minute, Mama Esther prodded gently, "So what are you going to do about your sister?"

Tamia exhaled a deep, shaky breath. "I don't know, Mama. Part of me knows that turning her over to the authorities would be the right thing to do. But another part of me is afraid of what will happen to her if the truth comes out. What if she's sent to prison for the rest of her life? Or what if she gets the death penalty?" Chilled by the thought, Tamia rubbed her hands up and down her arms to banish the goose bumps that had risen.

"I'm so torn, Mama Esther. I don't know what to do." She eyed her grandmother imploringly. "I was hoping you'd give me some guidance."

Mama Esther shook her head regretfully. "I'm afraid I can't, Tamia. You have to bear this cross, because you're the one who'll have to live with the consequences of whatever decision you make. But until you decide what to do, baby, you're gonna remain in prison."

Tamia frowned. "What do you mean, Mama? I'm not in prison anymore. I was acquitted over a week ago."

Mama Esther arched a dubious brow. "Then why are you still dressed like that?"

Tamia glanced down at herself, startled to discover that she wore the drab prison uniform she'd hoped to never see again.

"That's strange," she whispered. "I wonder why—"

But when she looked up again, her grandmother was gone.

Tamia's eyes snapped open, sweeping desperately around her sun-drenched bedroom.

"Mama Esther?" she called out hopefully.

It took her several dazed seconds to realize that the entire conversation had only been a dream—a dream that left her feeling bereft and lonely for her grandmother.

Rolling onto her back, Tamia flung an arm over her forehead and blew out a long, deep breath.

Suddenly her cell phone rang.

She hesitated for a moment, then reached across the nightstand and picked it up, grimacing when she saw Shanell's number on the caller ID. She considered letting the call go to voice mail, but she knew her best friend would only phone right back.

Heaving a resigned sigh, Tamia pressed the talk button. "Hey, girl."

"Hey, yourself," Shanell said suspiciously. "Why do you sound like you just woke up?"

"Um, because I did."

"*What*? It's after nine o'clock! Have you forgotten that Mark and I are supposed to be picking you up for the ten a.m. service?"

"No." Tamia hesitated. "Listen, girl, I'm not going to church this morning."

"Why not?"

Tamia wished she could tell Shanell the truth—that the pastor she revered was a lying, cheating, hypocritical scumbag who paid women for sex. But she'd promised to keep Honey's secret, and a promise was a promise.

So she settled for saying, "I'm just not feeling Bishop Yarbrough's ministry."

"So that's it? After attending *one* service, you're done?"

"Afraid so. But you and Mark enjoy yourselves, and I'll holla at you later."

Before Shanell could utter another word of protest, Tamia ended the call.

"Good morning."

Tamia looked across the room to find Honey standing in the open doorway with a spatula in her hand. Her hair was wrapped in a colorful satin scarf, and she wore a pink, two-piece pajama shorts set and fuzzy bedroom slippers.

"Hey, baby girl." As Tamia sat up in bed, she gave Honey a teasing look. "I hope you weren't planning to sneak in here and bludgeon me to death with that spatula."

Honey laughed, shaking her head. "I was just about to start breakfast."

Tamia raised a brow. "Can you cook?"

"Are you kidding? Girl, I can *burn* in the kitchen! My grandma taught me everything she knows."

"In that case," Tamia drawled, "maybe you'll earn your keep after all."

Honey eyed her hopefully. "Does that mean I can stay a while longer?"

"I didn't say all that." At Honey's deflated look, Tamia grumbled, "We'll see. Now go on and get breakfast started. I'm starving."

Honey grinned broadly. "Yes, ma'am. Coming right up!"

As the girl headed back to the kitchen, Tamia's thoughts turned to the dramatic events of last night. After Brandon left, two police officers had arrived to take Tamia's statement, which they would use to file charges against Dominic. As Tamia answered the officers' questions and allowed them to photograph her bruised throat for evidence, she'd felt as if she were having an out-of-body experience. Several hours later, she still couldn't believe that Dominic had shown up at her apartment in flagrant disregard of the restraining order. And then he'd had the nerve to choke and threaten her, proving that he was even crazier than she remembered.

Although she'd thoroughly enjoyed watching him get manhandled by Brandon, she knew there would be repercussions down the line. Dominic was a conniving, treacherous motherfucker who wouldn't rest until he'd taken Tamia and Brandon down with him.

Frowning at the thought, Tamia picked up her cell phone and called downstairs to the front desk. After identifying herself, she said crisply, "Correct me if I'm wrong, but aren't you supposed to call tenants when they have visitors?"

"Yes, Miss Luke," the attendant confirmed meekly. "I apologize for what happened last night. Mr. Chambers has already spoken to my manager and expressed his, ah, displeasure. As I explained to both of them, Mr. Archer told me he was here to see another tenant on the same floor—"

"Who?" Tamia demanded.

"I'm not at liberty to say," the man mumbled apologetically. "But the tenant confirmed that she was expecting Mr. Archer, so I had no choice but to let him get on the elevator. If I'd known about the restraining order, I would have personally escorted him to the apartment he was visiting. Rest assured that your safety is *very* important to us, Miss Luke. You have my word that nothing like this will ever happen again."

"I hope not," Tamia said tartly. "I've only been living

here a week, and the three visitors I've had were allowed upstairs without my clearance."

"If you're referring to Mr. Chambers, I did try to reach you last night when he arrived, but you didn't answer your phone."

Because a lunatic was holding me hostage, Tamia thought darkly.

"Since his name is on the lease," the attendant continued, "I figured you wouldn't mind if I let him up."

"Wait a minute." Tamia had gone still. "*Whose* name is on the lease?"

"Mr. Chambers. Your apartment's in his name."

Tamia was stunned. *"It is?"*

"Yes. Didn't you—" The attendant broke off as someone spoke to him in the background. After muttering a curse, he came back on the line sounding dismayed and apologetic. "I'm so sorry, Miss Luke. You weren't supposed to know that. *Christ*, I'm such an idiot."

A huge, elated grin had swept across Tamia's face. She couldn't believe it. Brandon had set her up in the luxury apartment. Not one of Lou's clients. *Brandon!*

On the other end of the phone, the distressed man was muttering anxiously, "I am *so* gonna lose my job over this."

"No, you're not," Tamia assured him. "I won't say anything to Mr. Chambers."

"You won't?"

"Nope. He obviously didn't want me to know, so we'll keep it that way."

"Are you sure?"

"Positive. Believe me," Tamia said wryly, "I'm *very* good at keeping secrets."

The man breathed a sigh of relief. "Thank you *so* much, Miss Luke. If there's *ever* anything I can do for you, please don't hesitate to let me know."

"I will."

After ending the call, Tamia sank back against her pillows with a dreamy smile on her lips. Brandon had provided a home for her. Despite the way she'd hurt and betrayed him, he'd still cared enough to ensure that she had someplace to live. And not just *any* place. One of the nicest, most expensive residences in Houston.

Mama Esther's imaginary words whispered through Tamia's mind.

Never underestimate the power of a man's love.

Chapter 24

Brandon

The sharp *click-clack* of high heels against Italian marble announced Brooke Chambers's arrival before she reached the open doorway of the den, where Brandon and Beau squared off across an antique chessboard. The two brothers had struck identical poses, an index finger to their temples, broad shoulders hunched over the board.

"Oh, good, you're both here," Brooke said briskly. "Now we can get—"

Brandon and Beau held up a finger, cutting her off midsentence.

Huffing an exasperated breath, she marched over to the table to see which player was winning.

"Your move," Brandon prompted his brother.

"I know." Beau's eyes narrowed as he scanned the board, mentally strategizing how to avoid getting checkmated.

Grinning smugly, Brandon leaned back in his chair, clasped his hands behind his head, and stretched out his long legs. "Any day now."

Beau shot him a dark glance.

Another minute passed as he silently debated his next move.

"Oh, for goodness' sake," Brooke muttered impatiently.

"Hey!" her brothers protested as she rearranged pieces on the board, sealing Beau's fate by capturing his king with Brandon's knight.

As Brandon began laughing, Beau glared at their sister. "What the hell'd you do that for? The game wasn't over!"

"Oh, please!" Brooke scoffed. "Brandon clearly had you in check. I don't have time for you to sit there prolonging the inevitable. I have a meeting to conduct."

Fresh out of church, Brooke wore a cream two-piece skirt suit that hugged her voluptuous figure and complemented her gorgeous mahogany complexion. Her makeup was flawless, and her shoulder-length black hair was perfectly flat-ironed, not a strand out of place.

Like her older brothers, she'd earned a law degree from UT. But after spending one year at a large law firm, she'd realized that she was better suited for planning social events than litigating cases. So she quit her job and became a consultant to Houston's movers and shakers, quickly establishing herself as a socialite, fund-raiser, and corporate power broker whose services were sought by everyone who was anyone.

It was only natural that Brandon, Beau, and Dre had turned to her to coordinate the agency's scholarship fund-raiser gala to benefit inner-city youth athletes. As expected, Brooke had tackled the project with her usual zeal and multitasking prowess. She'd chosen the perfect venue and caterer, scheduled guest speakers, created and distributed publicity materials, mailed out invitations, and secured an arsenal of VIP donors. And now, with the event just a month away, she'd called a meeting that afternoon to hammer out last-minute details.

Beau sauntered over to the polished bar tucked into a

corner of the expensively furnished den, one of many such rooms that composed the sprawling Mediterranean-style estate the three siblings had been raised in.

"Anyone want a drink?" Beau offered.

"Nah, I'm good," Brandon declined.

"I'll have my usual." Brooke shot a glance at her Cartier wristwatch and scowled. "And where is Dre? He told me he'd have no problem attending the meeting since the Texans have a bye this week."

Brandon chuckled, rising from the chess table to claim the oversized armchair before Beau beat him to it. "Since he has the day off, he probably decided to sleep in late."

Brooke was already whipping out her BlackBerry and speed-dialing Dre's number.

"Deondre Kendrick Portis," she enunciated in the cool, no-nonsense tone she reserved for unscrupulous vendors who attempted to overcharge her clients, "where the hell are you?" She paused, one foot tapping impatiently as she listened to his response. "If you're not here in thirty minutes, I will personally drive over there and drag your ass out of— What? You're on your way? That's what I thought."

As she snapped her phone shut, Brandon glanced over and caught the quick curl of a feminine smile that had his eyes narrowing.

Briskly clearing her throat, Brooke stepped out of her Prada pumps and lowered herself onto the antique sofa with her long legs folded beneath her. "I don't want to have to repeat things, so we'll wait until Dre gets here."

"That's cool," Brandon drawled, using the remote control to turn on the giant plasma television, "but if Mom and Dad get here before Dre, we're eating lunch first. I'm starving."

"Me too." Beau walked over and handed his sister a glass, then sprawled on the sofa beside her with his Hennessy and Coke.

After sampling her martini, Brooke divided a reproach-ful glance between her brothers. "I know I missed church last week because I was out of town, but why weren't either of you there today? Didn't we promise Dad that we'd attend service every Sunday until the election?"

"I never promised anything," Beau countered defen-sively. "I'm a sports agent, so Sundays are reserved for at-tending my clients' games. The only reason I'm not in Florida right now is that I got back from New York late yes-terday, so I needed to catch my breath."

Brooke snorted. "Give me a damn break. We all know you spent the night screwing your latest jump off, and *that's* why you couldn't get up for church this morning."

Beau grinned unabashedly. "What can I say? The woman has skills."

Brooke smirked. "You'd better hope that's *all* she has."

Beau laughed. "Don't be jealous just 'cause you ain't getting any."

"Oh, please. I'm not jealous of you and your sexca-pades. Unlike those gold-digging hoochies you mess around with, I have too much pride and self-respect to open my legs for every asshole who buys me a drink. Besides," she added with cool hauteur, "I'm Brooke Chambers. So you know damn well I can have any guy I want."

"All except one," Beau taunted, smirking into his glass before downing his drink.

Brooke blushed, darting a nervous glance toward Bran-don.

He raised a brow at her. "Is there something you wanna tell me?"

"Not at all." She tucked her hair behind one ear, a tell-tale sign that she was lying. But before Brandon could probe further, she turned the tables on him. "So what's *your* excuse for missing church today?"

He eyed her suspiciously another moment, then turned

his attention to the football game between division rivals Dallas Cowboys and New York Giants. "Not that I owe you an explanation—"

"I'm just asking," Brooke protested.

Brandon shrugged dismissively. "I just didn't feel like going today. It's been a long week."

"Well, your absence caused *quite* a stir. Cynthia and her parents cornered me after service to ask me where you were. Apparently they were suspicious because you *and* Tamia were AWOL today."

"Tamia?" Beau repeated quizzically. "Has she started going to Redeemed Life?"

"She visited last Sunday—her first Sunday outta the joint." Brooke sounded wickedly amused. "I can't believe I missed all the drama."

"Damn. So did I." Beau stared at Brandon. "What's going on, man? You hooking up with Tamia again?"

Brooke snorted. "He'd better not, unless he wants to be disinherited and disowned. I saw Mom and Dad talking to the Yarbroughs after church, and they didn't look too happy."

Beau grimaced, shaking his head at Brandon. "Are you sure you wanna be here when they get home?"

Brandon was beginning to wonder. He wasn't in the mood to hear another lecture about Tamia, especially after he'd spent a restless night battling the urge to drive back to her apartment to finish what he'd started earlier. One taste of her sweet pussy was all he'd needed to remember why he was still addicted to her.

"Poor little Cynthia," Brooke lamented with mock sympathy. "She must be ready to slit her wrists at the thought of losing you to Tamia *again*."

Beau snickered. "Can't you just see her and her ugly-ass mother getting down on their knees and praying for God to smite Tamia?"

Brooke howled with laughter.

Brandon merely shook his head at his siblings. Beau and Brooke had never made any secret of their dislike for Cynthia, whom they considered fake and manipulative. Brandon had always dismissed their concerns, insisting that they didn't know Cynthia the way he did. But lately he'd found himself questioning whether he knew her as well as he'd thought.

Beau grinned slyly at him. "So tell the truth, bruh. *Were* you with Tamia this morning?"

Before Brandon could respond, they heard the rapid approach of footsteps. Moments later their parents burst into the room, their enraged gazes locking on to Brandon with the lethal precision of a nuclear missile bent on total annihilation.

Brandon braced himself for the explosion.

"WHAT THE HELL HAS GOTTEN INTO YOU?" Bernard roared thunderously.

Brandon felt rather than saw his siblings shrink back against the sofa.

As Bernard stalked toward him, Brandon instinctively rose from the armchair, squaring his shoulders and planting his feet. He was a grown man, so he couldn't remember the last time his father had raised a hand to him. But he wanted to be prepared for anything, because right now the old man looked furious enough to rip his throat out.

"I just got off the phone with Mort Chernoff," Bernard raged, advancing on Brandon until their faces were separated by inches. "He called to tell me that Dominic Archer was arrested last night for violating a restraining order. When the police picked him up, his face looked like he'd gone ten rounds with a reincarnated Mike Tyson! He told the cops that *you* assaulted him! Is that true?"

"Yes, it is," Brandon said flatly.

Across the room, his mother gasped sharply. "My God! What on earth were you thinking?"

"Obviously he *wasn't*!" Bernard snapped, a vein throbbing at his temple as he glared at Brandon. "What the hell were you doing at that woman's apartment when you were supposed to be at a wedding with Cynthia?"

"I went to see Tamia," Brandon answered evenly, striving for composure. "When I arrived, Dominic Archer was there. She told me that he'd choked her—"

"So you decided to go Neanderthal on him?! Why the hell didn't you just have *her* call the police and press charges against him? It had nothing to do with you!"

Brandon clenched his jaw. "I beg to differ."

"You beg to differ?" his father echoed, eyeing him incredulously. "Do you have *any* idea what a public relations shitstorm you've just created for my campaign? Dominic Archer has retained an attorney, but not just *any* attorney. He hired Levi Dorsey, who only happens to be Russ Sutcliffe's nephew-in-law. Remember Russ, your arch nemesis at the firm? The man you just castrated in front of the other partners? The racist son of a bitch who's been gunning for me since I ran for lieutenant governor seven years ago? Remember him? As soon as he heard about the circumstances surrounding Dominic's arrest, he dispatched his nephew to the police station to offer his services to Dominic. Mort told me they're holding a press conference on Monday morning to announce their plans to file a lawsuit against you for assault and battery."

When Brandon showed no reaction to this news, his father shook his head in angry disbelief. "You still don't get it, do you? What do you think is going to happen when the viewing public sees Dominic Archer's battered face and hears him talk about how much he misses his beloved Isabel? When he explains how he only went to Tamia's apartment because he's seeking answers about his wife's murder, who do you think the public will sympathize with? You and Tamia? Or the grieving widower?"

"Are we talking about the same 'grieving widower' who blackmailed a woman for sex and may have killed his own wife?" Beau interjected sardonically.

His father rounded on him. *"Was I talking to you, boy?"*

A lesser man might have cowered in the face of Bernard's wrath, but Beau held his ground. "No, sir, you weren't talking to me. But come on, Dad. During the trial, Brandon did such a good job of painting Dominic as the villain that he's now the primary murder suspect. Do you honestly believe that anyone will suddenly see him as a victim just because he turns up with a black eye and sheds a few crocodile tears for the camera?"

"You have no goddamn idea what people will think! As I've learned in politics, it doesn't take much to turn the tide of public opinion against you!" Bernard spun back to Brandon, jabbing a finger in his face. "I thought I made it perfectly clear to you and your siblings that everything you do reflects upon me! *EVERYTHING!* Why the hell do you think I had such a problem with you and Beau appearing on that magazine cover looking like gangsters? By assaulting Dominic Archer, you've just given the GOP even more ammunition to portray you as a thug!"

Brandon was silent. He knew his father was right. The Republicans were going to have a field day with this story, as would the media. But even knowing that, Brandon couldn't bring himself to regret his actions. As far as he was concerned, Dominic had gotten off easy last night.

"I don't think you understand what's truly at stake here," Bernard continued, his voice vibrating with controlled fury. "Do you think this is just a game to me? Do you think I'm running for governor to satisfy some egotistical need for power?"

His piercing gaze encompassed Beau and Brooke. "I'm trying to make history by becoming the first black governor of Texas. I'm fulfilling a dream that was denied your forefathers simply because of the color of their skin. Do you *truly* understand who those men were? They were brilliant, educated, pioneering leaders who, despite their many accomplishments and contributions, were deprived of the right to hold the highest office of the state. Do you understand what it means to carry the legacy of your ancestors on your shoulders? Do you realize that what I'm doing today will impact your children, your grandchildren, your great-grandchildren, and generations of Chamberses to come? Do you understand that? *Do you?*" Bernard looked at each of his offspring in turn. "If you don't understand the importance of my candidacy, then maybe you don't deserve to bear this proud name!"

And with that scathing indictment ringing through the air, he pivoted with military precision and marched out of the room.

In the tense silence that followed his departure, Gwen Chambers glared accusingly at Brandon. "I wish to *God* you'd never met that damn woman!"

Before Brandon could respond, she turned and swept out the door with the righteous fury of a queen who'd just declared war against an enemy country.

For several moments afterward, Brandon, Beau, and Brooke stared at one another.

No one spoke.

After another minute, Dre appeared in the doorway. He took one look at the siblings' grim countenances and raised his brows. "Damn. What'd I miss?"

Chapter 25
Tamia

Later that morning, Tamia threw on some leggings, laced up her sneakers, and went jogging at nearby Discovery Green Park. While incarcerated, she'd kept herself in excellent shape by working out every day. Once she was released from prison, she'd vowed to maintain her exercise regimen—a goal made easier since she lived in a building that was equipped with a state-of-the-art fitness facility.

As she jogged along the trail, enjoying the crisp fall weather and the lush scenery that boasted a glistening lake, she came upon another runner approaching from the other direction. He was an attractive, middle-aged black man clad in a white Houston Rockets T-shirt and gray sweatpants.

When their eyes met, Tamia felt a jolt of recognition that was mirrored on the man's face.

Slowing his pace, he stared at her in surprise. "Miss Luke?"

Tamia was equally stunned. The approaching jogger was none other than Lester McCray, also known as Juror Number Eight.

What were the odds of her running into one of her jurors in a city the size of Houston, she wondered.

As they reached each other on the trail, Tamia greeted him with a friendly smile. "Hello, Mr. McCray. What a nice surprise."

"It certainly is." He gave her a discreet once-over, admiring the way her spandex leggings molded her curves. "How have you been?"

She grinned ironically. "Can't complain, especially considering that I was on trial for murder the last time you saw me."

He chuckled. "Good point."

"Speaking of the trial, I wanted to thank you and the other jurors for reaching the verdict you did."

"No thanks necessary," Lester countered graciously. "No one truly believed you were guilty of murder. Bad judgment, maybe. But not murder."

"That's good to know," Tamia told him.

Lester gestured toward the thirty-seven-story high-rise that overlooked the park. "Do you live at One Park Place?"

"No," Tamia lied, surprising herself. "I've been wanting to visit Discovery Green since the park opened years ago, so I just decided today was the day. What about you? Do you live nearby?"

"About ten minutes away."

"Oh, okay." Tamia smiled. "Well, it was nice to see—"

"Would you like to have dinner with me?"

Caught off guard, Tamia stared at him. "Excuse me?"

Lester looked sheepish. "I didn't mean to just blurt that out. And I realize that asking you on a date might be somewhat inappropriate, under the circumstances—"

"Um, probably," Tamia agreed. "You might be seen as having a conflict of interest."

Lester grimaced. "That's probably true. And the last thing I'd want to do is compromise your acquittal in any way." He sighed deeply. "I guess I just figured it wouldn't hurt to ask now that the trial is over. You're a very beautiful woman, Miss Luke. I have to admit that I've been attracted to you from the moment I saw you."

Tamia didn't bother to act surprised. "I'm very flattered," she said sincerely, "but I'm afraid I'll have to pass on dinner."

"How about drinks then? Surely there's no harm in us having a drink together?"

She shook her head regretfully. "We'd better not take any chances."

He shifted closer. "Are you sure I can't persuade you?" he persisted.

"Positive." She smiled to soften her rejection. "Maybe if we'd met under different circumstances—"

Lester chuckled wryly. "You wouldn't have looked twice at me. Not with a boyfriend like Brandon Chambers."

Tamia didn't deny it.

"Well, it was great to see you, Mr. McCray."

"You, too, Miss Luke." He smiled whimsically. "Who knows? Maybe we'll run into each other again the next time we're both at the park."

"Maybe. Enjoy the rest of your Sunday."

"Thanks. Same to you."

As Tamia turned and jogged away, she could feel his eyes boring into her. When she'd put sufficient distance between them, she hazarded a glance over her shoulder. Sure enough, he was still standing where she'd left him, watching her intently.

She felt a whisper of unease.

As she continued down the trail, some instinct told her she'd done the right thing by not letting Lester McCray know where she lived.

Chapter 26

Brandon

An hour after leaving his parents' River Oaks estate, Brandon drove to the Joe Corley Detention Facility. Before heading out there, he'd called one of his contacts at the prison to deliver a personal message to Dominic. He'd informed Dominic that he wanted to meet with him, but only if Dominic agreed not to speak to his attorney until after Brandon's visit.

Dominic had agreed.

So there they were, seated across from each other in the small, private room reserved for attorneys and their clients.

As Brandon silently assessed Dominic's black eye, bruised jaw, and busted lip, he didn't feel an ounce of shame or remorse. This should have concerned him on some basic level, but it didn't. Not even remotely.

Dominic returned his appraisal, eyes glinting with amusement. "So what's on your mind, Counselor? Or did you only come here to admire your handiwork?"

Brandon smiled narrowly. "I must admit you've never looked better, Archer."

"Think so?"

"Oh, most definitely. You were a little too pretty before." Brandon smirked. "You know how it is with you light-skinned brothas."

Dominic chuckled. "Right, right."

Brandon clasped his hands on the table, a deceptively casual gesture. "So . . ."

"So . . . ?"

"I hear you've scheduled a press conference tomorrow."

Dominic smiled. "That's what I admire about you, my man. You've always got your finger on the pulse of what's happening."

"Of course. Gotta stay ahead of the curve, you know?"

"Absolutely."

Brandon looked at Dominic, all traces of humor gone. "You know I'm gonna bury you, right?"

Dominic's smile wavered, but only for a moment. "When?" he challenged. "Before or after I take you to the cleaners?"

Brandon chuckled softly, shaking his head. "See, that's the thing I tried to explain to you last night, and really, it pains me to go there again, because I hate people who throw their wealth around. But you've given me no other choice, so let's try this one more time. You can't *take* me to the cleaners, Dominic. Between my inheritance, what I make at the law firm, and my earnings from the sports agency, my net worth is untouchable to you. Even if you were to successfully sue me for ten million dollars, you wouldn't come close to bankrupting me. And for what I did to you"—he pointed to Dominic's battered face—"no judge or jury will award you that kind of settlement. Especially not when you violated a restraining order and assaulted Tamia. And definitely not when the majority of the population thinks you murdered your wife. I'm an attorney. I know how these things work, so take my word for it."

Dominic stared at him, a muscle twitching in his jaw as he silently weighed Brandon's words.

"So here's the question you have to ask yourself," Brandon continued mildly. "Do you really want to escalate this war with me? Is it wise for you to send in more troops when I have the financial wherewithal, the connections, the means, *and* the motive to completely destroy you? Think long and hard about that before you answer."

He and Dominic stared each other down, the air between them crackling with challenge.

After several moments, Dominic leaned back in his chair and spread his hands wide. "If you're so confident that you have the upper hand, why the fuck are you here?"

Brandon met his gaze. "Because I want you to call off the press conference."

Dominic's lips hitched upward in a smile that, coupled with his black eye, made him look ghoulish. "What's wrong?" he taunted. "Afraid your violent temper might cost your father the election?"

"Let's just say I'd feel guilty for costing him even one vote."

"No doubt." Smirking, Dominic deliberately folded his arms across his chest. "Why should I cancel the press conference? What's in it for me?"

"We'll get to that in a minute. While I've got your undivided attention, there's something else I wanted to ask you." Brandon paused, his eyes narrowing on Dominic's face. "Last night you told me that I have interesting taste in women. What did you mean by that?"

Dominic eyed him blankly. "Is that what I told you?"

"Yes."

"Really? I don't remember saying that."

Brandon frowned. He didn't believe him.

"But assuming I *did* tell you that," Dominic drawled, "shouldn't it be obvious what I meant? Your ex-girlfriend is a former porn star who just stood trial for murder. If that doesn't make her *interesting*, I don't know what the hell does."

Brandon searched Dominic's face. "So you weren't talking about anyone else?"

"Like who?" Dominic smiled slowly. "Cynthia Yarbrough?"

Brandon just looked at him.

"Poor little Brandon," Dominic lamented mockingly. "Are you going to spend the rest of your life worrying that I'll get to every woman you fall in love with?"

Brandon clenched his jaw, forcing himself not to rise to the bait. If he lost his temper and went off on this motherfucker again, he'd be thrown out of there and he'd never get the answer to the question that had been nagging him for months.

"Who told you that Tamia was Mystique?"

Dominic sighed. "Ah, yes, that's the sixty-four-thousand-dollar question, isn't it? Who sold Tamia out?" He smiled slyly. "What's it worth to you?"

Brandon's eyes narrowed. "Are you trying to negotiate with me?"

"Maybe. Maybe not."

Their stares locked.

After several seconds, a slow, mischievous grin crept across Dominic's face. "Come now. If you couldn't get the answer out of me during the trial, what makes you think I'd talk now?"

Brandon slowly leaned back in his chair, feeling as if he were playing eight-dimensional chess with Hannibal Lecter.

"You still haven't watched the movies, have you?" Dominic murmured.

"What movies?"

"The *Mystique Slave Chronicles*. You still can't bring yourself to watch Tamia fucking other dudes, can you?"

Brandon didn't respond.

Dominic chuckled quietly. "You should check them out sometime. You'll gain a whole new appreciation for Tamia's amazing skills, and it might even help you get over the sense of betrayal that's been eating you alive for months." His eyes gleamed. "Or maybe not."

Brandon remained silent, refusing to give Dominic the satisfaction of knowing that he was getting under his skin.

But Dominic was determined to provoke him.

"I'm feeling generous this afternoon, so I'll let you in on a little secret." He propped his elbows on the table and leaned toward Brandon, lowering his voice as he confided, "Once when I was hitting it from the back, bruh, she called out your name."

Brandon swallowed hard. The surge of satisfaction he felt was quickly obliterated as his mind conjured images of Dominic and Tamia fucking doggy style.

"Yup," Dominic continued humorously. "Fucked me up when she did that. You know I couldn't let her get away with it, right? No, sir. Not me. So you know what I did? I wore the *hell* outta that pussy, and you'd best believe she never did that shit again."

Brandon glanced toward the closed door, wondering how much damage he could inflict on Dominic before the guard posted outside came rushing into the room.

That's when he knew it was time for him to go.

"Listen, asshole," he snarled, leaning toward Dominic. "I didn't come here to compare notes on who was better at banging Tamia. I let you get to me last night, but as much as I enjoyed fucking you up, I don't want my father's campaign to suffer behind my actions. Call off the press conference tomorrow and drop the damn lawsuit."

"Or what?" Dominic challenged.

"Don't play with me, motherfucker. I already told you I ain't the one. We're both businessmen, so I'm prepared to offer you something in return for your cooperation. But my offer's only good for a limited time. Once I walk out that door, it's on, and let the chips fall where they may."

Dominic glared balefully at him. "Tell Tamia to drop the charges against me."

"Hell, no. You disobeyed a direct order from the judge when you decided to roll up on Tamia last night, so you're gonna have to take your chances at the hearing tomorrow. If you're lucky, the judge will release you on bail and give you probation since it's your first offense. Quite frankly, I hope he locks your ass up and throws away the key. But that's just me. Name something else you want."

Dominic looked disgruntled. "I want my assets un-frozen so that I can continue sending money home to my family."

It was the first trace of humanity the man had ever shown, and it caught Brandon by surprise. "That's what you want?"

"Yeah."

"All right," Brandon said slowly. "I might be able to help you with that."

"For real?"

"For real."

"That'd be great," Dominic muttered, looking both relieved and embarrassed at having to ask Brandon for help. "My grandfather passed away last week. I hated like hell that I wasn't able to fly home and pay my respects to the man who practically raised me. Things have been really rough for my mother and grandmother, and the added funeral expenses didn't help. If there was any way for me to send them enough money to tide them over for a while, I'd appreciate it."

Brandon considered his adversary for a long moment. Dominic looked and sounded so sincere, he knew that the brotha was on the level.

"I'm sure the judge who froze your assets could be persuaded to set up an escrow account for your family," he proposed.

Dominic eyed him with grudging respect and awe. "You could really do that, couldn't you? Even though the police have me in their crosshairs, you could call in a favor and get the judge to set up that account for me."

"That's right." Brandon paused. "As long as you understand that the funds would only be available to your family, not you."

"I understand."

"Good." Brandon regarded him a moment longer, then shoved back his chair and rose from the table. "I'll be in touch."

Dominic nodded.

Brandon strode to the door and knocked, alerting the guard posted outside that his visit was over.

As the door opened, Dominic called out quietly, "Chambers."

Brandon glanced over his shoulder.

Dominic met his gaze. "It was never personal."

A cold, sardonic smile lifted the corners of Brandon's mouth. "It's *always* personal when you fuck another man's woman."

And with that, he turned and walked out.

Chapter 27

Fiona

Fiona rocked back and forth on the rickety porch swing, watching as rain fell from the night sky like glass-bead curtains. Because the inclement weather had chased her neighbors indoors like rats scurrying from light, the street was empty, and the old shotgun houses had an air of desolation.

Fiona took a deep drag on her blunt and exhaled, sending soft clouds of smoke floating toward the wet sky.

Ever since Tamia moved out, she'd been entertaining the idea of selling the house and striking out for greener pastures. God knows she made more than enough money now to afford a nicer place. Maybe she could move somewhere downtown that was close enough to Tamia to piss her off but not close enough to make Fiona seem like a stalker.

She scowled to herself. This was a free country. So there was nothing to stop her from packing up the house and moving on, just as her sister had done.

But this was the only home Fiona had ever known. Every time she pondered leaving, she was gripped by a sense of panic that immobilized her. So she wasn't going anywhere anytime soon.

Toking on her blunt, Fiona opened the old photo album she'd brought outside. On the first page were pictures of her as an adorable, chubby-cheeked baby with a head full of curly hair.

She began turning the pages, smiling nostalgically at images of herself nestled in her beautiful mother's arms, or propped up on Tamia's lap as they both beamed into the camera.

Her throat tightened painfully at a photo of Mama Esther. She was flanked by Tamia and Fiona, their small hands tucked into each of hers as they stood outside the house one Easter morning, dressed in their Sunday best.

As guilt assailed Fiona, she quickly turned the page.

When she came to a photo of her father, she froze.

Sonny Powell leaned proudly against a gleaming black Iroc-Z—a car he'd never admitted stealing, though everyone knew he had. He was a tall, good-looking man with a charming smile that seduced while masking a violent temper that made category five hurricanes look like child's play.

Fiona stared at Sonny's picture as she toked agitatedly on her blunt. The smoke that filled her mouth suddenly tasted as bitter as if she'd just inhaled ashes. She swallowed hard, then ran trembling fingers over her father's smiling image.

She'd hated and feared him.

Loved and revered him.

But she'd spent one too many afternoons sitting on the porch steps, waiting for him to show up and take her to all the exciting places he'd promised. But he never had. And with each broken promise, her love had grown dimmer and dimmer, slowly evolving into a cold, seething hatred that would eventually consume her.

Suddenly her cell phone rang, interrupting her reverie.

Swiping tears from her eyes, Fiona snatched the phone off the porch swing and answered, "Hello?"

There was no answer.

"Hello?" she repeated impatiently.

Silence.

A fine chill ran through her. Nervously she glanced up and down the dark, rain-washed street.

"Hello?" she croaked into the phone. "Is someone there?"

Still no answer.

Just as she was about to disconnect the call, a soft, eerie voice whispered, "*Guilty . . .*"

Fiona's blood ran cold.

Seconds later, the line went dead.

Chapter 28

Tamia

"To recap our top story this hour, local businessman Dominic Archer was denied bail at a hearing this morning after he was arrested for violating a restraining order filed by Tamia Luke. According to police reports and a statement issued by Assistant District Attorney Cal Hartwig, Archer went to his former mistress's home and assaulted her over the weekend. At today's bail hearing, the judge ruled that Archer poses a threat to Luke, so he will therefore be held until trial. Miss Luke, who was recently acquitted of the murder of Archer's wife, was absent from today's court proceedings and could not be reached for comment. In other news—"

Tamia cut the ignition, plunging her car into silence.

On one hand, she was glad to hear that Dominic would be spending more time behind bars. After everything he'd done to her, he deserved to get a taste of what she'd gone through.

On the other hand, she hated having her name back in the news. After the trial, she'd hoped to be forgotten by the media so that she could resume some semblance of a normal life. But thanks to Dominic's reckless behavior, she'd be dragged into another three-ring circus whereby the lurid details of their affair would be rehashed with renewed vigor.

If Tamia didn't know better, she would think that Dominic had gotten himself arrested on purpose. Because the timing of this incident couldn't have been worse. Not only had she begun making progress with Brandon, but she was scheduled to report for her new job at Chernoff, Dewitt & Strathmore today. She'd already expected to be the object of curiosity, stares, and whispers. But now, in light of Dominic's shenanigans, she might as well have a giant spotlight on her when she made her entrance.

Heaving a deep, resigned sigh, Tamia checked her reflection in the rearview mirror. Satisfied that her hair and makeup passed muster, she smoothed the creases from her gray pencil skirt and brushed stray strands of hair from her ivory blouse, then climbed out of her Honda Accord.

Armed with her leather attaché case, she strode across the underground parking garage to reach the elevator, which whisked her up to the forty-ninth floor of the building.

As she stepped off the elevator, she had a flashback to the last time she'd been there. It was the night she'd shown up unannounced to beg Brandon to take her back. But she'd never gotten the chance to make her appeal. When she'd arrived at his office, she'd found him fucking Cynthia like his life depended on it.

Shoving aside the painful memory, Tamia entered the elegant reception area paneled in rich, dark wood and gleaming marble. A middle-aged white woman wearing a phone headset sat behind the large reception desk, efficiently manning the phone lines.

When there was a lull in incoming calls, Tamia smiled at her. "Hello, Iris. How are you?"

"I'm doing jus' fine, missy," the woman responded with

a thick Southern accent that raised eyebrows even in Houston. "It's so good to see you again."

"Same to you." *So far so good*, Tamia thought. "How are your grandsons?"

Iris beamed. "Are you kidding? Those boys are as busy as ever! I'll have to show you their latest photos when you get a moment later."

"I'd like that," Tamia said warmly. "I bet they're growing up so fast."

"You know it! Anyway, hon, I was pleased as punch when Brandon told me you'd be working here. Which reminds me—" She retrieved a thick envelope from her desk and passed it to Tamia.

"What's this?"

"Some HR paperwork for you to fill out while you wait for Noemi to get out of her meeting and come fetch you."

"Okay. I know it's only nine-thirty, so I'm early." Tamia hesitated. "Is Brandon around, by any chance?"

"He's with a client. But I'll let him know you're here as soon as he's finished."

"Great. Thanks, Iris."

"Sure thing, hon."

As Iris returned to answering the phone, Tamia took a seat in the plush reception area.

No sooner had she pulled out her pen than she was joined by Cynthia, who sat down right beside her and crossed her legs, one Prada-clad foot tapping in the air.

"Since Brandon didn't have the heart to rescind his job offer," she said tightly, "I was hoping you'd have the decency to politely decline. But it's obvious that I gave you more credit than you deserve."

Tamia smiled coolly. "Hello to you, too, Cynthia. Are you the welcome committee?"

Cynthia smirked. "Very funny."

"*I* thought it was."

Cynthia glanced toward the reception desk, where Iris was pretending not to watch them as she spoke on the phone.

"Can we talk in my office for a moment?"

Tamia hesitated. "I'm waiting for Brandon's assistant."

"I'll take you to her cubicle when we're finished." Without waiting for Tamia's assent, Cynthia stood and started from the reception area.

Tamia sighed heavily. After tucking her paperwork inside her attaché case, she got up and reluctantly followed her nemesis down the corridor.

Once they reached Cynthia's small office, she closed the door and motioned to the lone visitor chair. "Have a seat."

"No, thanks," Tamia declined. "I won't be staying long."

Cynthia frowned, perching on the corner of her desk and folding her arms across her flat chest. "I think we need to have another woman-to-woman talk."

Tamia blinked innocently. "About what?"

Cynthia's eyes narrowed. "Nice try. I know what you're trying to do, Tamia. But I'm here to tell you it won't work."

"I have no idea what you're talking about."

"Don't insult my intelligence, bitch. You've been enjoying the role of damsel in distress—"

"Enjoying?" Tamia echoed in disbelief. "I spent the past five months confined to a prison cell not much smaller than this office. I was on trial for a murder I didn't commit, facing the possibility of serving a life sentence or worse. Please tell me what could *possibly* be enjoyable about what I've just described?"

"You know exactly what I'm talking about," Cynthia hissed accusingly. "You've been milking your misfortune to play on Brandon's sympathies—"

"What!"

"—and I'm sick and tired of it! Do you have *any* idea how much bullshit I've gone through for you? I could have been a total bitch when Brandon told me he planned to represent you, but I wasn't. I put aside my own personal feelings and supported his decision without ever once complaining, even though you tested my patience with your constant phone calls and needy demands. I held my tongue because I love Brandon, and I looked forward to having him to myself again once the trial was over. But I should have known you had no intention of leaving him alone!"

Tamia arched a brow. "You mean the way *you* left him alone when he was mine?"

Cynthia gave her a look of outraged innocence. "What the hell are you talking about? I *did* leave him alone! As I told you months ago, Brandon and I were just friends!"

"But you wanted to be more," Tamia shot back. "Every time I turned around you were there, hanging around him. I still remember the first night I met you. Brandon and I were supposed to be spending some time together, but when I got here, *you* were cozied up to him in his office. You'd let your hair down, kicked off your shoes, and made yourself *real* nice and comfortable. Remember that, Cynthia? Remember how you *innocently* fucked up my special evening with Brandon?"

Cynthia just looked at her, nostrils flaring.

"Yeah, you remember," Tamia jeered. "Deny it all you want, bitch, but you knew *exactly* what you were doing that night. So how does it feel now that the shoe's on the other foot? How does it feel now that Brandon's *your* man, but you find yourself feeling threatened by the other woman in his life, the one who simply refuses to go away?"

Cynthia swallowed visibly.

A slow, satisfied smile curved Tamia's lips. "It doesn't feel very good, does it? Tell me something. Have you and Brandon started arguing about me yet? Have you found yourself questioning his true feelings for you? Have you often wondered just what you have to do to make him see that you're better for him than *I* am?"

Cynthia glared at her. After several seething seconds, she pushed abruptly to her feet, stalked around her desk, and sat down hard.

"Get out," she snapped.

Tamia laughed. "Oh, *now* you want me to leave? And just when our woman-to-woman talk was getting good."

"I've said all I wanted to say to you," Cynthia spat.

"Is that right?" Tamia taunted, sauntering over to the desk. "Then allow me to offer *my* closing argument. I'm not going away, Cynthia. I love Brandon—"

"Some love!" Cynthia scoffed caustically. "You fucked another man and lied to Brandon about *everything*! If *that's* how you treat the people you love, God help everyone else!"

Tamia congratulated herself for not flinching with shame.

"You're right," she conceded humbly. "Cheating on Brandon was a terrible mistake that I will regret for the rest of my life."

Cynthia rolled her eyes. "Cry me a damn river."

Tamia frowned. "Mock me all you want. Quite frankly, I don't give a damn what you think of me. All you need to know is that I love Brandon, and if I'm lucky enough to get a second chance with him, I'm *never* letting him go."

Cynthia smirked at her. "That's so sweet, but let's keep it real, Tamia. Do you honestly believe that Brandon will ever marry you? You dated him for *nine months* before he reluctantly decided to introduce you to his parents. That should have clued you in to the fact that he's just not that serious about you. Yet you insist on clinging to the misguided notion that you could actually be the one. Why? Because you're a former porn star who knows a few tricks? Bitch, please. A guy like Brandon can get good pussy anywhere, so what else do you have to offer him?"

Tamia glared at Cynthia, wishing she could dismiss the

malicious barbs that had spewed from her mouth. But she couldn't, and they both knew it.

As Cynthia's expression grew even smugger, Tamia's gaze wandered across the desk to a framed photograph of Joseph and Coretta Yarbrough. It was one of those professional studio shots that made the couple look good enough to grace the cover of a magazine.

"Awww, isn't that sweet?" Tamia cooed mockingly. "You keep a picture of your parents on your desk."

Cynthia gave her a haughty look. "You make that sound like something to be ridiculed. I'm very blessed to have two wonderful parents who love each other so much. I hope to have what they have someday."

Tamia smiled sweetly. "I hope you do, too."

Cynthia's eyes narrowed.

At that moment, Tamia had an overwhelming urge to tell Cynthia her father's dirty little secret. The bitch would be devastated, and she'd undoubtedly confront daddy dearest to demand the truth. Once the scandal broke, Bernard Chambers would throw Bishop Yarbrough under the bus faster than President Obama had ditched Reverend Wright. And there was no way he or his wife would allow Brandon to marry Cynthia.

Which was exactly what Tamia wanted.

So what're you waiting for? an inner voice demanded. *You've been handed the perfect opportunity to eliminate your biggest rival. If the shoe were on the other foot, you know Cynthia wouldn't hesitate to use a damaging secret against you!*

But Tamia had promised not to betray Honey's trust. So no matter how tempted she was to revert to her old scheming ways, she had to honor her word. Right? *Right?*

Suddenly there was a firm knock at the door.

Before Cynthia could call out, the door opened to reveal Brandon standing there.

He looked from one woman to the other, then frowned.

"Iris told me I'd probably find you in here," he said to Tamia. "What the hell's going on?"

"Nothing," Tamia said smoothly. "Cynthia was just explaining to me how things work around here."

Brandon stared at Cynthia until her face reddened.

"Aren't you due in court this morning?" he asked softly.

"Yes." Nervously she began gathering papers on her desk. "I was just about to leave."

He regarded her another moment, then shifted his gaze to Tamia. "Come here."

She obeyed without hesitation.

When she reached him, he took her attaché case from her hand, then turned to Cynthia. "Whatever this was"—he pointed between her and Tamia—"don't let it happen again. You feel me?"

Cynthia's mouth tightened at the edges, but she nodded.

Brandon looked expectantly at Tamia.

She nodded. "I feel you."

"Good." Shooting one last warning glance at Cynthia, Brandon cupped Tamia's elbow and steered her out of the office.

As they started down the long corridor, Tamia felt compelled to defend herself. "Look, I'm not here to start any trouble—"

Brandon cut her off. "I forgot that Noemi had a doctor's appointment this morning. In case she doesn't return to the office today, she left a cheat sheet for you to review so you'll be ready to start shadowing her tomorrow."

Tamia nodded briskly. "I've been studying all weekend. I was pleasantly surprised to realize how much I remembered from my summer internships, not to mention all the legal research I did while I was awaiting trial."

"Glad to hear it. Noemi might be put on bed rest, so

there's a strong chance you'll be thrown into the fire sooner than we expected."

As Brandon guided Tamia through a labyrinth of mahogany cubicles that housed the department's administrative staff, she pretended not to notice the speculative stares and whispers that followed them. By the time they reached Noemi's cubicle, however, the drone of hushed voices seemed loud enough to rival the noise generated by a colony of bees.

Brandon obviously noticed as well. After setting Tamia's attaché case next to the spare computer that had been set up for her, he grabbed her hand and led her to the center of the nest of cubicles.

"Listen up, people," he announced.

Heat suffused Tamia's face as all eyes swung toward them. As an air of hushed expectancy swept over the area, several attorneys appeared in the doorways of offices along the corridor.

Satisfied that he had everyone's attention, Brandon took Tamia by the shoulders and positioned her in front of him. "This is Tamia. As you all know, she used to be my girlfriend, as well as one of the firm's clients. Now she's an employee. If anyone has a problem with that"—he deliberately glanced around the room—"come see me. Otherwise, please let her work in peace. Are we clear?"

There were nods and murmurs of agreement sprinkled with a few deferential "Yes, sir"s.

As Tamia and Brandon walked back to his assistant's cubicle, Tamia muttered under her breath, "I really wish you hadn't done that. Now everyone's gonna hate me."

Brandon chuckled softly. "No, they won't. But if they do, you can take comfort in that old saying."

"What old saying?"

" 'You're nobody until somebody hates you.' "

Chapter 29

Tamia

Tamia spent the rest of the day immersed in legal research for one of Brandon's new cases. Following the instructions provided by his assistant—who'd gone home after her doctor's appointment—Tamia pored through countless online articles, annotated statutes, and legal encyclopedias to identify all relevant case law that would help Brandon prepare his defense strategy. After retrieving as many supporting documents as she could, she organized and indexed the materials for the database, then took a stab at drafting a report.

She was so absorbed in her work that she lost track of time. One hour melted into another until she glanced out the window and saw that nightfall had arrived.

"You do realize that you're only supposed to be part-time," a deep voice murmured in her ear.

Tamia jumped, head snapping to the right.

Brandon was leaning over her shoulder, an amused expression on his face.

Tamia threw a hand over her racing heart. "You scared the hell out of me!"

He chuckled softly. "Sorry. I thought you would have heard me coming. In case you haven't noticed, it's a ghost town around here."

"No, I hadn't noticed."

"Obviously."

Tamia smiled into his eyes, enjoying his nearness. His lips were a breath away from hers, tempting her with their sensual fullness.

"Do you know how late it is?"

She shook her head, unwilling to break eye contact with him to check the time. "How late is it?"

"After seven."

She smiled playfully. "Wasn't that the name of an old nineties group?"

Brandon's eyes glimmered with amusement. "What you know about the nineties, little girl? Weren't you still in diapers?"

"I was not!" she sputtered indignantly. "For your information, I was born in 1982. But I can understand how you've forgotten that detail, seeing as to how your memory's starting to fail you."

"Now there you go with the old man jokes."

She grinned. "Hey, you started it, pops."

Brandon chuckled, tucking a strand of her hair behind one ear.

Tamia stared at him.

He stared back.

Seconds passed.

Disappointment swept over her when he pulled away to lean against the desk, thrusting his hands into the pockets of his suit pants as if he wanted to keep himself from touching her again.

Tamia smiled at the thought. "Are you just now getting back to the office from your meetings?"

"Yeah. And I didn't expect to find you still here. Didn't

we agree that your hours would be ten to four until Noemi goes on leave?"

"Yes, but I got busy and lost track of time."

He glanced at the stack of books on her desk, then nodded toward her computer screen. "What're you working on?"

She hesitated. "A report."

"Really? Can I take a look?"

"Not yet. It isn't finished."

"That's okay. I just want to see if you're on the right—"

"No, don't look!" Tamia protested, moving quickly to block his view of the computer screen. "Let me finish the report first, then I'll give it to you. Okay?"

Brandon chuckled. "So this is how it's gonna be, huh?"

Tamia grinned sheepishly. "Just until I feel more confident about my work."

"Fair enough." Brandon straightened from the desk. "It's late. You should start heading home."

"Not yet. I want to add more to the report while things are still fresh in my mind. I can't get over how much case law data are out there. Just on the Internet alone, the sheer volume of information is staggering."

Brandon smiled, squeezing her shoulder. "Welcome to my world."

Tamia wanted desperately to take his warm hand and hold it against her cheek, then lower it to her breast. But before she could act on the urge, her cell phone rang.

"I'll be in my office," Brandon told her. "Don't leave without saying bye."

"I won't." Tamia picked up her phone and checked the caller ID, frowning at the unfamiliar number. She considered letting the call go to voice mail, but her curiosity got the best of her.

"Hello?" she answered cautiously, thinking of the crank call she'd received over a week ago.

"Tamia?"

"Yes."

"Hey, this is Mark's friend, Gavin."

"Oh, hey, Gavin," Tamia said warmly.

"I hope you don't mind that Shanell gave me your new number."

"Not at all." Tamia glanced up as Brandon returned to the cubicle, arms folded across his chest. Smothering an amused grin, she leaned back in her chair and leisurely crossed one leg over the other, watching as Brandon's eyes tracked the movement. "So how's it going, Gavin?"

"It's going okay," he responded. "Still getting adjusted to being back home after a year in Afghanistan."

I know the feeling, Tamia thought grimly. Crazy as it sounded, she would have preferred dodging gunfire in a war zone to spending even *one* day behind bars.

"I'm sure your family is glad to have you back safe and sound," she told Gavin.

"Oh, absolutely. They haven't stopped blowing up my phone and coming over to bring me food." Gavin chuckled. "Speaking of food, I was calling to see if you've already had dinner."

"Dinner?" Tamia echoed.

Brandon cocked a brow at her.

"Yeah. Dinner. I know it's kinda late, but I just got home from work, and I really don't feel like dining alone tonight. So I thought I'd just take a chance and see if you've already eaten."

"Um, no, actually, I'm still at work. But—"

Without warning Brandon took the phone out of Tamia's hand. Before she could stop him, he told Gavin, "Wassup, man. This is Tamia's boss. I need her to stay and finish what she's working on, so she'll catch up with you another time."

Tamia eyed him incredulously as he ended the call and

stuffed her phone into his pocket. "I can't believe you just did that!"

"What?"

"*What?* Brandon, that was so rude and uncalled for!"

"Didn't you tell me that you're not interested in that dude?" he challenged.

"Yes, but that's not the point. You shouldn't have—Hey! Where are you going?" she sputtered protestingly as Brandon turned and sauntered out of the cubicle.

Huffing an exasperated breath, she jumped up and hurried after him. "Can I at least have my phone back?"

"I'm in the mood for Thai," he announced, tugging his tie loose as he headed down the corridor. He glanced over his shoulder at her. "You want some Thai?"

"Negro, you have lost your damn mind."

He chuckled. "I'll take that as a *yes.*"

At the end of the corridor, he strode through an open doorway.

Tamia followed him, her eyes widening as they swept over the plush corner office that featured an enormous mahogany desk, a dark leather sofa, gilt-framed oil paintings, and a wall of windows that overlooked the downtown skyline.

"Dayum," she whispered appreciatively. "Talk about movin' on up."

Brandon sent her a lazy smile as he crossed to the desk, picked up the phone, and speed-dialed the Thai restaurant.

"The usual?" he asked Tamia.

"Yes, please."

As he ordered their food, she wandered to the windows and stared out at the glittering skyline, remembering the night she and Brandon had talked on the phone while enjoying the views from where they stood—she on her balcony, he at the office.

"Fifteen minutes," he told her, hanging up the phone.

"Great." Tamia looked over her shoulder, watching as he shed his suit jacket and tie, undid the top three buttons of his shirt, unfastened his cuff links, and rolled up his sleeves.

Her mouth watered. She'd always loved his sexy after-hours look, and tonight was no exception.

Glancing up, Brandon met her gaze. "Are you hungry?"

Damn, am I drooling?

"Yeah," she said slowly, tempted to check the corners of her mouth for saliva. "Why?"

"Because I'm guessing you worked through lunch."

She grinned sheepishly. "Yes, but I ate. Iris brought me a turkey wrap from the café downstairs. Wasn't that sweet of her?"

"Very," Brandon agreed. "But I'm not surprised. Iris is good people."

"Most definitely." Tamia walked over to the leather sofa and sat down. "This office is amazing, Brandon. Partnership certainly has its privileges."

"You could say that. Would you like a drink?"

"Oh, my God. You even have a wet bar?"

"Yup," Brandon said with a chuckle as he sauntered to the private bar in question. "The firm's founding partners are throwbacks to the old days when you offered clients a stiff drink and a cigar before starting any meeting. So what'll you have, pretty lady?"

Tamia smiled, thoroughly charmed. "How about a glass of white wine?"

"Your wish is my command."

If only!

Settling more comfortably against the sumptuous leather sofa, Tamia watched as Brandon poured her wine and fixed himself a neat scotch. As he walked over to her, they stared at each other, the air between them pulsing with sexual energy.

By the time he handed Tamia her drink and sat down beside her, her nipples were so hard they burned.

"A toast," Brandon murmured, raising his glass to her. "To your first day on the job."

Tamia smiled. "I'll toast to that."

They clinked glasses and sipped their drinks, staring at each other.

"Thanks again for giving me this opportunity," Tamia said softly.

"You're welcome."

"I know Cynthia didn't approve, so I appreciate your willingness to put your neck on the line for me."

Brandon's lips twitched. "It's all good."

Tamia sipped more wine, then couldn't resist asking, "Where is she anyway? I'm surprised she's not working late."

"Actually, she is. She's having dinner with a new client."

Tamia nodded slowly. "No wonder she's not here." *Keeping a close eye on you*, she added silently.

As Brandon drank his scotch, she continued thoughtfully, "You know, now that I think about it, I'm surprised that this place is so deserted tonight. I remember when we were dating, there were *always* other attorneys around, working well past ten o'clock."

Brandon nodded. "It's still like that. But people typically cut out earlier on Monday nights. And don't forget Thanksgiving's right around the corner."

"Ah." Tamia nodded. "So even lawyers are susceptible to the holiday productivity slump."

Brandon chuckled. "Of course. We're human."

"Hmm, the jury's still out on that."

They shared a quiet laugh.

After staring into his glass for a long moment, Brandon asked suddenly, "Why weren't you at church yesterday?"

Caught off guard by the question, Tamia floundered for an answer before settling on the truth—or as close to the truth as she was allowed. "Well, like I told Shanell yesterday, I'm really not feeling Redeemed Life Ministries."

"Really? Why not?"

"Honestly? I'm not a fan of megachurches. They seem so impersonal and over the top to me, more like a theatrical production than a worship service."

Brandon chuckled. "Can't argue with that."

Tamia smiled faintly. "When I was growing up, the church I attended with my grandmother was a small community church where everyone knew one another, and it wasn't uncommon to be invited to the pastor's house for Sunday dinner."

Brandon nodded. "That sounds like the church I grew up in."

"Really?"

"Yeah."

"So what happened? Why don't you go there anymore?"

He shrugged. "Once my siblings and I left home for college, attending church wasn't a priority for us. And once my father launched his political career, he and my mom decided to join a larger church that had more visibility in the community."

"Of course," Tamia drawled. "Belonging to Bishop Yarbrough's megaministry is advantageous for any black politician seeking higher office."

Hearing the cynicism in her voice, Brandon grimaced. "I wish I could say my father wasn't motivated by political expediency, but I can't. Everything he does nowadays is a calculated strategic move to strengthen his candidacy." Brandon shrugged. "It is what it is."

"That's true." Tamia took a long sip of her wine. "But your father should be careful who he aligns himself with."

Shit! she thought. *Did I just say that out loud?*

"What do you mean?" Brandon asked her.

She swallowed hard. "I mean, um, he needs to make sure he doesn't align himself with anyone who could, um, compromise his campaign."

"Of course. Believe me, he knows that. It's all he's been lecturing us about since he announced his decision to run for governor. 'Don't do anything to make me look bad,' is his new mantra," Brandon said sardonically before downing more scotch.

Tamia was silent.

Lowering his glass, Brandon eyed her speculatively. "Anyway, were you speaking in general terms just now? Or did you have something specific in mind . . . ?"

Tamia stared at him, wishing she could tell him what she knew about Bishop Yarbrough. But Honey would never forgive her for revealing her secret. And after the way Bernard Chambers had rejected Tamia, he didn't deserve to be warned that his most important campaign surrogate was a scandal waiting to happen.

She smiled brightly at Brandon. "Of course I was only speaking in general terms. Any politician running for office needs to watch who they associate with."

Brandon studied her in that quiet, probing manner that always made her want to squirm. "Are you keeping something from me?"

"No," she said quickly.

One corner of his mouth lifted wryly. "Just like you're not keeping anything from me pertaining to you and your sister, right?"

Caught off guard, Tamia stammered, "W-What're you talking about?"

"I'm talking about your rift with Fiona—the mysterious argument you guys had that's kept you apart for the past several months. Just because I haven't brought it up in a while doesn't mean I no longer have questions."

Pulse thudding, Tamia could only stare at him.

He stared back.

Mercifully his desk phone rang at that moment.

While he went downstairs to meet the deliveryman, Tamia cleared space on the mahogany worktable, wishing she could improvise with a linen tablecloth, Wedgwood china dinner plates, and candles.

Brandon returned and closed the door behind him, then helped her set out the fragrant food on the table. They sat beside each other so they could share the generous portions of pad Thai, curry chicken, and spicy basil fried rice.

It felt so natural for them to be eating together that Tamia almost forgot about the past five months. When she fed Brandon a bite of chicken, watching as his succulent lips closed around her chopsticks, her throbbing pussy didn't care that he now belonged to another woman. As long as he was there with her, and not Cynthia, she would enjoy every last moment of their time together.

"Something else we never did when we were dating," she murmured.

Brandon met her gaze. "What?"

"Have dinner in your office."

When he said nothing, Tamia smiled ruefully. "You were always worried that the partners would think you were slacking if they walked in on us eating dinner together."

Nodding slowly, Brandon deftly twirled a few noodles around his chopsticks and brought them to her lips. She stared into his eyes as she opened her mouth, accepting the morsel of food.

"It seems," he murmured, gazing at her lips as she chewed, "that I deprived you of a lot of things. I'm sorry for that."

"You don't have to be sorry," Tamia whispered. "You were working toward an important goal. Sacrifices had to be made."

"True . . . but at what cost?"

Tamia was silent. It was the closest he'd ever come to acknowledging that he may have played a role in the disintegration of their relationship.

His soulful eyes lifted to hers. "I never meant to neglect you, or make you feel like you weren't good enough for me. I hope you know that."

Tamia searched his face, trying to quell her doubts even as Cynthia's malicious taunts echoed through her mind. *You dated him for nine months before he reluctantly decided to introduce you to his parents. That should have clued you in to the fact that he's just not that serious about you.*

Tamia shook her head, biting her lower lip. "I don't know, Brandon . . ."

"You don't know?"

"No." She swallowed tightly. "I don't."

His eyes flashed with sudden anger.

"Know this," he growled, swiveling her chair around to face him. "Despite everything that went down between us, I can't stop thinking about you. Even when I'm with *her*, I wanna be with you. Know this—"

"Brandon—"

"—the next time you even *think* about messing with another nigga, I'm going to jail for double homicide."

Tamia gasped. *"Brandon!"*

He cupped her face between his hands. "What you did to me was fucked up beyond belief, but I'm man enough to accept some responsibility for what happened between us. I took you for granted, and I behaved in ways that made you question my feelings for you. If I had to do it all over again, I'd do things a helluva lot differently. And I'll tell you something else, something I didn't even realize until a few days ago. Since we never had a picnic or made love in my old office like you always wanted to, I've been secretly saving this office for you."

Stunned, Tamia stared at him, afraid to believe what he was telling her. "You mean you and Cynthia never—"

"No." He shook his head once. "We haven't."

Tears welled in Tamia's eyes. "Baby—"

Before she could say another word, Brandon leaned forward and crushed his mouth to hers.

Chapter 30

Tamia

The moment he kissed her, Tamia forgot about the past and surrendered herself to the here and now.

Grinding his mouth against hers, Brandon reached beneath her skirt and seized her lace thong, dragging it off her legs and over her stiletto heels. He swept their plates of food aside, then lifted her onto the table and roughly shoved her thighs apart.

Tamia watched, heart pounding furiously, as he knelt between her legs and lowered his head to her pussy. She cried out as he licked her clit, then sucked the plump folds of her labia into his mouth.

"Brandon," she moaned helplessly, falling back against the table and wrapping her legs around his neck. "Ummm . . . baby . . ."

"Damn," he whispered gutturally as he slid two fingers inside her succulent wetness. "Missed the *hell* outta this pussy."

Tamia groaned as he fucked her with his fingers and his mouth. His tongue was a maestro, masterfully conducting a symphony that had her body writhing to the rhythm, her voice soaring to an operatic crescendo as she exploded in ecstasy.

She was still trembling uncontrollably as Brandon stood and hurriedly unbuckled his pants. One look at his long, thick dick, and her pussy started pumping all over again.

She pulled herself up, then reached out and curled her fingers around his hot, heavy shaft. He groaned as she stroked him, a sensual caress that seduced pearly beads of precum from the swollen tip.

Hungrily licking her lips, Tamia whispered, "I missed the *hell* outta this dick."

"Then let's get to it," Brandon growled, lifting her off the table.

She wrapped her legs around his waist as he carried her over to the sofa and sat down with her straddling him. She pushed to her knees, shivering as the blunt head of his dick nudged her creamy gates. She provocatively rubbed against him, making both of them shudder with arousal.

"I've been dreaming about this moment for so long," she confessed against his mouth.

"Me, too." Brandon kissed her, his tongue delving inside to tangle erotically with hers.

Tamia moaned, curving her arms around his neck as he shoved her skirt up to her hips and cupped her ass cheeks. They kissed deeply and feverishly before their mouths parted on a string of saliva.

As their eyes locked, Brandon lowered her onto his rock-hard erection. Tamia threw back her head, her hoarse scream blending with his savage groan as her pussy stretched to absorb his ten inches. As the curved tip connected with her G-spot, a wave of spasms tore through her body.

"Don't come yet," Brandon commanded, quickly lifting her off his shaft.

"I'm trying not to," she whimpered, "but I can't help it. You feel *sooo* fucking good."

"So do y—*Ah, fuck!*" he shouted as she impaled herself again, too horny and desperate to exercise any restraint. She bent her knees and planted her feet on the sofa, spreading her pussy lips wide as she rocked on his dick, making him groan.

As he began thrusting into her, she clung to his shoulders, her fingernails digging into the corded muscles beneath his shirt. She cried out as he slapped her butt cheek, the sound echoing sharply around the room. He struck the other side, making her flesh jiggle the way he loved.

She smiled into his glittering eyes. "You missed this juicy booty?"

"Fuck, yeah," he growled, slapping both cheeks so hard she nearly came.

Her erect nipples protruded through her silk blouse, twin beacons that lured Brandon to latch on and suck. She moaned, shivering at the wet heat of his mouth, the gentle scrape of his teeth.

As he pulled away she looked downward, watching as his dark cock pumped in and out of her. The pleasure was so raw and intense, she swore she'd start speaking in tongues at any moment.

Knowing she wouldn't last much longer, she picked up the pace, making her ass clap as she bounced up and down on his dick, riding him like their lives depended on it.

"Shit, woman," Brandon panted, sweat glistening on his forehead as he squeezed her flexing butt. "You tryna kill a brotha."

Tamia grinned wickedly. "I told you I was gon' wear your ass out with this starvin' pussy."

"Damn. You sure did."

Her throaty laughter dissolved into a groan as he quickened the tempo, pummeling her pussy so fast and hard she thought she was riding a bucking bronco at the Houston rodeo.

"Fuck, baby," she screamed hoarsely. "I'm coming!"

"Me, too!"

They erupted together, shouting each other's names as their bodies shuddered and convulsed violently.

Pulling out of Tamia, Brandon grabbed his dick and ejaculated all over her smooth-shaven mound. She purred with pleasure as he smeared his hot cum into her skin, lubricating her swollen pussy lips. Then, watching her face, he slid his wet fingers into her mouth, smiling as she sucked them dry.

She returned his satisfied smile, then tenderly kissed his damp forehead, his closed eyelids, and the strong bridge of his nose before stopping at his soft lips.

As she licked at his mouth, she slowly began unbuttoning his shirt. "Good thing you closed the door before we ate."

"Mmm." Brandon sucked her bottom lip. "Locked it, too."

Tamia chuckled. "Such premeditation."

He laughed softly.

She removed his shirt and tugged off his wifebeater, humming appreciatively as she beheld his hard, powerful chest. He quivered as she traced his ripped muscles with her fingers, then her tongue.

After torturing him for several moments, she climbed off his lap and stood before him. Holding his hungry gaze, she slowly unbuttoned her blouse and unzipped her skirt, letting both garments fall to the floor.

By the time she unhooked her bra and cupped her luscious breasts, Brandon's dick was standing at attention. When she pushed her tits together, raised them to her mouth, and flicked her tongue over her distended nipples, Brandon lunged from the sofa.

Laughing naughtily, Tamia backed away, evading his grasp as he reached for her.

He scowled. "Oh, so now you playin' with me."

"Umm-hmm," she teased, watching as he impatiently shed his pants, shoes, and socks. His buff, dark chocolate body was so damn sexy it was all she could do not to pounce on his fine ass.

As he started purposefully toward her, she murmured, "You owe me a cigar."

He paused. "A what?"

"A cigar." She arched a brow. "Didn't you tell me that your bosses never start a meeting without offering their clients a stiff drink and a cigar?"

Brandon's lips quirked. "Is that what we're having, Tamia? A meeting?"

"Of sorts."

His eyes roamed over her voluptuous body clothed in nothing more than her Christian Louboutin stilettos. He closed his eyes for a moment, nostrils flaring as he muttered darkly, "I swear you're gonna be the death of me one day, woman."

Grinning coquettishly, Tamia sashayed over to his desk and sat down in the leather executive chair that felt more like a throne. As Brandon watched, she propped her feet up on the desk and seductively crossed her legs at the ankles.

He stared at her, looking awestruck.

"Damn," he breathed. "You are *so* fucking beautiful."

Tamia smiled demurely as her clit hardened.

"Hold up. I have to capture this moment." Brandon grabbed his cell phone off the desk and held it up. Tamia winked and blew him a sensual kiss as he snapped off a few shots, shaking his head. "Sexy ass."

Her smile widened. "You'd better make sure those don't fall into the wrong hands," she warned teasingly.

"Hell, no," he growled, admiring the photos he'd just taken. "These are for my eyes only."

Setting down the phone, he rounded the desk and knelt beside her, slowly running his hand over her smooth legs. She moaned as the heat of his touch made her pussy cream.

"Where's my cigar, baby?" she purred.

He blinked at her. "Your what?"

"My stogie. I'm still waiting for it."

Brandon chuckled and shook his head before opening the bottom desk drawer and removing a hand-carved, camel bone chest that was filled with twenty premium Gurkha Black Dragon Cuban cigars—the most expensive brand in the world.

As Brandon retrieved one of the hand-rolled stogies, Tamia stared at him. "You're giving me one of your Black Dragons?" she breathed, knowing that the rest of his coveted collection was under lock and key at his condo.

"Isn't this what you've been asking for?" he drawled softly.

She shook her head. "Not one of those."

"Why?" He paused, searching her face. "You don't think you deserve the best?"

Tamia swallowed hard, wondering if they were still talking about cigars or something else entirely.

"Tamia."

"What?"

"I asked you a question."

Suddenly uncomfortable beneath his intent gaze, Tamia straightened in the chair and tucked her disheveled hair behind one ear. "Just forget it."

"Nah, let's not forget it." Setting the cigar down on the desk, Brandon planted his hands on either side of the chair and leaned close to her, his dark eyes boring into hers. "You got me fucked up right now, baby."

"What do you mean?" she mumbled.

"I was your man. It was my job to show you just ho... precious you are, how truly special. But it's obvious that I failed to do that."

"You didn't," she interjected, cupping his face between her hands. "It wasn't your fault I was ashamed of who I was and where I came from. That was on *me*, boo. Not you."

Brandon kissed her so tenderly that tears stung her closed eyelids. "If I never told you before, sweetheart, I'm telling you now. You deserve the best. And from now on, I'm gonna make damn sure that's exactly what you receive."

"Oh, baby." Tamia wrapped her arms around his neck, and they hugged long and hard.

After a while, she pulled away and dabbed at the corners of her eyes, embarrassed that she'd gotten so emotional. "Okay," she sniffled. "I'll take your Black Dragon."

Brandon grinned suggestively, stroking his dark shaft. "Thought you'd never ask."

Tamia let out a peal of laughter. "Excuse me, but I meant the cigar."

"Oh, so you don't want this?"

"Ummm . . ." Her pussy throbbed as she watched his thick cock swell in his hand, veins bulging. "That depends."

Brandon looked affronted. "On what?"

She grinned. "On whether I can have my stogie first."

"You still want it?"

"Yes, I still want it."

"All right." Brandon picked up the finely wrapped cig... and passed it under his nose, savoring the distinctiv... ...ly "Ahhh, nothing like a good Cuban. I can think ... other thing that would make it even better."

"What?"

Eyes glinting wickedly, Brandon took ...legs fro... ...shoulders. the desk, one at a time, and draped them ...

Her pulse raced.

Holding her gaze, Brandon eased the fat cigar between her pussy lips.

Tamia gasped as a rush of heat filled her belly.

"Mmm." Brandon's deep voice rumbled through her. "A honey-dipped cigar. Now *that's* what I'm talking about."

Tamia moaned as he slowly twisted the stogie inside her, sending delicious shivers up and down her spine. "This wasn't quite . . . what I had in mind . . . when I asked for— *Ohhh*—" She broke off with another moan as Brandon pushed the cigar deeper.

"You asked for it," he murmured, bending to suck one of her erect nipples, "so I'm giving you what you wanted."

As he began fucking her with the stogie, Tamia groaned and closed her eyes, her fingers gripping the padded arms of the chair.

By the time he removed the cigar, swept his desk clear, and lifted her onto it, Tamia was more than eager to feel the hot, velvety steel of *his* black dragon pounding her insides.

As he spread her legs apart, she wrapped them around his waist and crossed her ankles at the small of his muscular back.

And then he was inside her, thrusting so deep her spine contracted.

She screamed with pleasure, her back arching off the desk.

Brandon shuddered against her. "Damn, this pussy is tight," he groaned as he began pumping into her with long, penetrating strokes.

As Tamia rocked against his pelvis, she thought of the many months she'd fantasized about showing up unexpectedly at his office and having sex with him. This night had definitely been worth the wait.

She moaned and shouted encouragements to him as he fucked her with thrusts powerful enough to rock the humongous desk. Sweat coated her chest and poured from his brow as his taut stomach slapped against hers, the sound filling the room. She dug her fingernails into his round butt, feeling the muscles flex in and out as he ruthlessly pummeled her pussy.

"Ohhh shit, baby," she moaned as her stilettos clattered to the floor. "This shit is *sooo* fucking good."

Leaning down, Brandon licked at her parted lips. "Daddy doin' work?"

"Hell, yeah! Daddy puttin' it *down*!"

He gave a rough, sexy chuckle that curled her toes. "That's what's up."

She writhed with ecstasy as he cupped her bouncing breasts and rubbed her aching nipples before lifting her off the desk. As he held her in the air and pounded into her, she screamed, *"Fuck, I can feel you in my stomach!"*

Moments later she came, her body wracked with explosive tremors as she sobbed Brandon's name, her nails raking down his back. He followed within seconds, head thrown back, muscles quivering, hands tightly gripping her ass as he shot his load inside her.

They didn't take very long to regroup.

After another frenzied coupling on the huge desk, they moved to the wall, the worktable, and then the floor, sixty-nining each other into another mind-blowing orgasm. They fucked with the insatiable urgency of two lovers who had a lot of lost time to make up for, though they understood that the future remained uncertain.

Before the night was over, they'd christened every corner of the office before collapsing together on the sofa, where they'd started.

Savoring the heat of Brandon's sweaty body spooning hers, Tamia blew out a deep, exhausted breath and groaned softly. "I can't feel my legs."

Brandon chuckled, his warm breath fanning the back of her neck. "Legs? What are those?"

They both laughed.

After a while, Tamia looked over her shoulder and whispered, "I love you, Brandon."

He grew silent, his eyes searching hers.

Several seconds passed.

Just when she began to despair that he wasn't going to reciprocate the sentiment, his expression softened.

"I love you, too, Tamia," he whispered huskily. "I never stopped."

Chapter 31

Brandon

The next afternoon, Brandon and Dre met for drinks and a late lunch at Stogie's.

Seated across from each other at their favorite corner booth, the two friends were uncharacteristically silent as they ate, both preoccupied with their own private thoughts.

Brandon's humidor sat untouched beside him on the table. After what he'd done to Tamia last night, he knew it'd be a *long* time before he could look at another cigar without springing an erection.

Giving himself a hard mental shake, he grabbed his bottle of beer and took a deep swallow, watching as Dre poked disinterestedly at his steak with his fork.

Brandon frowned, setting down his drink. "What's up with you?"

Dre glanced up from his plate. "What do you mean?"

"Any other time, you would have inhaled that steak as soon as the plate hit the table. Now you're picking at it. So what's wrong?"

"Nothing. I just have a lot on my mind."

"Such as?"

Dre didn't respond.

Brandon angled his head to get a better look at his best friend's downcast eyes. "You know I'm about to put you on the stand, so you might as well just come clean."

Dre scowled. "Damn lawyers."

Brandon laughed. "Out with it."

Setting down his fork, Dre scrubbed his hands over his face and blew out a deep, ragged breath. "I fucked up, man. Fucked up *big-time*."

"Damn, bruh. What'd you do?"

"Not *what*," Dre countered sardonically. *"Who."*

Brandon went still, staring at him. "You'd better not tell me you slept with Brooke."

Dre frowned in confusion. *"Who?"*

"My sister," Brandon growled. "Unless you got a death wish, nigga, you'd better not tell me you're messing around with Brooke."

"Hell, no! Damn, B, where the hell'd you get a crazy idea like that? Brooke's like a little sister to me!"

Brandon nodded slowly. "Just making sure."

Dre shook his head, disgruntled. "I can't believe you just asked me some shit like that. You be trippin', man. Straight up. Have I ever given you any reason to think I'd push up on your sister?"

"No, and you'd better keep it that way." Brandon took a swig of beer. "So who were you talking about? Who did you fuck up with?"

Dre pushed out a long, deep breath and blurted, "I had sex with Fiona."

"What?" Brandon exclaimed. "Aw, hell, nah! Are you kidding me?"

Dre made a pained face. "I wish I was."

Glancing quickly around the restaurant, Brandon leaned

across the table and whispered sharply, "I thought I told you to leave that girl alone."

"I know," Dre said grimly. "Trust and believe, I had no intention of going anywhere *near* her."

"So what the fuck happened?"

"I don't know, man." Dre looked genuinely bewildered. "One minute we were arguing, the next minute I had her up on the printer."

"The *printer*?"

"Yeah." Dre grimaced, passing a trembling hand over his head. "We were in the copy room at the office—"

"What?" Brandon eyed Dre incredulously. "Where was everyone else?"

"Gone. It was Saturday night."

Brandon gaped at Dre another moment, then downed more beer, stunned by his friend's confession.

"It was crazy," Dre continued. "I don't know what the hell I was thinking. I mean, *you* know how much I hate Fiona's fucking ass."

Brandon smirked. "Guess there's a thin line between lust and hate."

"You ain't lying." Dre shook his head at Brandon, eyes wide with dazed wonder. "Just between you and me, bruh, I ain't never—I mean, *ever*—had no pussy like that before. Shorty almost had me getting down on one knee and proposing, that shit was so fucking tight. *Dayuuummm!*" he exclaimed before stuffing his fist into his mouth.

Brandon couldn't help laughing. "Damn, nigga, you sound straight-up whipped."

"Man." Dre shuddered, rubbing his hands over his face.

Brandon forked up a bite of steak and chewed slowly, eyeing his friend across the table. "You know you gotta leave her alone, right?"

"Yeah, yeah. I know." But Dre didn't sound too convinced.

Brandon frowned at him. "Seriously, man. You and Leah have been together almost four years. If she finds out about this, she'll be devastated."

"I know," Dre mumbled, his expression clouding with guilt and shame. "Believe me, the last thing I wanna do is hurt her. Ever since that night, I've been trying to tell myself that I wouldn't have fucked Fiona if Leah hadn't been holding out on me for so long. But I know that's just a cop-out. The bottom line is that there's absolutely *no* justification for cheating."

"That's right," Brandon agreed, even as guilt gnawed at his insides at the memory of what he and Tamia had done last night. Although he'd asked Cynthia for some breathing room, they were still a couple. So, technically, he'd just cheated on her.

Who're you kidding? his conscience mocked. *You've been cheating on her since Tamia got out of prison.*

Brandon frowned. Although he felt guilty for betraying Cynthia, he couldn't bring himself to regret making love to Tamia. What they'd shared last night . . . mere words couldn't begin to describe just how phenomenal the experience had been. His mind was *still* blown.

"I owe you an apology, bruh."

Pulled out of his reverie, Brandon shot Dre a surprised look. *"Me?"*

"Yeah." Dre hesitated, fidgeting with his beer bottle. "Last time we were here, I gave you a hard time about renting the apartment for Tamia and letting her back into your life, and I lectured you about being unfair to Cynthia. But you and Tamia have history, so while I might not approve of everything you've done for her, I know it can't be easy to get over someone you loved that much."

"You're right," Brandon agreed quietly. "It's *not* easy. Not by a long shot."

Dre nodded understandingly.

After several seconds, he cleared his throat and added sheepishly, "Not to go there, but as you recall, I've seen the Mystique videos—"

Brandon's eyes narrowed dangerously.

"—so I already know Tamia ain't no joke. But if her pussy's even *half* as good as her sister's, it's no wonder you can't get enough of her. *Ooo-wee!*"

Brandon laughed, shaking his head. "You a damn fool, you know that?"

"Just keeping it real, my man." Grinning wickedly, Dre raised his beer in a toast. "To the sisters."

Brandon hesitated for a long moment, then clinked his bottle against Dre's. "To the sisters. And may God help *both* of us."

When Brandon returned to the office later that afternoon, he forced himself not to make a beeline to the cubicle that his assistant now shared with Tamia. Even though he'd been out all day and was dying to see her again—to see her smile and hear her voice, to talk and laugh with her, to check out what sexy shoes she was wearing—he had to remember that he was her boss and this was a place of business. So he had to play it calm and cool, and not act like a sprung schoolboy who'd just gotten his first taste of pussy.

And, of course, there was the matter of Cynthia to contend with.

Even before Brandon and Tamia hooked up last night, he'd known that his relationship with Cynthia was in trouble, maybe even doomed. But he'd been willing to try to make things work because he genuinely cared about her, and because they'd always been such good friends, he'd hoped that she could be the one. But he'd only been fooling himself. After last night, he knew beyond a shadow of a doubt that there was no way he and Cynthia could continue dating. Not when he was still in love with Tamia, and *definitely* not when he found himself counting down the hours until he and Tamia could be alone again to enjoy an encore performance.

He knew it wouldn't be fair to string Cynthia along. So he had to do the right thing and break up with her. Sooner rather than later.

Dreading that conversation, Brandon unlocked the door to his office. The moment he crossed the threshold, his mind was bombarded with carnal images from last night. He saw Tamia on the sofa, knees bent, glistening pussy lips spread open as she rode his dick. He saw her sauntering provocatively to the desk, looking like every man's erotic fantasy with her voluptuous breasts, bodacious ass, and killer legs. He saw her juicy butt jiggling as he bent her over the table and fucked her from behind, saw her luscious tits bouncing up and down as he rammed into her. When he looked down at the floor, he saw their naked bodies thrusting, gyrating, rolling around so vigorously it was a miracle they didn't get a bad case of carpet burn.

Everywhere his gaze fell was a land mine of orgasmic nirvana.

He swallowed hard, loosening the knot of his tie as he strode to his desk and sat down. Almost at once, his mind flashed on the memory of Tamia occupying that very same chair, her stiletto-clad feet propped on the desk, a naughty smile curving her lips.

Ignoring the blinking message light on his phone and the stack of paperwork demanding his attention, Brandon retrieved his cell phone and pulled up the pictures he'd taken of Tamia. He clicked through them before lingering on the one of her blowing him a kiss.

As he stared at the seductive photo, he could feel his dick pushing against his zipper. He wished he could send everyone home, call Tamia into his office, and feast on her for the rest of the day, and long into the night.

Suddenly the phone rang, startling him.

When he saw the number to the state capitol in Austin, he smiled wryly, recognizing the irony of having his lustful daydream about Tamia interrupted by his father.

"Please hold for the lieutenant governor," a woman's familiar nasal voice instructed Brandon.

After several moments, Bernard came on the line, his resonant baritone crackling with authority even as he issued a simple greeting. "Hello, son."

"Dad," Brandon drawled, leaning back slowly in his chair. "To what do I owe the pleasure of this call?"

His father took umbrage. "What? I can't call my firstborn just to say hello and see how your day is going?"

Brandon chuckled dryly. "Considering that you practically disowned me the last time we saw each other—"

Bernard guffawed. "Don't be ridiculous. I would never disown you, son. You're my heir. My pride and joy. But you made an egregious mistake, and you needed to be corrected."

"Hmm," was Brandon's noncommittal response.

"Speaking of which, I've been meaning to call and thank you for handling the situation with Dominic Archer. Mort phoned yesterday morning to inform me that Archer canceled the press conference and dropped the lawsuit against you. And when reporters asked him about his injuries after the bail hearing yesterday, he recanted his story about being assaulted by you. He told the reporters that he got into some bar fight after leaving Tamia's apartment on Saturday night."

"I heard about that," Brandon said drolly.

His father laughed. "So how did you persuade that conniving son of a bitch to cooperate? Not even his attorney knows what the two of you discussed."

Brandon smiled wryly. "Let's just say even Satan has a soft spot."

"You didn't do anything illegal, did you?" Bernard half joked.

"Only if calling in an old favor is illegal," Brandon murmured, thinking of yesterday's private meeting with the judge who'd agreed—albeit reluctantly—to set up the escrow account for Dominic's family members.

"Well, needless to say," Bernard continued, "Russ went on a tear when he found out. Speaking on behalf of his nephew, of course, he called a meeting with Mort and the other founding partners to rant about how you'd gone rogue and obstructed justice by striking a deal with Archer behind his attorney's back. Mort said ole Russ was the epitome of moral outrage." Bernard's tone dripped with amused satisfaction. "So have you seen him since yesterday?"

"Haven't had the pleasure," Brandon drawled. "But I'm sure he'll make his way to me eventually."

"After he's finished sulking and licking his wounds, that is."

Father and son shared a low chuckle.

"So how *is* your day going?" Bernard asked conversationally.

"Busy. I've been in meetings all day."

"You're not taking on any major cases, are you? When Mort and I were talking, I suggested to him that you should probably keep a low profile for the next year. You know, just until the election's over."

Brandon rolled his eyes and shook his head at his father's obsession with ensuring that nothing compromised his candidacy. "You'll be happy to know that I don't have any major cases on the horizon. Not at the moment, anyway."

"Good," Bernard said approvingly. "Let's keep it that way."

Brandon frowned. "I'm a defense attorney, Dad. Do you honestly expect me to spend the next year shying away from potentially controversial cases just to protect your campaign from any negative backlash?"

"That's exactly what I expect."

Brandon clenched his jaw. "Dad—"

"Look, you've already accomplished more in your short career than over half the attorneys at that firm. After your masterful handling of the Quasar Diagnostics lawsuit, you deserve to take a breather. Let yourself ride high on the success of this past year's accomplishments."

Brandon narrowed his eyes. "Who are you, and what have you done with my father?"

"Beg your pardon?"

"Come on, Dad. When have you ever been an advocate for taking a breather? Haven't you always taught us that the key to success is never resting on your laurels or being satisfied with yesterday's accomplishments?"

"Well, of course," Bernard conceded gruffly. "And I stand firm by those life lessons I instilled in you and your siblings. But it's not as if I'm telling you to go on sabbatical or anything that drastic. I'm simply encouraging you to take time to smell the roses. You went straight from the Quasar trial to Tamia's, and then you made partner. Starting after the holidays, you're going to be traveling and campaigning heavily on my behalf. Which reminds me—don't forget you're scheduled to speak to the Hispanic Chamber of Commerce in San Antonio to help me shore up the Hispanic vote."

"I haven't forgotten, Dad," Brandon muttered. "It's on my calendar."

"Good. Anyway, son, I have to run to a meeting. Gotta crack the whip on some of these troublemaking senators who're holding up the passage of a budget bill."

"Uh-oh," Brandon drawled. "They must not know about you."

His father laughed. "They must not. Anyway, think about what I said, Brandon. You've more than earned the right to take time to smell the roses."

Brandon sighed. "I'll think about it, Dad. Good night."

"Good night, son."

Brandon disconnected the call and set down the phone, his thoughts churning.

Although he resented the hell out of his father's strong-arm tactics, he knew there'd been some merit to the old man's argument. Brandon had spent the past eight years toiling slavishly to make partner, sacrificing everything—including his relationship with Tamia—to achieve that coveted goal. Regret assailed him every time he thought of the romantic getaway they'd hoped to take that summer but had never gotten around to scheduling. It was Dominic, not Brandon, who'd whisked Tamia away to St. Croix. Although their trip had been a disaster—served them right—it still haunted and angered Brandon that another man had made the time to arrange an exotic weekend tryst with *his* woman.

Now that he'd been named partner and had won the firm its most lucrative case of the year, there was nothing stopping Brandon from taking a few days off to "smell the roses," as his father had put it.

And there was absolutely no reason he couldn't take Tamia on that trip they'd been robbed of months ago.

Brandon drummed his fingertips on the desk for a few seconds, then picked up his phone and made a few calls before he could change his mind.

Chapter 32

Tamia

Tamia eyed Noemi Garcia sympathetically as the expectant mother rubbed her humongous belly, grimacing every now and then as her unborn baby stretched and rotated inside her womb.

"Are you sure you don't want to go home?" Tamia asked her.

Glancing up from her computer, the petite, dark-haired young woman smiled wanly. "I'm okay."

"You don't *look* okay," Tamia countered skeptically. "You look like you're in a lot of pain. What's that little man in there doing to you?"

Noemi grinned wistfully. "The 'little man' isn't so little. Although I'm only thirty-four weeks along, he already weighs five pounds—"

Tamia whistled softly.

"—and his weight is putting a lot of pressure on my sciatic nerve, which causes my lower back and legs to hurt. It feels worse every time he moves."

Tamia pursed her lips for a moment. "Okay, I'm not

even gonna pretend to know what a sciatic nerve is, but what you've just described sounds painful, and it's clear to me that you should be at home with your feet up, letting your husband rub your back and wait on you."

Noemi giggled, brown eyes twinkling. "You're so funny, Tamia."

"I'm serious. I know we only met this morning, but I like you, and I hate to see you suffering like this." Tamia glanced at her watch. "It's after four anyway. Who's gonna care if you cut out a little early?"

Noemi grimaced. "Not that I wouldn't love to, but I really shouldn't. It's bad enough that I didn't come back to the office after my doctor's appointment yesterday. Which reminds me, I am *so* sorry for deserting you on your first day."

Tamia waved off the apology. "Don't worry about it. You left me great instructions, so I had plenty to do. And the template you provided for writing a report was extremely helpful, so thank you."

"You're welcome. I'm glad it helped. I'm taking your report home with me tonight, so I'll give you my feedback tomorrow."

"Great! And remember what I said earlier. Be brutally honest with me. I can take it."

Noemi grinned at her. "We'll see."

Tamia laughed.

Seconds after Noemi had returned her attention to her computer, she was back to rubbing her stomach and wincing.

Tamia sighed. "Okay, you really need to go home."

Noemi met her exasperated gaze. "I can't—"

"Yes, you can. Look, for all you know, those pains you're having could be contractions. So you could be in labor right now. If I don't know what a sciatic nerve is, I damn sure don't know the first thing about delivering a baby. Besides," Tamia continued pragmatically as Noemi opened her mouth to argue, "you just said you'd be reading my report this evening, right? So, technically, you're taking work home."

"Well," Noemi conceded slowly, "that's true."

"Of course it's true. So what is it you need to do before you leave this evening? Maybe I can take care of it for you."

Noemi wavered, biting her lower lip. "If you're sure . . ."

Tamia gave her a pointed look. "I wouldn't offer if I wasn't."

"Well, I need to make copies of the minutes from last week's partners meeting. As the newest partner, it's Brandon's responsibility to provide copies for everyone before the next meeting. Never mind that the minutes are saved on the network and everyone downloads them to their PDAs anyway," Noemi added with a disgusted eye roll. "All that matters to Russ is that they've been printing hard copies for years, so he insists on maintaining the status quo."

"Russ?"

"Sutcliffe. One of the firm's senior partners"—Noemi lowered her voice—"and a major league asshole. Just to give you a heads-up, he and Brandon are sworn enemies. I'm talking Superman versus Lex Luthor, and you know which one is the despicable villain. Russ has always hated Brandon's guts, and he was strongly opposed to his hiring you. So just keep your head up and watch your back, 'cause Russ Sutcliffe can be a spiteful son of a bitch."

Tamia nodded slowly. "Thanks for the warning."

After Noemi left, Tamia got up and headed to the copy room, relieved to find it empty. She had a lot of copying and collating to do, and she didn't feel like waiting on anyone else. She also craved some privacy to daydream about Brandon and the incredible night of lovemaking they'd shared.

She was disappointed that she hadn't seen him all day, but she understood that he was very busy. She'd checked out his schedule, so she knew that he'd spent the entire day running from one meeting to another. But she wondered whether he, like her, had found himself frequently losing his concentration as he replayed memories of last night. She hoped he had. And she hoped that he didn't regret what they'd done. Didn't regret telling her that he loved her.

She was so absorbed in her thoughts that she didn't realize someone had entered the room until a woman's voice drawled, "Hey, new girl. We don't allow that around here."

Startled, Tamia glanced up from the humming Xerox machine to encounter the coolly amused gaze of an attractive, thirty-something brunette wearing a two-piece power suit and kitten-heel pumps.

Tamia blinked at her. "Sorry. What did you say?"

"I said we don't allow that around here," the approaching woman repeated. She was conspicuously empty-handed, which meant she'd either left behind what she wanted to copy or was there for the sole purpose of meeting Tamia.

"Allow what?"

"Daydreaming."

Tamia flushed, glancing away.

When she offered no denial, the brunette chuckled knowingly and sidled up to her. "Judging by the smile on your face, girlfriend, that must have been some *gooood* dick."

Tamia gasped, taken aback by the crude remark and the woman's bold familiarity. Raking her with an annoyed look, Tamia said tightly, "I'm sorry. I didn't catch your name."

"Addison." She stuck out a manicured hand. "I'm an associate here."

Tamia hesitated, then shook the brunette's hand. "I'm—"

"No introduction necessary. Everyone knows who you are." Cool, assessing green eyes roamed across Tamia's face and body—a frank appraisal that ended with Addison shaking her head. "I must admit. You're downright gorgeous in person. No wonder."

Tamia narrowed her eyes. "No wonder what?"

But Addison merely smiled. "So how's it going so far? This is, what, your second day on the job?"

"That's right." Tamia turned back to the copy machine, which was slowly cranking out the collated pages of the meeting minutes. She wished Addison would take the hint and leave, but no such luck.

After glancing toward the doorway, Addison leaned close to Tamia, further invading her personal space as she confided, "I'm sure it won't surprise you to hear that there were some grumblings among the administrative staff when you were hired. Certain people were offended that you were hired with practically no legal experience. Most of the assistants who work here have bachelor's or associate's degrees in paralegal studies, so they're rightfully insulted by the notion that you think you can just waltz in here and do their jobs with limited training."

Tamia nodded slowly, keeping her expression neutral. "I can certainly understand their concerns. If I were in their shoes, I'd probably feel the same way."

"Wow." Addison stared at her with a combination of surprise and admiration. "*That* was a very mature response."

"I'm just speaking the truth."

"I know. Which was what made it so . . . refreshing."

Tamia gave her an amused look. "I'm sorry you didn't get the reaction you were obviously expecting or hoping for. But you didn't tell me anything I didn't already know. The other assistants resent me for getting a job I'm unqualified for, so as an act of protest, they've decided to give me the cold shoulder."

"Pretty much," Addison confirmed.

Tamia gave an unconcerned shrug. "That's their prerogative. I've never cared about winning popularity contests, and I'm not about to start now."

A slow, delighted grin stretched across Addison's face. "I think you and I are gonna get along just fine, Tamia Luke."

Tamia had her doubts about that, but she kept the thought to herself.

As she checked the progress of her copy job—wishing the damn machine would collate faster—Addison eyed her with fascinated curiosity. "So what's he really like?"

"Who?"

"Brandon."

"Brandon?"

"Yeah." Addison looked amused. "You know, your ex-boyfriend slash lawyer slash new boss."

"Got that part. What I *don't* get is why you're asking me what he's like."

Addison smiled. "I'm curious. I mean, Brandon has so many different facets to his personality. He's a consummate professional at the office, a total gentleman who opens doors for the ladies, and a sweet guy who remembers people's birthdays. But then he's a ruthless mercenary in the court-room and in meetings with people he doesn't like. Since I've never had the pleasure of hanging out with him after work, I just wonder whether he's one of those brothas—"

Tamia's brow shot up.

"—who lets it all hang out when he gets around his friends. Does he get loud and rowdy? Does he curse like a sailor? Does he act really silly and playful?" Addison chuck-led softly. "I just figured, next to Deondre, you know Bran-don better than anyone else."

Tamia eyed her suspiciously. "And you want to know all these things about him because . . . ?"

Addison shrugged nonchalantly, twirling a strand of dark hair around her finger. "Like I said, I'm just curious about him."

"Ohhh, I see." Tamia nodded knowingly. "You're one of those."

"One of what?"

"An MSWG."

Addison frowned. "What's that?"

Tamia hesitated, then decided since Addison had been so forward with *her*, she'd return the favor. "MSWG is an acronym my best friend made up. It stands for Mandingo-Seeking White Girl."

Addison gaped at her for a moment, then threw back her head and laughed. "I love it!"

"You do?"

"*Yes!* I'm totally gonna start using that."

Tamia smiled sardonically. "I'm glad you weren't offended."

"Not at all." Addison's green eyes twinkled. "I love black men, and I make no apologies for that."

"Umm-hmm." *I see I'm gonna have to keep an eye on this heffa*, Tamia thought.

"I hope I'm not interrupting this, ahem, bonding session."

Tamia and Addison glanced toward the doorway. Cynthia stood there smirking at them, a manila folder in her hand.

"Hey, Cynthia." Addison made an exaggerated show of glancing at her watch and gasping in shock. "Oh, my goodness! It's after five and *you're* still here?"

Cynthia's mouth tightened, but only for a moment. "Of course I'm still here," she said with stinging sweetness as she entered the copy room, "but I'm surprised that *you* are. I heard you totally bombed in court today, flubbed your closing argument so bad that the judge may have to declare a mistrial." She tsk-tsked. "Poor baby. Better luck next time."

Addison's face reddened.

Watching the barbed exchange with keen interest, Tamia thought, *Well, what do we have here?* Was it possible that she'd finally met someone else who didn't belong to the Cynthia Yarbrough fan club?

Recovering her composure, Addison plastered on the fakest smile and volleyed back, "Gee, thanks for your concern, Cynthia. It's remarkable that you have time to keep up with *my* cases when you have so much on your own plate, which apparently includes planning your wedding. Or was that someone else's bridal magazine and invitation sample book on your desk?"

Tamia stiffened with surprise.

Cynthia darted a glance at her before glaring accusingly at Addison. "What the hell were you doing in my office?"

Addison smirked. "I went to ask you a question, but you weren't there. Your door was open, so I decided to leave you a note. But after I saw all the wedding paraphernalia on your desk, I got distracted and left." Addison raised a brow at Tamia. "Did *you* know that your boss was getting married?"

Tamia glanced at Cynthia, who looked like she wanted the ground to open up and swallow her whole. "No," she murmured. "I didn't know."

Addison sighed. "I don't think *he* knows either. Especially considering what I overheard last . . . Well"—her wickedly amused gaze met Tamia's—"*that's* another story for another day."

Tamia's face flamed at the realization that Addison had overheard her and Brandon last night. Although most of the offices had appeared dark and empty, Addison must have been lurking around somewhere. She'd shamelessly eavesdropped at the door as Tamia and Brandon rocked each other's worlds, which might explain why she'd been asking all those weird questions about Brandon and had known what Tamia was daydreaming about.

Tamia looked back at Cynthia. Her eyes were narrowed suspiciously.

Blushing harder, Tamia turned back to the Xerox machine, relieved to see that her copies were finally done.

Cynthia advanced into the room, glaring venomously at

Addison. "For your information, the bridal magazine and sample book belong to my cousin who just got married. I had pulled them out of my desk drawer so I'd remember to give them back to her when she returns from her honeymoon."

Addison snorted. "Nice try, but that was the December issue of *Brides* magazine, which didn't hit the stands until *after* your cousin's wedding."

When Cynthia said nothing, Addison taunted further, "What's in that folder? Are you making copies of the wedding invitations that you liked?"

"Bitch, whatever," Cynthia hissed.

As Tamia turned from the Xerox machine, she ran smack-dab into her nemesis. Caught off guard, she lost her balance and stumbled backward, dropping her armful of copies. As she watched in dismay, the papers scattered across the floor.

"Oops." Cynthia smirked at her. "My bad."

Tamia shot her an evil glare, then bent down to gather the strewn papers.

"Guess you'd better watch where you're going next time," Cynthia jeered. "Or better yet, stop wearing those hooker heels to the office so you can keep your balance."

Tamia's face burned with anger and humiliation.

As Cynthia stepped around her to reach the copy machine, she left a shoeprint on one of the fallen sheets of paper, adding insult to injury.

"Oh, for God's sake." Heaving a sigh of disgust, Addison sank to her haunches to help Tamia while glaring at Cynthia. "That was *real* classy, Yarbrough. Way to show the rest of us those Christian values your parents taught you."

"I agree."

All three women's heads whipped toward the doorway.

Brandon stood there, his face hard with suppressed fury as he surveyed the scene before him.

Cynthia actually withered against the copy machine. "Hey, baby," she said weakly. "You're back."

"Unfortunately for you." Without sparing her another glance, Brandon stalked across the room.

As he knelt down to help Tamia and Addison gather the rest of the papers, Cynthia stammered out, "I-I would have helped too, b-but I'm sort of in a hurry and I, uh, needed to, uh . . ." She trailed off pathetically.

Deliberately ignoring her, Brandon cupped Tamia's elbow and gently assisted her to her feet. "Are you okay?"

She nodded quickly, clutching the stack of copies to her chest.

He touched her cheek, then looked at Addison. "Thanks, girl."

She winked at him. "Anytime, handsome."

Brandon's gaze shifted to Cynthia. "Can I see you in my office?" His curt tone made it clear it wasn't a request.

Cynthia wavered, then gave a jerky nod, looking so miserable that Tamia actually felt sorry for her. She watched as Cynthia followed Brandon from the room with the reluctant dread of a misbehaving child who'd been summoned to the principal's office.

As soon as they were gone, Addison grinned broadly at Tamia, her eyes gleaming with malicious satisfaction. "That couldn't have turned out better if I'd planned it myself."

Tamia was silent, making another copy of the page that Cynthia had stepped on.

Addison laughed. "Oh, come on, Tamia! Tell me that didn't feel good, watching that phony bitch finally get her comeuppance."

Tamia grimaced. "As someone who's been on the receiving end of Brandon's anger—and rightfully so—let's just say I sympathize with Cynthia."

Addison snorted rudely. "She sure as hell didn't sympathize with *you*. I seem to recall her floating on cloud nine for weeks after you and Brandon broke up. And call me jaded, but I think she was secretly relieved when you went to prison. She enjoyed having you out of the picture so she could have Brandon all to herself."

Tamia smiled wryly, shaking her head at Addison. "There you go again, telling me things I already know."

Addison laughed.

As they started from the room, Addison suggested, "We should do lunch sometime. I'd love to pick your brain and learn your secret."

Tamia frowned quizzically. "My secret to what?"

Addison grinned. "Keeping a man like Brandon Chambers wrapped around your little finger."

Chapter 33

Brandon

Brandon closed the door behind Cynthia, then strode to the windows and began pacing, too angry to be confined to his chair.

Cynthia watched him nervously. "Brandon—"

"What the *fuck* was that?" he exploded, rounding furiously on her.

She swallowed visibly. "Can you please keep your voice down? Plenty of our colleagues are still here—"

"I don't give a fuck!"

Cynthia made a whimpering noise. "I-I don't understand why you're so upset. What did I do that was so terrible?"

"Are you kidding me?" Brandon thundered. "How can you even ask that question after the way you just showed your ass? Even *Addison* was embarrassed for you! Do you realize that? You got taken to task by a woman who's not exactly known for being Miss Congeniality. So you should feel *real* small right now," he snarled, raking her with a look of disgust that brought tears to her eyes.

"You don't understand," she insisted. "You weren't there. *Tamia* bumped into *me*—"

"I saw the whole damn thing!"

Cynthia looked stricken. "You . . . did?"

"Damn right I did! I was looking for you, and someone told me you were in the copy room. I got there just in time to see what happened between you and Tamia at the copy machine. So I saw what you did, and I heard *exactly* what you said. And I gotta tell you, sweetheart, that was some petty, spiteful, mean-girl bullshit right there. If you're not ashamed of your behavior, then you're *definitely* not the woman I thought I knew!"

She gaped at him for a moment, then burst into tears. "I'm sorry! Okay? I was wrong. I let my emotions get the best of me, but it won't happen again!"

Brandon regarded her skeptically. "Are you sure that's all it was? Your *emotions*?"

Cynthia stared at him through tear-glazed eyes. "W-What do you mean?"

He frowned. "Ever since Tamia got out of prison, I've seen a side of you that I never knew existed. I know you're not a saint, and I never expected you to be. But I also never expected you to have such a vicious mean streak. And it's not just that. Before we started dating, you used to complain about how bougie and overbearing my parents are. Now you run to my mother about every little goddamn thing. Before we hooked up, you presented yourself as this proud, strong, fiercely independent sister, and I totally admired that about you. Now you're clingy and smothering as *hell*."

Her face reddened as Brandon shook his head, staring at her as if he'd never seen her before. "It's like you're a completely different person from the woman I thought I knew. So I have to wonder whether you've been conning me all this time. Are you the sweet, sassy, caring woman I met three years ago? Or are you the catty, cold-blooded bitch who just acted a damn fool in that copy room?"

Cynthia swallowed audibly and dropped her gaze to the floor, nostrils flaring, eyes blinking rapidly. "I *love* you—"

"That's not what I asked you," Brandon snapped.

"My love for you is all that should matter—"

"Bullshit! If you've been running game, *that* matters! If you're not the person I thought you were, *that* matters! So again I ask. Would the real Cynthia Yarbrough please stand the fuck up!"

At that her head snapped up, and her glittering eyes locked onto his. "You wanna know who I am? I'm the woman who loves you unconditionally and would do anything for you! I'm the woman who was there for you when that lying, treacherous bitch broke your heart! I'm the woman who swallowed my pride and supported you when you rode to her rescue without thinking twice about my feelings! Don't you *dare* stand there and pretend not to understand why I've been behaving the way I have! If I've become a 'catty, cold-blooded bitch,' it's because *you've* turned me into one!"

"WHAT?"

"You heard me! *You're* the one who gave Tamia a fucking job when even the janitor knows she's not qualified! *You're* the one who's been sneaking off to her apartment for lunch and God knows what else! *You're* the one who selfishly jeopardized your father's campaign because you lost your temper and went caveman on Dominic Archer! And for what? Because he choked Tamia? Have you *seen* any of those filthy *Slave Chronicles* videos? Have you *seen* the perverted things she used to do with her fellow 'actors'? The anal sex? The gang bangs? That disgusting whore probably *enjoyed* being choked by Dominic!"

Brandon had gone still.

Pulse pounding, eyes narrowing, he stared at Cynthia so

long that she took a step backward, then another, as if she were preparing to take flight.

In a deceptively soft voice, Brandon said, "I'm going to ask you a question. And I'm going to give you one opportunity to tell me the truth. *One*. So think long and hard before you answer."

Cynthia gulped hard, her eyes wide with something akin to fear.

"Have you ever met Dominic Archer?"

"What?"

"You heard me. Have you ever met Dominic Archer?"

Cynthia frowned. "Why are you asking me that?"

"Just answer the damn question."

"No, I've never met Dominic Archer."

Brandon searched her face, his mind racing with unthinkable possibilities. "So you had nothing to do with him blackmailing Tamia?"

"What?" Aghast, Cynthia stared at Brandon. "Of course I had nothing to do with Dominic blackmailing Tamia! How can you even ask me something like that?"

Brandon clenched his jaw. "*Someone* told that son of a bitch that Tamia was Mystique."

"Well, it wasn't me!" Cynthia's lips twisted sardonically. "Believe me, if I'd known that your girlfriend was a former porn star, I would have told you as soon as I found out. Not only because we were friends, but because the truth would have set you free of her *a lot* sooner."

Brandon's eyes narrowed speculatively. "When did you watch the Mystique videos?"

Cynthia swallowed visibly. "When?"

"When."

"I don't remember the exact date," she hedged.

"Try."

Her eyes darted around the room before she shrugged, feigning nonchalance. "I guess it was about two months ago.

I remember we'd been discussing Tamia's porn career because the prosecution wanted her movies entered as evidence of her shady character, and you were glad that Judge Perlman had granted your motion to suppress the videos. Anyway, I couldn't understand why you insisted on keeping them if you never intended to watch them, as you claimed. And I'll admit that I was curious to see just how raunchy they were. So one night while you were out, I snuck into your office and found the videos." Cynthia wrinkled her nose in disgust. "Believe me, *one* was all I could stomach."

Brandon frowned. "Why didn't you ever tell me that you'd watched one of the movies?"

Cynthia's face flushed. "I was embarrassed. And, quite frankly, I was intimidated by the fact that my competition was a former porn star who knows more sexual positions than I could ever begin to imagine."

Upon hearing that, Brandon could have assured Cynthia that he had no complaints about their sex life. But there was no point. They were through.

"Anyway," Cynthia continued, starting toward him, "I don't want to waste any more time arguing about Tamia. What we have is too special to be poisoned by her, or anyone else. I'm sorry for what happened earlier, but just remember that if *you'd* never hired her, I wouldn't be forced to deal with her."

Brandon smirked. "So it's *my* fault that you behaved like a childish, vindictive bitch."

Cynthia flinched, pausing midstride. "Can we stop with the name-calling?"

"I just call 'em like I see 'em."

Cynthia sneered. "Except when it comes to Tamia, right? When it comes to *her*, words like *whore, cheater, fraud,* and *ghetto* are apparently off limits—even though they describe her to a fucking *T*."

Brandon shook his head, mouth grimly set. "I didn't want to do this here at the office—"

"Do what?"

He looked her in the eye. "It's over, Cynthia."

She recoiled as if she'd been slapped. "What's over?"

"Our relationship. It's not working anymore."

She gasped, eyeing him fearfully. "Don't say that. *Please* don't say that."

"I'm sorry." And he meant it. "I wanted this to work. I really did. But it's not."

"What do you mean?" she cried. "Why are you doing this? Because of what happened in the copy room?"

"No," Brandon said quietly. "That's why I was looking for you this afternoon. I was going to suggest that we go somewhere private, because I wanted to let you know my decision as soon as possible."

"Your decision to break up with me?"

He nodded. "Yes."

"I don't believe this!" she shrieked, on the verge of hysteria. "She's only been home for eleven days, Brandon! *Eleven days!*"

His chest tightened. "I never meant to hurt you, Cynthia. You know that. But I can't keep lying to myself—or to you."

"Lying about what?"

"My feelings for Tamia. You know they haven't gone away. It was a mistake for us to get involved. It wasn't fair to either of us."

She eyed him incredulously. "Don't talk to me about *fair*, Brandon Chambers! It isn't *fair* that you allowed me to believe we had a future together! It isn't *fair* that you keep choosing that bitch over me! It isn't *fair* that—" She broke off, her face crumpling into tears.

Brandon blew out a deep, ragged breath and scrubbed a

hand over his face. He wasn't immune to the sight of Cynthia crying. He hated to hurt her like this, which was why he'd been dreading this conversation all day. He knew he probably should have waited until tonight to speak to her, but after what he'd witnessed in the copy room, he'd been so angry and disgusted with her that he couldn't put off the deed another second.

He exhaled another deep breath. "Cynthia—"

She lifted her head, her face ravaged by tears. "*Please* don't do this, Brandon. You don't have to end our relationship! If it's space you want, I've already moved out of your condo, and I promise not to call you so much every time we're apart! And if you really want me to, I'll apologize to Tamia for the way I behaved. I'll do whatever—"

"This isn't one of your cases, Cynthia," Brandon gently interrupted, shaking his head at her. "You can't plea bargain your way out of this. I've made my decision, and you need to respect that."

"*No!* You're asking me to just give up on us, and I can't do that!"

Brandon sighed. "Cynthia—"

"Please don't do this, baby," she begged, rushing forward and throwing her arms around his midsection. "I love you so much! I *need* you!"

He grasped her arms, peeling her off him and holding her firmly at arm's length. "Listen to me, sweetheart. You need to let this go and get back on your A game, all right? I didn't want to mention this before, but some of our colleagues think you're slipping."

"*What?*" Cynthia burst out, her red-rimmed eyes widening with shocked outrage. "Who told you that? Addison? You know you can't trust a word that bitch says. She's always spreading malicious lies about me!"

"It wasn't just Addison," Brandon countered gently. "I had a meeting with Mitch yesterday, and he shared some of the same concerns. You know he's always been in your corner, but he's worried that you're hurting your chances at making partner next summer. You and I discussed this when we first started dating, remember? We both agreed not to allow our relationship to interfere with our jobs. But I think I've become a distraction to you, Cynthia, and others have obviously noticed as well."

She sneered at him. "That sounds like just another sorry excuse to justify your decision to break up with me."

Brandon frowned with frustration. "You're not listening to me. Remember how you once told me that next to your family, making partner is the most important thing in the world to you? Remember that?"

She hesitated, then nodded grudgingly.

"Refocus your energies on achieving that goal, Cynthia. I'm telling you that as someone who knows how hard you've worked to make partner. I'm telling you that as a friend who wants you to succeed and be happy."

Cynthia held his earnest gaze for a long moment, then wrenched free of his grasp and stepped back. "Thanks for the pep talk," she said bitterly, taking an angry swipe at her wet cheeks, "but I don't need your damn friendship."

Brandon gave her a look of genuine regret. "I'm sorry you feel that way."

"Save your fucking 'sorry,' " she spat viciously. "If you were *really* sorry, you wouldn't be doing this to me. But you know what, Brandon? Karma's a straight-up bitch. So when that scheming whore betrays you again—because I know she will—don't come crawling back to me with your balls tucked between your legs. You had your chance to be with a good, faithful woman who truly loves you, and you blew it. So fuck you, and *fuck her*!"

With that, she spun on her heel and marched to the door, yanking it open so hard she nearly sideswiped herself. Skewering Brandon with one last glare, she turned and stormed out.

Chapter 34

Tamia

"Mamacita! Welcome back!"

Tamia beamed with pleasure when she arrived home that evening to find Lou and Honey sipping cocktails in the living room.

"Hey, papi," she called out warmly.

"*Hola*, working girl."

After setting down her attaché case and stepping out of her high heels, Tamia made her way over to the sofa. She laughed as Lou caught her around the waist and pulled her onto his lap.

She kissed his pockmarked cheek, then drew back and smiled into his eyes. "I didn't know you were stopping by today."

He grinned. "Honey invited me over for dinner. She's been telling me for months what a great cook she is, so I decided to see for myself."

Tamia grinned at Honey, who sat curled up on the love seat. "You definitely won't be disappointed. Baby girl can throw down." She winked at Lou. "Which is why I'm still keeping her around."

Honey pretended to pout. "And here I thought it was because you enjoyed my company."

Tamia laughed, snagging Lou's glass and stealing a sip of his drink. "Mmm," she murmured appreciatively. "She even makes good mojitos."

"I know." Lou's voice was slightly slurred. "I can't stop drinking 'em. I'm on my fourth glass."

"Fifth," Honey corrected.

"Really?" He winked at her. "If I didn't know better, I would think you were trying to get me drunk so you and Tamia can take advantage of me."

Honey sighed. "I wish, but Tamia doesn't do three-somes. I already propositioned her."

Lou burst out laughing.

Tamia just smiled and sipped more of his mojito.

"Which reminds me," Honey mused, tapping a manicured finger to her lips as she regarded Lou, "how come Tamia's the only actress who never had any girl-on-girl scenes?"

After exchanging amused glances with Tamia, Lou explained, "That was one of her stipulations. No girl-on-girl action, and her identity had to be hidden from viewers at all times. She wouldn't sign the contract unless I agreed to her terms."

"Dayum." Honey gazed admiringly at Tamia. "You were only, what, twenty?"

"Nineteen."

Lou chuckled reminiscently. "Even back then, she was a savvy businesswoman who knew what she wanted. And after watching her audition performance, I would have been crazy not to sign her."

"Wow." Honey looked impressed. "Now *that's* what you call a powerful pussy."

Lou and Tamia laughed.

"Before you got home, Tamia, Lou and I were joking about how scandalized your neighbors would be if we went skinny-dipping in the pool after dinner."

"Aw, hell, nah! Don't even think about it," Tamia warned.

When Honey and Lou traded conspiratorial grins, Tamia shook her head at them. "Okay, I think you've *both* had too many mojitos. And speaking of dinner, Honey, whatever you're cooking smells wonderful."

The girl beamed. "I'm making my grandmother's jambalaya and corn bread."

"Mmm. Sounds delicious." Tamia smiled softly. "You know, I'd love to meet your grandma sometime."

Honey grinned. "Funny you should say that. I was gonna invite you home with me for Thanksgiving next week. That is, if you don't have any plans."

Tamia's expression clouded at the thought of Fiona, the only real family member she had. They'd always spent the holidays together. Even when Fiona was incarcerated, Tamia had made a point of visiting her so neither of them would feel lonely. It was sobering to realize that this would be the first of many Thanksgivings they would spend apart.

Observing her downcast expression, Honey said gently, "You don't have to let me know right away. Take your time."

Tamia mustered a grateful smile. "Thanks for the invitation. I'll get back to you soon."

"Whenever. No rush." Honey set down her drink and rose from the love seat. "I'm gonna check on dinner."

After she left the room, Lou kissed the top of Tamia's head. "Thanks for letting her crash here. I really appreciate it."

Tamia waved off his gratitude. "You don't have to thank me. She's a sweetheart, and I'm enjoying her company. Not to mention that I haven't had to cook since she's been here."

Lou smiled, but only for a moment. "I know she came here because she had a fight with her boyfriend."

Tamia was silent, neither confirming nor denying what he'd said.

His expression darkened. "She doesn't want me to find out what happened because I told her what I'd do to that motherfucker if he ever hit her again."

"You don't have to do anything," Tamia gently assured him. "She can stay here as long as she needs. She hasn't been taking any of his calls, so he doesn't know where she is. This building has a twenty-four-hour front desk attendant. So she's safe here."

"Yeah, but for how long?" Lou countered grimly. "That asshole's a cop, so he has resources. Once he realizes that she's serious about leaving him, all he has to do is triangulate her cell phone to trace her exact location."

Tamia hadn't considered that possibility. "So we'll need to get rid of her phone and get her a new one."

"Assuming it's not too late. We both know that if he shows up here and flashes his badge, he'll be allowed upstairs—no questions asked."

Tamia frowned, remembering how easily Dominic had gotten to her on Saturday night. Since learning that one of her neighbors had vouched for him, Tamia had been on her guard, viewing everyone with suspicion.

Lou growled, "I don't want to give that motherfucker a chance to find Honey—or you, for that matter."

Tamia saw the leashed violence in his eyes, could feel the tension radiating from his body. Even the serpent tattooed onto his neck seemed to be quivering with lethal anticipation.

She swallowed. "Don't do anything crazy, Lou."

A muscle hardened in his jaw. "If that's what it takes—"

"No." She cupped his face between her hands, forcing him to meet her intent gaze. "Listen to me, papi. Are you listening?"

He hesitated, then gave a tight nod.

"Back in May, I came to you for help with Dominic. Remember that? I asked you to send a warning to him so he'd leave me alone. I was scared, desperate, and at the end of my rope. But I was wrong for requesting such a favor from you. Thank God Dominic was out of town at the time, and thank God you never made that phone call to—"

"Because I was gonna take care of that crazy motherfucker myself," Lou said through clenched teeth.

"Thank God you didn't! Don't you see? If you *had* done something to Dominic, you'd be locked up right now, and I never would have forgiven myself. So I'm asking you not to go after Honey's boyfriend. I'll notify the front desk to alert security if he ever shows up here. And since Brandon already put the police on notice over Dominic, maybe we can ask him to make a phone call to Keyshawn's supervisor—"

"Of course," Lou drawled mockingly. "How could I forget about our powerful secret weapon who makes problems go away with the snap of his fingers?"

Tamia stared at Lou, taken aback by his sarcastic remark. "What's that supposed to mean?"

Instead of answering her question, he took the glass from her hand and downed the rest of his drink.

But Tamia wasn't about to let him off the hook. "Aren't you the one who's always bragging about how great it is to have friends in high places? Aren't *you* the one who nicknamed Brandon 'the rainmaker' after he got the feds off your back?"

"Yup." Lou's lips twisted into a bitterly sardonic smile. "It seems we *all* owe your boy a debt of gratitude. Honey told me that you're working at the law firm as his assistant. So allow me to offer my congratulations. Didn't I tell you everything would work out for you?"

"Yes. You were right." Tamia paused. "Did you know Brandon was going to offer me a job?" *Like you knew about the apartment*, she added silently.

"Nope. I had no clue." Lou set his empty glass on the table with a sharp *clink* that made Tamia wince. With mounting discomfort, she watched as his hazel eyes roamed down her bare legs and pedicured toenails. When she felt his dick harden against her backside, she knew their friendship had just veered off into dangerous, uncharted territory.

"I don't know what he's paying you, mamacita," Lou said, "but I guarantee you would have made *way* more if you'd come to work for me."

"Maybe," she conceded, unnerved by the undercurrent of jealousy in his voice. "But I told you I didn't want to work at the escort agency."

"Right." Lou smirked. "After all, we can't have the wife of the future attorney general working as a madam."

Tamia stared at him, searching his face for some sign of the man she'd always trusted and adored. "Where's all this coming from, Lou?"

He returned her stare. "Where do you think?"

She swallowed hard.

Seconds passed.

When she moved to climb off his lap, his arm tightened around her waist, restraining her.

Their eyes locked.

Tension crackled between them.

"I think you've had too much to drink," Tamia said quietly.

"Maybe." A shadow of cynicism touched his mouth. "Or maybe that's what you'd prefer to believe."

Tamia shook her head slowly. "Don't."

Something like pain flashed in his eyes. "Don't what, Tamia? Don't tell you that I love—"

"Okay, folks," Honey announced, returning to the living room. "Everything's just about ready."

"Great!" Tamia exclaimed, jumping off Lou's lap with

such haste that Honey's eyes narrowed. "I'ma go, um, freshen up before we eat."

"Okay," Honey said slowly, dividing a speculative glance between Tamia and Lou. "I thought we could have dinner on the balcony. It's such a beautiful night."

"That's fine. Whatever." As Tamia headed quickly from the living room, her cell phone rang on the foyer table. She grabbed it, pressing the talk button without checking the caller ID. "Hello?"

"Hey, it's me," Brandon murmured.

"Hey, baby." She glanced self-consciously at Lou. He met her gaze for a moment, then rose from the sofa and prowled to the windows, his hands shoved into the pockets of his dark jeans.

"I'm coming up," Brandon said.

Tamia's pulse thudded. "You're *here*?"

"Yeah. Getting on the elevator right now."

"Okay." She gulped a shaky breath. "See you soon."

When she snapped her phone shut, Honey asked excitedly, "Brandon's coming over?"

"Um, yeah."

"That's great!" Honey enthused, heading back to the kitchen. "He can have dinner with us."

"Sure," Tamia said weakly, stealing another glance at Lou. After what had just transpired between them, she didn't know whether having him and Brandon at the same table was such a good idea.

But she didn't have time to worry about that.

Tamia went to the front door and opened it just as Brandon raised his hand to press the doorbell.

"Hey," he murmured. "Perfect timing."

Tamia smiled, then leaned up and hugged him. Her body tingled at the memory of having him inside her, bringing her to one mind-blowing orgasm after another.

As she pulled away, he brushed her hair off her face, his

eyes probing hers. "You left the office without saying good-bye."

"I know. I wasn't sure how much time you and Cynthia would need, and I didn't want to be there when . . ." She trailed off awkwardly.

Brandon nodded slowly. "I understand."

Tamia cautiously searched his face. "Is everything . . . okay?"

He hesitated. "Can we talk inside?"

"Of course." She stepped aside to let him enter, then closed the door behind him. As she led him down the long entryway, she explained, "I have company, so we can talk in my—"

"Hey, Brandon!" Honey called out as she emerged from the kitchen and walked over to greet Brandon, her eyes glint-ing with feminine appreciation as she looked him up and down. "You probably don't remember me, but we met briefly at Tamia's homecoming party. My name's Halima, but every-one calls me Honey."

Brandon smiled, shaking her hand. "Nice to see you again, Honey."

"You, too," she purred.

When she clung to his hand longer than necessary, Tamia shot her a dark glance.

Honey grinned, reluctantly letting him go. "You're just in time for dinner, Brandon. I made—"

"Let me guess." He inhaled deeply. "Mmm. Jambalaya and corn bread."

Surprised, Honey laughed. "How'd you know?"

"My great-grandmother used to make that all the time."

Honey beamed with pleasure. "Really? Is she from New Orleans?"

"She was. She passed away several years ago."

"I'm sorry to hear that."

"Don't be. She was ninety-six, so she enjoyed a nice long life."

Honey smiled, looking like she wanted to curl up on Brandon's lap. "Is your brother single?" she blurted.

Tamia gasped. "Honey!"

Brandon laughed, amused by her boldness. "Beau is . . . selectively single."

Before Honey could ask him to elaborate, Lou emerged from the powder room located off the foyer. His eyes briefly met Tamia's before they shifted to Brandon. "Wassup, Counselor."

Brandon smiled. "Wassup, Saldaña."

As the two men exchanged handshakes and friendly greetings, Tamia was relieved to see that Lou appeared to be back to his normal self. Outwardly, at least.

He flashed a half grin at Brandon. "You gonna grace us with your presence for dinner?"

"Yes," Honey interjected before Brandon could open his mouth. "He has to taste my jambalaya and tell me if it's as good as his great-grandmother's. And I want to hear more about his 'selectively single' brother," she added with a wink.

Brandon chuckled. "I guess I'm staying, then."

"Yup."

Tamia glanced at Honey and Lou. "Would you two excuse us for a few minutes?" she murmured before taking Brandon by the hand and escorting him to her bedroom.

She closed the door behind them, then led him over to her neatly made, queen-size bed. She wanted to kiss his soft, succulent lips and undo the remaining buttons on his shirt, then shove him back onto the mattress and straddle him. But she figured she'd better wait until she knew where things stood between him and Cynthia.

They sat on the edge of the bed.

Staring down at his hands clasped between his legs, Brandon said quietly, "I broke up with Cynthia."

Tamia's heart soared. If Brandon had been looking at her, he would have seen the look of sheer joy that crossed her face before she managed to control herself and ask gently, "Are you okay?"

He hesitated for so long that Tamia wondered whether he'd even heard her question.

She waited anxiously.

Finally he met her gaze. "It wasn't easy. The last thing I wanted to do was hurt Cynthia. We've always been good friends, and my feelings for her are real."

"Meaning that . . . you really love her?"

Again Brandon hesitated, then nodded slowly. "In my own way, I do. Despite the way she behaved today, I know she's a good person, and I believe she really loves me."

"She does," Tamia agreed quietly. "I may not like or trust Cynthia, but one thing I can't deny is that she genuinely loves you, Brandon. I saw it in her eyes when I confronted her at your father's campaign launch party. She's crazy about you, so I know she must be pretty devastated right now."

Brandon said nothing.

Tamia sighed heavily. "Maybe you could have worked things out with her," she surprised herself by saying.

"I don't think so." Brandon exhaled a deep, ragged breath. "Honestly, Tamia, I probably just need to be alone for a while to clear my head and figure out what I really want."

Her heart sank. "I know what you want," she told him. "You want me."

"Baby—"

"Listen," Tamia said urgently, sliding off the bed to kneel between his legs. "I know you're feeling confused and guilty right now because of what happened between you and Cynthia, and God knows I don't want to give you any more to worry about. But we made a powerful connection last night, Brandon. Not just sexually. *Emotionally*, too. You told me that you've never stopped loving me, and I know you were speaking from the heart."

"I was," he admitted, stroking the side of her hair. "I can't get you out of my system, no matter how hard I try. But as I told you before, we've still got some issues to work through. Every time I think I'm over what you did, something happens to remind me that I'm not. Seeing Dominic at your apartment on Saturday night really fucked me up. I know you didn't invite him over here," he said when Tamia opened her mouth to protest, "but seeing him all over you in the hallway just took me back to that night in May when I found out that you'd been sleeping with him."

"It didn't mean anything," Tamia insisted, capturing his hand and holding it to her heart. "What you and I have means *way* more to me than the cheap sex I had with Dominic."

"Maybe," Brandon conceded grimly, "but I'm a man, Tamia, and any man in my shoes would have a damn hard time getting over the thought of his woman fucking some other dude. Why do you think I haven't been able to watch your Mystique videos? I know you were just acting, and I know you did those movies *years* before we ever met, but just the thought of seeing you like that . . ." He trailed off, shaking his head at her. "I don't even wanna *think* about it."

"Then don't," Tamia urged him. "Put it out of your mind."

His lips twisted sardonically. "I wish it were that simple."

She eyed him beseechingly. "I can't undo the past, baby. If I could, you know I would."

"I know." He held her gaze for a long moment, then slowly pulled his hand away and blew out a deep breath. "Anyway, I just wanted to see if you were all right, and talk to you face-to-face about what happened."

Tamia nodded. "You're still staying for dinner, right?"

"Yeah." He smiled wryly. "Even though Lou probably doesn't want me to."

Tamia went still, staring at him. "What're you talking about?"

"You think I don't know that Lou has feelings for you? It's so obvious."

"Not to me! We've never been more than just friends."

Brandon chuckled, shaking his head at her. "No offense, Tamia, but you're not the kind of woman that guys only want to befriend. You're beautiful, and sexy as hell. And Lou has seen what you can do . . . in the bedroom. So he'd have to be crazy *not* to want you."

Frowning, Tamia rose from the floor and reclaimed her spot on the bed. "I'm not interested in Lou, or any other man. You're the only one I want, Brandon, and nothing's going to change that. So whenever you decide you're ready for a relationship, I'll be here."

Brandon gently caressed her cheek, his eyes probing hers.

Several seconds went by.

"Do you have a passport?" he asked suddenly.

Tamia blinked. "A passport?"

"Yeah." He paused. "I want to take you on a trip."

She stared at him. "A . . . trip?"

Brandon made an exaggerated show of glancing around the bedroom. "Damn, is there an echo in here? Why do you keep repeating everything I say?"

Tamia laughed. "Because I want to make sure my ears aren't deceiving me! Are you asking me to go on a trip with you?"

"That's exactly what I'm asking you. I want to make up for the trip we never took this year. We'd leave on Friday and come back next Friday. So we'd be gone for Thanksgiving."

"But what about work? I just started on Monday. Isn't it too soon for me to take a vacation?"

"Don't worry about that. You're only part-time until Noemi goes on leave, and the office will be mostly deserted next week anyway. So what do you say? Yes or no to the trip?"

"Are you kidding? One thousand percent *YES*!" Tamia squealed excitedly, throwing her arms around his neck and hugging him.

Brandon laughed. "Don't you at least want to know where we're going first?"

"I don't care! As long as we're together, baby, it doesn't matter *where* we go!"

"Good," Brandon said, smiling into her eyes as they drew apart, "because I wasn't going to tell you anyway. It'll be a surprise."

Tamia beamed. "I can't wait."

A knock sounded at the door. "I hate to interrupt whatever you lovebirds may be doing," Honey called in an amused voice, "but dinner's on the table, and Lou and I are ready to throw down. So come on, you two!"

Tamia and Brandon grinned at each other.

As they rose from the bed and walked to the door, Tamia basked in the knowledge that she'd have her boo all to herself for an entire week. She intended to make the most of their time together. And if all went well, she'd be back in the running to become Mrs. Brandon Chambers by the time they returned home.

Chapter 35

Tamia

Two nights later, Tamia and Honey went on an excursion to the downtown facility that housed Pinnacle Sports Group, the agency founded by Beau Chambers.

As they entered the lobby, Tamia glanced toward the barber shop to ensure that there was no sign of Fiona. Before heading over, she'd anonymously called the shop to see whether her sister was working that night, because she had no desire to see or speak to Fiona. Thankfully, she'd been told that Fiona had class tonight.

Looking through the shop's glass windows, Tamia was relieved to see that her sister's workstation was indeed empty. The other barbers were tending to customers, which included Houston Texans running back Arian Foster and Kevin Martin of the Houston Rockets. The place was abuzz with loud music and raucous laughter as the men bantered about whatever it was that men discussed in barber shops.

"Oh, my God!" Honey squealed, pointing excitedly toward the shop. "Girl, look at all those ballers in there!"

Tamia chuckled. "I see them," she drawled, steering

Honey toward the wellness center across the lobby. "But that's not why we're here, remember? We're supposed to be waiting for Beau to come downstairs any minute so that you can 'accidentally' run into him."

"Right," Honey agreed, throwing one last glance at the barber shop. "But I still don't understand why we couldn't just ask Brandon to introduce me to his brother. Wouldn't that have been easier?"

"Maybe," Tamia agreed. "But Brandon told me that Beau absolutely hates matchmaking schemes. Their mother is always introducing him to the daughters and nieces of her bougie society friends, so Beau adamantly refuses to date *any* woman that he suspects he's being set up with. Even if his brother is doing the matchmaking."

"Well," Honey drawled, licking her glossy red lips, "I'm definitely no debutante."

Tamia laughed, surveying Honey's weaved mane, cleavage-baring blouse, skintight leather pants, and stiletto boots. "You can say that again."

As they strolled into the general nutrition store that fronted the wellness center, Tamia wondered whether Dre was working tonight. No sooner had the thought crossed her mind than he emerged from the back.

When he saw Tamia, he nearly dropped the box he was carrying.

As they stared at each other, Tamia had an unpleasant flashback to the last time she'd seen Dre at Brandon's father's campaign launch party in May. She'd made the mistake of donning a black mask that had jolted Dre into recognizing her as Mystique, whose porn videos he'd apparently been watching—and jerking off to—for years. After he outed Tamia to Brandon, everything had gone downhill for her.

And now as she faced Dre, Tamia realized that she hadn't completely forgiven him for the way he'd treated her. Although he'd claimed that he was only looking out for Brandon, Tamia felt that he'd been judgmental toward her, as if *he'd* never made any mistakes in his life. She looked forward to the day that he'd do something that would jeopardize his relationship with Leah. After all, he was a man. So it wasn't a matter of *if* he'd fuck up, but *when*.

Following the direction of Tamia's gaze, Honey murmured, "Oooh, he's sexy. Do you know him?"

Tamia nodded tightly. "That's Brandon's best friend."

"Oh." Suddenly remembering what she'd been told about the role Dre had played in Tamia's downfall, Honey nodded understandingly. "*Oh.*"

Recovering his composure, Dre glanced away from Tamia and carried the box over to one of the store clerks who was stocking shelves.

"Wait a minute." Honey eyed Tamia speculatively. "Did you know he'd be working tonight?"

"Nope. I didn't even think about it."

Honey snorted. "Yeah, right."

Tamia ignored her.

As Dre turned and started toward them, Honey announced under her breath, "I'm gonna look for some vitamins. Please try not to make a scene while I'm gone. It might hurt my chances with Beau."

Tamia chuckled dryly, watching as Honey sashayed away before she turned and began wandering down an aisle filled with various diet and nutritional supplements.

"Wassup, Tamia," Dre greeted her.

Glancing around, she gave him a cool, narrow smile. "Hello, Deondre."

His brow lifted at the formal address. "Damn. So it's like that?"

"Like what?"

"I'm Deondre now?"

Tamia blinked innocently. "Isn't that your name?"

Dre frowned. "Come on, Tamia. You know damn well that none of my friends call me Deondre."

"Oh, are we friends?" Tamia countered coolly. "Did you ever visit me while I was in prison? Did you ever send a word of encouragement or a simple hello through Brandon? Did you show up for one single day of my trial? Did you even support Brandon's decision to represent me?"

Dre was silent, guilt flickering in his eyes.

Tamia smirked at him. "Then we're not friends."

With that, she turned and walked away.

Dre followed her. "Look, if you expect me to apologize for looking out for my best friend—"

"I don't expect anything from you, Deondre," Tamia cut him off. "I know you may find this hard to believe, but I don't give a damn what you think of me. The only one who has ever mattered to me is Brandon. Despite the terrible mistakes I made, he never stopped loving me and wanting the best for me. Despite the way you and his parents tried to poison his mind, he never gave up on me." She paused. "We're going away together, did you know that?"

Dre looked surprised. "Nah, he didn't tell me that."

Tamia couldn't suppress a satisfied smile. "Well, it's true. Brandon's taking me on a trip. He already told his parents that he wouldn't be home for Thanksgiving. I'm sure they didn't take the news too well. But it doesn't matter. Because if Brandon and I are meant to be together, there's nothing his parents—or you—can do about it. Now if you'll excuse me."

This time when Tamia walked off, Dre let her go.

As he returned to the back with his tail tucked between his legs, Tamia went in search of Honey. Rounding the corner of the aisle, she caught sight of Beau stepping off the elevator across the lobby, briefcase swinging at his side. As he sauntered toward the glass-fronted entrance to the wellness center, Tamia couldn't help staring at him. Clad in a pin-striped navy suit with no tie, the brotha looked good enough to lick like a melting chocolate bar.

As he reached the wellness center, his steps slowed and his eyes widened as he stared through the windows.

Following the direction of his riveted gaze, Tamia saw Honey leaning over to retrieve a bottle of vitamins from the bottom shelf of a display case. The sight of her round, thick ass sheathed in black leather had Beau practically drooling all over his expensive Italian threads.

Tamia smiled to herself. *Houston, we have take off.*

But before Beau could enter the wellness center, he was intercepted by none other than Joseph Yarbrough.

Shit! Tamia thought. She watched as the two men exchanged friendly handshakes before her gaze swung back to Honey. As the girl straightened from the vitamin display case, she glanced out the windows and froze at the sight of Beau talking to Bishop Yarbrough. Seconds later she whipped her head toward Tamia, her eyes wide with panic.

What the hell should I do? she mouthed.

Hide! Tamia mouthed back.

As Beau and the bishop stepped through the entrance, Honey ducked down an aisle.

Hoping to distract the two men long enough for Honey to make her escape, Tamia stepped forward with a bright smile. "Well, isn't *this* a nice surprise?"

Beau and Bishop Yarbrough glanced around. When Beau saw Tamia standing there, his face broke into a broad smile. Yarbrough, on the other hand, frowned with displeasure.

"Hey, Tamia." Beau came forward to greet her with a warm bear hug before he drew back and grinned. "Wassup, girl. What brings you here tonight?"

Tamia smiled at him. "Brandon told me that you guys have the best selection of vitamins."

"He's right," Beau confirmed. "Since Dre works as an

athletic trainer, he has a lot of contacts in the health and fitness industry. So we get many new products before they even hit the market. Have you had any trouble finding what you need?"

"Oh, I just got here, so I'm still browsing." Tamia looked at Joseph Yarbrough. "Hello, bishop. Nice to see you again."

"Miss Luke." Joseph offered a thin, condescending smile. "We've missed you at church. Was it something that I said?"

"Not at all," Tamia murmured. "I'm just used to a different type of worship experience. No offense."

"None taken," Joseph countered smoothly. "Not everyone is spiritually mature enough to receive God's word the way I'm led to deliver it."

Here he goes again with this sanctimonious bullshit! Tamia thought darkly.

"When someone is living in sin," the bishop continued piously, "their heart is hardened to the truth of the Gospel."

Without missing a beat, Tamia volleyed back, "Well, as the Bible says, 'Let he who is without scandal—I mean *sin*—cast the first stone.'"

Joseph's haughty expression evaporated.

As his face reddened, he shot a nervous glance at Beau. But Beau had missed the entire exchange, too busy looking around the store for Honey.

As the bishop's eyes narrowed suspiciously on Tamia's face, she smirked at him.

When Honey emerged from another aisle and began heading for the rear exit that backed to the parking lot, Tamia blurted to Beau, "Your brother tells me that you're close to signing Damarion Griggs. Congratulations."

Beau smiled at her. "Thanks, Tamia. Of course it's not a done deal yet since he hasn't officially declared for the NFL draft. But everything's falling nicely into place."

"That's wonderful, Beau. I'm so happy for you." Over his shoulder, she could see Honey darting quickly out the back door. Tamia waited another moment, then glanced down at her watch and sighed. "Well, I'd better get what I came for so I can head home and finish packing."

"Oh, yeah," Beau said, his eyes glinting with mischief as he added, "You and Brandon are going on a trip, right?"

"Right," Tamia confirmed, thoroughly enjoying the look of stunned outrage that swept across Joseph's face. "We're leaving tomorrow morning. Brandon won't tell me where we're going; he wants to surprise me."

Beau grinned. "He swore me to secrecy, but I *can* tell you that you're going to be very pleased."

Tamia beamed. "I can't wait," she enthused as Bishop Yarbrough's expression grew darker. She relished the thought of him breaking the news to Cynthia that Brandon was whisking Tamia off on a romantic getaway. Oh, to be a fly on the wall when *that* conversation went down.

Ten minutes later, after buying a bottle of vitamins that Beau recommended, Tamia left the wellness center and met Honey outside at the car. "Girl, that was a close call."

"I know," Honey agreed, climbing into the passenger seat and closing the door. "Bishop Yarbrough doesn't know that we're friends. If he'd seen me there with you, he probably would have freaked out. The last thing I need is his crazy, paranoid ass calling me every damn hour to find out if I've told you anything."

Tamia shook her head as she reversed out of the parking space. "I don't know how in the hell you put up with that self-righteous, hypocritical motherfucker."

Honey laughed. "Trust and believe, he's not quoting any scriptures when I'm giving him head and riding his little dick."

Tamia sucked her teeth in disgust. "Okay, that was just

too much information. Damn. Anyway, what the hell was he doing here?"

Honey grinned wryly. "Probably replenishing his supply of male enhancement pills so he'll be ready for me the next time we—"

Tamia held up a hand. "I get the point."

Again the girl laughed. Sobering after a few moments, she sighed deeply. "Damn, Beau's even hotter in person."

"I told you." Tamia grinned slyly. "You had that brotha's tongue hanging out of his mouth when you were bending over."

"He saw me?"

"Hell, yeah. He was about to approach you when Bishop Yarbrough arrived."

"Damn," Honey lamented. "Talk about a cock-blocker."

"I know." Tamia gave the girl an encouraging smile. "But don't worry. If you and Beau are meant to meet, you will when the time's right."

Honey brightened. "You really think so?"

Tamia nodded. "I do."

And she meant it.

Chapter 36

Fiona

Fiona sauntered slowly through the dark foyer of the large, two-story house.

The spiky heels of her six-inch stilettos tapped softly against the polished hardwood floor. It was the only sound that penetrated the silence of the house, and it wasn't loud enough to alert the home's occupant to her presence.

But soon enough, he'd know she was there.

Smiling wickedly at the thought, Fiona twirled the belt strap of her short trench coat as she rounded the corner. Wearing no panties, she could feel the plump folds of her pussy lips rubbing together, tingling in anticipation of what was soon to come.

She reached the end of the corridor and stepped through the open doorway of the master bedroom suite. Excitement pulsed through her veins at the sight of Dre sprawled upon the enormous bed, bathed in moonlight that poured through a pair of French doors. His chest was bare, and he had one arm flung over his forehead with the covers resting across his waist.

He was snoring lightly, and didn't awaken when Fiona entered the room.

She walked to the foot of the bed, untied her trench coat, and slipped it from her bare shoulders. As it landed on the floor with a soft rustle, Dre stirred slightly but remained asleep.

Fiona stepped out of her stilettos, then climbed onto the bed and crawled her way up his body. Straddling his legs, she carefully pulled down the heavy covers. To her everlasting delight, Dre was already naked, his black dick lying against his abdomen like a drowsing snake. Not even erect, and the thing was *still* huge.

Pussy throbbing, Fiona wrapped her fingers around the thick base and pumped slowly upward.

Dre moaned softly in his sleep.

As his shaft hardened in Fiona's hand, she lowered her head and eased his twelve inches into her mouth.

"Ohhh, shit," Dre groaned, nearly choking her as his hips surged off the bed, forcing his dick down the back of her throat.

She swallowed and relaxed her jaw, then began deep-throating him with hungry pulls of her mouth.

He let out another rumbling groan of pleasure. "Damn, baby . . . what the hell happened at the hospital tonight?"

Fiona didn't answer, licking and sucking his cock while massaging his engorged balls with her hand.

Moaning and writhing beneath her, Dre jammed his fingers into her long, silky hair and gripped the back of her bobbing head.

Moments later his hands stilled.

"Wait a min—*Oh, fuck*!" he screamed as Fiona sucked the swollen head of his dick. As he exploded, she swallowed the hot, creamy jet of cum that filled her mouth.

After she'd milked him dry, Dre quickly reached across

the nightstand and switched on the lamp. His eyes bulged with shock when he saw Fiona straddling him.

Yanking himself out of her mouth, he shouted hoarsely, "What the fuck are you doing here?"

Fiona smiled slyly, wiping a trickle of cum from the corner of her mouth. "Isn't it obvious?"

"Are you fucking *crazy*?" Dre demanded, even as his lustful gaze swept over her luscious breasts and the shaved mound of her pussy. "How the hell did you get into my house?"

"Wouldn't *you* like to know?" Fiona purred, stroking his muscular chest. "And don't try to pretend you didn't know whose mouth was locked around your dick just now. We both know Leah has *never* given you head the way I just did."

At the mention of his absent girlfriend, Dre shot a panicked glance at the clock on the nightstand. It was 11:57. "Yo, you gotta get outta here!"

Fiona pouted. "Why?"

He eyed her incredulously. "*Why?* 'Cause Leah will be home any minute, that's why!"

"Are you sure about that?" Fiona countered, provocatively rubbing her wet pussy against his shaft, which hardened immediately. "'Cause I'd be *awfully* disappointed if I had to leave here without riding this black python of yours."

Dre swallowed visibly, his erection throbbing against her sex as he stared at her chocolate-tipped titties, wrestling with temptation. *"Shit,"* he whispered under his breath.

Taking advantage of his momentary indecision, Fiona rose to her knees, then slowly lowered herself onto his pipe. It was so thick and long she had to take him inch by swollen inch. By the time he was fully embedded, both of them were groaning with arousal.

Grabbing her buttocks, Dre began ramming into her, his

penis stroking her walls like no other man's had ever done before. Was it any wonder he'd been dominating her thoughts since Saturday night? Could anyone blame her for calling the hospital to confirm that Leah was working late, then breaking into the couple's crib to have her way with Dre?

"Fuck," Fiona moaned uncontrollably, her breasts bouncing to the beat of his pummeling thrusts. "Oooh, Daddy . . . fuck me, baby . . . *fuck me*!"

"Crazy-ass bitch," Dre growled, his nails digging into her clapping ass cheeks as he ruthlessly pounded her insides. "Just couldn't leave shit alone, could you?"

"No." Fiona flexed her inner walls, making him cry out sharply. "And you didn't want me to, either."

The nigga knew better than to deny it.

He cupped and squeezed her titties as she rode his dick, her hips bucking furiously against his. She matched him stroke for stroke until they were both dripping with sweat and the room was filled with their harsh breaths and the slapping sounds of wet skin.

As she felt her nut building in her stomach, Fiona leaned back on Dre's thighs and drew her knees up, and together they watched his cock drill her pussy like a jackhammer.

Moments later they erupted with loud, guttural screams.

Pulling out of Fiona, Dre painted her breasts and stomach with his hot cream.

With a breathless laugh, she collapsed beside him, only too happy to imprint her scent into Leah's side of the bed.

Dre closed his eyes, chest heaving rapidly as he fought to catch his breath. "We can't keep doing this shit," he panted.

"Why not?" Fiona purred, leaning close to nibble his earlobe. "No one has to know about us."

Dre frowned. "That's not the point, shorty. I'm in a relationship—"

"—with a woman who doesn't know how to satisfy you."

He turned his head on the pillow to glare at Fiona. "How the hell do you know that?"

She smiled lazily, caressing his damp pectoral muscle. "I overheard you and Leah talking in your office on Saturday evening. So I know she's been withholding the pussy for over a month."

Dre scowled at her. "Crazy *and* nosy. Ain't that some shit."

Her smile widened. "Say what you want about me, Deondre, but one thing you can't deny is how good we are together. You *love* this pussy. It's all you've been thinking about since we fucked that night."

He smirked at her. "Considering that I've been deprived for over a month—as you just reminded me—*any* pussy would have done the trick."

Fiona sucked her teeth. "Nigga, please. You know that's a damn lie."

"Maybe. Maybe not. The point is, little girl, you and I could never work."

"Why not?"

"Because I don't trust you."

She frowned. "Brandon does."

Dre made a face. "Brandon's always been way more trusting than he should be. It's one of the few character flaws he possesses."

"So you still don't think he should have hired me."

"Nope."

Fiona glared accusingly at Dre. "Can I ask you a question? Why the hell do you think you're better than me? You grew up in the projects and were raised by a single mother *just* like I was. Shit, we probably have more in common than you and that stuck-up girlfriend of yours."

Dre snorted. "Not hardly. And speaking of Leah"—he glanced at the alarm clock—"you really need to bounce before she gets home."

No sooner had the words left his mouth than they heard the sound of the garage door opening.

Dre bolted upright. *"Shit!"*

Fiona smirked. "This ought to be interesting."

Dre gave her a panicked look. "Yo, where'd you park?"

"Down the street."

"Thank God!" Dre lunged from the bed and rushed around to scoop her trench coat and stilettos off the floor. Marching over to her, he grabbed her hand and hustled her across the room to a walk-in closet that was twice as large as her bedroom.

"Stay here," he commanded, shoving her coat and shoes at her before snatching a thick bathrobe off a hanger. "And don't make a fucking sound!"

Fiona gave a mock salute, lips twitching with laughter. "Yes, sir."

Dre shot her a warning glare before shutting the closet's double doors on her face.

As Fiona quietly slipped on her trench coat and high heels, she heard Dre spraying the room with air freshener.

The next sound she heard was Leah's rubber-soled clogs slapping softly against the hardwood floor as she walked through the bedroom door.

"Hey, baby," she greeted Dre. "I saw the light on when I pulled up. What're you still doing awake?"

"I couldn't sleep, so I decided to wait up for you." Judging by the direction of Dre's voice, Fiona assumed he'd gotten back into bed just in the nick of time.

There were soft kissing noises.

"How was work?" Dre asked.

"Exhausting." Leah paused. "Have you been spraying air freshener?"

"Yeah." Dre sounded sheepish. "I had baked beans with dinner, and you know what beans always do to me."

Leah chuckled dryly. "Yeah, I know. For that reason, I think I'll sleep in one of the guest rooms tonight. I have to be up early, so you can't be keeping me awake with your noxious fumes."

As Dre laughed, Fiona silently marveled at his cleverness. If Leah slept in another room tonight, he would have time to change the cum-stained bedsheets.

Of course he's smart, Fiona mused. *The brotha does have a PhD.*

"I've been covered in blood all day," Leah announced around a tired yawn, "so I'm gonna take a nice, hot shower."

"Sounds good," Dre murmured. "I'll give you a massage when you come out."

"Mmm. Just what the doctor ordered."

"You know it."

As soon as Leah went inside the bathroom and started the shower, Dre let Fiona out of the closet, grabbed her hand, and hustled her from the bedroom with such haste she nearly tripped over her stilettos.

When they reached the front door, she asked breathlessly, "When can we hook up again?"

"Are you crazy?" Dre whispered sharply. "This was the last fucking time!"

"You don't mean that." Fiona guided his hand underneath her trench coat and rubbed his fingers against her wet pussy lips. As his nostrils flared, she smiled with wicked satisfaction. "I know you still want me as much as I want you."

"Be that as it may—"

She kissed him hard, silencing his protests. As she sucked his juicy bottom lip, he groaned softly and pushed his middle finger inside her throbbing pussy.

Fiona moaned, gyrating against his hand as he stroked

her fleshy canal. "Fuck me one more time," she whispered against his mouth, "and I promise to leave you alone."

Dre swore gutturally and darted a glance over his shoulder. Still hearing the sound of running water, he turned back to Fiona and lifted her off the floor. As she wrapped her legs around his waist, he opened his robe and thrust into her.

They gasped into each other's mouths, her arms looping around his neck as his hands gripped her ass cheeks. As he began fucking her against the front door, it was all she could do not to scream in ecstasy. She couldn't get enough of him. For the first time in her life, she was straight-up dick-whipped. She'd hooked up with Shane last night after class, but he was no substitute for Dre. So there was no way in *hell* she was leaving this nigga alone.

Two minutes of Dre pounding her pussy was all she could handle before she started creaming and coming all over his shaft. He followed seconds later, his body wracked by deep shudders as he shot and shot inside her.

His dick was still pumping when the overhead light suddenly snapped on, followed by Leah's outraged exclamation, "WHAT THE HELL IS GOING ON HERE?"

Dre had barely jerked out of Fiona and spun around before Leah was upon them, catching the two lovers off guard. She wore a bathrobe that matched Dre's, and her face was contorted with fury as she attacked Dre with flying fists.

"You sneaky, cheating motherfucker!" she screamed. "How dare you bring that ghetto bitch into my house while I'm *right* down the hall! *Are you crazy?*"

"Baby, listen—" Dre began pleadingly.

"Don't you 'baby' me, you lying bastard!"

Though Dre attempted to restrain Leah, she broke free of his grasp and lunged at Fiona, who lost her balance and stumbled back against the front door. Before she could recover, Leah punched her in the face and viciously grabbed a chunk of her hair.

Fiona swung blindly, landing blows on Leah's jaw and chest before Dre dragged the skinny heffa away.

"You trifling bitch!" Leah shrieked, struggling wildly in Dre's arms. "How dare you step foot in my house!"

Fiona smirked, ignoring her split lip. "I did a *whole* lot more than that, trick. Just ask your man."

To her everlasting satisfaction, Leah promptly burst into tears.

"You bastard!" she screeched accusingly at Dre. "How could you betray me like this? *What the hell were you thinking?*"

Before Dre could respond, Fiona interjected smugly, "He was thinking about how pussy-whipped he's been ever since he fucked me on Saturday night."

As Leah's eyes widened with wounded disbelief, Dre rounded furiously on Fiona. "GET THE FUCK OUT!"

"Well, okay, if you insist." She smiled coyly, then turned and opened the door. Unable to resist, she glanced back and gave Dre a slow, provocative once-over. "If you want more of this sweet pussy, Daddy, you know where to find me." As Leah lunged toward her, she winked at Dre. "See you at work tomorrow."

She sashayed out the door seconds before it was slammed behind her. As she started down the brick walk, she could hear Leah cursing and screaming hysterically at Dre.

Fiona chuckled, but her satisfaction was short-lived.

Because she knew that she'd not only jeopardized her job at the sports agency but also probably ruined any chance she'd had of becoming Mrs. Beau Chambers.

Chapter 37

Tamia

"I can't believe I'm in *Italy*." Tamia sighed contentedly, her head nestled against Brandon's shoulder as their gondola glided down the moonlit canals of Venice. "Someone please pinch me and tell me I'm not dreaming."

Brandon chuckled, cuddling her closer. "You're not dreaming, sweetheart."

"Are you sure? Because this *definitely* feels like the best dream I've ever had."

"Well, I can't argue with that."

They smiled warmly at each other.

Tamia had been enthralled with Venice from the moment they'd arrived at the airport that afternoon and boarded a water taxi that ushered them into the city in the most exhilarating of welcomes. They'd disembarked from the taxi and checked into a five-star luxury hotel located in the heart of Venice. Tamia's jaw had dropped when they entered their opulently furnished suite, which boasted glass chandeliers, gold-trimmed ceilings, marble columns and floors, and breathtaking views of the island of San Giorgio from a private terrace.

She'd nodded, smiled, and kept her composure as the English-speaking concierge offered helpful suggestions for where to eat, shop, and sightsee. But as soon as he left the room, she'd squealed excitedly and leaped into Brandon's arms, making him laugh as she rained kisses all over his face. When he carried her over to the enormous bed, she'd tugged him down with her, and together they'd rolled around in the sumptuous silk sheets before getting naked and devouring each other.

Afterward they'd showered, changed, and headed out to enjoy a romantic candlelight dinner at a cozy restaurant overlooking the Grand Canal. As music played softly in the background, they sat close together at the table, sipping from the same glass of vino and feeding each other succulent forkfuls of carpaccio, spice-encrusted sea bass, and risotto with black truffles.

After dinner, they'd strolled hand in hand through the busy streets, savoring the sights and sounds of the enchanted city on water. With its beautiful architecture, winding alleys, scenic bridges, and glittering waterways, Tamia could see why Venice was considered one of the most romantic places in the world.

From the moment Brandon told her where they were going, she'd looked forward to taking a gondola ride by moonlight. Despite the crowd of spectators peering down at them from bridges, the experience was as breathtakingly romantic and enjoyable as she'd hoped.

She sighed dreamily as the gondola drifted along the canal, steered expertly by the gondolier who was traditionally garbed in a striped shirt and black pants. Other than to point out a landmark here and there, the man was silent, leaving Tamia and Brandon to their private enjoyment of the passing scenery.

As the moon spread a path of silver on the water, Tamia

glanced up at the dark sky and pointed. "Look! Do you see that?"

Brandon had been nuzzling the nape of her neck. At her delighted exclamation, he followed the direction of her gaze and smiled. "It's a full moon. Surrounded by stars." He paused, looking at her. "Didn't you tell me how rare that is?"

Tamia nodded quickly, pleased that he remembered the conversation they'd had weeks ago.

"So that just confirms it."

"Confirms what?"

His smile softened. "How special tonight is."

Tamia's heart melted. "That's exactly what I was thinking," she whispered.

As they stared at each other, Brandon leaned close and kissed her. Gently at first, then with growing hunger, his tongue stroking hers until her nipples hardened and her clit throbbed.

As he began easing his hand underneath her cashmere sweater dress, she whispered against his mouth, "What're you doing?"

"What does it look like?" He caressed her bare thigh, sending delicious shivers to her pussy.

Pausing to suck his tongue, she murmured, "Have you forgotten that we're not alone?"

"Dude won't care. He's Italian."

Tamia grinned. "Meaning?"

"Italians perfected the art of PDA. But if it makes you feel better"—Brandon's hand crept higher—"I'll pay him to look the other way."

"I don't think so." Chuckling, Tamia pulled away and discreetly rearranged her dress over her legs. When she and Brandon glanced back at the gondolier, the man grinned and gave Brandon a conspiratorial nod of approval.

Brandon winked at Tamia. "What'd I tell you? That's *amore, bella signorina.*"

She just laughed.

At the end of their romantic ride, Brandon generously tipped the gondolier, who kissed Tamia's hand and invited them to come back for another tour before they returned home.

Even though it was late, and they'd already had a long day, Tamia and Brandon didn't immediately head back to the hotel. Venice was the kind of city that lured you to explore, to soak up all it had to offer. So they continued their leisurely stroll, losing themselves in the winding twists and turns of narrow alleys and side streets. Eventually they came upon a small piazza where the crowds were thinner, and secluded corners awaited them at every turn.

Holding Tamia's hand, Brandon guided her down an alley way bathed in soft moonlight. Her pulse raced as he backed her against the brick wall, braced his hands on either side of her head, and slanted his mouth over hers.

She moaned with pleasure, aroused by the feel of his hard dick pressed against her stomach. As their tongues mated, she hooked her leg around his calf and rubbed her pussy against his thigh, making him shudder and groan.

"I've been dying to get inside you again all night," he confessed against her mouth.

"You know we're still out in public, right?"

"Makes no damn difference."

She smiled. "You're crazy," she whispered.

"Crazy about you," he whispered back.

Her heart soared.

As the kiss intensified, Brandon lifted Tamia off the ground. She wrapped her legs around his waist, and he quickly unzipped his pants and pushed aside her lace thong. Moments later she cried out as he impaled her against the wall.

With his feet braced apart on the ground, he began thrusting into her. Tamia closed her eyes and moaned as she grabbed his butt, feeling the muscles clench and unclench as he plunged inside her. She heard voices and laughter at the entrance to the alley as people wandered by. The threat of getting caught only heightened her pleasure and excitement, and she sensed that it was the same for Brandon as he drove into her pussy with deep, relentless strokes.

They exploded together, mouths locked as they swallowed each other's screams of ecstasy.

After several moments of shuddering and panting heavily, they looked at each other and chorused, "Round two. Hotel."

They made it back in record time, rushing up to their suite as if the streets had suddenly been placed under a mandatory evacuation order.

Tamia smiled naughtily as Brandon kicked the door shut behind them, then began stalking her, step for step, across the room. His eyes glittered with fierce arousal as she deliberately pushed the long sleeves of her dress down her arms, then peeled the soft material past her breasts and stomach and over her hips. As the dress slid to the floor, she unhooked her bra and let it drop, then slowly rolled her thigh-high stockings and thong off her legs.

Brandon's nostrils flared as his hungry gaze devoured her voluptuous nudity.

Never taking his eyes off her, he tugged off his shirt and tossed it aside, then toed off his boots and socks. With his chest and feet bared, he looked so damn sexy and primal that Tamia's pussy dripped.

As he reached her, she sank to her knees before him and yanked down his pants and dark briefs. As his erection bobbed free, she took him down her throat and back up again, a move reminiscent of a fire-eater swallowing flames.

Brandon swore hoarsely, shoving his hands into her hair as she repeated the erotic motion, this time hollowing out her cheeks as she suctioned him deep.

"Fuck!" he hissed, his hips thrusting forward as his shaft thickened inside her mouth.

She sucked him voraciously, swirling her tongue around his length as her fingers kneaded his heavy balls.

He groaned huskily. "Oh, shit, I'm about to—"

"Feed me," she whispered encouragingly as he exploded inside her mouth, his head flung back, his hands clenched tightly in her hair.

She drank him dry, savoring his creamy taste and texture. When she'd swallowed the last drop of his cum, Brandon gave another deep shudder and slowly opened his eyes to stare down at her.

"Damn, woman," he growled softly. "You and that mouth are gonna be the death of me."

Tamia smiled seductively. "Nah, baby," she purred. "You can't die—I'm not finished with you yet."

His eyes glinted. "Good. 'Cause I'm just getting started with *you*."

He picked her up, carried her over to the bed, and set her down near the edge. Holding her gaze, he parted her legs and knelt between them, then stroked his tongue over her clit.

Tamia arched off the bed with a choked cry of pleasure.

Her hips writhed against Brandon's face as he licked her labia, then sucked the swollen flesh into his mouth. By the time he curled his tongue into her pussy, she was coming and calling out his name.

She'd barely caught her breath before he flipped her over, hauled her onto all fours, and entered her from behind. She cried out sharply as he filled her, stretching her walls. She looked over her shoulder, meeting his ravenous gaze as he started pumping into her with long, thick strokes.

"Brandon," she moaned in octaves as his hands stroked her bouncing breasts. *"Ohhh, baby . . . you feel so damn good!"*

"So do you, baby. *Fuck*."

She whimpered as he slapped her round butt cheek, making the flesh jiggle beneath his hand. When he slapped her again, she nearly came.

Guttural cries and moans blended with the sound of Brandon's pelvis slapping Tamia's backside as he rammed into her. The pleasure was blisteringly intense, and though she didn't speak Italian, she was pretty sure she was screaming in a foreign language as her orgasm tore through her.

Brandon followed moments later, shouting her name as he pulled out and splashed off on her back and ass.

Before the night ended, they'd made love all over the suite and outside on the terrace, taking each other to indescribable heights of ecstasy. Afterward, thoroughly spent, they collapsed upon the bed, whispered tender endearments to each other, and fell into a deep, satiated slumber.

For the next seven days, Tamia and Brandon had not a care in the world.

They dined on delicious cuisine and drank fine wine while enjoying glorious sunsets. They made love like there was no tomorrow. Night and day, day and night. They went sightseeing, immersing themselves in the history and charm of the Peggy Guggenheim Collection, the Basilica, and the Piazza San Marco, which was populated with the shops of Italy's most famous designers and jewelers. Brandon spent lavishly on Tamia, buying her shoes, handbags, and clothes by Dolce & Gabbana, Prada, and Versace, as well as a Cartier diamond bracelet. They explored ancient marble churches and palaces that graced the banks of the Grand Canal. They befriended locals who directed them to the best restaurants and markets that were off the main tourist drag.

One evening they danced until sunrise at an underground club, where they smoked the best weed they'd ever had. Afterward they returned to the hotel and fucked each other senseless before pigging out on room service.

Wanting to explore Venice's scenic countryside, they spent one night at a cozy bed and breakfast, where they celebrated Thanksgiving with a romantic picnic the next day. Afterward, as they snuggled together on the lush hillside while gazing up at the vivid blue sky, Tamia asked thoughtfully, "Do you believe in the power of dreams?"

"What do you mean?"

She raised her head from Brandon's chest to search his face. "Let me rephrase the question. Do you believe that the dead can communicate with the living through dreams?"

"Hmm," Brandon murmured. "I don't know. I guess I've always had a healthy dose of skepticism when it comes to stuff like that."

"Supernatural stuff?"

"Yeah. I don't really believe in ghosts and things that go bump in the night." He gave Tamia an amused look. "Why? Something you wanna tell me?"

She hesitated, biting her lower lip. "I've been having dreams about my grandmother."

His expression softened. "The one who was murdered ten years ago?"

Tamia nodded. "Ever since I went to prison, I've been dreaming about her."

"Good or bad dreams?"

"Hmm. It's hard to say."

"What do you mean?"

"Well, on one hand, I'm very happy to see her and spend time with her. But on the other hand, there's an undercurrent of sadness to all of the dreams. Like we both know our time together won't last very long."

Brandon tenderly stroked her cheek. "You wake up missing her even more, don't you?"

"I do," Tamia murmured, soothed by Brandon's gentle

touch. "You know, I've spent the past ten years wondering who killed her, hoping for a breakthrough that would help the police solve her murder. But during the dreams, it never occurs to me to ask Mama Esther who killed her. Isn't that weird?"

"Not necessarily. Since you know you don't have a lot of time with her, maybe you don't want to dwell on unpleasant things, like her death."

Tamia sighed. "Maybe."

"What do you two talk about?" Brandon asked curiously.

"Everything."

"Everything?"

Tamia nodded. "The dreams are so realistic and current. I mean, we have conversations about things that are happening in my life right now, not just in the past."

Brandon's eyes probed hers. "Maybe that's your subconscious way of staying connected to your grandmother, since you were so close to her. If she were still alive, you'd still be able to confide in her. So when you've got things weighing on your mind, you dream about unburdening yourself to her."

Tamia nodded slowly, pondering his words. "That makes a lot of sense."

Brandon grinned crookedly. "Of course. I *always* make sense."

Tamia snorted a laugh. "I wouldn't say all *that*."

"Oh, really?" he challenged, his eyes glinting with humor. "When don't I make sense?"

"Well," Tamia purred, smiling wickedly, "when I've got you speaking in tongues during sex—"

With a shout of laughter, Brandon rolled her onto her back and covered her body with his. "Speaking of which . . ."

Tamia smiled, wrapping her arms around his neck as his warm mouth captured hers. "Happy Thanksgiving," she whispered to him.

"It has been," he murmured, staring into her eyes as he kissed her. "One of the best ever."

Tamia wholeheartedly agreed.

No matter what tomorrow may bring, she knew she would never forget this amazing week she'd spent with Brandon.

Chapter 38

Brandon

The day after Brandon and Tamia returned from their trip, Brandon went into the office to catch up on some work so he wouldn't feel bombarded come Monday morning. Since Tamia had errands to run, they'd agreed to meet back at his place by five o'clock so they could have dinner together. Afterward he was supposed to meet Dre for drinks.

Dre had called that morning to tell Brandon that Leah had put him out. Before he could elaborate, he'd been interrupted by the arrival of one of the Texans' players, who needed some physical therapy before tomorrow's football game. Dre had promised to give Brandon the lowdown when they met at Stogie's, but Brandon already knew that his best friend's troubles had something to do with Fiona. He could only hope, for Dre's sake, that he hadn't been careless—no, *stupid*—enough to get caught in the act of cheating.

As Brandon sat down at his desk to check his voice mail messages, his mind was still on the romantic, relaxing week he and Tamia had spent in Italy. So when he gazed out the windows, he saw moonlit canals and a lush green country-side dotted with villas instead of the steel and glass sky-scrapers that formed Houston's downtown skyline. He wished he and Tamia could have stayed away another week—hell, another month. Because while they were in Venice, they hadn't thought about the tumultuous past year, or the obstacles they still had to overcome. When they were taking a romantic gondola ride or making love beneath a glittering canopy of stars, they could have been the only two people in the universe. Nothing and no one else had mattered.

"I take it by the smile on your face that you and Tamia enjoyed your trip."

Snapped out of his soft-focus reverie, Brandon swiveled away from the windows.

When he saw Cynthia standing in his office doorway, he inwardly groaned. He wasn't in the mood for another confrontation with her. He'd hoped to have more time to savor the memories of Italy before reality intruded.

So much for that.

"Cynthia," he murmured, setting down the phone receiver without listening to the rest of his messages. "How're you doing?"

"Not as well as *you're* doing, obviously," she quipped, her arms folded across her chest as she leaned on the door-jamb with her ankles crossed. She wore a belted cardigan sweater over black leggings and suede moccasins.

"How was Italy?" she asked.

"Italy was wonderful," Brandon said evenly. "But I'm sure you don't want to hear the details."

"No," Cynthia agreed, lips twisted sardonically. "My imagination has tortured me enough."

Brandon said nothing.

"I didn't expect to see you back in the office until Monday," she continued, "but I'm glad you came in today because there's something I need to discuss with you. And since hardly anyone else is here, we can have some privacy."

Brandon instinctively tensed. "What do we need to discuss?"

Cynthia hesitated, biting her lower lip. "Mind if I come in?"

Brandon shook his head, then watched with mounting tension as she entered the office, closed the door behind her, and crossed to his desk.

"I decided to heed your advice and refocus my energies on making partner," she explained, settling into one of the leather visitor chairs and crossing her legs. "As painful as that conversation was, you were right. I lost track of my priorities when we started dating, and I became the type of woman I swore I would never become. Thank you for making me see that."

Brandon inclined his head. "That's what friends are for."

Cynthia winced, no doubt in response to the word *friends*. "Yes, well, I appreciate your honesty, though I didn't at the time. I needed the reality check, and now I'm back on track, focused on achieving my most important goal."

"That's good," Brandon murmured.

She nodded slowly, her eyes moving past him to stare out the windows. "There's just one problem, though."

"What's that?"

She met his gaze directly. "I'm late."

Brandon stared at her. "Late for what?"

She just looked at him.

As comprehension dawned, the bottom dropped out of his stomach.

Reeling with shock, he leaned back slowly against his chair and scrubbed an unsteady hand over his face.

Cynthia watched him, silently observing his stunned reaction.

After several excruciating moments, he found his voice—or a weak imitation of it that managed to whisper, "You're pregnant?"

Cynthia nodded. "I think so."

"You *think* so? Have you taken a pregnancy test?"

"Not yet," she said almost defensively.

"Why not?"

"I've been so busy with work that I haven't had a chance to schedule a doctor's appointment. But I plan to do that on Monday."

"What about taking one of those home pregnancy tests?"

She shook her head. "I don't trust those, because I know too many people who've gotten inaccurate results. I'd prefer to wait until I can have a blood test done at the doctor's office. But I know my body, Brandon. I'm *never* late—certainly not five whole days late."

He frowned. "You've been on the pill for about a month, right?"

She hesitated. "Right."

"Well, couldn't *that* be throwing your cycle off?"

Cynthia looked him in the eye. "I've been on the pill before, Brandon, and it's never interfered with my cycle. *Ever*."

He regarded her a moment longer, then shoved to his feet and stood at the windows with his hands jammed into his pockets. The high he'd been riding before Cynthia's appearance had evaporated, possibly for good.

"I guess it was too much for me to hope that you'd greet this news with tears of joy," she said bitterly.

Brandon looked over his shoulder at her. "What do you want me to say, Cynthia? You come to me and tell me that you think you might be pregnant, even though you haven't taken so much as a home pregnancy test. Why didn't you wait until you knew for sure before you brought your suspicions to me?"

"Are you serious?" Cynthia demanded, eyeing him incredulously. "While *you* were off traipsing around Italy with your fucking porn star, *I* spent the past week agonizing over the possibility that I might be carrying the child of a man who no longer wants me. Forgive me for wanting to confide in you the moment you got back. Forgive me for wanting to give you a heads-up that you might be the father of my unborn baby!"

Guilt gnawed at Brandon's insides. "I'm sorry. I didn't mean to come off like—"

"A selfish bastard? Too late for that."

Brandon clenched his jaw, then exhaled a deep, weary breath and dragged his hands over his head. "Look, if you're pregnant—"

"There's no *if* about it."

"—you know I'll be there for you."

"I truly hope so." Cynthia's hand went to her stomach, an instinctively protective gesture that further shamed Brandon. "I have no desire to raise this baby alone, B. It took two of us to create this life, so it'll take two of us to nurture and sustain it. I'm not looking for financial support from you, because we both know that between my salary and the generosity of my parents, no child of mine would ever want for anything."

Brandon scowled. "There's no fucking way I'd ever let someone else—grandparents or not—assume responsibility for my kid. What kind of man do you think I am?"

Cynthia's expression softened, her eyes probing his. "I hope you're still the man I fell in love with nearly three years ago. The kind of man who understands the importance of providing a stable, loving home for a child because that's how *he* was raised. The kind of man who'd put his child's needs above his own selfish desires."

Brandon silently absorbed her words, understanding the implications of what she was asking. She wanted him to choose between their unborn baby and Tamia.

"Our child doesn't need someone with a bottomless bank account," she continued with quiet resolve. "What he or she needs is a father they can count on to always be there for them. And I need a partner, Brandon. Someone to help me raise the precious offspring we brought into this world together. Someone to share the ups and downs, the trials and triumphs of being a parent." Holding his gaze, she uncrossed her legs and slowly rose from the chair. "I hope you won't let me and our baby down."

Brandon eyed her for a long moment, then turned back to the windows.

"Get a blood test," he said gruffly.

"And then?"

He closed his eyes. "Then we'll go from there."

Chapter 39

Tamia

"It's almost time, chile."

Tamia looked at her grandmother, who sat beside her on the gently rocking porch swing, her fingers deftly working her knitting needles.

"Almost time for what, Mama Esther?"

The old woman met Tamia's curious gaze. "Almost time for you to decide what to do about your sister."

Tamia heaved a deep sigh. "I don't want to think about that right now, Mama Esther. Not when things are going so well between me and Brandon—"

"You can't put it off much longer, Tamia. He won't let you."

"Who won't let me? Brandon?"

But Mama Esther was suddenly staring off into the distance, her eyes filled with worry. "Trouble's coming, chile."

A chill swept through Tamia. "What kind of trouble?"

Her grandmother shook her head slowly. "The kind that's been coming for years."

"Years? What are you talking about, Mama? You're starting to scare me."

"I don't want to scare you, baby. But I want you to know that your sister needs you. So when the time comes for you to go to her, don't hesitate." The old woman's eyes bored into Tamia's. "Do you understand what I'm telling you?"

Tamia swallowed nervously, then nodded.

"Good."

Silence lapsed between the two women, punctuated by the click-click-click of Mama Esther's knitting needles.

After a while, Tamia looked down at the unfinished knitting on her grandmother's lap. "I think I know who you're making that blanket for."

Mama Esther's fingers stilled. "Oh?"

Tamia nodded. "Brandon's assistant is having a baby boy. So maybe I'm supposed to give her a blanket at her baby shower next weekend."

"Maybe." The knitting needles were back in motion. "But that's not who I'm making this one for."

"It's not?"

"No, chile."

Tamia frowned at her grandmother. "Then who's it for?"

Mama Esther wore a quiet, enigmatic smile. "You'll know soon enough."

Tamia opened her eyes, jarred awake by the ringing of the doorbell.

Rolling over in Brandon's king-size bed, she peered at the alarm clock. She was surprised to see that it was past noon. She hadn't meant to sleep so late, but she'd been exhausted from jet lag and hours of lovemaking with her boo. So the errands she'd planned to run would probably have to wait until tomorrow.

Assuming Brandon doesn't keep me in bed all day, she thought slyly, stretching against the luxurious cotton sheets.

The doorbell rang again, sounding more insistent this time.

Tamia sighed, then climbed out of bed, padded to the walk-in closet, and retrieved Brandon's bathrobe. The sleeves were too long, and the hem nearly reached her feet. But it was perfect, she mused as she snuggled into the soft fabric, savoring Brandon's clean, wonderful scent.

It felt so good to be back in his bed, his home, his life.

This is where I belong, she thought contentedly, moving through the condo to reach the front door.

Since Brandon hadn't mentioned that he was expecting company, she couldn't imagine who was on the other side of the door.

Trouble's coming, her grandmother's sage warning whispered through her mind.

Tamia frowned, chilled by the thought even as she reminded herself that she'd only been dreaming.

Her voice trembled as she called through the door, "Who is it?"

"Gwen Chambers," came the tart reply.

Tamia froze, her eyes widening with shock. What the hell was Brandon's mother doing there?

Take an educated guess, her conscience mocked.

"Um, just a second." Tamia combed shaky fingers through her hair and tugged the lapels of Brandon's robe together, then drew a deep, calming breath before unlocking and opening the door.

Gwen Chambers stood there seething with haughty indignation. She was an elegantly attractive, maple-toned woman who was a dead ringer for the actress Diahann Carroll. She wore a cashmere trench coat with a silk Hermès scarf and a black Birkin handbag on her arm.

Tamia forced a polite smile. "Hello, Mrs. Chambers."

The woman raked her with a look of scathing contempt. "I don't appreciate being kept waiting on the doorstep like some trespassing salesman."

"I apologize," Tamia said levelly. "I was asleep. Would you like to—"

Before she could complete the invitation, Gwen swept past her and through the door as if she owned the condo, the building, and the land it was built upon.

Alrighty then, Tamia mouthed as she closed the door.

Striving for composure, she asked politely, "Can I offer you something to drink, Mrs. Chambers?"

Gwen eyed her disdainfully. "Do not speak to me as if I'm a guest here. This is *my* son's apartment. If I want something to drink, I can get it myself. Anyway, this isn't a social call."

"Color me surprised," Tamia quipped under her breath.

Gwen's eyes narrowed with displeasure. "I'll get right to the point. How much will it take to make you disappear from my son's life?"

Tamia stared at her. *"Excuse me?"*

"I don't believe I stuttered, Miss Luke. How much will it take to make you go away and leave Brandon alone?"

Tamia eyed her incredulously. "Are you trying to pay me off?"

"If that's what it will take to get rid of you." Gwen reached inside her Birkin and removed a checkbook and a pen. "Name your price."

Tamia shook her head slowly, numb with shock. "I don't believe this."

Gwen's lips twisted scornfully. "Please don't insult my intelligence by pretending to be outraged, Miss Luke. Bribery is the only language that a woman of your ilk understands. As I recall, you were more than willing to become

Dominic Archer's sex slave in exchange for his silence. So I know you won't turn down cold, hard cash." She opened her checkbook. "How does $250,000 sound?"

"I don't want your damn money," Tamia said, coldly and succinctly.

Gwen snorted. "Who are you kidding, Tamia? We both know you're nothing but a gold-digging whore who's been after my son's money from the day you met him. So don't stand there and pretend you don't have a price, because I know damn well that you do. So what is it? I'm feeling generous today, so I'll up the ante to $350,000."

Tamia shook her head in wounded disbelief. "I think you'd better leave."

"I'm not leaving until we've reached an agreement."

"That's not going to happen," Tamia snarled. "I don't want your fucking money. I love Brandon—"

"Give me a damn break!" Gwen interjected contemptuously. "You don't love my son! You don't know the first goddamn thing about love, or you wouldn't have hurt and betrayed Brandon the way you did! See, you may have fooled *him* into believing that you've changed your ways, but *I* know the truth, and the truth is that you're a scheming, manipulative, selfish little bitch who'll go to any lengths to get what you want. But if you think for one second that I'm going to stand by and let you ruin my son's life, you'd better think again!"

"How dare you!" Tamia exploded, choking with pain and fury. "You don't know the first damn thing about me! And the last I checked, Brandon is a grown man who's more than capable of deciding what's best for him!"

"Which sure as hell isn't *you!*"

"That's not your call to make!" Tamia raked the other woman with a look of incredulous disgust. "And what the hell kind of mother tries to bribe people into leaving her son?"

"The kind of mother who wants to protect her son from making the biggest damn mistake of his life!" Gwen roared.

Tamia raised her chin in defiance. "Well, you wasted your time coming here, because I have *no* intention of taking one damn cent from you."

"Suit yourself," Gwen hissed, shoving her checkbook into her handbag. "You're going to regret turning down my generous offer when Brandon sends you packing, which he eventually will. Why? Because you're nothing but a novelty to him, Tamia. The girl from the wrong side of the tracks is *always* appealing at the very beginning. But Brandon's no fool. He's going to be our state's next attorney general, then he's going to run for the U.S. Senate. With his God-given talents, combined with his family connections and the backing of President Obama, the sky's the limit for Brandon. Do you honestly believe that he's going to jeopardize his future by marrying a former porn star who was recently acquitted of murder? He knows you're not wife material, Tamia. Not only that, but he doesn't love you. He loves Cynthia. If he hadn't been distracted with your criminal trial this past year, he and Cynthia probably would have been married by now. *She's* the one he belongs with, not you!"

Tamia swallowed tightly, the woman's venomous diatribe cutting deep. "If what you're saying is true," she challenged, "why are you here talking to me? If you're so confident that Brandon doesn't love me, why go to the trouble of trying to bribe me to go away? Why take the risk that I'll go to the media to tell them about this conversation?"

Gwen's eyes narrowed. "You wouldn't dare."

Tamia sneered. "Don't be too sure about that. I think voters have a right to know that the lieutenant governor's wife—a powerful federal judge—is capable of resorting to bribery. I'm sure that revelation wouldn't go over too well with your employer, not to mention all those criminal defendants who felt they didn't get a fair shake in your courtroom.

Once they learn that you're not above *offering* bribes, it's only natural that they'd question whether you've ever *received* bribes. And once that seed is planted, well . . ." Tamia trailed off deliberately, smirking at Gwen. "You can infer the rest."

Nostrils flaring with fury, Gwen advanced on Tamia until their faces were separated by mere inches. "You conniving little bitch," she snarled. "If you breathe a word of this conversation to *anyone*, including Brandon, I will become your worst fucking nightmare. If you thought the five months you spent in prison were bad, you haven't seen *nothing* yet. Cross me at your own peril, little girl."

With the vicious threat issued and received, Gwen turned and marched out of the apartment, slamming the door behind her.

Chapter 40

Fiona

Fiona was sweating bullets as she drove home that afternoon.

A man from the district attorney's office had called her while she was at the barber shop, tightening up a customer's fade. He'd introduced himself as Cal Hartwig and explained to her that he was preparing to bring murder charges against Dominic Archer, but first he wanted to ask her some questions about her estranged father.

Fiona had panicked.

If the prosecutor had connected Sonny Powell to Isabel Archer, then it was only a matter of time before the trail would lead right to Fiona.

She couldn't allow that to happen.

After promising to return the man's call when she got off from work, she'd finished the rest of her appointments, then bounced.

Twenty minutes later, she whipped into her driveway and hopped out of her SUV while it was still rocking. Although it was sixty degrees outside, sweat dampened her forehead, and her armpits were soaked beneath her sweater.

Heart pounding, she burst through the front door and raced to her bedroom. She grabbed a large suitcase from the closet and tossed it down on the bed, then hurriedly began throwing clothes inside.

Ever since Tamia threatened to turn her in to the police, Fiona had been preparing herself for the day she'd have to skip town. She'd been stockpiling her earnings and the generous tips she received from her clients, so she had more than enough money to set herself up nicely wherever she wound up.

She had no intention of going back to prison. So she had no choice but to flee.

Satisfied that she'd packed enough clothes to last her at least three weeks, Fiona snapped the suitcase shut, hoisted it off the bed, and started across the room.

But just as she reached the doorway, she heard a sound.

The soft scrape of a boot against the hardwood floor.

She froze, the fine hairs rising on the back of her neck.

Someone was inside the house.

Swallowing hard, Fiona moved backward, retreating from the door even as the intruder's footsteps drew nearer.

Then suddenly a tall, dark figure filled the doorway.

And Fiona found herself staring into the face of the man she thought she'd never see again.

"Going somewhere?" Sonny Powell drawled, one arm behind his back.

Shaking with fear and dread, Fiona whispered, "Daddy?"

A slow, sinister grin cut across his face, which was as handsome as she remembered. Thick eyebrows, high cheekbones, a strong nose that whispered of some distant Native American ancestry.

"Didn't I tell you I'd come back for you someday?"

Fiona nodded slowly, remembering the malevolent presence she'd sensed that night in the cemetery, followed by the eerie phone call she'd received. *Guilty*, the voice had whispered.

She'd dismissed the call as a prank, but deep down inside, she'd known that her day of reckoning was near.

Sonny stepped into the room, his dark eyes searching her face. "Do you know why I'm here, baby girl?"

She gulped a shaky breath but didn't respond.

"I loved her."

Fiona remained mutinously silent.

Her father crept closer. "Did you hear what I said? I *loved* her, and you took her away from me."

Disregarding his words, Fiona beamed at him. "What're you hiding behind your back, Daddy? Did you bring me a present?"

His face hardened.

"No present," he said very softly. "Not this time."

As Fiona watched, he brought his arm from behind his back and pointed a gun at her.

The blood drained from her head. "Daddy . . . ?"

"Call your sister."

Fiona eyed him fearfully. "Why?"

A cold, narrow smile curved Sonny's mouth. "We're gonna have a family reunion."

Chapter 41

Tamia

"Thanks for dropping everything to have lunch with me," Tamia said to Shanell that afternoon.

The two friends sat inside the cozy warmth of Tamia's car, which was parked at the curb in front of Shanell's one-story stucco house.

Shanell waved a dismissive hand. "Girl, please. *I* should be thanking *you* for getting me out of the house for a few hours. I love Mark's family, but having them here for Thanksgiving has stressed me the hell out. I've lost count of how many children his siblings have."

Tamia chuckled. "Do they still harass you and Mark about starting your own family?"

Shanell snorted. "You know they do. But I've learned to tune them out. When God says it's time for me and my husband to become parents, I'll get pregnant. Besides, the more I'm around Mark's nieces and nephews, the more I appreciate my clean, peaceful home."

The two women laughed.

"Anyway," Shanell continued, "I enjoyed catching up with you and hearing all about Italy. You and Brandon had such an amazing time together. Sounded like a honeymoon."

Tamia sighed. "I wish."

Prior to Gwen Chambers's visit, she'd been optimistic about her future with Brandon. But now that she realized his parents would never accept her, she wasn't feeling so hopeful anymore. And she couldn't help but wonder if there'd been a grain of truth to the things Gwen had told her. *Was* she just a novelty to Brandon? Would he and Cynthia already be married if he hadn't been preoccupied with Tamia's trial?

Observing her troubled expression, Shanell gently probed, "Are you sure there's nothing else you want to tell me?"

Tamia met her friend's speculative gaze. After her confrontation with Brandon's mother, she'd been so upset that she'd called Shanell to vent. But Shanell had been busy with her houseguests. By the time she returned Tamia's call, Tamia had decided not to say a word about Gwen's bribery attempt. She was too humiliated, for starters. And she was just paranoid enough to believe that Gwen had her phone tapped.

She smiled wanly at Shanell. "There's nothing else. I'm just trying to take things one day at a time with Brandon. Italy was a dream, but now it's back to reality, and the reality is that we still have a lot of issues to overcome."

"True. But if you love each other, you can overcome anything." When Tamia was silent, Shanell leaned over and hugged her. "Everything's going to be fine."

Tamia just smiled, wishing she shared her friend's optimism.

After dropping Shanell off, she was on her way back to Brandon's condo when her cell phone rang. Even before she checked the caller ID, she knew who was calling. She'd been expecting to hear from her sister ever since she'd awakened from the dream.

As she reluctantly answered the phone, Mama Esther's admonition whispered through her mind. *Your sister needs you. So when the time comes for you to go to her, don't hesitate.*

"What is it, Fiona?" she asked without preamble.

"I know you told me not to call you anymore," her sister said tremulously. "But I need to talk to you, Tam-Tam. It's important."

Trouble's coming. . . . The kind that's been coming for years.

Tamia swallowed nervously. "Is everything okay, Fee?"

Her sister paused for a long moment. "I'd rather talk to you in person."

"I'm on my way."

Fifteen minutes later, Tamia pulled into the driveway behind Fiona's SUV and cut the ignition.

As she surveyed the white shotgun house, nothing seemed out of place. Yet she felt a sense of foreboding that made her pick up her cell phone and call Brandon.

"Hey, it's me," she told his voice mail. "I'm meeting Fiona at our old house, so I'll be running late for dinner." She paused. "If I'm more than an hour late and you can't reach me . . . call the police."

After shoving her phone into her back pocket, Tamia climbed out of the car and slowly walked up to the house. When she reached the front door, she turned and glanced up and down the silent, shadowy street. She could remember a time, not long ago, when the neighbors had congregated on their porches every night to gossip, play cards, and watch the comings and goings of others. Now it seemed that most people preferred to remain indoors, isolated from one another.

Drawing a deep breath, Tamia turned around and twisted

the doorknob, her nerves tightening when she discovered that it was unlocked.

She hesitated, then cautiously entered the house.

Moments later, she let out a shocked gasp.

Fiona was strapped to a chair in the living room, her arms and legs bound with wire, her mouth sealed with duct tape. Her eyes were wide with terror.

"Oh, my God!" Tamia cried out, rushing to her sister's side. "Who did this to—"

"Hello, Tamia. So glad you could join us."

Tamia whipped her head toward the voice.

Her blood ran cold at the sight of Sonny Powell sauntering casually into the living room.

He had a gun pointed right at her.

Fear pulsed through Tamia's veins. "W-What are you doing here?" she whispered faintly.

A grim parody of a smile twisted Sonny's mouth. "As I told your sister, I thought we were long overdue for a family reunion."

Memories assailed Tamia. The terrifying roar of his voice as he shouted curses at her mother. The sound of flesh striking flesh as he punched Lorraine, his rage untempered by her shrill screams and pleas. The heavy thud of his boots against the floor as he stormed out of the house, disappearing for days at a time.

Although he'd rarely struck Tamia or Fiona, the violence he'd unleashed upon their mother had been damaging enough to leave the two sisters permanently scarred.

He looked Tamia up and down, his eyes glinting with appreciation. "Lorraine wasn't much of a cook or housekeeper, but she sure knew how to make some beautiful babies."

Tamia swallowed tightly as nausea crawled up the back of her throat. "Why are you here, Sonny? What do you want?"

"I want justice."

"For who?"

He met her gaze unblinkingly. "Isabel Archer."

Tamia's heart pounded into her throat. "I didn't kill Isabel."

"I know." Sonny looked past her to Fiona. "Your sister did. And you let her get away with it, so that makes you just as guilty."

Exchanging troubled glances with Fiona, Tamia nervously licked her dry lips. "I don't understand. What does Isabel's death have to do with you?"

Sonny's gaze returned to hers. "I was in love with her."

It was the *last* thing Tamia had expected him to say.

Stunned, she gaped at him for several moments before whispering, "But . . . Isabel was married."

"To a worthless motherfucker who didn't appreciate what a good woman she was." Sonny smirked. "But I don't have to tell you that. *You're* part of the reason Isabel was leaving Dominic. Which is a damn shame. I know your grandmother didn't raise you to be no homewrecker."

Tamia didn't respond. Her mind was reeling as she struggled to comprehend what he was telling her. "So you and *Isabel* were having an affair?"

"It didn't start off that way. Believe me, she tried her damnedest to honor her vows and make her sham of a marriage work." Sonny paused, frowning suspiciously at Tamia. "You're standing too damn close to your sister."

As Tamia edged away from Fiona, he gestured to the sofa with the barrel of his gun. "Just sit the fuck down."

She obeyed without hesitation.

"I've been back in Houston for over a year," he continued once she was seated, perched tensely on the edge of the sofa. "You don't need to know where I was before that, or what I was doing. All you need to know is that I was laying low, trying to keep myself out of trouble." His lips twisted sardonically. "Your mama always said that trouble followed me wherever I went. So I was determined to prove her wrong. But times were hard. When I came back to Houston last year, I had to stay in a shelter until I could find a job and get back on my feet. Isabel was volunteering there, and that's how we met. She helped me find a construction job, and unlike most rich motherfuckers who only do charity work to make themselves feel good, Isabel actually gave a damn about me as a person."

He glared accusingly at Fiona. "She was a good woman. She didn't deserve what you did to her."

Fiona made a whimpering noise behind the strip of duct tape plastered across her mouth.

"Wait a minute." Tamia stared at her sister, struck by a horrifying realization. "Did you know who Isabel was before I told you about her?"

Tears welled in Fiona's eyes.

"Of course she knew," Sonny jeered, stalking over to Fiona and viciously ripping the tape off her mouth. "She went to Isabel's house that night to kill her!"

"Oh, my God." The blood drained from Tamia's head, even as she shook it in denial. "That can't be true. You told me it was an accident, Fiona!"

When Fiona said nothing, Sonny pressed the barrel of the gun to her temple. "Tell your sister the fucking truth. *Tell her!*"

"ALL RIGHT!" Fiona exploded, spittle flying from her mouth. "It's true! I killed that bitch on purpose!"

Tamia gasped sharply, staring at her sister with shock and horror. "Why, Fiona? Why'd you do it?"

"Because I hated her!" Fiona screamed, her face contorted with outraged fury as she glared at her father. "She had the nerve to visit me one day while I was locked up. Did you know that? She said she was a close friend of yours, and

she was concerned about you because you hadn't forgiven yourself for not being a good father. She wanted to know whether I was willing to reconcile with you. When I asked her how the fuck that was any of her business, she said she loved you, and she wanted you to be happy." Fiona's tone hardened with bitter accusation. "You told a complete stranger about me, Daddy, but you didn't even care enough to come see me yourself! You've *never* wanted me or loved me, but you loved *her!*"

"So you killed Isabel so I couldn't have her?" Sonny demanded furiously.

"Yes!" Fiona sneered at him, heedless of the revolver pressed to her temple. "The stupid bitch thought I came over to talk about you. When I pulled my gun out, she got scared and tried to run. But she never stood a fucking chance."

Tamia stared at Fiona, chilled by her words and the cold, calculating gleam in her eyes. How could she not have known the extent of her sister's mental illness? Her depravity? How could she have missed all the warning signs? *How?*

"I don't believe this," Tamia whispered, shaking her head at Fiona. "It wasn't an accident. You didn't panic because Isabel threatened to call the police. You went over there to kill her, knowing that I was supposed to meet her that very same night. You murdered her, and you deliberately let me take the fall for it. How could you, Fiona? *How could you?*"

Her sister's gaze was disturbingly calm. "I knew you wouldn't be convicted—"

"Bullshit!" Tamia raged. "You knew no such thing! *No one* knew how the trial was going to turn out! I could have been convicted and sent to prison for the rest of my life. I could have gotten the *death penalty*, Fiona! But you didn't give a shit! All you cared about was getting rid of an inno-

cent woman who never did a damn thing to you. I hope you rot in *hell* for what you did to Isabel!"

"Because that's where I belong, right?" Fiona spat, her eyes flashing with bitter resentment. "I've always been the fuckup, the black sheep in a family full of black sheep. Mama never expected me to amount to anything, so she never bothered to encourage my dreams. *You* always thought you were smarter than me just because you went to college, even though you whored yourself out to pay your fucking tuition. You thought you were better than me just because you snagged yourself a rich boyfriend while I was still running around with broke hood rats. When I got in trouble with Marquis, you *never* let me forget what a stupid mistake I'd made by trusting him. You threw that shit back in my face every chance you got—"

"I did not!"

"Did, too! As I recall, I had to check your ass about it earlier this year. So I considered it poetic justice when *you* turned around and got yourself caught up with Dominic's mess."

"Oh, my God," Tamia breathed, eyeing her sister incredulously. "So *that's* why you set me up? To get back at me for *criticizing* you?"

Fiona smirked at her. "You know what they say. What goes around, comes around."

Tamia felt sick to her stomach. "You need help."

"You don't know the half of it," Sonny interjected darkly.

Tamia looked at him. "I don't understand something. If you knew she killed Isabel, why didn't you come forward sooner?"

"I didn't know for sure," he admitted grimly. "At first I thought Dominic may have killed Isabel because he'd somehow found out about us. She'd always warned me how vindictive he could be, so I knew I couldn't put anything past him. But my gut instinct told me Fiona had done it. When you got arrested and went on trial, I knew you were protecting her, just like you'd always done when you two were children. But the stakes were much higher this time. So I kept waiting for you to crack under the pressure and tell the truth. But you never did. After you were acquitted, I waited some more to see whether you'd do the right thing and turn your sister over to the police. As you can see"—he dragged the barrel of the gun down to Fiona's throat—"my patience has worn thin. So I've decided to take matters into my own hands."

A chill ran through Tamia. "W-What does that mean? What are you planning to do?"

Sonny met her stricken gaze. "I was a terrible father to you and your sister. I had a nasty temper that caused me to hurt your mother, and I know that our constant fighting traumatized you and Fiona. I'm not proud of my behavior, especially since I know I created a monster. I can't change the past, so there's only one thing left for me to do." As he cocked the trigger, Fiona whimpered fearfully and squeezed her eyes shut.

"Please don't kill me, Daddy," she begged.

Sonny sneered. "Maybe I should have a long time ago. If I'd gotten rid of you back then, your poor grandmother would still be alive."

Tamia went completely still, staring at Sonny. "What are you talking about?"

He looked at her. Even before he opened his mouth to speak, icy foreboding settled over her heart.

"Your sister was mad at me for breaking another promise to come see her. She wanted to get back at me, so she told your grandmother that I'd been molesting her for years." Sonny's expression hardened. "Esther believed her. She went to your mother and urged her to call the police and

Child Protective Services, or she'd do it herself. When your mother confronted me about Fiona's accusations, I went to Fiona and told her to tell the damn truth before the police threw me in jail."

"I never wanted that to happen!" Fiona burst out desperately. "I just wanted to get your attention, Daddy. That's all I ever wanted!"

"So what happened?" Tamia whispered, her body quaking with fear and dread. "Tell me what happened!"

Fiona looked at her, her eyes glistening with tears of shame and regret. "I told Mama Esther that I'd made up the whole story about my father, but she didn't believe me. She thought I was just trying to protect him. She insisted that she was going to call the authorities first thing in the morning." Fiona shook her head slowly. "I couldn't let her do that. I couldn't let them take away my daddy."

Tamia stared at her sister with mounting horror. "No," she whispered. "Please tell me you didn't—"

"Late that night, while you and Ma˙ were sleeping, I took Ma's car keys and snuck out of the house. I was fifteen, remember, and I'd just gotten my learner's permit. I drove to Mama Esther's house and parked a few blocks away, like I did that night at Isabel's." Silent, mournful tears streamed down Fiona's face. "I had a baseball bat. Mama Esther was fast asleep in her bed. She . . . she never saw me coming."

"NO!" Tamia screamed.

Fiona was trembling violently. "After I h-hit her, I t-took all her money and s-some jewelry so it would look like a r-robbery." Her face crumpled, and she began weeping uncontrollably. "I'm so sorry, Mama Esther. . . . *I'M SO SORRY!*"

With an anguished wail that was wrenched from her soul, Tamia launched herself at her sister—clawing, slapping, and punching Fiona before Sonny grabbed her around the waist and hauled her back.

Tamia kicked and flailed against him, sobbing hysterically. "She killed our grandmother! *Oh, God, she killed Mama Esther!*"

"I know," Sonny said soothingly. "And she's going to pay for it."

Suddenly the front door crashed open.

"POLICE!" an authoritative voice boomed. "Nobody move!"

Tamia watched as several armed police officers rushed into the house.

Moments later, everything went black.

Chapter 42

Tamia

One week later, Tamia and Brandon sat beside each other on her living room sofa. They were alone in the apartment, since Honey had not yet returned from visiting her family in New Orleans.

Tamia's hands were wrapped around a steaming cup of hot chocolate Brandon had brought her. She'd been taking small sips, hoping to chase away the chill that had settled deep into her bones and wouldn't let go.

Although an entire week had passed since that harrowing night, she was still struggling to process everything that had happened. Overcome with shock and horror, she'd fainted when the police arrived at the house that evening. When she came to, she'd found herself peering into the concerned faces of Sonny and Brandon, who'd called 911 and rushed over after listening to Tamia's cryptic voice mail message.

As it turned out, the police had already been camped outside the house, along with Assistant District Attorney Cal Hartwig. After Tamia regained consciousness, Sonny had explained to her that he'd struck a deal with the D.A.'s office. In exchange for Sonny's assistance with solving two homicides, the prosecutor had agreed to grant Tamia immunity for concealing the identity of Isabel's murderer.

When Sonny showed up at the house on Saturday night, he'd been wearing a wire. He knew Fiona would never willingly confess her crimes to him, so he'd ordered her to call Tamia. Everything had gone according to plan.

Sonny revealed to Tamia that he'd stayed away for the past ten years because he'd feared that Fiona would maliciously try to implicate him in Mama Esther's murder. In light of everything Tamia had just learned about her sister, she realized that Sonny had been wise to keep his distance.

She couldn't believe that after all these years, she finally knew who'd killed her grandmother. And it was the absolute *last* person she would have ever imagined.

After confessing to the two murders, Fiona had waived her right to a jury trial, opting to be tried and sentenced by a judge. She was refusing visitors, and Tamia had made no attempt to go see her. She knew it would be a very long time before she could even *think* about forgiving Fiona.

Observing her haunted expression, Brandon said softly, "I'm really sorry about your grandmother."

Tamia nodded, staring at the foamy surface of her hot chocolate. "Losing her the first time was devastating enough. Knowing that my own sister killed her . . . it's like losing Mama Esther all over again."

Brandon nodded, gently rubbing the nape of her neck. "Have you had any more dreams about her?"

She shook her head. "Not yet. I've been waiting all week, hoping to see her and talk to her. But she hasn't come back. Maybe she doesn't need to anymore, now that her murder has been solved."

"Maybe."

In the silence that followed, Tamia reflected on the last

dream she'd had. Mama Esther had come to her to warn her of pending trouble. But Tamia now realized that she'd never been in any danger. Her grandmother had summoned her to the house knowing that Sonny had no intention of hurting her.

"I wish you'd told me the truth about Fiona," Brandon said quietly, his voice breaking into Tamia's thoughts.

Swallowing hard, she risked meeting his gaze. He looked more disappointed than angry.

"I know I should have been honest with you," she confessed. "I was genuinely trying to protect Fiona, but it was wrong of me to keep you in the dark. I'm truly sorry."

Brandon was silent.

She remembered what he'd told her the night Dominic showed up at her apartment. *If I find out that you're lying to me about anything—absolutely anything—I promise you there won't be any second chances.*

A knot of dread tightened in her stomach.

She was going to lose him. Again.

She anxiously searched his face. "Do you accept my apology?"

He hesitated for a long moment, then heaved a deep breath and nodded shortly. "I do."

"You do?" Tamia echoed hopefully.

"Yes." A small, humorless smile touched his mouth. "I think you've gotten so used to keeping secrets, you don't know any other way to be."

Tamia couldn't deny it, though she desperately wished she could. And judging by Brandon's disappointed expression, he probably wished the same.

After a prolonged silence, he asked casually, "Have you heard from Dominic?"

Caught off guard by the question, Tamia shook her head. "No. Why?"

Brandon shrugged. "Just curious."

In the wake of Fiona's confession, Dominic had been cleared as a suspect in his wife's murder. After Tamia dropped the charges against him, he'd been released from prison, where he'd been waiting to stand trial for violating the restraining order. His assets had been unfrozen, and once he collected on Isabel's multimillion-dollar life insurance policy, he'd be richer than ever.

Tamia sipped her hot chocolate. "Now that his wife's killer has been caught, Dominic has no reason to bother me anymore."

Brandon gave her a long, dark look. "Don't be too sure about that."

Tamia was silent. She was suddenly remembering something, a fragment of the dream that had been forgotten in all the madness of the past week.

She looked at Brandon. "Is Cynthia pregnant?"

Startled, he stared at her. "What?"

"In the dream I told you about, my grandmother was knitting a baby blanket. She wouldn't tell me who it was for. She just said I'd know soon enough." Tamia paused, pulse hammering. "Is Cynthia pregnant?"

Brandon held her gaze for a long moment, then nodded slowly. "Yes."

The bottom dropped out of Tamia's stomach. "When did you find out?" she whispered.

He hesitated. "Last Saturday, after we got back from Italy. She told me when I went into the office that she suspected she was pregnant. Her doctor confirmed the results on Wednesday."

"I see." Tamia swallowed painfully. No wonder Cynthia had been all sunshine and smiles at the office this week. "When were you going to tell me?"

Brandon looked grim. "I was waiting for the right time. You've been dealing with a lot this past week."

"You're right," Tamia said shakily. "I don't think I could

have handled hearing this news before today. I'm not handling it very well right now."

"I'm sorry," Brandon murmured.

"For getting Cynthia pregnant? Or for the decision you've already made to be with her?"

Brandon met her accusing gaze. "I don't want my child to be raised by a single parent, especially one who'll be struggling to balance the demands of motherhood with a busy law career."

Tamia wanted to tell him that women juggle motherhood and careers all the time. But she knew she'd come off sounding horribly selfish and insensitive. And she knew that *she'd* want and expect Brandon to marry her if *she* were carrying his child.

When all was said and done, the sad truth was that she was still reaping from her treacherous behavior. If she'd never cheated on Brandon, she wouldn't have opened the door for Cynthia to step into the picture. Ultimately, Tamia had no one but herself to blame for driving Brandon into the arms of another woman.

Still, she couldn't help but wonder whether Cynthia was really with child. She certainly wouldn't be the first woman who'd faked a pregnancy to trap a man into marriage. Mama Esther had been smiling when she'd told Tamia that she would find out soon enough who the baby blanket was for. Would she have smiled when she knew that Cynthia's pregnancy would devastate Tamia?

"Are you sure she's telling the truth?" Tamia blurted.

Brandon sighed heavily. "Yes. I spoke to her doctor myself."

"Oh. I see." Blinking back tears, Tamia forced a wobbly smile. "Then I guess congratulations are in order. So . . . congratulations."

Brandon reached over and gently cupped her cheek. "I'll never forget Italy."

"Neither will I," Tamia whispered achingly.

They gazed at each other for several moments.

As Brandon slowly withdrew his hand, Tamia swiped tears from the corners of her eyes and cleared her throat. "Sonny told me about a job opening for an advertising assistant at the construction company he works for. He said he'd put in a good word for me if I'm interested. I think I am."

Something like regret flashed in Brandon's eyes. But he merely nodded.

"I see that your father's political opponents wasted no time capitalizing on Fiona's arrest," Tamia said cynically. "They ran a spot on TV this morning that referenced your involvement with me—a former porn star and murder defendant whose sister just confessed to killing two people, including her own grandmother. The ad made me and Fiona sound more depraved than the Manson Family."

Brandon grimaced, shaking his head in angry disgust. "I'm really sorry you had to see that shit. It had Russ Sutcliffe's sleazy fingerprints all over it."

Tamia waved a dismissive hand. "You don't have to be sorry. I understand that politics is a dirty business, and I knew it was only a matter of time before they'd come after me. Let's face it. I'm a gold mine of scandal." She sighed heavily. "On the bright side, once they find out that you and I are no longer involved, they'll have to sling their mud elsewhere."

She thought of Joseph Yarbrough's secret relationship with Honey. She hoped, for Honey's sake, that Bernard Chambers's political rivals never caught a whiff of her scandalous affair with the bishop.

"Brandon?"

"What, baby?"

"If we ever meet in another life," Tamia said softly, "I hope we'll have less obstacles to overcome to be together."

Brandon smiled sadly. "Me too."

A heavy silence lapsed between them.

Reaching a decision, Tamia set her cup down on the table, rose from the sofa, and held out her hand to Brandon. "Come with me," she whispered.

He stared at her hand for a long moment, then slowly raised his eyes to hers. She saw his internal struggle, his desire for her warring with the sense of responsibility he felt toward Cynthia and their unborn child.

Slowly he stood, shaking his head at her. "I shouldn't."

"One more night." Tamia's throat tightened with raw emotion. "We'll make it a long good-bye."

Brandon's expression softened.

After an agonizing eternity, he took her hand and allowed himself to be led to her bedroom . . .

Chapter 43

Cynthia

Cynthia carefully smoothed down the pleated skirt of her white silk dress. It wasn't the Vera Wang gown she'd already selected for her wedding because, technically, today wasn't the "big day." Or at least not the big day she'd always envisioned whenever she'd fantasized about exchanging vows with Brandon.

The kind of lavish society wedding she wanted—and intended to have—would take months of planning and preparation. Unfortunately, she couldn't wait that long to get Brandon down the aisle. She'd had a hard enough time convincing him to marry her in a small, intimate ceremony at the justice of the peace. He'd claimed not to want a shotgun wedding, but Cynthia knew better. The only reason he preferred a long engagement was to give himself more time to change his mind. Because as long as Tamia was around, he would always feel torn between doing the right thing and succumbing to temptation.

It would be Cynthia's duty, as his wife, to purge temptation from his system.

And she intended to do just that.

Joseph and Coretta Yarbrough were seated across the small table from Cynthia. Their wedding guests—which included some close relatives, friends, and members of Brandon's family—awaited them inside the room where marriage ceremonies were officiated. Afterward, more guests would join them for an elegant reception at an upscale waterfront restaurant.

Coretta sighed, breaking the heavy silence that had permeated the room. "I'm looking forward to doing this the *right* way at our church in a few months. You know the sanctuary will be packed, and the banquet hall will be decorated to perfection."

Her husband grunted. "I still don't understand why we couldn't just wait to have a proper wedding ceremony. No daughter of mine should be getting married at no damn justice of the peace." His eyes narrowed on Cynthia's face. "What's the rush if you're not pregnant?"

Cynthia and her mother shared a glance.

They'd both agreed not to tell Joseph or his four sons about Cynthia's pregnancy. Although the Yarbrough men already considered Brandon part of the family, they'd always been overprotective of Cynthia. So there was no telling how they'd react to the news that Brandon had gotten her knocked up . . . especially if he jilted her at the altar today.

Cynthia forced a smile for her father. "If you think about it, Daddy, Brandon and I spend so much time in court, it seems only fitting that we'd get married inside a courthouse."

Her father wasn't amused. "You shouldn't have to settle for a shotgun wedding, formality or not. If this was Brandon's idea—"

"It wasn't, Daddy. It was mine."

"That's even worse." Joseph checked his watch and scowled. "Where *is* Brandon anyway?"

Good question, Cynthia thought darkly. "I'm sure he's on his way."

Joseph and Coretta exchanged wary glances.

"Please stop doing that," Cynthia snapped. "He'll be here. He's just running late."

Her parents didn't look convinced.

And with good reason.

Brandon was twenty minutes late. If he didn't show up soon, they'd have to reschedule the ceremony.

Assuming he hadn't gotten cold feet.

Cynthia eyed her silk clutch purse on the table. She wanted nothing more than to grab her cell phone, call Brandon, and ask him where the hell he was. But she couldn't let her parents see that she was just as worried as they were.

She sent another discreet glance at her diamond-encrusted wristwatch—an engagement present from Brandon's mother. *You patiently waited on my son for over two years*, Gwen had told her, explaining the symbolism of the gift. *You proved that timing is everything, darling.*

And speaking of timing . . .

Cynthia glanced toward the closed door, silently willing Brandon to walk through it, flashing those sexy dimples as he smiled at her.

Any moment now.

But he didn't.

Fighting to stave off hysteria, Cynthia smiled brightly at her parents. "Thank God this is just a dress rehearsal. I promise you he won't be late to our *real* wedding ceremony."

Her parents shared another dubious glance but remained silent.

Cynthia kept her eye on the door, hoping and waiting . . .

Chapter 44

Tamia

Tamia sat alone at a cozy table tucked into a corner of Da Marco, the Italian restaurant Brandon had taken her to on their first date. She sat with her back facing the entrance because she didn't want to appear too anxious, checking the door every two minutes, looking hopeful every time someone new arrived. And if four o'clock came and went without Brandon showing up, she didn't want the other diners to witness her devastation.

Which she would be if Brandon went through with marrying Cynthia.

She'd spent the past week struggling to accept his decision to be with the mother of his unborn child. But no matter how hard she tried to convince herself that Brandon was doing the right thing, the honorable thing, she just couldn't bring herself to let him go.

Not without a fight.

So she'd picked up the phone yesterday and called him.

When he answered, she'd laid her heart on the line. "I love you, Brandon Chambers. I love you so damn much. I know we've had our ups and downs, but after everything we've been through, our feelings for each other haven't changed. If anything, my feelings for you have only gotten stronger. And even though I promised not to say anything, I know you rented the apartment for me. You wouldn't have done that if you didn't love me, if you didn't care what happens to me. I don't want to lose you again, Brandon. If you agree that we belong together, meet me at Da Marco tomorrow at four."

Silence had greeted her fervent declaration.

Without awaiting Brandon's response, Tamia had quietly ended the call.

And now she sat perusing the restaurant's dinner menu, though she had no appetite. How could she possibly think about food when her future hung in the balance?

When her cell phone rang on the table, she nearly jumped out of her skin. Drawing a shaky breath, she picked up the phone and checked the caller ID, relaxing when she saw Honey's number. She'd been wondering whether the chick had decided to remain in New Orleans.

"Hey, girl," Tamia answered warmly.

"Hey, Tamia." Honey sounded frantic. "You're not gonna believe who just called me."

Tamia frowned. "Don't tell me—"

"It was Keyshawn! Oh, God, Tamia, he knows about me and Bishop Yarbrough!"

"*What?* How did he find out?"

"I don't know! He must have followed me to one of my dates with the bishop! He told me that if I'm not back home by tomorrow, he's going straight to the media. And he's even got the diamond bracelet that Bishop Yarbrough gave me— the one with his initials on it!"

"Shit!" Tamia swore under her breath.

"I know." Honey groaned loudly. "Everything's so fucked up. That's why I'm leaving for Houston tomorrow morning."

"No! Don't do that!" Remembering her whereabouts, Tamia lowered her voice to an urgent whisper. "You know what will happen if you go back to Keyshawn. He's gonna beat the shit out of you—or worse!"

"What other choice do I have?" Honey wailed. "I can't risk him talking to reporters about me and Bishop Yarbrough!"

"I know," Tamia acknowledged, drumming her manicured fingernails on the table, "but I don't want you putting yourself in harm's way. So I'm gonna call Lou—"

"No, don't. I'll call him. He doesn't wanna talk to you."

Tamia's fingers stilled. "What?"

"I'm sorry." Honey sounded sheepish. "I didn't mean to just blurt that out."

"Lou told you he doesn't want to talk to me?"

"Not in so many words," Honey hedged. "But he told me what happened that night at the apartment before Brandon showed up. I think he was hurt and embarrassed because he put himself out there, and you couldn't get away from him fast enough."

"Oh, papi." Tamia sighed, guilt gnawing her insides. "I figured that was why he hadn't returned any of my calls."

"That, and he's been in Puerto Rico since Thanksgiving. He's supposed to be coming back tonight, so I'll call him and let him know what's going on with Keyshawn. Something tells me I'm gonna need all the help I can get."

"That's probably a safe assumption," Tamia said grimly.

"I'll call you tomorrow when I'm on the road," Honey promised.

"Yes, please do that. And be safe."

Tamia ended the call and set her phone down on the table, her mind racing, veering into several directions at once.

She felt him before she saw him.

Suddenly her skin heated, tingling with awareness.

And then he appeared beside her at the table, his hands

thrust into the pockets of his Armani suit pants, the sliver of a platinum Rolex glinting beneath the recessed lights.

Her heart galloped past her ribs to leap into her throat.

Slowly, deliberately, she raised her eyes from the table to look into his face.

Her smile froze.

Because the face staring back at her wasn't the one she'd been expecting to see.

"Dominic . . ."

Don't miss the latest book in the Exposed series
by Naomi Chase

Betrayal

On sale now!

Prologue

Moaning with pleasure, Tamia tightened her thighs around the sweaty, muscular back of her lover.

He groaned her name, his hips pumping up and down as he drove into her. Deeper, harder, the slap of their naked bodies echoing around the shadowy room.

Tamia clung tightly to his shoulders, her nails breaking his skin as his thick, hard shaft pounded her core. He felt so good inside her, hitting all her sweet spots. It was as if they'd never been apart.

Gazing into her eyes, he lowered his mouth until his warm breath fanned her lips. "You thought I'd let you walk out of my life?" he whispered, the husky rasp of his voice sending shivers through her. "Is that what you thought? Huh?"

Lost in sensation, Tamia could barely breathe, let alone speak.

He thrust faster, his dark eyes boring into hers. "I'm never letting you go, Tamia. Never . . ."

Chapter 1

Tamia

Time ground to a halt as Tamia stared up at Dominic Archer, stunned speechless.

She couldn't believe he was standing at her table, looking like he had every right to be there with his hands casually tucked into his pockets, a smile playing at the corners of his full lips. She couldn't believe he had the audacity to approach her after the way he'd nearly ruined her life, blackmailing her for sex by threatening to expose her past as a porn star.

As fury quickly replaced her shock, Tamia spat, "What the fuck are you doing here?"

His eyes glinted with amusement. "Hello to you too, Tamia."

"Don't 'hello' me, motherf—" Glancing around the elegant restaurant, she lowered her voice to an angry hiss. "I don't know what the hell you think you're doing, but we have *nothing* to say to each other."

"I disagree," Dominic said calmly. "I think we have plenty to talk about."

"I don't give a shit what you think." Tamia turned her head, darting an anxious glance toward the front entrance. The last thing she wanted was for her ex-boyfriend Brandon to show up and see Dominic standing at her table. There was no telling what Brandon would think—or do.

"You need to leave, Dominic. I'm serious."

"Why?" His eyes gleamed. "You expecting someone?"

Tamia scowled. "Not that it's any of your damn business, but yeah, I *am* expecting someone. He should be here any moment."

Or so she hoped.

For the past twenty minutes, she'd been anxiously waiting for Brandon to join her at Da Marco, the Italian restaurant he'd taken her to on their first date. She'd told him to meet her there at four o'clock. It was now ten minutes past the hour.

He's coming, she assured herself. *He's just running late.*

She didn't want to consider the alternative. That Brandon was at the justice of the peace this very moment exchanging vows with his fiancée, Cynthia Yarbrough. She couldn't bear the thought of it.

"Let me buy you dinner," Dominic drawled.

Tamia gaped at him, incredulous. "What part of 'I'm expecting someone' did you not understand?"

He looked amused. "Come on, Tamia. You don't really think he's coming, do you?"

Her eyes narrowed with suspicion. "How the hell do you even know who I'm waiting for?"

Dominic chuckled softly. "I think I can safely assume that you're waiting for Brandon. Which is unfortunate, since I heard through the grapevine that he's getting married today." He raised a thick brow at Tamia. "Did I hear wrong?"

She glared at him. "How did you know I'd be here?" she demanded, ignoring his question. "Have you been following me?"

"Of course not," he said with lazy amusement. "I had a business meeting this afternoon, but my client had to cancel. I was just about to leave when I saw you."

Tamia didn't believe him, not for one damn second. This was the same conniving motherfucker who'd had an affair with her while he was married. She couldn't believe a word that came out of his lying mouth.

Before she could light into his ass, the waiter appeared. After topping off Tamia's water, he divided a friendly smile between her and Dominic. "Will you two be dining together this evening?"

"No," Tamia said so sharply that the man looked startled.

Dominic smiled at the waiter. "Give us another minute."

"We don't need another minute," Tamia interjected through clenched teeth. "He's not joining me for dinner. I'm waiting for someone else. In the meantime, I'd like to order the grilled scampi with orange honey salad."

"Excellent, *signorina*." The waiter shot a sympathetic glance at Dominic before moving off.

Tamia picked up her crocodile Dolce & Gabbana handbag, one of many expensive gifts Brandon had lavished upon her during their recent trip to Italy.

"I'm going to the ladies' room," she coldly informed Dominic as she rose from the table. "I expect you to be gone when I get back."

With that, she turned and stalked off, feeling Dominic's gaze on her ass until she rounded the corner and disappeared from view.

Once inside the empty restroom, she slipped into the nearest stall and retrieved her smartphone from her handbag. After taking several deep breaths, she pulled up Brandon's number and pressed SEND.

Her heart sank when her call went straight to his voice mail.

"This is Brandon. Keep it short and sweet."

Tamia inhaled a shaky breath, debating whether or not to leave a message. If he'd gone through with marrying Cynthia, there was nothing she could say or do at this point. But if he was somewhere having second thoughts, she had to at least *try* to get through to him.

The beep sounded, prompting her to speak or hang up.

Gripping the phone, she nervously moistened her lips. "Hey . . . it's me. I'm at Da Marco waiting for you. I hope . . ." She trailed off, not wanting to sound too desperate. "I hope to see you soon."

She disconnected, closed her eyes and held the phone to her thudding heart.

Please don't let it be too late, she silently prayed. *Please let Brandon be on his way to the restaurant, not the court-house.*

Drawing another deep breath, she stepped out of the stall and crossed to the row of sinks to inspect her reflection in the mirror. Her sleek bob was freshly straightened, her red lipstick was perfectly intact, and she wore a Dolce & Gabbana tapestry-print dress that molded her voluptuous curves. She'd been delighted when the Italian saleswoman had told her that the dress wouldn't hit the U.S. market for another four months. She enjoyed being ahead of the curve.

With a parting glance at her reflection, Tamia left the restroom and headed back to her table.

When she saw Dominic sitting there, a wave of incredulous outrage swept through her.

This motherfucker!

As she marched over to the table, he stood and smoothly pulled out her chair for her. Ignoring the chivalrous gesture, she thrust her hands onto her hips and spat, "What the fuck do you think you're doing?"

His lips twitched. "You might want to keep your voice down," he advised. "People are staring at you."

"I don't give a shit." But even as the angry words left her mouth, Tamia couldn't help glancing around. Meeting the curious stares of several other diners, she scowled.

Not wanting to cause a scene, she reluctantly sat down and allowed Dominic to push her chair back in. But as soon as he reclaimed the seat across from her, she began looking around for the waiter so that she could request her food to go.

"I ordered a bottle of Chianti," Dominic said, gesturing to the wineglass in front of her. "It's good. Have some."

"I don't think so." Tamia glared at him. "I thought I told you to leave."

"You did," Dominic said mildly.

"So why the hell are you still here?"

"I thought you could use some company." He raised his glass to his lips, his eyes dancing with humor. "Were you able to reach Brandon?"

Tamia's face heated. "None of your damn business."

Dominic laughed, leisurely sipping his wine.

Tamia hated him with every fiber of her being. But not even she could deny how fine he was with his hooded dark eyes, juicy lips framed by a trim goatee, broad shoulders, and muscular six-four frame dipped in Armani. His lazy West Indian accent only added to his immense sex appeal.

But it didn't matter how gorgeous he was, or that he was by far one of the best lovers she'd ever had. From the moment Tamia had met him, he'd wreaked pure havoc on her life, ultimately causing her to lose everything. Now that she was trying to pick up the broken pieces and move forward, she wanted absolutely nothing to do with him. The sooner he got that through his thick head, the better.

Tamia took a sip of her water and glanced impatiently around the restaurant. "Where the hell is that damn waiter?"

"Probably taking care of our order," Dominic drawled.

Tamia's eyes snapped to his. "*Our* order?"

"Yeah." He drank more wine. "I canceled your salad and ordered dinner for both of us."

"Excuse you?" *The nerve of this motherfucker!* "Who the hell told you to do that?"

He smiled lazily. "We're both here. We might as well eat together. Besides, this will give us a chance to discuss my proposal."

Tamia's eyes narrowed. "What proposal?"

"Glad you asked. I'd like to—"

"You know what?" Tamia cut him off, holding up a hand. "I don't even wanna hear it."

He frowned. "Why not?"

"Why not? Why not? Hmm, let me see. Maybe because the last time you approached me with one of your so-called proposals, I lost my boyfriend and my job, and I went to prison for murder."

Dominic grimaced, leaning back in his chair. "All of that was unfortunate—"

"Unfortunate?" Tamia echoed in angry disbelief. "Getting a speeding ticket is unfortunate. Falling on your ass in public is unfortunate. What happened to me was absolutely devastating, Dominic, and none of it would have happened if you'd stayed the hell out of my life. So, no, I have absolutely no interest in hearing your proposal, so you can just go fuck yourself."

Dominic hung his head, looking contrite for the first time since she'd met him. "I know I did you wrong, Tamia. That's why I'd like to make amends."

"How? You nearly destroyed my life, Dominic. There's nothing you can say or do to make amends for that."

"Maybe not," he conceded, "but I'd at least like to try."

"Why? To ease your damn conscience?"

"Nah," he murmured, watching as she agitatedly sipped more water. "This isn't about making myself feel better. It's about rectifying a mistake, righting a wrong—"

Tamia snorted derisively, shaking her head at him. "You are so full of shit, Dominic. And you're out of your damn mind if you think I'd be stupid enough to ever trust you again."

He looked at her with solemn eyes. "Everyone deserves a second chance, Tamia."

"Not everyone." She set her empty glass down on the table, then grabbed her purse and stood so abruptly she got lightheaded.

As she swayed for a moment, Dominic frowned in concern. "Are you okay?"

"I'm fine," she snapped.

"Maybe you should stay and eat something."

Tamia sneered. "Nice try, but I'd rather go back to prison than stay here and have dinner with you." She jabbed a finger at him. "You wanna make amends? Stay the fuck away from me."

With that, she turned and strode from the table without a backward glance.

Grab the Hottest Fiction
from
Dafina Books